IN THE WAKE

OF THE

NORTHERN LIGHTS

IN THE WAKE OF THE NORTHERN LIGHTS

By
Charles Daudert

HANSA-HEWLETT PUBLISHING COMPANY
CHICAGO

Printed in the United States of America
Library of Congress Catalog Card Number 88-80455

ISBN 0-945732-00-7

Published by Hansa-Hewlett Publishing Company

THIS BOOK IS FOR PAM

Author's Note

This is a work of fiction. However, many of the scenes in the novel are based upon actual events, and there may be persons who took part in incidents similar to those described in the book. But with the exception of the character Billy Meister, who is based upon the author's uncle, Jesse (Billy) Meeker, and the recognizable public figures associated with this historical period, the people portrayed are purely fictional.

The exceptions are: Judge Freisler of the People's Court in Berlin, the members of the White Rose and July 20th organizations he sentenced to death, the members of the Black Square underground, and the infamous Nazi leaders.

The Schildwache and all characters associated with that underground organization are purely fictional. However, they are representative of those Germans who opposed Hitler, not because the Nazi regime was evil, but because it failed.

Part One

The Wreck of the Tres Belle

THE WRECK OF THE TRES BELLE

Lashed to the helm, all stiff and stark,

With his face turned to the skies,

The lantern gleamed through the gleaming snow

On his fixed and glassy eyes.

Henry Wadsworth Longfellow

FORWARD TO
WRECK OF THE TRES BELLE

On November 11, 1940, the worst storm of the century struck Lake Michigan. Four men from the South Haven station put out in a small Coast Guard lifeboat in a vain attempt to rescue two foundering fishing tugs from that city. For twenty-seven hours, the relatives of the lifeboat crew and the friends and relatives of the missing fishermen waited at the South Haven station for word of the missing men.

All hope was given up when a body and wreckage were found on the beach north of Holland.

The storm had already sent the *Davock* and *Minch* to the bottom of Lake Michigan south of Ludington, when it drove the Canadian freighter *Novadoc,* bound from Chicago to Fort Williams, aground off Pentwater. The ship broke her back at Little Point Sable and lay at the mercy of the pounding seas for two days and two nights. For reasons still unclear, the Coast Guard failed to rescue the men freezing on the ship. But a little fishing tug from Pentwater put out in the storm. The waves were running so high the tug's captain could see nothing until the boat lifted on a crest.

The tug came up in the lee of the *Novadoc* and ran a line to the stricken freighter. But the tug pounded bottom in the shallow water, and found herself in danger of foundering.

The crew of the Coast Guard boat from South Haven, as well as the three-man crew of the Pentwater fishing tug, were hailed in the press and on the radio as national heroes.

However, the brave men of the Pentwater fishing tug were called less honorable names by men of the local Coast Guard, who loudly denounced them as glory-seekers.

Part One of this book, THE WRECK OF THE TRES BELLE, is a fictionalized account of these two incidents.

One

It was the third day of the storm; and it was bitter cold in the fish tug that morning when the dark-haired Austrian immigrant, Karl Meister, stepped aboard. A black beard covered the scar on his face. A black glove hid his mangled left hand.

The wind howled over the wooden boat's tar-paper roof. The big diesel engine, sitting in the bilge and showing only its three cylinder heads above the workroom floor, was ice to his touch.

Karl Meister leaned against the iron rail around the engine well and slid the small plate on the number one cylinder to the side. Directly in front of this opening was a nozzle, which sprayed oil into the manifold. He pumped six powerful strokes on the pre-heater, opened the valve on the nozzle, and lit the vaporized stream with his cigarette lighter. Blue flame shot into the opening.

Then Karl went to the number two and number three cylinders, each as massive as a tree trunk, and repeated the procedure.

When the diesel heads were warm to his hand, he closed the nozzles, snapped shut the access plates, and pressed the starter button. The number one clyinder fired with a whoosh, followed by number three and then number two; and as the engine warmed, the whoosh sound developed a more solid thumping noise. The engine took on a steady rhythmic whoosh-boom-whoosh, not loud but singularly powerful in its long strokes.

Today, we'll be netting men, he thought. Frozen men from the *Tres Belle*, if they're still alive, God willing, and he added coal to the pot-bellied stove which stood against the bulkhead.

Warming his hands at the boat's coal stove, Karl heard a tramping of heavy boots on the wooden dock. The side hatch slid open. In stepped

Indian Joe and Corky Reiley, with their bulky watchcoats turned up around their necks, and with their black knit caps pulled down over their ears.

Snow and sleet stuck to their caps and jackets and they stamped their feet on the boat's heavy planks and banged their hands.

"Damn cold," Corky said. "Fecken truck wouldn't start."

"Yer battery," Joe said. "Told ya it wouldn't last the week."

"Warm up, boys," Karl said. "We're shoving off."

He stepped around the hot stove, climbed up to the pilothouse, reached behind the wheel, and switched on the bilge pump. A low whirr came from below, followed by the gurgle of water above the engine's steady thump and the crackling and spitting of coal in the workroom stove, as the electric pump emptied the boat's bilge into the river.

Then he heard Corky's voice from below. "Hell, Karl. Don't you ever make fresh coffee?"

"Secure the boat and pole off," Karl said, resting his hands on the wooden spokes. "You can have your fresh coffee when we get back—and I'll buy."

Through the starboard window he saw a long pole hook the bow line from the forward piling, and then push off. Slowly, the tug's snub bow swung and pointed out to the river.

"Stern lines clear," Joe's hoarse voice came from below.

"Going ahead half!" Karl shouted.

He felt a solid thud, as he pulled the clutch handle and moved the heavy bar forward, engaging the engine, then the steady vibration under his feet when he pushed the throttle lever to half speed.

The whoosh noise of the cylinders disappeared. The engine took on a heavy, slow drum roll as the tug surged forward into the current. Already he could feel the slow rise and fall of the boat in the long swell which rolled down the channel, reflected off the river bank at the bend, and angled up to meet the *Three Sisters*.

This was where he must make his decision. There was no turning back once he entered the channel—there was too little room to come about between the concrete piers; and even if he could have swung her around, there was always a good chance of capsizing in a huge roller.

"Well, men," Karl yelled below, "I'm not making this decision alone."

Corky popped up on the left and Joe on the right, and both stood beside Karl in the pilothouse. "We'll know when we round the bend," Karl said. "We're the only hope for those boys on the freighter. But we aren't damn fools. We go only if it'll work."

The tug rounded the bend and rose on the first long swell—and there it was—that seething, heaving caldron boiling in the channel. Mountainous waves tumbled over the south pier, crashing against huge crests which curled around the lighthouse and marched in.

The water pushed and heaved its way up the channel to the Coast Guard Station, where the waves crested over the concrete banks, flooded the sandy beach, and then dropped to deep troughs in the river between the piers.

"Damn!" Joe cried out, "She'll hit bottom for sure, Karl. Those troughs go right down to the mud."

"We only need three feet, Corky. I think we've got that much. What do you say, boys?"

"Go!" said Corky.

"Aw, shit! Let's go get 'em," Joe said.

"Then hit it, Corky! Give me everything you've got! We'll need a helluva lot of power in that mess!"

Turning to Joe, he said, "Brace the hatches! We'll get waves from the side as we go out!"

Karl gave a long blast with the tug's horn to alert the Coast Guard and laughed. Captain Bennett would take no small delight in fishing me out of the channel with a grappling hook, he said to himself.

The wind and surf came to him in a muffled roar over the boat's engine as they plowed toward the station. The boat plunged down the first trough, sinking dizzily, until the pilothouse windows went below the normal water level markings on the concrete piers.

An endless groaning, squeaking and creaking echoed in the pilothouse, as the boat strained over the next crest, which left the bow hanging high. The tug raced down and hit the next wave hard in the trough. The bow went under as water curled over the boat; and as the tug staggered up, Karl saw a man stumbling and sliding along the wet rocks, which lay between the concrete pier and the boat house. It was a dark figure in a Coast Guard uniform, waving both arms wildly. The man, standing knee deep in the swirling overflow among the rocks, motioned vigorously with his right hand.

"Back! Go back!" Karl imagined Captain Bennett's open mouth shouting, for he could hear nothing above the turbulent seas and raging wind.

"Bennett," Karl said to himself, "you ass. Get back before you're washed off your feet and crack your stupid skull."

Glancing quickly at the flagpole high over the white tower, Karl saw the storm warning flags stretched taut in the wind.

Karl looked up at Captain Bennett, now above him as the tug sank in a trough, and just then he was thrown to his knees by a sudden and unexpected force. The tug shuddered and ground momentarily to a stop on the channel mud. The next wave crashed over the boat; and as Karl struggled to his feet, he looked quickly around. The pilothouse windows had cracked. But the

Three Sisters was still pointing out the channel, gaining headway again, as it rose through the foaming water.

"Holy Christ!" He heard Corky yell below. "We hit bottom, Karl!"

***

The storm had roared in on Monday.

Jacque DuPays, a tall, thin French-Canadian in his early thirties with rust hair, green eyes, and a closely-cropped mustache, shoved his captain's hat to the back of his head, folded his arms comfortably over the binnacle's brass housing, and turned his attention to the music of a Chicago station on the radio direction-finder above the *Tres Belle's* pilothouse window.

That day had broken with the most beautiful sunrise he'd ever seen. He'd found himself in the middle of a rainbow of purple, red and violet; with the sun a painted backdrop, all transparent rose and ballooned many times its normal size.

The young captain had plotted a course north to clear Little Point Sable and was hugging the Michigan shore of the lake; and coming south along that same shore, steering 217 degrees, SW3/4S from the Manitou Passage were the *William B. Davock* and the *Anna C. Minch.*

Captain Charles W. Allen on the *Davock* pressed the button on his radio-telephone, pinpointed his position north of Ludington, and remarked that the weather was unusually mild, despite the lateness of the season. That was the last transmission ever made by the *Davock.*

The *Tres Belle*, a 253-foot Canadian Steamship Company canaller, was out of Michigan City that morning with a crew of nineteen officers and men, bound for Fort Williams on the Lake Superior shore. She was riding low in the water with a load of powdered coke; and the early morning music from Chicago was becoming increasingly difficult to hear in the the unusual static.

The ship had white deckhouses and a black hull. A white deck with hatches almost flush with the plating ran between the deckhouses. The pie-shaped fo'c'sle containing the windlass, ship's anchors, and the forward crew's quarters was set back all around from her spar deck, allowing seamen space to walk around it to reach the mooring bits.

The pilothouse with its high narrow windows, which sheltered the ship's wheel and the navigation systems, was over the oak-panelled captain's office in the fo'c'sle.

The bronze bowl holding the Great Lakes compass card was ahead and to the right of the spoked brass wheel. It was sealed by a plate-glass cover, heavily gasketed, and filled with a liquid containing forty-five percent grain alcohol and fifty-five percent distilled water. In contrast to the shore compass used by woodsmen and surveyors, in which the needle waves over a graduated scale, the compass card turned on a jeweled bearing and the direction was read directly from the dial in reference to a fixed line in the bowl called the lubber line.

The *Tres Belle's* fine-tuned engine, a triple-expansion masterpiece with a thirty-six inch stroke which produced one thousand horsepower at ninety revolutions per minute was located in the stern section under the after crew's quarters. Early marine engines employed the single-expansion principle in which steam from the boilers was fed into the cylinders, where the pressurized vapor expanded and then was exhausted. With improvements in boilers and higher pressures, the exhaust from one cylinder was used to power another low-pressure cylinder; and with development of the triple-expansion engine, the steam went on to yet a third cylinder, eliminating the need for carrying large supplies of coal.

Most freighters on the Great Lakes were built and designed for the specific purposes they served. By the first decade of the Twentieth Century, ore carriers six hundred feet long and with a beam of sixty feet were plying the lakes. At a little over two hundred and fifty feet, the *Tres Belle* was a much smaller ship. During the winter of 1920-21, she had gone to the yards of the Great Lakes Engineering Company at River Rouge, Michigan, where she was shortened by twenty-four feet to fit the Welland Canal and the small St. Lawrence River canals, then sold to the Canadian Steamship Company. The canaller was the Great Lakes version of the ocean tramp freighter, and the *Tres Belle* became a familiar sight at Port Colborne, Port Weller, and dozens of towns along the St. Lawrence, carrying diversified cargo; packaged freight, grain from Buffalo to Montreal, taking on coal at Buffalo for delivery to Marquette or Chicago, bringing back pig iron for the Buffalo mills.

The crew housed at the ship's stern consisted of the engineers and oilers who attended to the steam power plant, the cook and his helper, who prepared meals in the galley over the engine rooms, and the black-hole firemen and coal-passers who slaved at her two Scotch boilers, eleven feet in diameter and twelve feet in length, each with two furnaces, and producing a working steam pressure of one hundred and sixty pounds per square inch.

Over the spar deck on each side of the aft cabin, lifeboats swung in davits, each equipped with a full compliment of oars and a rudder with yoke lines. Lashed securely under their canvas covers were life preservers, one galvanized iron bucket with lanyard to be used as a head, a second galvanized bucket to serve as the galley, one bailer, a two-inch card compass, one lantern containing sufficient oil to burn at least nine hours, an extra gallon can of illuminating oil, one carton of friction matches wrapped in a waterproof package and carried in a box fastened to the underside of the stern thwart, a watertight metal case containing twelve self-igniting red flares capable of burning two minutes, a sea anchor, and a five-gallon can of heavy oil to be spread upon the raging waters.

Captain DuPays reached up and adjusted the radio's tuning control when the Chicago signal was temporarily lost in a burst of static. It was a little after nine in the morning, and WGN was broadcasting national news. The news was of a terrible storm marching in from the west. The young French Canadian strained to hear the weak voice over the background noise. He heard the announcer say the storm was moving with violent winds, and leaving death and destruction in its wake. Fifty-three duck hunters had frozen to death in boats and blinds on the bottomlands of the upper Mississippi River in Minnesota. The storm had struck suddenly with heavy rain and sixty-five mile-per-hour winds, followed by blinding sleet. The balmy temperatures dropped forty-five degrees in ten minutes.

Steaming south four hours astern of the *Davock*, Captain Donald A. Kennedy of the *Minch* personally took down the weather forecasts. He was running close-in, taking advantage of the calm waters near shore and making good progress; and he realized immediately he was in trouble. Suddenly, the wind shifted violently from southeast to southwest, where a ragged bank of low-hanging clouds rolled in disarray. He called for more power and spun the wheel to starboard, beginning his desperate clawing away from shore. It was too late. The wind struck with force and the heavily-laden ship shook and heeled. The bow swung slowly back. The captain had too little power to bring her into the wind—it would be another fifteen minutes, or so, before the boilers were up enough to swing the sluggish freighter in that fierce onslaught; and then the grain in the hold shifted.

All along Lake Michigan the sky turned black, the waters boiled, the waves grew and pounded the steel hulls of waddling freighters. Those who could, immediately hauled around into the wind and building waves and away from shore. The *Davock* never made the turn and went to the bottom with its crew of thirty-two before the day was over. The *Minch* followed her down with twelve additional seamen a few hours later.

Captain DuPays found himself in the same predicament. The *Tres Belle* would not come about. At first it was a race between the wind and the boilers. By the time he had enough steam to overcome the wind forces, the waves had built and the heavy masses of water smashing against the iron sides set the bow back each time she swung.

By late afternoon, he'd managed to bring her no more than another half mile away from shore; and it was no longer a question of making progress against the huge waves. The question was now one of degrees. How far could he swing her before the crunching waves brought her to a stop? He couldn't risk pounding too sharply into those gray curlers. Each time he did, the ship shuddered and slowed, and soon he wouldn't have steerage, and then she'd start a hard roll and the powdered coke in the holds would shift.

He glanced at the first mate at his elbow, then at the young wheelsman. "It's a balancing act now."

The first mate nodded, he understood. He'd come to the pilothouse to report to Captain DuPays personally. "I just made an inspection of the engine room." The slim, dark-haired first mate paused and puffed on his pipe. "And I came up to make sure you knew our situation—we can't get more out of her."

DuPays nodded. The wheelsman spun the spokes to port as a gray slab of water water carried the bow ten degrees in.

"The hull's working something fierce, sir," the first mate continued. "Screaming like a banshee, she is, Captain. I can hear rivets popping down there." He paused and studied the captain's grim face, then continued. "Even the deck plates are moving. I can feel 'em under my feet. I thought you should know that."

Captain DuPays nodded thanks. It was what he suspected. The last few tons had set her well below her marks, the ship was overloaded for these conditions. And it was his fault. Damn, it was getting harder and harder to make a profitable run. The weather was perfect, that's why he chose the shorter run along the Michigan shore of the lake, he'd shave several hours off his schedule that way. It was a risk, that he'd known. Most heavy weather came from out of the west, and you wanted lots of room between the ship and a lee shore. Well, he'd gambled, and now it looked like he might lose out. There was no calling for help. The radio-telephone had gone out on the trip down, and it would have been another delay for repairs at Michigan City, with no assurances. Two days, three days? he had asked. "Well, it appears to be a short in the electrical system, and you never know with these things," was the answer. So they sailed without radio.

After the *Titanic* careened off an iceberg and went to the bottom with fifteen hundred souls in 1912, the International Wireless Convention was held in London, making it mandatory for vessels with more than fifty people on board to be equipped with wireless and keep qualified operators on duty at all times. The Great Lakes passenger ships quickly adapted to the new Radio Act of 1913; and although not required a good many of the lake freighters added a wireless room and took an operator.

Surprisingly, many grizzled captains looked upon the wireless operators with contempt. They'd sailed about these inland seas for years with nothing more than a little bit of weather sense, a lot of luck, a compass, a clock, and a taffrail log which dragged a long rope with a propeller at the end from the stern, ticking off the miles as the line spun. With some justification, they felt the new men who talked to the home office in dots and dashes were spies, no doubt commenting upon the captain's performance as well as the messages the old man had printed out for transmission.

This hostility mellowed in the early thirties when the space-hogging wireless sets gave way to the compact ship-to-shore radios. Gone was the stranger tapping out shrill code on a key. Now the captain himself could talk to shore by pressing a button on his microphone.

The first radio-telephones were made by the Lorain County Radio Corporation in 1934, and went aboard the *Tres Belle* immediately, even though they would not become mandatory for another twenty years.

Captain DuPays was a systematic and orderly man who had spent his apprenticeship as a seaman, where he learned to limit his belongings to the absolute necessities. In his cabin which doubled as his office below the pilothouse, there was strong evidence that the old habits persisted. There was a place for everything and everything found its place. His varnished desk was a model of neatness.

In the pilothouse above, each chart was carefully rolled, banded, and placed in its proper numerical sequence. The pencils in the chart desk were pin-point sharp. The log was kept punctiliously exact and up to the hour; and everything on the ship reflected in the highly polished brass.

The highest gloss of all was on the brass clock in the pilothouse over the center window. With a thirty-hour Seth-Thomas movement, it kept precise time when wound every day at exactly the same time. The young captain had made it a standing order, the helmsman would wind the clock at exactly eight bells, four o'clock in the afternoon each day, before assuming his evening watch. The captain knew the clock performed at maximum efficiency when its thirty-hour movement was never allowed to unwind—and he made sure the helmsmen knew it too. He watched to see whether the man handled the chore with reverence toward the honored timepiece, or whether he displayed a lack of affection for the instrument. If he fell into the latter category, his name was entered on the list for replacement; and if ever, God forbid, the poor man overwound the clock, or worse, forgot altogether, the accursed seaman was relieved from duty on the spot and shipped home from the next port.

The stern captain had been below at his desk when the storm struck, his mind occupied with contracts, tonnage commitments, fueling, repairs, provisioning, and the endless details of cargo steamer operations. The second mate was in charge of the pilothouse, reserving for the evening and long night the greater skills of the captain and first mate. Captain DuPays felt the ship shudder, then heel over, as the wind screamed across the ventilators and rose to a high pitch around the wires supporting the loading masts. He rushed to the pilothouse just as the second mate took over the wheel. The captain gave the command through the voice tube for the chief engineer to make all possible steam. But it was too late. The ship never completed the turn. Now there was no choice but to pound ahead. The wind had come up so suddenly and the seas risen so quickly and ominously that he was powerless in their grip. The waves were rolling out of the southwest. He could do no more than bring the vessel onto a westerly heading, and each few feet he gained in the trough were lost on the next crest. The ship was crabbing slowly north and east, ever closer to shore.

One thing was building on another. Now the problem was compounding. The coal in the bunkers was so poor, the chief engineer was having difficulty getting additional heat into the boilers. Many of the men had stayed home that trip, off to enlist with the British and Canadian armed forces to carry on the war against Hitler's Germany. The new black-hole crew were getting seasick in that hot, rolling coffin down below.

In the pilothouse, the captain now sweated at the wheel, even though the temperature had already dropped below freezing. The cables were binding somewhere in the ship, he could feel the resistance building each time he spun in response to a huge sea which exploded over the ship's bow, flinging spray high over the masthead and peppering the windows. The ship was twisting somewhere along its length and the cables were binding, of that he was certain. How much longer they could steer the ship was another question. Well, he thought, when the time came, it would be two men on the wheel, using all of their strength, until the cables snapped. After that, there was no choice but to go to emergency steering. That iron wheel was in the open, aft of the stern cabin, and connected directly to the rudder post top by a worm gear. If conditions deteriorated so that seas sweeping down to the stern bashed the poor man senseless, he'd take his place, and lash himself to the wheel. He'd done it before, when he was first mate on a rusty cargo ship, and his quick action had saved the dazed captain and the demoralized crew, and earned him his own command.

They'd put into Muskegon then. But now he wondered whether he'd ever make that distant harbor. With these seas running, there wasn't much chance of bringing the ship into one of the little towns along the shore. Even if he'd somehow manage to make the narrow channel entrance, most likely she'd stike bottom in a trough and veer off against the concrete piers. So the only thing left was to keep going. If his luck held, they'd ride out the storm.

Already, movement from the pilothouse to the stern quarters had become impossible. Stinging sheets of hard-driven sleet blotted the aft section from view. For long periods of time, the low deck between the two structures was smothered with boiling water. Except for the voice tube and the unreliable telephone, there was no way to get a message to the stern.

Captain DuPays hadn't eaten, had nothing warm to drink, since early that morning when he drank the last of the black coffee and took the wheel from the first mate. "Oh, I could use some of Rene's onion soup now," he said with a grin and handed over the wheel to the first mate. They were trading off every half hour now, the captain, the first mate, and the regular wheelsman. Even with the shorter intervals at the wheel, the young captain's muscles ached from the strain.

Normally, the job of changing watch in the pilothouse was a clear-cut routine accomplished with precision under the command of Captain DuPays. The officer in charge remained at his post at a window facing forward near the engine telegraph, the levered instrument connected to the engine room by cable, and with which he signaled the required speed. He turned over the watch data rapidly and clearly to the relieving officer, giving any special orders from the captain which must be carried out, giving the position of the ship and how it was obtained, the weather, sea, and wind conditions; and finally, the course, which was clearly and distinctly repeated by the relieving officer, who at that moment stepped next to the telegraph and took charge of the vessel.

Then the wheelsman stepped away from the helm after being relieved, faced the new officer in charge, and repeated the course he had just given to the relieving wheelsman.

This would have been the procedure followed at four o'clock, when the new helmsman came on duty and carefully wound the clock. But Captain DuPays stayed on the bridge. On a night like this, he never trusted the ship completely to others.

The ship's crew, except for those in the pilothouse and those sweating over the engine and at the boilers, kept to their snug and warm quarters, heated by the steam lines from the boiler room.

The cook's helper braced his feet against the bulkhead as he washed and dried the last dishes from the hasty supper. None of the foredeck men had come aft to eat, and the cook wrapped the left-over chicken and biscuts in newspapers and pushed them down between the flat rail and the outside bulkhead, where the temperature was down to about forty degrees.

In the pilothouse, Captain DuPays shoved his hands into the pockets of his peacoat and shook his head. "It's dustin' up a bit," he said softly to the first mate. He wiped the condensation from the pilothouse window and peered ahead through the flying spume and scud. Behind them, the stack rising above the deckhouse at the stern belched black smoke from the rotten coal in the ships burning belly; a thick black cloud which the wind flattened and spread low over the water, until it disappeared in the heaving seas.

They were rolling hard and being set back by the waves, taking them over the port bow. The captain turned and walked to the small portholes at the rear of the pilothouse. Below, the deck passageways on both sides were being flooded regularly.

The wind rattled all the windows now and hammered and shook the steel door leading to the narrow bridge deck outside the pilothouse. The ship began desperate, sickening rolls as the helmsman tried to hold her quarter to the seas that were now cresting well over twenty feet. There was pitching, becoming very pronounced, with the bow going completely under the gray-green water.

There was nothing to do but plug ahead. Captain DuPays took down the red flare gun and checked the dates on the flares. They were still valid, and they'd work, he knew they had to work. They had nothing else. If they went aground, it would be only a matter of hours before the ship started breaking up; and a grounding was the better of the two alternatives they faced. At any moment, the seas could maul open the ship's hatches, and then she'd take on water faster than they could pump. Even if the hatches held, the cargo could shift, and then she'd lay caught in the trough on her beam ends, held there by the wind and seas until she slowly filled and slipped below the raging surface.

These were the thoughts which ran through the young skipper's mind as he reached next to the chart desk for the copper cylinder which contained the crew list. When the time came, he would add to this the nature of the disaster as best he could, the assumed location and any other information that might be helpful in strengthening her sister ships. The polished cylinder was cork-lined with a watertight screw-on lid. At the very last moment, he would surrender the small metal drum to the victorious sea as the ship went under.

***

Watching from the placid surface of that vast water wasteland far north of Chicago that first morning, Karl Meister saw the dawn of that day come, softening the lake with its peculiar gray tint. Before his dark eyes the unfolding morning first danced on the high cliff tops, bathing them in light. Slowly, the sullen clouds in the east began to blush, then to glow red. Karl spun the spoked wheel with his good right hand, and his trawler came about to face the sun, now a transparent blood-red disk, one hundred times its normal size, rising above the dark cliffs.

The angry clouds, in shades of rose, yellow and purple, climbed higher above that shimmering mass, and everything reflected as darker tones in the still water below. He shook his head and muttered to himself, "Red sky in the morning, sailor take warning." His hand tightened on the wheel. This was the month of death—November—the month of all those terrible storms which took their annual toll of lakemen; storms so violent that more than two hundred seamen had gone down in a single day. All the fishing boats trapped out then, most no bigger than than the *Three Sisters* which now rocked gently beneath his feet, splintered in the waves.

Karl Meister thought of himself as a prudent man. Prudence sustained the ordered direction of his life like a cautious hand upon his shoulder. But no one succeeds in everything. There comes to all of us a time when the prudent hand upon the shoulder falters and vanity leads us astray. Such a time began for Karl on that day, November 11, 1940.

While he watched that burning sky, a sea gull dropped with a thud to the deck. Two other gulls circled above, shrieking loudly to their sister on the boat, who staggered to her feet, blood frothing from her beak. The birds had come from the open water, and when the exhausted gull regained its senses, it leaped into the air with a frenetic scream, joined its siblings and glided to the quiet shore.

Already it was warm. Karl Meister peeled his wool sweater from his hot back and laid it on the large bunk behind him in the pilothouse. The unusual weather was not a good sign.

Turning to the wheel, he recalled the words of the old gray-beard at the Southport Navigation School: "Like the sea," the old man had said, puffing on his briar pipe, "these lakes demand certain qualities of mind and character in those who extract a living from the water. There is a time for caution—and a time to make for port."

"Yes," Karl said to himself, "a time to make for port." His throat went dry when he remembered Elias Figg.

Elias Figg, Karl's neighbor, was a simple man with a simple wife and many simple children, who cast pornographic figurines in a small foundry behind his house and went to mass every day. Late last night, Elias Figg had come running and pounding on Karl's door. When Karl finally struggled awake and opened the door, he found Elias Figg on his knees in the grass, arms stretched to the northern sky, palms up. "Lord Jesus, Lord Jesus, Lord Jesus," Elias cried out. Then he clasped his hands to his face, slumped to the ground, and screamed, "Take this miserable sinner!"

North over the lake, Karl saw the shower of light caused by the electrical discharges in the upper atmosphere which induced Figg's act of contrition—rapidly shifting and dancing columns of various hues, stretching up to a luminous circle near the zenith. Filaments and streams of pure white light arched from the dazzling circle to meet the vari-colored columns. The second coming of Christ could not be more splendid.

That warm night had come after a clear day of bright hot sun and soft shore breezes.

The quiet foreboding gnawed at him still that Armistice Day morning, when Karl pointed the forty-foot tug down the dark channel to Lake Michigan, passing the red lighthouse at the end of the south pier and feeling the solid, slow rumble of the heavy Kahlenberg diesel below his feet.

The boats were big enough, but they were frail craft. With thin planks nailed to two-by-fours on top of a wooden hull. He thought they looked more like sardine cans. In the middle, rising three feet above the flat tar-paper roof, were the windows of the pilothouse. Behind the windows, the smokestack, which carried a symbol identifying the owner.

At the stern, there was always the spoon-shaped platform. The bottoms of the newer boats were covered with metal sheathing. But most rested on wooden planks which worked in heavy seas.

The knot in Karl's stomach grew tighter when he saw the startling sunrise that morning. The mangled hand under the black glove was his barometer. Its signals were loud and clear; and he pulled a steel flask from his pocket and gulped the apricot brandy, then waited for the sweet liquor to numb the pain.

Now, as the *Three Sisters* made a slow turn into that dreadful glow, he stepped below into the workroom. Glancing out the stern door past the silouettes of his half-breed Indian helper, Joe Bear, and the stout Irish net-puller, Corky Reiley, he saw a low-hanging bank of darkness hugging the horizon. "Boys," he said softly, pointing through the opening, "we're in for a blow."

"Plenty of time," Corky replied in his broad Irish accent, straightening and peering out the open hatch. "Don't look that bad, Karl. We've got three more nets to throw, ya know."

Indian Joe chewed his cigar and spat a brown stream out the side hatch. "Could be grim," he said with a nod of his head. "But hell, Karl, it's the first day. I got a family to feed. Let's lay net."

"All right boys," Karl said, turning and pulling himself up the pilot-house steps, "set another."

At the wheel, Karl pressed his face to the window. High overhead were frazzled gray-reddish clouds rolling and tumbling lazily. Below the clouds, water ripples told him the easterly breeze was shifting rapidly and rising in strength from the southwest.

This time he jumped the three steps to the workroom.

The men stood outside on the stern platform, with a wooden box of neatly flaked net at their feet. Corky lashed one end of the net to a new pole.

Lying still on the flat green water behind the fishing tug were silver bobbers supporting the net they had laid to catch the whitefish and trout upon which the season opened that day. The net was attached to a tall pole flying a black eagle on yellow banner. In the distant haze were three other flags, marking the nets they'd laid earlier that morning.

Karl studied the men's faces a moment—he knew his reputation was to run scared. "We're goin' in. A blow's coming up, sure as hell!"

"Damn," Corky groaned, and swore low.

The half-breed Indian grinned, showing his big, tobacco-stained teeth.

"Prudence," said Karl, and smiled at the men.

"Yeah, prudence." Indian Joe climbed through the small hatch door, and sat on a box, stretching first one leg and then the other. "Two weeks," he muttered, "and they're still tender as butter."

"Yer lucky to have legs at all," Corky growled through thick lips. "And ya still owe me ten. Where'd ya be, ya fathead, had I not pulled ya from that caldron? Dumb Injun. Next time we close down the Antler ya won't be so eager for yer balancing act."

Joe savagely chewed his blunt cigar and spat out the side hatch.

Karl eyed the men uneasily. They were all stone drunk then, he remembered. When Joe claimed he was the bravest of the three, Karl had bet too.

"Okay," Joe had cried out, "ten dollars says I can walk the four sides." Joe stepped out onto the eight-foot tank, where fish nets boiled over an oil-fired heater. Karl saw immediately Indian Joe wouldn't make it. He swayed on his second step, and tipped slowly into the bubbling caldron.

Quickly sobered, Corky grabbed Joe's plaid jacket, while Karl caught his flaying arms; and lifting together, they jerked him bodily from the steaming water, took three steps, and threw him into the river. But Joe's waders were full of scalding water and he was screaming when he came to the surface. When they removed the long rubber boots, Karl stared at the pink flesh beneath Joe's woolen socks.

Where was my prudence then, he wondered, as they chugged steadily in from the lake toward the red lighthouse.

"Lord," Corky cried out. "The *Sioux Chief.* She's coming out. Karl, let's turn back. We've got a full day yet."

"It'll be no day for the *Chief.*" Karl shook his head. "She's a big and heavy boat, but she's coal-fired. That weak steam engine's no match for what this lake can kick up." Spinning the tug's wooden wheel to pass the *Chief* on the port side, Karl said, "She was damned lucky last year. That's all. Damned lucky. Sailed to Chicago because she couldn't come about in those big seas. Damn them, don't they realize November is the devil's month out here? Can't they see that sky? If one of those rollers hit her boilers it'd be all over—that quick." Karl snapped his fingers. "And you don't fire up wet coke in a November gale."

A young man in a knit cap leaned out from the *Chief's* pilothouse and shouted, "Got trouble, Karl?"

"McKay," Karl yelled back to the *Chief,* "a storm's brewin'! Ya'd best put in!"

"Not as long as the *Bradley's* out." McKay pointed to the north, where a small white dot puffed black smoke.

"My G-God!" Karl stammered. West of the *Bradley*, on the horizon where he had seen the low-hanging bank of darkness, a black mountain now rolled steadily in. It was less than an hour away; and below the jagged cloud structure, he saw a dark swirl meet the water.

"McKay! McKay!" Karl waived his arms frantically toward the horizon. "That's rain, hail—surface water—blown along by one helluva a wind!"

The young man leaned from the rear window of the *Chief's* pilothouse and waved back across its flat roof, as the big white tug wallowed into the distance, its red-striped stack blowing soft smoke balls.

"Damn! He didn't hear me," Karl said to the men behind him.

"It's nothin' but a rain squall," Corky growled with disdain. "It's too warm for a big storm. Hell, they'll fill their nets and be in by sundown, fat with fish."

Ignoring the remark, Karl gave a short blast of the boat's horn as they approached the Coast Guard Station in the channel. His brother, Billy, waved marine glasses from the white tower and gave a knowing nod. Then Billy cupped his hands and shouted down from the open window, "It's prudence again, is it, Karl?"

He could see Billy's broad grin as the boat passed the tower. And Karl gave him a hand-salute.

At the boat dock, Karl glanced ahead to the large thermometer nailed to the fish shanty's weathered wood. He shook his head as he walked the narrow planks from the dock. "Seventy-four degrees," he murmured to himself. "That's too damned warm."

A gust tugged at his short-visored hat, and he turned and looked down the quiet river to the weather vane over the Coast Guard tower. "Now see," he said calmly to Corky, "it's shifted to the west." Then looking at his watch, Karl said softly, "It's nine-fifteen. That's mighty unusual, Corky. Mighty unusual."

Corky cocked his head and looked at Karl with a sparkle in his eye. "I'll drop off Joe and be over for your good Irish coffee." After a pause, Corky continued, "If we still have good weather at noon—what do you say—let's go out then, huh?"

Karl shrugged his shoulders. "I'll make the coffee. Then we'll see."

***

Karl lit the kitchen stove and set a coffee pot on the blue flame. He listened a moment for sounds of stirring from the bedroom where his invalid wife slept late. Then reaching to the old Atwater-Kent radio on a shelf over the ice box, he spun the yellow dial to 95.5.

"Well this is one for the books," the oval speaker blared forth.

Karl quickly adjusted the volume, and the radio went on, "We have a report here from Indianapolis. The airport tower says . . . yes . . . It's a duck . . . Stuck in the wind, right in front of the window, and blocking the view—it's blowing that hard there, folks.

"And here's another one—from station W I N D in Chicago. They've lost one of their transmitting towers. W I N D to the wind, I guess, folks.

"To give you some idea how hard it's blowing, the U.S. Weather Service in Chicago reports that the gale forced a five-foot drop in Lake Michigan. The Calumet River is flowing backwards into the lake.

"Where does all this come from? Well, the meterologist at the weather service reports that a tremendous low-pressure system off the Washington coast moved inland with fierce, cyclonic—yes, that's cyclonic, folks—winds. This was joined by another low-pressure disturbance far to the south, which crossed the Rockies, shot over the plains—and there's more—teamed up with warm, moist, Gulf air rushing into the central Mississippi Valley. These three weather systems converged fifty miles southwest of Chicago. The temperature dropped sixty degrees. I kid you not, folks, that's sixty degrees. All in one hour. And it's coming over the lake—right at us. So take heed. Get your feet down from that pot-bellied stove and put the cows in the barn. I'ts going to be a rough one!''

Karl listened while the radio forecast winds up to seventy miles per hour over the next twelve hours.

At his elbow, the white-enamel percolator bubbled its last. He poured a hot mug, sank into a straight-back chair, and shook his head. The waves were less than a foot when they came in. But Karl knew they'd build fast in seventy-mile winds; they'd reach thirty feet in a few hours, perhaps go to forty feet before the day was out. "My God," he said to himself, "those boats better keep a sharp weather eye out."

No tug can long survive in that, he thought; and he also knew there were few men who could slide a trawler between the narrow concrete piers in those conditions.

"And now for the news," the radio announcer said, "Neville Chamberlain, the former British Prime Minister who met with Hitler and promised 'peace in our time,' died this morning in his sleep at his country house in Hampshire, England. Mr. Chamberlain was in a coma during his final hours. But for weeks he had listened to the drone of Nazi planes winging their way to nightly raids on London.

"The State Department in Washington is absolutely opposed to it, but the question of breaking diplomatic ties with Germany may come to a head soon. New evidence gathered by the Dies committee reveals that German consuls in the United States are activily supporting subversive activities here, and are also channeling funds to agents. Nazi fifth columnists are now the plague of Latin America, operating almost openly in Uruguay. These agents have diplomatic immunity and can't be arrested."

Karl clicked off the radio and sipped his coffee slowly. Hitler had annexed Austria. Now she's part of the Third Reich, he thought. Dragged into another war—not just an ally, but a Nazi country. "Better dead than that," he muttered to himself. "Damn Nazis."

Pushing open the glass door, he walked slowly through the narrow dining area to the living room, where Sylvia now sat in a wooden wheelchair before the fireplace, a blue shawl covering her lap, and holding in her right hand a worn prayer book. A black rosary lay loosely in her left hand on the shawl.

Karl kissed her softly on the cheek.

"I knew you'd be back when I heard the wind." Sylvia was glaring at him from behind thin glasses. "We're two months behind on the mortgage—three boat payments overdue. We don't even own a car. It's God's blessing we never had children."

Karl Meister stirred the glowing embers and placed two pine logs on the grate as a freshening wind whistled in the fireplace. The logs snapped and crackled. New flame licked the dry bark. A pine scent filled the room.

Rising slowly from the fireplace, Karl shrugged his shoulders and faced Sylvia with a look of apology. "It'll be fierce before the day is out." He put a hand on her shoulder and smiled. "We'll double up on the nets tomorrow," he said softly, remembering the doctor telling him there would be days—weeks—when Sylvia would be irritable and irrational.

Sylvia shook Karl's hand from her shoulder. "Always tomorrow, isn't it, Karl?"

"Chicago reports seventy-mile winds," he said calmly. "It'll hit here soon."

She looked at him with her strange blue eyes. Her flaxen hair fell in tangles about her shoulders. "Seventy-mile winds?" She stared quietly at Karl, echoing his words. "I suppose you know best," she said dryly. "You always do."

Karl, ignoring the scorn in her voice, turned and poked at the logs in the fire. Damn, he thought, it must be the medicine—and the disease, too. He wondered if a vibrant body ever became chair-ridden without souring the disposition. No more polka for Sylvia, he thought.

He looked over his shoulder and studied Sylvia for a moment. "The waves will be high and heavy before the day is out.''

She frowned. "How will we pay those?'' She waved a hand to the open, roll-top desk, where Karl knew bills lay unpaid.

He shrugged again and sat on the floor, leaning against the fireplace brick, accepting her judgment of him. How many times had she pleaded for him to leave fishing; become a mechanic, a carpenter, anything steady. "You're a cautious man,'' she had told him. "But caution don't pay for coal, or engine repairs, or nets, or boat fuel.''

Sitting there and feeling very tired, Karl let his eyes roam over her. Sylvia's face was white and drawn, and she looked fragile in her tiny, steel-rimmed glasses and pearl-gray smock.

His eyes traveled across the bay window with its padded seat to the corner of the room where an easel with an unfinished canvas tacked to its board stared back. The paint box sat unopened on the shelf below the canvas and he could see a month's dust collecting on the wooden lid. Several minutes passed, and Karl then said, "If you'd start another picture–"

"Never!" She interruped belligerently

Karl fingered his neat black beard and with steady eyes looked at the canvas. He could see the outline of Sylvia's dead father leaning against the pilothouse of the *Merry B*. At the bottom of the charcoal sketch, she had stenciled the title: "Near Life's End."

A rattle of the front door startled him. Karl rose to see Corky's dancing eyes above a broad nose and handle-bar mustache peering through the small paneWaving Corky to the back door, Karl strode quickly through the dining room, hearing Sylvia say behind him, "Your fishy-stinking partner," and he closed the frosted-glass door.

"Good God, man," Karl said to Corky, who walked into the kitchen from the porch, "don't you ever wash?" You reek of fish!"

Corky's laughter shook the kitchen. "We're fishermen," he bellowed, slamming the table with his thick hand. "The Lord knows when this body needs a bath—"

"Aye! But you don't listen to 'em! The good Lord gave you a nose but it does you no good. It's your damned mustache, Corky. You slap on too much candle wax—"

"Honey wax." Corky interrupted.

"Yes . . . God praise the day you shave it off and learn what stink we live with."

Corky gave a quick snort, sat down and rubbed his heavy hands. "I'll cut it off the day you shave those ugly whiskers. Now, let's have at the brew." The wooden chair creaked as he leaned back. "It's gettin' damned cold out there, Karl."

Karl slid two pewter mugs onto the white metal table and pulled a whiskey bottle from over the sink. "Half and half, as always." He laughed and poured black coffee and whiskey.

Corky tapped the Austrian eagle on his mug. "You won't be goin' back there for a while. This damned war's spreadin' fast."

"Too fast," Karl answered, pulling a chair to the table. "Too damned fast. But I'm an American now, Corky."

"Hell yes," Corky said. "And so am I—and here's to stayin' out of it." He raised his mug. "We Irish ain't for goin' in on the British side, you know." He looked at Karl expectantly. "You must feel about the same."

Karl didn't answer. A solemn look crossed his grave face. His black eyes burned with a bitter light; and after a long pause, he said slowly, "Better dead than Nazi."

Corky thumped his mug on the table and his face went hard. Then the softness faded and his big mouth smiled a half grin, not showing his teeth. He nodded his head but his face remained oddly rigid. "An Englishman's enemy is an Irishman's friend."

Karl studied the broad-faced man quietly for a moment, then rose quietly and cranked the wall phone. "Central, give me three-seven-four, please." After a pause, Karl spoke, "Billy, what's the weather?"

"Blowin' all hell," his brother answered over the phone. "Visibility's less than three miles. Waves over ten feet. We haven't seen the *Bradley* since ten-thirty, and I lost sight of the *Chief* about five minutes ago."

Karl glanced at Corky. "That settles it."

"We've had gale warnings since six-thirty," Billy continued. "I knew that's why you came in."

"Yeah. It looked pretty awful out there. Have you heard the radio?" Karl asked. "Terrible reports out of Chicago."

"We've got 'em too," Billy said. "But Karl, I think it will blow over in an hour or so."

"No—I don't think so. Not really. Look, Billy, we're in for a big one. It could be as bad as 1913. A real monster's coming in. I can feel it."

"Hold it, Karl," Billy said. There was a long pause, then Billy returned to the phone. "The captain wants volunteers. I'm going out."

"Billy—."

The operator's voice came on the line. "Billy's disconnected, Karl. I think he hung up. Do you want me to place the call again?"

"No . . . Thanks, Linda."

Karl placed the receiver on its hook and turned to Corky. "The Coast Guard's going out to look for the *Bradley* and the *Chief*... Billy's with them ... I'm going down."

Karl turned his wool collar up against the cold as they stepped outside. When they rounded the corner, wet sleet hit him full in the face, driving him back against Corky.

"Christ," Corky yelled, and it sounded to Karl like a faint whisper in the roaring wind. "I've never seen ..."

Two

With Corky struggling along beside him, Karl fought his way along the surging river bank toward the Coast Guard Station on the channel. Red storm-warning flags snapped from the tower. Looking up through the stinging sleet as they rounded the bend, he saw an open lifeboat on a wheeled cradle slide down iron rails and splash into the black swell. Four guardsmen were in the gray boat, knit caps pulled down over their ears, dark peacoats buttoned tightly around their necks, and wearing faded gray, cork-filled life preservers.

The small craft plowed out the channel, rising and falling on the building swells as it chugged into the tempest between the concrete piers, wind whipping exhaust vapors which rose from the white foam behind the boat.

Leaning and pushing hard against the gale, each step an energy-draining effort, he turned to Corky, who's waxed mustache was blown flat against his red checks. The stocky man was shouting, but no words came to him from Corky's lips, two feet away—his voice was lost in the wind.

At the station, Karl forced the wooden door open against the onslaught and motioned Corky through. Inside, it was suddenly quieter now when the door slammed shut, and the storm's roar became a low-pitched moan in Karl's ears, as the structure vibrated to a resonant hum.

Karl led the way through the damp boat house, past the closed door of the Captain's office and up the narrow gray-painted stairs to the crew's billet.

They walked around canvas pipe bunks and into the adjoining storage area crowded with emergency folding cots and extra equipment, and climbed the spiral stairs to the watch tower.

"Karl," Timothy Bennett spoke first and held out his hand, "by God, it's been years."

"Hello Bennett," Karl replied, and motioning toward Corky said, "Your brother-in-law told me you'd made captain before it hit the papers, and I shouldn't have waited six years to congratulate you." Karl smiled, shaking the fist of the man who had cost him his hand.

Bennett returned the handshake, and slapped his brother-in-law, Corky, on the shoulder, and turning back said, "Karl, things have changed since you were with us. Our power boat was a thirty footer, then, with that damned two-cylinder, twelve horsepower Superior."

Assuming a commanding posture, fully aware of his current status, the short officer turned to the window and rubbed his neck. Looking down to where Karl could see the new lifeboat struggling out the channel, Bennett said, "She's thirty-six feet, and fitted out with a four-cylinder Gray. Puts out fifty-two horses."

The captain's face went serious as Karl stepped to the window. "Damn, it's buildin' faster than we thought," the officer said. "I don't think those tugs could make the channel now—even if we towed them."

Outside the tower window, the seascape was wild and terrifying, and somehow also beautiful and hypnotic in the size of the waves thundering onto the beach and exploding against the piers with a sound like a thousand cannons.

The tower shook under the buffeting of the gale winds.

Bennett pulled on a silver chain and lifted a flat watch from his vest pocket, flipping open the shiny lid with his thumb. "Twelve-thirty," he said, snapping the watch shut and returning it to his pocket. "Its building damned fast."

Karl's heart jumped when he saw the open boat stagger clear of the channel and drive straight up an in-coming roller. He snatched marine binoculars offered by Bennett from a shelf over the window, and on the next wave he saw the surfboat wobble up a steep comber, stand on its end, and plunge through a foaming crest. Three men stretched a canvas cover from the bow to the steering pedestal. Karl recognized his brother's big, burly figure behind the wheel, leaning back against a rope-sling which ran to each side of the boat. "Billy's steering?" asked Karl.

"Oh, yes. He's in command," Bennett said haughtily.

Directing the glasses to the lake once more, Karl saw sky and sea as one now, an indistinguishable mass of snarling gray cloud and water, welded together in turmoil. His eyes darted to Captain Bennett. Karl said crisply, "Those waves are over twenty feet! They shouldn't be going out in this! And The *Chief* won't survive. You should be setting beach patrols!"

Bennett's jaw went slack and he blew through quivering nostrils and said nothing.

"The *Bradley* might last," Karl spoke up, "if she runs off and doesn't broach . . . or if she heads into it. But I don't think the lifeboat could safely cut the channel now. And those waves are still building."

Bennett returned Karl's gaze with a flinty look in his gray eyes. "They'll make it,"he said defiantly and turned toward the storm."They . . ."

Just then, Karl saw a curling wave break over the lifeboat, and Bennett's voice turned strangling, then harsh, then timid, and trailed off. Karl looked sideways at the officer and saw an anguished look on his face. When Karl looked back into the boiling storm, the lifeboat was gone.

He waited anxiously for it to appear on the next wave and glanced nervously over his shoulder at the anemometer on the wall, where the needle rose to sixty-seven knots. Damn, he thought, that's well over seventy miles per hour.

Out on the lake, between slate walls of water, the small boat was nowhere to be seen. Karl saw very high waves now. Gray masses which heaped up, marching steadily in, with long, overhanging crests that toppled, tumbled, and rolled down the greasy slopes. Foam at the crests broke off and blew away in streaks along the direction of the wind; and as the storm built, more foam blew from wave tops in bigger patches of dense, white streaks. The tumbling of the sea became heavy and shocklike. Rain, mixed with hail, peppered and rattled against the window in front of Karl.

Glancing again at the wind gauge, he saw the pointer strike seventy-five knots; and out the window, the wave crests were now blown everywhere into froth. The air was filled with foam, spray, sleet and rain. The red lighthouse disappeared in a blanket of wind-blown spray. He could barely see where the water met the beach, one hundred yards away.

Captain Bennett coughed and staggered back from the window. "My God," he gasped, "they're gone!"

"You've sent them to their death!" Karl screamed at the distraught officer. "First my hand—and now Billy!"

"Easy, Karl!" Corky screamed, stepping between the men and pushing Karl back. "Yellin' won't do any good."

"We'll . . . We'll get a party out . . . along the beach," Bennett cried out from behind Corky. "We'll find 'em, Karl. We'll find 'em!"

***

The little double-ended lifeboat turned north after clearing the channel at Southport that morning to search for the fishing tugs Billy Meister knew were making heavy weather. He gripped the wheel, chanting one ditty after another to keep up the crew's spirits, and watched the seas mounting higher and higher all around. Suddenly, he heard a roar astern, and turned to see a huge wave, much larger than anything he'd ever seen, with a broken crest tumbling down its gray face. "It's coming aboard!" he cried out.

As the mountain of water broke over the stern, he wrapped both arms around the wheel post. The sea went over him. The next thing he felt was a force of water around his body so great he was slammed against the wheel and then forced down, his locked arms sliding to the pedestal base. He knew the boat had broached, starboard side down. He pulled himself up until he could get his hands on the wheel. By that time the boat had righted herself and the waist-high water was pouring out the scuppers. One man was over the side, pulled along by his safety line. He shouted to the men thrown into a heap under the canvas hood. They grabbed the line and heaved.

Then they wobbled over another crest and down into a trough. The engine behind him in its wooden box purred on. He put the wheel hard over to port. Half full of water, the boat was in a dangerous condition, another breaker could send it spinning over, perhaps tear the wooden cover off the engine, and then it would be all over for them.

The water drained to the floor boards before they met the next wave, this time head-on. The man overboard had been retrieved. They were soaked and shivering. But for the moment, they were back in control. He knew they had to give up the search. There was no hope for the two tugs. It was now a matter of their own survival.

His heart sunk when he stared at the compass ahead of the wheel. It was cracked and the fluid was running out. The gimbled scale canted to one side, no longer swinging. Well, he thought, it made little difference anyway now. There was only one course open to them, straight into those mammoth waves. And when the storm finally passed, he would use an old trick he'd learned from Captain Bennett. Hell, half the fresh water captains on the lake navigated that way. Take out your pocket watch, point the hour hand at the sun, and estimate due south to lie exactly midway between the hour hand and the figure twelve on the dial.

But in this seething caldron of mixed water and air, there was no sun. And if the storm kept on? he asked himself, if they were still plowing into those waves when night fell, what then? Well, he'd just have to feel his way along, maybe he could keep the boat into the waves by the lift of the bow.

***

Karl, Corky, and four surfmen searched the beaches throughout the afternoon, walking two miles north, and then two miles south, of the river; looking for signs of wreckage, survivors or bodies. Not a trace. Karl shook his head as he stumbled along the swirling sand, water, and now, hard-driven snow.

On the next trip through the boat house, he glanced at the thermometer and saw it register twenty-six degrees. "A drop of forty degrees," he said to Corky. As they walked from the boat house and onto the south beach once again, he turned to Corky and said, "Unless they've lashed themselves to the boat and gone straight down, they'd have washed up by now."

With hands in his pockets and chin tucked into his collar, he left Corky standing on the beach and walked to the water's edge. Leaning against the snow-spitting wind and flying water, he muttered to himself, "The boat's watertight, I know it. Unsinkable." His mind raced on, seeing Billy at the wheel, fighting through the froth. Lifting his face to the raging gale, he smiled. "Keep your peckers up, boys!" he shouted into the wind. "I know you're out there, and you're in for it now."

"Karl," Corky said to him as he returned from the surf, "let's give it up for a while. Come back later. I'm freezing. What do you say? A beer at the Antler?"

"Go on. Go ahead, Corky. I'm taking one more trip up the north beach. I'll be along later."

Karl followed behind two wind-whipped surfmen fighting their way up the north beach in the black night. With the wind from the southwest, he thought, this is where the boat would wash ashore—or the bodies—or both.

The two dark figures in front of him carried lanterns and Coston signals, the same flare-like signaling device used by Karl fourteen years earlier to warn vessels too close to shore, or to let ship-wrecked sailors out on a sandbar, know they were spotted.

That damned Corky is drunk by now, Karl said to himself after they had trudged along the beach for two hours and reached the northern boundary of the patrol. There, fifty yards above the high-water line, he saw a surfman shine his lantern on a black box supported by a wooden post. Nothing had really changed, Karl thought. He watched the lead man take a key from his belt pouch and open the metal box. Taking a still larger key from the box, the surfman pushed it into a timeclock, which swung on a leather strap from his shoulder, then twisted the key, marking the date and time on a paper dial inside the clock.

"A fitting memorial," Karl said quietly to himself as he watched the men in the swirl of driven sand and snow. But only Karl knew the key post was a headstone for Big Mike Curla. Karl had buried him there long ago, with a flat coal shovel.

It was a cold July in 1926, he remembered. He was twenty years old then. Al Capone came in on the *City of Southport*, a three-tiered, gleaming white side-wheeler. Karl met him at the Williams Company docks. Karl sat behind the wheel of a black Dodge touring car. A big Packard sedan, also black, was parked in front of him. Three more of the big cars waited behind to drive the Capone entourage to the Pirate's Cove Resort, farther up the lake.

Karl watched from under the car's tan canvas top, as Big Mike lumbered down the gangplank behind Capone's white panama, dragging a thin, short-haired girl behind him. When Curla reached the Dodge, he shoved the girl, whose name Karl later learned was Flora Nagel, into the back seat and slid in behind her. Flora was a bobbed brunette, with glassy black eyes and a constant giggle on her sensuous lips.

Two rough looking men, wearing the same rumpled, black silk suits and white ties in which Curla was dressed, squeezed into the front seat next to Karl. It was apparent to Karl that Big Mike was not to be crowded.

"*Bitte*—please," Karl stammered, trying to work the long, curved floor shift around the knee of the garlic-smelling man seated next to him.

"You a damned Hun?" Big Mike boomed from the back and kicked the driver's seat twice.

"*Nein* . . . No. Austrian," Karl answered in a thick accent. Then the heavy Packard in front leaped ahead, and he followed the black car up the Michigan Avenue hill, with the old Dodge touring car straining and its transmission growling in first gear.

When they reached the top, the lead car turned, and Karl followed it over the Dunckley Street Bridge. Three blocks later, they turned north along the lakeshore. After driving two miles, he followed the Packard through the resort's wrought iron gates.

Al Capone stepped from the car ahead. Setting the parking brake, Karl went to the rear door and opened it for Flora. A big hand shot past her and locked Karl's wrist in a steel grip. "Nobody but me opens the door for Flora, see!" Big Mike barked.

"Ya. Ya. Sure," Karl said.

Flora looked straight at Karl, and very slowly, almost mechanically, closed her left eye in a long wink. "I like uniforms, soldier," she said softly. Karl blushed under his visor.

Reaching from the opposite door, Big Mike pulled Flora across the rear seat and jerked her to his side. It was then that Karl saw her turn sideways from the big man, run her tongue slowly over her full lips, and wink again.

Karl returned the car to the big garage across the courtyard, and hanging his gray gaberdine tunic on a hook behind the green door, lay down on the small cot in his room over the cars. It would be three days before he reported for duty at the Coast Guard building. There, he also had a bed. But it was an uncomfortable pipe berth in a crowded room. He was glad that the new regulations permitted other part-time employment and sleeping off-station, so long as he was never more than five miles away. Six days on and three days off was his schedule. The resort met the additional requirement of a phone, so that in an emergency he could be on his bicycle and at the station in less than twenty minutes.

The extra money was saved for his younger brother's passage, as Karl's compensation at the resort included free meals; hot food that had cost him thirty of his sixty-dollars per month pay from the Coast Guard.

The resort manager was happy to meet this schedule, for Karl was a skilled carpenter and kept the buildings in good repair, tended the lawns and occasionally chauffeured resorters about the small town. In the colder fall weather before the Chicago schools opened and the resort closed, he stoked the furnaces.

But by midnight it was down to forty-five degrees and he heard the manager bang on his door. "Capone wants heat! Fire the boilers!"

Karl swung his feet to the cold tiles. "Ya. Ya," he shouted through the closed door. "I'm coming." He pulled on his gray pants and drew the suspenders over his bare shoulders.

Running down the sand-blown sidewalk past the tennis courts, he entered the basement of the "Parrot's Beak," the twenty-room building where Capone and his mob were quartered. It was dark on the basement stairs. He felt his way down to the first landing, where he pulled the string of a single light hanging by its cord. Walking down the second flight of stairs, he saw kindling in the corner. Ah, good, he thought. At least we have something left from last year. He shredded an old newspaper he had brought with him and laid it on the boiler's grate. Then taking the dry wood from the corner, he placed it in squares over the paper. In the middle, he stacked pieces of hard coal he had split with a hammer.

When the fire blazed and crackled, he added more coal from the bin with a narrow flat-bladed shovel. Stepping back and closing the boiler door, he heard a long low whistle from the stairwell. Turning quickly, he saw Flora on the landing, wearing a maroon-colored robe, slightly open at the front, and under which he could see she wore nothing at all.

"Hi, soldier boy," she said coming slowly down the stairs with a brown bottle in her hand. "Want a drinkie-pooh?"

"No thanks," Karl said and backed as she now advanced across the basement floor, clutching her robe about her. Then her hand was on his tunic, unbottoning it, and quickly flat along his naked chest, as he stood against the wall.

"You son-of-a-bitch!" Big Mike Curla rushed down the stairs.

Karl pushed Flora aside and stepped forward, arms raised in defense. Big Mike flashed past and grabbed Flora by the throat. She gurgled and then went quiet, as Curla squeezed his big hand tight around her graceful neck. Then she sank, and still he did not release his powerful grip.

Shaken, Karl watched. Big Mike was choking the life out of the girl! Or was it a bluff? Seeing Curla's face, as he pushed Flora to the ground, twisting her into the black coal dust, Karl knew the answer. The man was more purple than red, eyes narrowed, brows crushed together, lips curled in a fierce snarl and hissing between his teeth.

With his right hand, Big Mike pulled a long razor from his hip pocket and flicked it open. He raised it high, ready to strike, and tightened his grip around Flora's neck.

Without knowing what he was doing, Karl lunged with the coal shovel and chopped deep into Curla's neck. The blunt blade struck at the base of the skull. Big Mike crumpled and rolled, blood pulsing onto the dust covered floor.

Flora staggered to her feet and fell back against a post, gasping and sobbing, and then slid again to the floor.

Karl stared at Curla. Gurgling noises and red froth came from Big Mike's mouth. Then he stopped breathing.

A cold shiver of revulsion passed over Karl. He could taste the bile rising in the back of his throat. Sickness churned his stomach. He'd killed the man.

Karl fought the intense urge to vomit and opened the dead man's coat, avoiding those cold, accusing eyes.

"Here," Karl said to Flora, taking two fifty-dollar bills from Curla's wallet, "take this . . . And go home."

Flora, now sitting against the post and rubbing her neck, nodded and looked at Curla's body with wide eyes.

Karl helped her to her feet, pressing the bills into her palm. "Go home," he said again. "This is no place for you."

She walked slowly toward the stairs, looked back with a bewildered and questioning glance, and ran up the basement steps.

Karl could hold it back no longer, and clutching blindly for the ash bucket, he emptied his stomach.

After several long minutes while Karl mumbled "Hail Marys" and fought for control of his tumbling insides, he pulled Big Mike's dark suit coat from the heavy body and hung it on a post hook. He leaned the dead man against the post, slipped the coat behind his head, and tied the sleeves tightly around his neck. Next, he took the dead man's right wing-tip and hid it above a support beam.

Then he slid the body along the floor, bumped it up the wooden steps, and lifted it into a wheelbarrow from the tool shed.

He listened and heard nothing other than the waves rolling to the beach below the resort.

Seeing no movement behind the lighted, upper windows, he pushed the wheelbarrow through the dark courtyard.

The iron wheel dug into the loose dirt at the bluff; and when the wheel finally buried in the sand, he spun around and pulled it backwards over the dune.

The barrow was slipping and sliding down the loose sand now, as he pulled it to the beach below.

Stopping and looking at his watch, Karl saw that it was nearly two o'clock. He'd have to hurry. There was barely time before the next surfman came to punch his clock at the key post, one-hundred yards down the beach.

When he could no longer drag the wheelbarrow through the loose sand, he tipped it on its side, spilling the body on the beach. Too many resort dogs, he thought. I've got to get the body down to the key post, where the fence will keep them out—and then dig deep.

He dragged Big Mike through the sand, opened the gate, and pushed the body in, then rushed back to the wheelbarrow and grabbed the coal shovel. Running again to the body, he stopped suddenly. Down the beach he saw the swinging lantern of a surfman.

Looking quickly around, Karl threw the shovel into low bushes, grabbed the dead man by the arms, and pulled him into the brush.

Karl was breathing heavily and now held his breath as the surfman walked up to the gate, ten feet away.

"Damn kids," the surfman said. "In here again. And left the gate open." The surfman raised his lantern and peered about. Karl crouched low in the bush as the light hit his eyes. He saw the guard take two steps toward him, stop, and look at his watch.

"Oh, God," Karl said to himself. He recognized the man's face in the lantern light. "It's Jake."

Jake looked down, his eyes following the marks in the sand to where Karl held his breath in the dark bushes.

"Looks fresh," Jake said, bending to touch the sand. Rising again, Jake lifted the lantern high and pointed it along the path Curla's body had made from the wheelbarrow. "Went that way, did you," Jake said. "Damn resorters."

Karl's lungs were bursting. He exhaled slowly. He was in luck. The Coston beam didn't reach the barrow lying in the black shadows.

Waiting until Jake had punched the clock, and his lantern was no more than a small speck down the beach, Karl opened the gate, dug a trench to the side of the post, and pushed the body in. He covered it quickly, using the coal shovel, and smoothed the sand with a tree branch.

Returning the wheelbarrow to the tool shed, he swept up the blood-stained coal dust in the basement. Then he took the wallet and shoe to the garage across the courtyard. There, he carefully brushed the shoe and dropped it on the Dodge's back seat with the wallet.

After opening the garage doors and looking quickly around, he mashed the starter button, and backed the car into the courtyard. Then he smiled to himself. It would be even better, he thought as he roared off, if someone saw the car leave.

Karl drove to the Dunckley Street Bridge over the Black River, where he stopped the car. The street was empty, and he pulled the car's throttle lever sharply down, aimed for the side of the bridge, and dropped his head to his hands over the wheel, as the touring car struck the wooden rail.

The car splintered the rail and dove to the river below, hitting the water with a huge roar, which Karl was certain awakened the entire town.

He swam from the car and watched it float down the dark river, hood under water and square trunk stretching to the starlit sky.

By the time he reached the grass-covered bank, only large bubbles swelling to the surface marked the place where the car had sunk from view.

The next morning, Karl went to the manager's office and reported the touring car missing. Later in the afternoon, the manager told him Curla must have taken the car and lost control on the bridge. "Crashed through the rail," he said in the lounge, and leaning closer to Karl over his coffee, whispered, "The Nagel girl's gone too. They both must have drowned. The sheriff's dragging the river now. Found the car . . . and Curla's shoe and wallet, but no bodies yet," and looking nervously over his shoulder to where Capone dealt three other men cards, the manager said quietly with a nod of his head, "Our guest doesn't like all this publicity. He's leaving on the morning boat."

These were the things that tumbled through Karl's mind in the storm as he stood on the beach, the wind at his back, watching the surfman slide the time clock into its leather pouch. Flora had gone home, and Capone died without ever learning the truth. I don't believe the bastard's interrogation would have been very gentle, Karl said to himself.

Surfman Decker's broad face startled him from his thoughts. It was less than a foot away and shouting. "It's a good sign!" Decker said. "They would have washed ashore! Right here . . ." Decker waved an arm to the south, "had she broken up or gone over!"

Decker thumped Karl's shoulder a reassuring blow, and the three men trekked southward, pausing occasionally to search the boiling lake for signs of the two fish tugs and missing Coast Guard boat. Karl followed behind, glancing north over his shoulder. He didn't completely share Decker's confidence. The tugs sure as hell capsized in that, Karl thought, looking out at the wind-swept seas. And it's more likely they've blown far north in this southwester. Then it came to him. A trip farther north might yield evidence of the wrecks, or survivors, and maybe the lifeboat as well.

***

In the pilothouse of the *Tres Belle*, Captain Jacque DuPays pulled the collar of his peacoat tight around his neck. The temperature in the wheelroom had plunged shortly after the chief engineer tightened down the valve to the ship's steam radiators. DuPays had ordered all possible measures to conserve steam for the hard-working engine, including shutting down the steam generator and starting up the old emergency gasoline auxillary in the engine room which produced only half the ship's normal electrical requirement.

Below, the firemen were suffocating in the heat. Flames shot high in the air of the cramped space as the black-hole crew raked burned coal from the fireboxes into the ashpits. Gray clouds obscured the scene like a fog. Then taking long iron bars, they pried away the clinkers which plugged the grates, reducing the efficiency of the furnaces; and as the glowing clinkers fell upon the deck, they extinquished them with a hose. With the furnace doors open for that long operation, all the metal surfaces in the dust-choked room grew hot enough to scald the skin off a man's hand, should he forget and reach out for a bulkhead. They were priming the boilers for maximum steam.

Ahead the seas and sky were all one black mass. They had done all that could be done. They were buttoned up. Doors dogged down. Hatches secured; and now the ship was putting on its unlovely coat—its burden of ice which set it ever lower on its marks, the white lines indicating the maximum load lines on the hull for summer and winter conditions. With the weight growing on its decks and cabin sides, the old ship rolled a little farther out with each passing hour.

Now that the lifeboats had carried away, there was no choice but to accept the ship's destiny as theirs. She could break any moment and go to the bottom that way. She could roll far out, and the coke could shift, and she'd keep right on rolling. Or one or more of the hatch covers could be clawed off by the raging waters, and there'd be nothing to be done about it, she'd fill and then take her plunge; and if none of those things happened, they'd probably run aground.

After total darkness enveloped the ship, Captain DuPays had no idea where shore was, except that, with the ship's speed ever dropping, and the waves building, he knew they were being set, and at the same time, the shore was coming out to meet him, running at an angle to the northwest along this stretch.

But if he could only clear Deer Point, they might have a chance yet, because beyond that narrow sliver projecting into the lake, the shoreline turned eastward, and they would have another two-hours of running time before it swung to the west again just south of Muskegon.

The captain picked up the voice tube and piped the engine room.

The chief engineer had just come up the five iron steps from the boiler room. "We're gaining a little on her, sir." He screamed into the tube. "Taylor and Shipley are working their asses off," he said, referring to the green firemen and coal passer they'd picked up at Sturgeon Bay. The job of replacing engine room and black-hole crew went to the chief engineer, and he was justly proud of the new men who toiled below, although they were wretchedly seasick now.

The old ship's masthead lights swung in ever-wider, horrifying arcs. Black mountains pounded aboard every few seconds, thundering against the forward deckhouse and cabin bulkheads, roaring along the spar deck and clutching at the hatches. But the hatches held.

They were the usual wooden hatch covers, oak timbers bolted together in groups of four, with heavy canvas stretched over them and driven home with wooden wedges.

One after another the seas climbed aboard, rolling, pounding, twisting, and straining her hull. The wind had risen yet higher. The captain in the pilothouse heard it and knew higher waves would follow. The storm was screaming and whistling overhead, strumming the windows with a hollow sound and rising to a higher pitch as it encirled the wire shrouds and radio mast. The full force of the destructive combination of wind, snow, and sub-freezing temperatures boomed around the struggling ship. With the deck under seething water half the time, the forward crew was virtually marooned. Captain DuPays had handed the last of the water from the pilothouse jug to the laboring wheelsman. At least the wrenching action had done some good. By some unknown miracle, the steering cables had freed, leaving considerably more play in the wheel than the captain would like to see.

Ice had long since carried away the taffrail log trailed astern to record the distance through the water and speed made good. It made no difference now, Captain DuPays told the second engineer who reported it missing over the voice tube, they were going mostly sideways, and no man could have gone on deck to read it anyway.

Part of the time, Jacque DuPays could not make out the lights of the aft cabin, or see more than half the length of the deck. And he was wondering about the after end crew, knowing that the men in the firehold and engine room were going through sheer hell. He turned to the mate on watch. "How's the glass look?"

"Still falling rapidly, sir."

The captain rubbed his chin. "It was just too damned high yesterday. I don't like to see a barometer go that high." He paused and looked out through the frosty pilothouse windows. "It's not good at all. Once she starts down there's no telling how far she'll fall when she's gone that high."

They'd steamed from Chicago to Michigan City the night before; and all that long evening, the pilothouse windows were open and he'd had a man stationed outside in the balmy air, keeping an eye out for the heavy ship traffic.

In his sixteen years of lake experience, the captain had never seen such a vivid display of Northern Lights, nor such a rapid change in the weather. If they went down now, there was little chance of surviving for more than a few minutes in the freezing air and icy waters churned up from the depths by that terrible storm.

Now they continued on through the night. The battered ship rolling on her beam ends, smothered in white foam. In the galley, a cupboard door sprang open and dishes cascaded from their racks. The pans clamped on the old coal range broke loose and slid off onto the deck. Portholes in the aft cabins were cracking from the strain of the twisting metal bulkheads and water spurted everywhere. Dogged down watertight doors sprung. The cabin sides were bending in.

Down below, the boiler doors swung back and forth, sometimes slamming shut, just as a firemen advanced with a shovel of black coal. Carpets of loose coal slid back and forth along the steel plates; and the men working there, the fireman feeding the boilers and the coal passers with their stubby iron wheelbarrows, found themselves on the deck on all fours half the time. But the word had been passed. "Make steam, it means your very life, man!"

The overstrained hull was working all around them. Rivets popped and and whistled overhead. Below their feet, the deck plates were beginning to buckle. The steel used in such ships is known as mild steel; it's tough and pliable and so treated that it is less affected by heat and cold and stress than tool steel. But the forty-one-year old plates of the *Tres Belle* had seen too much stress; and now they were giving way in those murderous seas.

Soon the coal-passers' wheelbarrows and the firemen themselves were sliding from side-to-side along with the coal. The big fire-grate doors clanged back and forth. Tools and shovels slid everywhere and slammed against the bulkheads. Ash buckets spilled and spun about the floor.

In the engine room, the third engineer sweated and hung onto his levers, slowing the ship's screw each time the stern rose high on a wave. But even this couldn't stop the pounding vibration that threatened to shake loose the propeller shaft at any moment.

Then the powdered coke in the holds started to shift. It would be suicide to send men down there with shovels in that weather to trim the load, Captain Jacque DuPays told himself; and so he waited and watched the list to starboard grow steadily, putting off as long as he could the order.

As the chief engineer scribbled the engine-revolution count into the log, pondering the unexplained drop in steam pressure over the last few minutes, a sweating, black-faced fireman, panic in his eyes, rushed up to the desk where he stood.

"For God's sake, Chief, come quick and take a look! There's water in the firehold! Lots of it!"

When the chief reached the boiler room, the water was already ankle deep, and the men, shovels and wheelbarrows were sliding around in the coal-blackend mess with each roll of the ship. He stumbled back up the short iron ladder to the engine room platform and whistled up the captain.

"Forget trying to hold engine speed," DuPays yelled. "Get the pumps going—all of them!"

On the captain's orders, the engineer cut down the engine revolutions to provide more steam for the pumps. Then he returned to the boiler room to see what effect the extra steam had—it was very little—the water was building up in the firehold. Already it lapped into the ash pits on each roll, sending up clouds of acrid fumes.

He got the captain on the voice pipe. "Water in the firehold is gaining rapidly, sir, despite the pumps . . ." He waited for the reply and listened to the strange moaning in the communication tube. Somewhere along the twisting length of the ship the voice pipe had parted. He grabbed the bridge telephone and cranked the magneto. No answer. They'd lost contact with the pilothouse. In the boiler room, desperate firemen were working in water up to their knees.

Three

When Karl entered the Coast Guard Station, leaving the din of the storm behind him, he turned to find Captain Bennett addressing the relatives of the four missing guardsmen: wives, mothers, uncles and aunts, and brothers and sisters, all crowded into the boat house with other citizens of the small city, each feeling that the latest news would undoubtedly come to that place.

Bennett's voice was high-pitched, rising and falling in what seemed to Karl an hysterical manner. "It'll be all over in an hour, or so. Or less! Ah . . . less, much less," Bennett stumbled on and looked at his watch. His eyes darted out to the lake and back from the window to the uneasy throng huddled before him. When his eyes at last fell upon Karl, the captain smiled nervously and seemed to plead for his help.

Of the fourteen men who served in the Coast Guard with Karl during those prohibition years, only Bennett remained, now promoted from Number One surfman to station captain with rank of warrant officer.

Karl shrugged his shoulders in disgust. He had no confidence in Bennett then, and less now—it was remarkable that such an incompetent ass could gain charge of the station merely by attrition.

Near the back, Karl saw Muriel, Billy's wife of two weeks. She held her father, old John McKay, by the arm. She must be doubly troubled, Karl thought, her young brother on the old tug and her new husband after him in an open life boat. Karl knew he should go to her and tell her something—that Billy and her brother—the entire crews of the three vessels, would see dawn snug in port. But he felt his face would betray him. Let Bennett speak with the voice of authority, he thought, looking quickly away. They believed Bennett because they wanted to.

Karl stood, quietly listening to Captain Bennett's shrill voice over the raging storm, his eyes roaming over the wet and cold throng, his left hand throbbing in the black glove at his side.

He thought back to the storm of April 1929. That was a dark day—but the weather had started out good then, too. It was already late spring, and he hadn't expected a big blow. Karl was a Coast Guardsman in the watch tower, noting the fishing tug's names and times of departure in the log, as he watched the small boats set out to tend their nets.

The storm came suddenly, and wind blasts followed a few short, innocent puffs, and shook the tower. Minutes later, the wind was a fifty-mile gale, and snow, coming from nowhere, pelted the window before his face. The wind died. Then the snow came down heavy and wrapped the tower in a thick blanket; and the wind came back and whipped the snow-blanket into a raging blizzard. The temperature plunged, and Karl wished for his peajacket, down in the warm billet below, while he rushed to close the side window where the cold air curled in, turning the tower ice cold.

Pulling the window shut, Karl glimpsed the *Bradley* far out on the lake, making for the channel, with the *Chief* at her heel, and the *Merry B.* farther behind. Then he lost the boats in the swirling snow again.

He entered the time of sight in the log, and peered through marine glasses for some sign of the vessels. An hour passed, and he saw nothing on the lake. Suddenly, the tugs loomed closer now, and bearing off to the north, away from the channel and Karl realized the captains had given up the idea of running the channel in that weather, they were trying to bring the boats into the wind. He could see they had insufficient power to overcome the northwesterly's force against their box cabins, which ran the full length of each boat, topped by the dog-house windows ahead of the belching smoke stacks.

He jerked the white rope which ran on pulleys to ring the bell in the crew's quarters below. Having sounded the alarm, he returned to the window for a bearing on the tugs.

Just then the *Merry B.* rolled her rusty bottom to the leaden sky, as two large curlers converged and struck her flat side when she struggled for balance in a trough.

Karl ran down the wooden tower steps and burst into the boat house as Captain McKenzie barked commands to the surfmen struggling with the little power boat on its cradle.

"The *Merry B.*'s gone over," Karl shouted. "Let me crew!"

Karl knew McKenzie wouldn't refuse his request to go to the aid of his father-in-law, the captain of the *Merry B.*

"Take the port seat!" McKenzie motioned toward the little boat where a red-haired surfman jumped aside.

Karl spilled over the gunwale as the lifeboat raced down the ramp and smacked the water. Then the Number One surfman pulled the starter, the engine coughed and the surfboat bounced down the channel, its two cylinders beating out a steady tatoo against the wind and waves.

The little surfboat rose on a swell near the end of the piers, and Karl saw the *Bradley,* now alongside the capsized *Merry B.* A line flew through the air from the side hatch near the *Bradley's* bow and missed the turtled vessel.

The surfboat cleared the channel, rose high on a wave, and headed north toward the stricken ship.

When Karl realized Bennett, the Number One surfman, was steering straight toward the *Bradley,* he shouted out, "Go around! Go around!"

Bennett looked at Karl. "The lee side?" His forehead wrinkled and he shrugged his shoulders. "We wouldn't get back!" he shouted; and charging straight down on the capsized tug, Bennett said, "We'll come about between the two tugs. Stand by! Fend off on your own judgment!"

The *Bradley* veered quickly away to the north as its captain powered around for another run at the sinking vessel. The surfboat bobbed to the windward side of the *Merry B.*, and upon command from Bennett, two grappling hooks clattered over its tin bottom. The hooks held, and the surfboat drifted down toward the rusty hulk.

Karl's father-in-law, Nate Sunstrand and his two fishing partners clung to warps streamed to leeward of the stricken vessel, assuming help would swing past the disabled tug, turn back into the wind, and approach from the protected side of the boat. When grappling hooks clanged against tin overhead and dug into the metal seams, they realized too late that rescue lay to windward.

Karl and the red-haired surfman pulled on the lines, while Bennett worked the shift lever, cranking the wheel left and right, and maintaining a parallel position, while they closed on the rusted plates of the *Merry B.*

Fixing hard eyes directly on Timothy Bennett, the Number One surfman, Karl leaned forward. "We've got to go around and come up leeward—leeward, Bennett. Otherwise we'll bash to pieces against her!"

The Number One surfman paused for what seemed to Karl a full minute, and as Bennett finally opened his mouth to reply, a foaming swell lifted the lifeboat and set it hard against the tug's metal bottom. Karl lost his balance when the wooden boat hook broke in his hand, and he slipped to the bottom of the rocking boat.

Before he could regain his feet, a wave curled overhead and slammed full against the small boat. The heavy blow knocked Karl flat and he felt other men, ropes, and gear about him under the water. Foaming and swirling water was everywhere above him; and then he felt wooden planks of the smashed lifeboat all around.

At last, his cork life jacket carried him to the surface. The huge wave had washed the little boat completely over the wallowing tug.

Ahead, he saw two fishermen clinging to lines from the *Merry B.*, and around him he counted the heads of three guardsmen.

Looking for his father-in-law, and struggling through the icy water to take a line alongside Leonard Nesmith, one of the fisherman, he realized his left hand was broken and mangled—ripped flesh showing white bones.

Mr. Nesmith, cut the sleeve from Karl's peajacket and tearing it into three strips, wrapped the hand tightly while Karl clung to the line. Using the third strip from the jacket, Nesmith tied it firmly around Karl's head, stopping the blood flow from the gash across his cheek.

"Where's Sunstrand?" Karl asked above the wind's roar.

"Gone, Karl! Gone! Yer boat came down on 'em!" Nesmith explained that the lifeboat wreckage came over the tug in a wash of water, sliding down the rusty hull of the inverted tug and landing directly on Captain Sunstrand. He'd watched the lifeboat debris bubble to the surface with the Coast Guard men, but his captain never surfaced. Pointing to torn canvas and cork floating with the lifeboat's broken planks, Nesmith shouted, "There it is—his life preserver!"

Although the wind screamed overhead, it was strangely peaceful in the sinking tug's lee. But Karl knew the old boat was going under and wouldn't break the crashing seas much longer; and he also knew there would be a terrible suction when the hulk raced to the bottom. "We've got to swim for it!" Karl shouted to Nesmith, pointing to the lifeboat's inverted bow section which bobbed in the tug's eddy, supported by its ballast tank.

"Aye," Nesmith replied. "Can you make it, Karl?"

"Cut the rope and bring it along," Karl said. "I can make it."

Nesmith passed the word to his partner, who also cut his line, and the three men swam to the floating bow section. There, they passed the long lines back and forth over the shattered planks, running the ropes under their arms, and back over the bow again to the man on the other side, who did the same. Thus, balancing the floating debris and treading water, they slowly worked away from the sinking tug.

Now Karl and the two fisherman were out of the tug's shelter, and the wind and waves pushed them steadily to the beach. Hearing a hissing noise over his shoulder, Karl turned to see the old tug roll on its side. Then there was a loud boom, followed by a blast of water and air rising high from the tug's open side hatch. The *Merry B.* again rolled its bottom to the gray sky. Then the stern rose, showing its three-bladed prop, and the boat slid silently beneath the foaming waters.

In the distance, far beyond the massive bubble which marked the tug's exit, Karl saw the *Bradley,* fighting for its life.

Looking around, he saw the *Sioux Chief* cut the channel entrance. By God, he thought, old man McKay is one helluva seaman.

But now it was time to work for shore, and the men paddled furiously with their free hand, for they, like Karl, knew that exposure in the cold water was the true enemy; and after twenty minutes of hard work, Karl felt the bottom under his feet. A few minutes later, he was able to stand, leaning against the undertow, while they struggled to shore. At last, freeing himself from the rope lashing, he stumbled through the surf and fell upon the wet, sandy beach.

"Get up, Karl. Get up." he heard Nesmith screaming in his ear. "This is no good, Karl. Keep moving."

Karl struggled to his feet in the wind. Surfmen from the station were all around him now. On the road beyond the beach, he saw an ambulance, its red light flashing.

In the ambulance, Karl looked through the open doors and saw the *Bradley* hit bottom, spin broadside to the waves and roll its flat tar-paper roof toward the beach. Surfmen ran along the shore, dragging a two-wheeled cart through the sand. They'll shoot a line, Karl said to himself. As the ambulance doors closed, he turned to Bennett, who sat across from him.

"Karl, I told you to shove off," Bennett said in an anguished voice. "I saw it coming . . . Why didn't you shove off?" Karl watched his face take on odd lines, defiant, yet terrified, and also angry and fearful, and Bennett's eyes rolled from side to side as if wanting to be sure the other men heard. "Why didn't you shove off?" Bennett asked again, his voice strangling and trailing off at the end.

Looking straight at the oddly rigid face with its quivering jaw, Karl said, "God forgive you now, Bennett."

At the hospital, Karl learned that the *Bradley* crew had jumped to the shallow water and stumbled ashore when the fired line missed the tug. It's captain was the last man off. Before he left, he opened seacocks, letting the boat settle firmly into the sand. Fortunately, a lanky surfman told Karl, the *Bradley* heeled, with its bottom breaking the force of the waves, and would suffer little damage. When the weather cleared, the crew could float her off.

The *Chief* had come safely to port. Yes, Karl thought, only old McKay could thread the channel between those slate-gray walls.

Sitting in the operating room, with his battered hand held over a small table, Karl watched as Dr. Keith poked and pulled at the puffy mass. The doctor had closed the wide gash on his cheek with twenty-seven stitches; and now he turned his attention to the hand. "All we can do now, Karl," the doctor said dryly, "is clean it out and and sew it up. I'll set the broken fingers as best I can. But I'm not promising anything. You'll need several operations. Tendon and nerve sections missing. Bone fragments. No—it doesn't look good, Karl. You've lost two small bones in your palm—they're entirely gone."

Karl stared at the doctor for a moment, unable to speak. Then finally he said very slowly, "Doctor Keith, I work with that hand—everyday. Do you mean—?"

"I'm not a specialist, Karl. The orthopaedic men will take over from here. Dr. Nielson in Grand Rapids is a good man. I'll be referring you to him, unless you have someone else in mind. And from what I see, he should be able to do some bone grafting. The bones in the palm will have to be fused. You should have some movement in these two fingers." Dr. Keith managed a wan smile. "At least you're right-handed, Karl."

"Dr. Keith, I have to leave the hospital today. Nate Sunstrand drowned. I think I should be the one to tell Sylvia about her father."

"Yes. We'll make up a sling. Keep it high. I'll give you a second pain injection when we're done here, and a prescription. If the pain pills aren't enough, give me a call tonight. And then be back here tomorrow at ten. I'll make the arrangements with Dr. Nielson, give you another shot, and you can have someone drive you to Grand Rapids."

Dr. Keith laid down his instruments, pushed his glasses up on his nose with a gloved hand, and shook his head. "Sylvia may need a sedative, Karl. She was very close to her father. And this is going to be a real shock. Why don't you see her priest, Father Malloy. Maybe he should be the one to tell her. I'll stop by a little later."

The yellow taxi the nurse had called for him was waiting in the drive when Karl left the hospital. He slid into the back seat and said to the gray-haired driver, "St. Monica, Charlie."

"The Catholic church?"

"Yes. On the lake."

The taxi stopped in front of the gray stucco convent where a high bluff overlooked the south beach. Karl crossed the brick paving to St. Monica's Cathedral. Inside, he dropped to one knee and made the sign of the cross. "Help me dear Lord," he prayed slowly, "to find the right words. The old man was her life."

Walking to the back of the empty church, Karl found Father Malloy in the small chapel. "Our Lord Jesus," the short priest cried out, "by the sorrows you suffered in the garden, your agony upon the cross and your death, have mercy on the soul of my friend Nate Sunstrand; deliver him from the dire torment he must endure, and admit him to your most sweet embrace in paradise."

Yes, Karl thought, he'll not make heaven without serving penance, for in fact the entire town knew he loved the dear widows too much.

Karl felt a special sorrow for the square-faced priest who mourned for his bearded friend, one of the few men in the small fishing town able to match his skill at chess.

After greeting the priest, Karl returned to the rear of the church, lit a candle for his departed father-in-law, and placed it in the checkered holder behind the last pew. From the chapel behind the main altar, he could hear the mournful chant of the parish priest. Then Father Malloy joined him with a serene and soft smile, and he followed the priest through the double doors and into the cold of that black and chilly day in April.

The church's passionate death bell tolled behind him as Karl followed the priest along the concrete walk. He remembered following another priest long ago in Eisenkreutz, when the death bell had also yielded to the clapper and toned along the narrow path from the village to his uncle's farm on the hillside above.

The Austrian priest was a head taller than Father Malloy striding ahead of him, and Karl had been unable to see over that tall priest's narrow shoulders.

He had followed the village priest into his uncle's farmyard, holding a lantern high in front. When Karl pushed the door open, they stepped quietly into the wide hall where his uncle, aunt and cousins knelt in front of a crucifix, chanting a bittersweet "Hail Mary." His sturdy, dwarf-like, uncle rose to wobbly feet, sobbing uncontrollably, and the village priest followed him through a narrow hall, up worn steps, and into a dimly lit garrett.

Karl's father, Captain Jacque Meister, lay on an iron cot under a shuttered window, and Karl could see the rising sun's first gleam through its louvers.

"Do you hear me, Jacque?" the fragile priest anxiously asked the pale man in the bed.

It wasn't right, Karl thought. They'd brought his father home by train and wagon to die of mustard gas two days after the War of Nations ended—not clear in his head, blind and unable to recognize his sons, and speaking to their dead mother he saw before him. Was she his angel of death? Karl wondered.

"The cross," his father said weakly from his death bed.

The priest wiped the dying man's face and held the crucifix for him to kiss. Karl listened while the priest blessed his father and administered the sacraments. Then the priest methodically gave his father the last Holy Communion. "Forgive us our trespasses," Karl heard his father hiss through burned lips; and then the priest took Karl's hand and placed it around the dying man's raw fingers. Bringing little Willi from the corner, the priest then joined hands with the three and they said the Lord's Prayer and one Hail Mary.

"Amen," his father sighed and closed his eyes for his final sleep.

It was at that moment that Karl thought he saw his dead mother's image, all white and wispy, step from the shadows and take his father's hand. But he realized the vision must have been the candlelight which danced upon the wall, reflecting from the Holy Water on the clean white cloth over the small altar at the foot of the cot.

Then the priest exchanged his purple stole for white to administer the Viaticum, annointing his father's eyes, ears, nostrils, mouth and feet with oil; chanting Latin prayers which Karl didn't understand.

Do we ever understand anything? Karl wondered now, thinking back to that sad day in 1918; and then he felt coldly alone and stepped quicker to reach the little priest's side as they turned up the walk to his house in Southport.

Sylvia opened the door and stepped back. She stared at the bandage taped to Karl's face, then looked at his arm in the sling with bandaged hand, and then at the priest, and she lowered her eyes. "Come in Father," she said quietly. "Do you have bad news for me?"

She received the messenger of death with a quietness and sereneness Karl had not expected; and he slipped outside and stood in the wind while the priest and Sylvia chanted the sorrowful mysteries of the rosary.

Karl returned to the house as the priest rose to leave. But Sylvia was unable to stand. When they helped her to her feet, she couldn't walk.

"A small stroke—nothing more," Dr. Keith told them. "Not a surprising result from such a shock."

But Sylvia didn't recover, and in the fall Karl took her to a specialist in Grand Rapids who treated her for hysteria.

Soon the money ran out. "Sylvia," Karl told her that fall, "I've found a boat. She's up for sale by an old fisherman's widow at Muskegon." Karl sat down, pulling his stool closer to Sylvia's wheelchair. "Let's mortgage the house," he said. "I can make good money fishing. Let's buy the boat. Its the only way now."

Sylvia agreed. Two weeks later Karl set his first net from the new boat—then the stock market crashed.

A month later, Crandall Fisheries in Chicago defaulted on a large shipment, leaving Karl with no funds for the Grand Rapids doctor. The following week, Karl packed his bag and boarded a Chicago-bound train.

At the Crandall Fisheries bankruptcy hearing, belligerent creditors and irate fishermen pressed and pushed about the defunct company's musty warehouse. A platform made from old planks and covered with worn wool carpeting from the office stood near the center of the back wall. In the middle of the platform was a mahogany bench, behind which sat a bald and bespeckled magistrate. To Karl, the varnished bench and the scrubbed, scarecrow of a judge looked equally out of place in the dingy building.

But when the judge spoke, his voice boomed with authority; and with a roar which sounded as if it must come from somewhere other than the timid-looking man behind the bench, the judge let forth with a volley, and the warehouse went silent. My God, Karl thought, I never expected to hear a judge swear so splendidly.

The shouting and shoving stopped everywhere, and although Karl had not understood any of the procedures, he suddenly recognized the judge's chant as an auction sale. Machinery and equipment were offered up; and each time bids fell short of a predetermined price.

"Bulk, bulk," went up in a chant from the men in vests near the front.

Then the mass of men turned, as if one, to a loud voice behind Karl near the freight elevator. "Seventy-five thousand, lock, stock and barrel," the voice bellowed.

"That does it," said a thin man in a blue suit at Karl's elbow.

Then the crowd parted, making a path for the owner of the booming voice. He wore a white panama, and waved a fat cigar at the judge. "Come on. Come on," he said, "you know its the best offer you'll get," and then turning to the crowd, he yelled, "Is there a man here who can top the offer?"

Having received no reply, the big man pointed his cigar at the judge and said, "Draw up the papers. We don't have all day, Judge."

"Its Dutch," the thin man next to Karl said. "No damn fool would top his offer."

"Going at seventy-five thousand," the judge yelled out. "Once, twice—sold!" And he rapped the bench with his gavel.

The big man with the cigar turned to a frail woman behind him. She handed over an envelope. Karl recognized the large, black eyes. She was Flora Nagel.

The judge took the papers handed up by the big man and stepped to a table where other papers were laid out. These were signed first by the judge and then by Dutch.

A green-visored clerk reached over and stamped the papers as they were signed.

The judge returned to his high bench and whacked his gavel, crying out for order. The din and clamor in the smoke-filled room fell off to low whispers and grumbles.

"All claims are to be in writing!" the judge shouted. "Forms are here." He pointed a long, bony hand to a stack of papers on the clerk's desk. "Now gentlemen," he continued, "claims are to be on affidavit. Any fraudulent or overstated claim will be investigated by the marshall, and prosecuted. The penalty is four years." Removing his glasses and waving them at the crowd, the judge said, "Payment is only thirteen cents on the dollar. Now that isn't worth four years in the cooler—so go easy, boys."

Karl was hot and damp under his wool sweater and the scar under his trim beard itched as he nervously pushed through the musty throng and took a form from the table. He folded his trench coat onto the platform and printed his claim with a stubby pencil.

"No," Flora said from a desk on the platform, as he stretched up his hand, "Put it in the box." She pointed to a gray, metal tray.

"Boys!" Dutch stood next to the judge, who thumped his gavel. "Listen up. Your claims will be paid by the court. You won't get much. And that's past business." He poked his cigar at the up-turned faces below. "But you'll be dealing with Dutch Schultz now." He beamed a wide smile. "Honest bills will be paid with good money. Those who want to do business with us, step forward and sign up over there." He waved his cigar to the table on the platform. "You fishermen sign up with that man. His name's Isadore Steinhertz. Izzy, stand up!"

A thin man in shirt sleeves with a hawk nose, wearing a herring-bone vest, stood and raised a pale hand to the crowd.

"The gal on Izzy's right is Flora," Schultz said. "She'll be in charge of funds. Call her if you have a problem. Now, Flora has an information sheet for those who need it."

Dutch Schultz stepped back from the platform edge and turned to the judge. "Kill it," Karl heard him growl to the judge, who then whacked his gavel three times and motioned to the clerk. Nodding his head, the clerk rose and chanted in a loud voice, "Special session of the Bankruptcy Court for the Northern District of Illinois is now closed!" The judge banged his gavel a final time.

Karl joined the line of anxious men who shuffled slowly around the platform and up the three steps to the narrow table, where the man in the herring-bone vest took their sheets, examined each paper closely, and handed it to Flora, who entered names and addresses in a large, red ledger.

Flora looked up as Karl neared the table. Fixing her eyes on him in a quick, interrogative way, she continued to study him, looking puzzled.

"It's the beard," Karl said as she continued to stare at him with a singular, direct gaze.

Flora took Karl's sheet from the vested man, and then a small smile spread on her lips as she glanced over the paper.

"Yeah," Karl answered. "It's me." The blood spread hot in his face. His eyes traveled to the vested man next to Flora; and seeing the man was busy with papers, said, "Karl . . . from Southport."

"Soldier boy?" she asked. Her smile was broader now.

Karl nodded and looked nervously at the vested man, who now glared and motioned for him to move along.

"Don't worry," Flora said quietly and leaned forward. "Wait for me."

She pointed to the sliding doors leading to the loading docks. "There. Outside."

She looked fresh and exciting in her red dress, and Karl smiled in spite of himself.

The vested man laid a stack of papers at Flora's elbow. Then his colorless eyes turned on Karl and examined his face with a long, hard look.

Outside, Karl stood on the loading dock in a light drizzle. He tapped a Chesterfield against his watch, lit the cigarette, and drew a short puff. Then he turned, pulled his coat collar tight, and walked slowly down the concrete steps and along the wet paving stones to the train station.

The following Tuesday, Karl looked up from mullets he packed in ice for shipment to Kalamazoo, and saw an old Buick with wood-spoked wheels enter the yard. The dark-blue car stopped before the fish shanty, and the Southport station master motioned from the driver's seat. Karl stepped up to the running board of the old sedan and the station master handed him a manila envelope.

"No receipt," the mustached station master said, and quickly backed the Buick down the gravel drive.

Karl opened the envelope. Wrapped in a Crandall Fisheries purchase order, he found ten fifty-dollar bills.

For the next two years, Karl packed herring, lake trout, whitefish and perch in wooden boxes, layered them with salted ice, covered them with straw, and shipped them by rail to the Crandall Fisheries in Chicago. Each Tuesday, the station master came to his shanty with a manila envelope. Inside were always fifty-dollar bills; sometimes, one thousand dollars, or more, wrapped in an invoice acknowledging the last shipment and a credit memo, showing the prior week's advance. These documents were always signed by Flora Nagel.

In those days, Karl was the only Southport fisherman who prospered; and at times he'd pass along his good fortune by purchasing from other boats to fill out an order.

He paid off the house mortgage, purchased a used 1929 Ford roadster, which he greatly admired, for it had a convertible top with a rumble seat, and was painted canary yellow with black trim.

At last, he traded in the old tug for a new boat, with a three-cylinder, hot-bulb, Kahlenberg semi-diesel engine, which produced ninety horsepower.

"Well, hell," Karl sighed out loud now at the Coast Guard Station where anxious relatives gathered before Timothy Bennett, "those were damned good years." Then the blustery storm was brought back to him in all its fierce intensity by Captain Bennett's shrill voice. "Get the watch down!" he shouted over the heads of the huddled group. "The tower's likely to go any second now."

At that moment, James Swift, the owner of a cottage on the bluff eight miles south of town, looked up from a book he was reading. A lashing wind had just shaken the cottage, flapping its roof shingles and driving sleet against its windows. Looking out on the lake, he saw the swaying lights of a ship, seemingly close to shore. He went to the kitchen, poured a cup of hot coffee, and returned to the window. The lights were still there. But he'd missed the three quick flares fired by Captain DuPays from the pilothouse window. "Maybe the night is playing tricks with my eyes," he said to himself. "What damn fool would come that close-in during this kind of weather?"

He watched the lights for a few moments and noted slow progress along the window pane. "By God," he muttered, "I wouldn't want to be in their boots. It's as bad out there as 1913, maybe worse." He remembered the violent storm which struck that November, when the wooden piers and docks at Southport were swept away and beach cottages reduced to kindling.

Out on the water, the *Tres Belle* slid into a trough between giant seas and slammed against the lake bed. Then she shuddered and rolled heavily, showing her rusty bottom plates. Seamen were sent flying from their bunks, dishes in the galley cascaded from the cupboards and the galley stove broke loose.

Down below, firemen, coal passers, wheelbarrows, and coal slid in an avalanche. The engine crew grabbed the brass railing to keep from being thrown into the pounding piston rods.

"Port! Port!," screamed Captain DuPays, and then lunged for the wheel himself, spinning it to the left. The ship shook free of the bottom on the next wave, then slammed down again, harder this time, taking the next wave full across her length. The three men in the pilothouse were knocked to the deck and the entire structure moved in almost half a foot, bending stanchions and beams, and then the pilothouse windows flew away, one by one.

Four

Karl had heard enough of the insufferable Captain Bennett, and he had no desire to spend a long vigil in the presence of that despicable creature, so he left the Coast Guard Station and trudged along the river to the Antler.

The bar was crowded and boisterous. Karl peered through the heavy smoke and spotted Corky and Joe at a table near the back. They sat near the juke box, which blared out Glenn Miller's "I've Got a Gal in Kalamazoo." Corky was at it again—he'd dumped a dollar's worth of nickels into the machine and punched the selector for that tune twenty times. He hated the song, and when well fortified by Kessler's whiskey, carried out his determined plan to destroy the obnoxious platter once and forever.

After three weeks of Corky's campaign, Skipper Nelson, the bar's owner, had agreed not to replace "I've Got a Gal in Kalamazoo" once the Irishman succeeded in wearing it out. It wasn't that he was intimidated by Corky. He knew the recording was good for thousands of trips on the turntable. But after listening to that disk night after night, he'd grown to hate it too.

As Karl threaded his way through the crowded tables in the smoke-filled room, he saw Corky poking a finger earnestly at Joe. The half-breed leaned over the table, waving his cigar under Corky's nose.

"Saints be with us," Corky said to Karl, "the answer man commeth."

Karl hung his black coat on a hook next to the juke box and sat down at the greasy table.

"The old man is seventy and not a buck left," Indian Joe shouted to Corky in a harsh voice.

"He's a liar," Corky screamed at Karl. "There's bound to be gold in his boots."

Karl made a quick count of the empty beer bottles at the table: seven, and who knows how many whiskeys.

"Whoa, boys. Whoa. Now Corky, don't be callin' Joe a liar," Karl said.

"He's a liar," Corky shouted again. Karl could see Joe growing tense and hot in the face. "De Havilland's a liar—and he's got money to burn."

Karl scowled at Corky. "De Havilland?"

"De Havilland' a Tokyo liar. He lost his Jap law practice when war broke out." Corky's handle-bar mustache danced over thick lips.

"Wait!" Karl held up his hand. Then he started a low chuckle, and finally broke into roaring laughter. "You mean l-a-w-y-e-r," Karl sputtered.

"That's what I said. A l-i-a-r," Corky spit back at Karl, his black eyes fire. "What's so damned funny?"

Joe Bear rolled back in his chair, tears of laughter streaming down his cheeks.

Taking a seat at the table, Karl explained to Corky the confusion caused by his thick accent.

Corky now laughed with them, and leaning back in his chair, slapped the waitress on the behind as she passed and ordered beers around.

Joe Bear's face went serious and he leaned toward Karl. "It ain't right, though," he said. "Hell, both his daughters are movie stars. They could do a lot more for the old man."

"Well the name explains one!" Corky said, leaning forward and stabbing a stubby finger on the newspaper between the men. "Fontaine ain't shit for a name—its French! And the dumb ass married a Jap and that explains the rest!" Corky shouted, slapping the table with his thick hand and sending bottles spinning to the floor.

Then Corky's voice went treacherously mild. "If they had kids, they'd all be piggly half-breeds."

Karl's hand shot out, grabbed Joe's raised arm and held it tight. "Back off, Corky!" And turning quickly to the halfbreed, he said, "Now take it easy, Joe."

Karl had learned from his Indian grandmother in Austria that the instincts of the red race were for generosity, love of nature, and endurance. But Injun Joe, his half-French, half-Indian crewman, had been insulted twice by Corky now, and Joe's endurance had limits—and both men had long passed reason to alcohol.

The big half-breed twisted free and struggled to his feet, showing his large, tobacco-stained teeth. Karl jumped after him and held the men apart. He knew his lanky frame was no match for the vibrating muscles of the two drunken fishermen, and he waited for a blow from either side.

Just then, the door of the Antler swung wide, and a shrill voice came to his ears over the room's din. "A freighter's run aground off Deer Point!" Everyone turned to the gaunt woman swaying in the tavern door.

In a noisy wave of excitement, the drunken occupants of the Antler Bar spilled into the gravel parking lot and surged toward rusty sedans and pickups waiting there.

Karl wired shut the door of Corky's Chevrolet truck as they bumped through puddled water in the tavern's drive.

Corky turned south along the lake bluff, and drove seven miles to the dirt road leading to Deer Point. The battered truck squealed to a stop high over the beach as other cars pulled along each side. Corky, Karl, and Joe slid down the sandy bank and scrambled along the shallow creek bed to where the beach turned to stones at the water's edge.

Karl saw nothing but the black night and sleet slanting through the glare from the headlights behind him. Then he saw a light beyond the sandbar, dim and flickering in the distance.

"They think its the barge tug *Calico Ray* outbound from Indiana Harbor," a man said at his elbow. "Bill Mills heard her radio, saying she'd broken her rudder cable. Seas were monstrous. They were making efforts to repair the cable under way, but were sure they'd go aground."

"Where's Bennett?" Karl shouted. "We need a beach cart down here, with a breeches buoy."

"I dunno," the man answered. "Someone said he wasn't coming. Said Bennett's waiting for your brother, Billy, in the powerboat."

"What?" Karl gasped. "Those men aren't within miles—if they're on the water at all!"

Karl turned and ran up the sandy bank to the small lighthouse above the point. The keeper pulled open the door in response to his determined pounding.

"I didn't hear ya over the wind!" the red-faced man shouted. Karl smelled strong whiskey as they went up the narrow stairs to the watch room.

"She ain't much. But I keep her oiled and polished," the keeper said proudly, and patted the brass rail leading to the frensel lens overhead. "I could see her masthead lights," the stocky old keeper went on. "Rollin' and swayin' out there," he pointed to the black lake. "They were a rollin' somethin' fierce. I figured then she was bein' hard driven by those curlers tripping over the backwash from the sandbar."

Stinging sheets of snow and sleet struck the lighthouse windows. In a lull, Karl saw a light blink beyond the sandbar. "There, look!" Karl pointed in the lights direction. "See it?"

"I know," the keeper replied. "I saw it before. But Captain Bennett don't believe me. 'The waves are up to thirty feet,' he says, 'and ain't likely to be any survivors on that old wreck. Deckhouse made of wood—it'd be swept clean away by now,' he told me." The old man peered out into the black. "But that sure didn't look like some small barge tug to me. Them masthead lights was at least a hundred feet apart!"

"Can I use the line?" asked Karl.

"Sure."

Karl grabbed the field phone and cranked the handle. "Bennett!" he yelled into the mouthpiece. "Get me Bennett!"

After a pause, Bennett came on the line. "Kreuer," he said, "what the hell do you want now?"

"This is Meister," Karl answered.

"Karl, what are you doing there?"

"Look, Bennett, I think that's a mighty big ship out there—Bill says one hundred feet between the mastheads—"

"Kreuer's a drunk," Bennett interrupted. "Karl, get the hell out of my lighthouse!"

"I saw a light, Bennett! Where's the beach crew? You've got to shoot a line!"

"Look, Meister, your brother's a good man. But you . . . you stay out of my way! You've been a pain in the . . ." Bennett trailed off and Karl could hear voices of the assembled men and women at the boat house. "Just get out of my lighthouse. That's an order!"

Karl dropped the phone into its pouch and shrugged his shoulders.

The old lighthouse keeper blinked his eyes, and said in a clear voice, "I know he thinks I'm just an old drunk. But I ain't. And I know there's freezen men out there."

Karl studied the bow-legged man. He saw a mild look of protest in the man's deep blue eyes, and the man's lips seemed to tremble.

"Freezin' men out there," the keeper said again, and turned to the roaring weather. "Do something," he turned his head and said to Karl over his shoulder, as Karl went down the stairs.

In the surf below the lighthouse, Karl saw a black object in the water, rolling and sliding with each wave. He shouted to Corky and Joe, and they came running with three other men.

When the water surged out, they all ran down the slippery stones to the water's edge, where Karl reached down and grabbed a white hand. Then the water roared in again and swirled up to their knees as they braced against its force. Corky grabbed an arm, and a third man the dark coat of the sodden body. When the water again receded, they ran the body to shore and up the sand to below the sharp grasses of the lower bluff.

Standing stiff against the icy wind, Karl watched Injun Joe pull a folded black purse from the dead man's coat and take a white card from an inside pouch and hold it in the light from Corky's battery lantern. "It's the cook from the *Tres Belle*," Joe said over the wind. "Canadian ship."

"Joe, tell the keeper to report this to Bennett," said Karl. "And let's start a fire here." He turned to the remaining six men. "As soon as it's going, cut the car lights and save the batteries."

Corky pulled a diesel fuel can from the Chevrolet pickup, and soaked driftwood the men had gathered from the beach. Taking a rag from his back pocket, he dipped it in the diesel fuel, held it out on a stick, and touched it off with a cigarette lighter. The rag glowed orange and whistled in the wind, and Corky plunged it into the fuel-soaked wood. Flames flattened out with a whoosh, and sparks and fire balls spun off in the direction of the wind.

"The wood's wet," Karl yelled in Corky's ear. "But it should dry quick in that heat."

Then Joe ran up to where the men stood around the fire. "Bennett said do nothing and wait for the Coast Guard. Kline's will be out for the body."

"My feet are numb," Karl shouted to Corky. "And I'm frozen to the waist." He looked at his pants, stiff with ice. His left hand ached under its wet leather glove, and his right hand was red and raw in the firelight. "Come on, it's Bennett's show. Let's get some dry clothes." Grabbing Joe's arm and pulling him along, he shouted through the wind to the men around the fire, "We'll change and come back!"

In the truck, Corky turned the heater knob to high, and Karl reached down and felt the hot blow from the coil under the seat. He had no feeling in his toes. He pulled off his boots and massaged his feet as the pick-up lumbered north along the bluff to Southport.

They stopped at the white fence in front of Karl's house, and he turned to the two men as he stepped from the cab. "It's not likely Billy's survived this long," he said grimly. "And I'm sure both tugs have gone down."

"Look, Karl," Corky said, peering around Joe's bulk and poking a finger in Karl's direction, "I think you're right about the tugs. They're gone for sure. But Billy's in a stout little boat. If they don't freeze, they'll make it . . . somewhere."

Karl rubbed warmth into his stiff left hand. "It's damned rough out there, Corky. But if anyone can do it, I guess Billy's the man." He leaned into the cab. "Now get some dry clothes on and pick me up. I want another look at that freighter—*Tres Belle* was it?"

"Yes," Joe replied, "*Tres Belle*. A Canadian ship. . . French-Canadian.

***

Sylvia woke with a start when Karl came in. She was seated in her wheelchair before the fireplace, a white bowl resting on a towel in her lap. She had sliced two potatoes into the bowl, and then started thinking, remembering when she was a young girl on her bicycle, flying down the hill to her father's fish market. The market was on the other side of the bridge, and she remembered her long, blonde hair streaming in the wind as she crossed the bridge, her school books strapped to the luggage rack.

She stopped her bicycle next to her father's shed where the *Merry B.* had docked before it was lost and her father drowned. She took the fish from the salt brine, and put them in a clean box, where she washed them with clear water from a hose outside the fish shed so they would take an even smoke.

As they were rinsed, she had always placed them one by one in a galvanized pail. When it was full, she struggled to the fish house. Inside, she laid the fish on chicken wire racks, being careful they didn't touch, so they would smoke evenly on all sides.

"Too much dry oak," her father had explained, "and you burn the fish. Too little," he continued, "and you'll smoke 'em all right, but they won't be cooked."

She sold the smoked fish inside the tiny market, where everything was painted fresh white, and the glass cases were always clean.

The surfmen passed the market on their way to patrol the north beach. Many of the men stopped to buy a small piece of smoked white fish or lake trout, to eat on their lonely trek; and that was how she met Karl.

Karl, with his intense black eyes and long straight hair curling over his forehead, spoke halting English. She thought he was quite handsome with his wide-set eyes and strong jaw, although she did feel his nose was too long for his face. Yes, all-in-all, she thought when he first peered down at her over the scales, a strikingly handsome man, in his navy-blue uniform, with its wide collar buttoned tight against his neck.

She sighed and sliced an extra-thick piece of smoked trout, wrapped it in wax-paper, and handed it to him with a trembling hand.

In the summer, Karl took her boating. But most of all, it was the dancing she loved. The ballroom was on the second floor of the Williams Company warehouse, directly across the river from her father's fish market. The high school boys no longer interested her then, and she thought they had become rather silly; and none of them could dance like Karl.

In the spring, after he walked her home from the prom, they paused on the dark porch. "My mother's ring," Karl said, holding a bright gold band in the light from the window. "Our custom is just one—first on the left for the engagement. And on the right for the wedding. I'll talk to your father tomorrow."

"And our custom is to ask the girl first." She turned quickly, on her heel and ran inside. Then she hurried upstairs to her bedroom window in the dormer over the porch. There, she watched Karl disappear toward the Coast Guard Station. Rather a brisk walk, she thought, as Karl marched into the black night

He reappeared on her porch the next afternoon, a bright Sunday, just as she knew he would. She'd seen him at church that morning and turned her head; and there he was now, tall and undeterred, coming up the porch steps. "Good afternoon, Sylvia," he said. "Will you sit with me on the porch swing?"

As they sat there, rocking gently in a soft, spring breeze, he finally told her he loved her. "Now will you marry me, Sylvia?" Karl looked at her anxiously.

"Yes, Karl. I will."

"Then I'll speak with your father," he said, taking her hand, and gazing into her eyes with a certain solemnity in his grave face.

Sylvia, too, was worried. She'd already talked to her mother, and then her father. It was true that Karl was twenty-one, she told them. But she'd be eighteen herself in a month, and graduating the month after that. And this wasn't the middle ages—this was 1927.

"We'll talk it over," her mother said.

"He hasn't come back, yet," her father added. "When he does, and if he asks you to marry him, we'll worry about it then."

Now that Karl finally did ask to speak to her father, Sylvia left the two men in the parlor and busied herself in the kitchen, where her mother rolled out a pie crust. "I think . . ." She leaned over the table to her mother. "I think Karl's asking Dad now," she said nervously.

"I know," her mother replied and wiped her hands on her apron. "And Dad will agree."

Her father came into the kitchen with an amused look in his gray eyes, and stroked his white beard. "Sylvia," he said quietly, and took her by the shoulders, "your young man wants to talk with you in the parlor."

They walked to the lake. At the bluff, it occurred to her that she'd left the house without saying good-bye to her parents, or telling them where she was going—it was the first time she'd ever done that. They'll understand, she thought.

"How beautiful it is today," she said to Karl. She marvelled at the blue water below the bluff and the blue sky above the water; and standing out in sharp contrast to the deep blue, was the red lighthouse at the end of the pier; and over it, crisp, white clouds. "Love makes the picture sharper," she said to him. "The colors brighter."

"Yes," he answered, his dark eyes steadily on her. Then looking out over the water, he said, "And the wind smells as fresh as the Vienna woods."

***

"You were sleeping," Karl said with a smile, and set his wet boots by the fire. "There's been a wreck." He looked at her, deciding not to tell her about the body washed ashore or that Billy was missing. "I think Captain Bennett plans to take the crew off in the morning, when the wind's down."

"Karl, you're soaked," she said in a weary voice, looking at his dripping pants.

"I slipped off a rock," he said.

"Just like a little boy." She nodded weakly. "Can't stay away from adventure. She raised her face to him and there was a a faint sparkle in the pale blue eyes behind her thick glasses. "You went down there, didn't you?"

"Oh, sure. With Joe and Corky. They went home to change. We might help somehow. Gotta go back, Sylvia."

"Yes, Karl, I know," she said with a wan smile. "But be careful, okay?"

"You know I will."

He looked at the bowl in her lap. "Potatoes—for poor man's soup?'

"Yes. And we have some butter and a little corned beef."

"Ah, good," he said. A little butter and corned beef added to the potatoes, onions, salt and pepper always brought the soup to life.

Sylvia listened to Karl pull open drawers for dry longjohns and open the closet door for clean denim trousers. Then suddenly, she realized that Karl had changed from his wet clothes and stood beside her, and was talking to her.

"You were sleeping again," he said softly.

"No," she answered with a smile. She knew only that the pain in her back was gone for a while; and now the numbness, which crept daily along her arm, came slowly back.

They ate silently in the living room, listening to the wind's song in the fireplace. When they finished, Karl took the soup bowls and rinsed them in the kitchen sink. Then Corky and Joe came and banged on the door, and Karl left with the men in the truck.

Five

The fire had gone out during the night and it was cool and damp in the house in the morning. Sylvia crumpled papers, as she had done so long ago when smoking fish. Kindling was in an iron bucket next to the fireplace. With it, she built a square over the rumpled newspapers on the grate. On top of this, she balanced three pine logs. Then she lit the paper under the wood, closed the screen, and leaned against the wheelchair's cane back.

Outside, the wind still howled. Perhaps even louder than yesterday, she thought. Behind her, from the large Grundig floor radio under the wall clock in the living room, she heard Tommy Dorsey's band playing. The Grundig, imported all the way from Germany. Karl wanted the best for her. Nothing was too much for their fifth wedding anniversary, he had told her.

Karl had come in very late last night; and he'd slept fitfully next to her, tossing and turning in the bed. He was still sleeping now, and she wheeled to the bedroom door, and opening it a crack, listened to his heavy, even breathing. Well she thought, he won't be going out today, so let him sleep.

The new fire crackled before her in the wheelchair and dry heat rolled out. She pulled her quilt tight around her shoulders, thinking of the bacon and eggs she would fry to go with the fresh coffee in the kitchen. I'll slice in potatoes and onions, Karl's Austrian favorite. Farmer's breakfast, he called it.

Then the music stopped. A man's voice came on the radio, sounding strained and tired.

"Storm damage reports keep coming in," the deep voice said. "Guardsmen, who kept a vigil throughout the night, have little hope for recovery of the twelve men lost in the storm yesterday. The three boats simply disappeared into the lake, and have been unreported since.

"Missing from early yesterday are two fishing tugs. The *Henry Bradley*, owned by Captain George Madison, went out at seven. The *Sioux Chief*, owned by John McKay, who was not aboard, and piloted by his son, John Jr., left port about nine o'clock.

"The Coast Guard boat left around noon, shortly after the storm struck here, in an attempt to locate the missing vessels. Aboard the power lifeboat were Boatswain's mate William Meister, in command, and three surfmen, all from the Southport station.

"Karl!" Sylvia cried out. "Billy's gone missing on the lake. Karl! Karl! It's Billy. Unreported—since yesterday!"

"I know, Sylvia. I know." Karl stumbled into the living room, rubbing his face awake.

"It's on the news," she said, spinning her chair to face the radio. "Billy's missing in the storm, Karl!"

"I know, Sylvia," Karl said again, rushing to her side.

"Karl . . . you didn't tell me!"

"Billy will make it. He'll be all right, Sylvia." Karl clasped her hand in his, and kneeling before her wheelchair, staring earnestly into her face, said, "I know they consider him lost. Even Bennett. But I walked the beach Sylvia. And guardsmen have searched all night. Nothing's been found. Listen to me, Sylvia," he said, shaking her by the arms. "The boat's unsinkable. It's built for storms. Unless they've washed over, or capsized, they're still on the boat. And if they'd gone over the side, they'd have washed ashore long ago."

Sylvia sat and looked at Karl. She'd heard what he said. One word stood out. "Capsized, Karl? Do you think it's capsized?"

"No. No, Sylvia. And even if it had, the boat would have kept right on rolling and come up again. The boat's designed that way, Sylvia. And I saw them go out—Billy's strapped to the wheel."

She bent forward, gripping his hands, her face now ashen. "Take me to the beach," she pleaded.

"Sylvia, that's impossible." Karl rose and went to the door. "Look at it out there."

Snow and sleet, driving in horizontal lines, flew across the door in the gray light. The wind howled and screamed.

Karl shook his head and pushed the door closed. "Later. When it lets up," he said. "If there's no news by then, I'll take you to the station in Corky's truck."

"The *Tres Belle*," the radio broadcaster continued, his voice calmer now, "a Canadian freighter, has gone aground at Deer Point. The body of the cook washed ashore last evening. And Captain Bennett of the Coast

Guard told us there was little hope for any life on the vessel."

"We saw a light," Karl said.

"And up and down the lake," the announcer continued, "several steamers reported serious problems in the seventy-mile winds and mountainous waves.

"The storm has also reeked havac on shore. A blacksmith shop on US-31, belonging to Sherm Andrews, was smashed to the ground during the night. Large cottonwood trees crashed into the home of Alfred Newton, at 816 Glenn, around five this morning. And the Casco Township hall was blown off its foundation. Police report that all roads to the city are closed this morning by downed trees.

"Huge swells continue to roll down the channel at Southport. But boats tied along the river's banks are reported holding fast with no damage."

"Muriel!" Sylvia swiveled her chair to look directly at Karl. "Where's Muriel?"

"I don't know. She was at the station last night, with old McKay."

"Poor Muriel," Sylvia sobbed. "Her brother out there . . . And Billy, too. Oh, God. Not our Billy." Sylvia struggled in her chair, pushing down hard on the wooden arms and trying to rise to her feet. Then she sank back. "Not our Billy."

Karl snapped the radio off and returned to her side.

She felt his strong, firm grip on her shoulder, and heard his voice, sounding as if it came from a distant echo-chamber.

"Call Muriel," he said to her. "She'll need your help."

Sylvia looked at Karl standing before her. His face was hard and white above his soft beard, and his brows were drawn together in a deep furrow. "I'm going to check on the boat," he said. "I'll let you know the minute I hear anything about Billy."

"Take something with you," she said. And her eyes were staring and unblinking. "I'll be all right. Sausage and cheese are in the icebox. I made bread yesterday. Take some along."

After Karl left, she wheeled to the radio and turned it on. She listened to the soft music and watched the bay window lighten in the gray dawn. The wind in the fireplace stirred sparks in the snapping logs. More wind buffeted the house and rattled windows in their loose frames.

Still unreported, she thought. Such a small boat. But Karl says there's still hope.

The mellow radio voice broke into her thoughts. "It's reported from Shanghi that large concentrations of Japanese troops are standing by at Haipong, awaiting orders to board ships for an attack against the French naval base at Saigon, farther south on the Indo-China coast.

"President Roosevelt, in Armistice Day celebrations at Arlington

Cemetery yesterday, declared that the men who suffered and died during the war to end all wars were not sacrificed in vain. The President stated his faith that democracy was 'the new order of the ages,' and will survive the present era of modern feudalism and dictators."

"On the national scene, the Reverend Michael Whetlew, in his speech on the Christian Hour yesterday, used the term 'Fifth Column Termites' in urging alertness to the destructive work of foreign influences who are seeking to destroy our unity. 'There was never a time in our history,' he said, 'in which it was so essential that we remain calm and clear, free from all hysteria and fear, in dealing with the detestable, underhanded work of the alien element in this country.'"

Sylvia stiffened. This was too much. With Colonel Lindberg speaking for isolationism, while others countered with tales of atrocities by the "Huns," fanning embers of hatred lain dorment for over twenty years, there was a growing sense of distrust of all foreigners in America.

Turning to the radio again, she heard: "It is feared the death toll may rise to sixteen in the fierce storm which struck Michigan yesterday, raged throughout the night, and continues unabated this morning. Little hope remains for the crews of the two fishing boats and the Coast Guard rescuers from Southport. All are now feared drowned."

"Poor Muriel!" Sylvia cried out and wheeled her heavy chair to the kitchen. "Central," she said, pulling down the long-necked mouthpiece, "give me eight-two-four, please."

She held her breath and listened to the hollow buzz in the receiver: two shorts and one long. Her left hand, holding the receiver to her ear, shook. Not home, she thought, and gave a long, low sigh, as the two short rings continued, followed by a longer tone.

Reaching up, Sylvia clicked the wall phone's cradle twice. A soft, woman's voice responded. "Number please."

"Muriel's Style Saloon," she said. "I don't have the number.

"Six-two-seven," was the patient reply.

"Muriel's Saloon. Bertha speaking."

"Muriel, please."

"She won't be in today, ma'am. Her husband's on the lake with the Coast Guard. Can I help you?"

"Would you tell me where I can reach her, please?"

"She's at the Coast Guard Station, ma'am. Can I take a message?"

"No. Thank you . . . Thank you very much."

Returning to the living room, Sylvia paused by the fire. She felt a cold draft on her back, and knew the logs would not warm the house that day. But there was little coal money for the winter, and she felt they must make do until Thanksgiving. After that, Karl could stoke the hungry basement furnace.

Sitting quietly before the burning logs and sipping a hot coffee, she listened to the wind. It's as bad as ever, she thought, and freezing cold on the lake, now too.

She'd been out on that lake. Even in the early winter when gales blew up. Some of the times she had napped in the pilothouse bunk, snug in a thick quilt, behind her father at the wheel. The big bed was high, almost as high as her father's head. From there, she could turn on an elbow and see out the portholes to the stern, or read a book in the light from the window at her head. But usually she fell asleep, and awoke with a start to a new roll or pitch of the white pilothouse. When her father was below, she could see the spoked wheel in front of her, turning slowly to the left, stopping, and then back to the right.

Sometimes she would lift her head from the huge pillow, and peer out the round portholes past the black roof of the puffing tug, where she would see white and gray sea gulls, swooping over the boat's stern platform. They were telling her, "We're going in. We're going in," with their shrill cry. She knew the gulls never ventured far from shore in the cold months.

In those fresh gales were endless, white wave-horses, galloping in every direction, as far as she could see. Most times, she remembered, the crests were racing with the tug. If the wind was from the west, which it usually was at that time of year, it meant they were headed home. There were also times when the tug had stopped. Then she would slide under the warm quilt, and listen to the clanking drum, pulling fish-loaded gill nets from the cold water. That was also a good sound, she remembered, because it meant nets were being pulled, and she knew her father would run off home soon.

She remembered that her father, like Karl, was cautious. Her father never tested the gale more than twenty minutes. "There's always a tomorrow," he told her; and they would race for home and glide between the Southport piers, never more than an hour after the first gusts struck. Those were the days when fish were plentiful, and at a premium in the big city markets. Now, she was no longer sure there would always be a tomorrow.

This storm, this great evil monster which screamed continually in her ears, was different, she knew. Never had it blown so hard, so long. She looked up through the bay window's lace curtains. It's killing people, she thought. Good men, like Billy and John McKay, Jr.; and the leaden sky and whipped spruce she saw through the window told her the storm had not grown tired. "It'll live longer than Billy," she sobbed. "And God is letting it happen."

She retreated from the window and switched on the big radio. The dial glowed as the radio warmed.

". . . body of the cook," the faint voice on the radio said, growing stronger as its tubes came to life, "was from the *Tres Belle*. It washed ashore at Deer Point last evening. But no sign of life has been seen on the stricken freighter.

"And now for Oxydol's own Ma Perkins . . . "

Sylvia turned down the radio and wheeled to the bedroom. She lifted her rosary and prayer book from a stand under the window. Returning to the living room, she drew near the radio, and half listening to the monotonous soap opera, recited the rosary. She progressed, black bead by bead, through the string, pausing occasionally to pray for Billy, the missing fishermen, and all seamen lost on the lakes. Then she said ten "Hail Marys" for her father and ten for Billy. "Lord," she said hard and loud, leaning back in the wheelchair, "hear my prayer."

Praying for Billy out on the lake, she thought of when he came to America. "Karl and I had been married only six months," she said to herself, smiled, and leaned her head back against the chair's cane webbing. And Billy was such a small boy to be traveling by himself. But Karl had made all the arrangements, and written careful letters of instruction. In July, Billy traveled by train from Vienna, transferred at Berlin, transferred again at Hamburg, and finally arrived at Bremen, where he boarded the Lloyd Steamship *Weser Stern*.

Two weeks passed, and then they received the telegram Billy sent from New York upon his arrival, coming just as Karl had written it, with Billy filling in the date and time of arrival in Kalamazoo.

She closed her eyes, thinking of the red-brick station.

She chuckled, seeing Billy standing on the train platform in his gray, leather shorts.

"Lederhosen," Karl had called them. "And this is Willi," he said, pounding the stout, fourteen-year-old across the shoulders, until Sylvia thought his bones would break.

The boy blushed pink, lifted his green leather hat, bowed low, and then stretching out his hand said, "I am very pleased to make your acquaintance, madam."

"Oh, my!" Sylvia exclaimed, rushing past the out-stretched hand, "not so formal." And she hugged him tightly. She took his face in her hands and beamed down. "You're a perfect Billy—That's what we'll call you—'Billy.'" Then taking his hand, she said, "This is my mother. And my father."

"I am very pleased to make your acquaintance, madam. I am very pleased to make your acquaintance, sir." With each greeting, Billy held out his hand, which was ignored by rushing arms of Sylvia's thin mother, and then her bearded father, as they embraced the boy.

"Your luggage," Sylvia asked as they pushed through the station's oak doors, "is it on the train?"

"I have none," Billy said, shaking his back pack. "Everything's in here." And he smiled a wide grin.

"But, Willi," Karl said. "Your clothes. You had a trunk!"

"I know," Billy said, looking sheepish, "I lost it."

"Well, Billy," Karl said. "I guess it's time to get new clothes to go with your new name."

Packing Billy's rucksack into the old Reo's trunk, Sylvia's father said, "You speak very good English, Billy. And you even have an English accent."

"It's the school," Karl said. "The Austrian middleschool. They teach 'em British English. And Billy's a good student." He looked at his brother proudly. "Much better than me."

In the car, Sylvia turned to Billy, sitting between her and Karl in the back seat, and said, "You'll be fifteen in March, Billy. Isn't that right?"

"Yes, ma'am."

"Then you will be in the ninth grade of our high school," Sylvia's mother said cheerfully.

"And a good weight for football," her father said over his shoulder from behind the wheel.

"Yes—fussball—football," Billy said. "I know the game."

"It's different here, Billy." Karl broke in. "But kickin' is the same, almost. You'd make a good kicker, Billy."

"Center," Sylvia's father interrupted. "Maybe tackle. But he's got a good weight for center."

"The boy isn't even home yet," Sylvia said with a laugh. "You men! And you've already got him playing football."

Well, she thought now, listening to the radio's forecast of continued stormy weather, Billy did play center after all. And he was the kicker too. The best punter Southport had seen. And the coach said Billy was their most valuable player when the school won the Class C championship. Billy graduated with honors, and then joined the Coast Guard.

"To get out from under your feet," he had said to her in the wheelchair. She smiled again. Only Billy could make her laugh at herself. "Now he's lost on the lake, Lord," she murmured and raised the crucifix to her pale lips. "Dear, dear Lord," she said quietly, "bring him home safely . . . And soon."

Outside, a stronger gust burst against the house, and Sylvia dropped her head and sobbed.

Six

When Karl entered the fish shanty, he found Corky Reiley stretched out along the wall on old netting, his feet toward the pot-bellied stove, behind which lay Indian Joe. Both men were fast asleep.

The odor of alcohol was heavy in the air, and Karl knew the men had gone straight to the shack, where they drank into the morning hours after closing the Antler Bar.

Karl added coal to the stove. Then he listened to the labored breathing of the two men and the cold wind outside for a moment, smiled to himself, and pulled a ragged net to his chair.

While his fingers worked new twine into the old net with a flat, wooden needle that morning, Karl thought about his last Armistice Day in Austria.

He remembered trudging along the stone road, his field coat turned up against the chilly mist. The sentry at the military caserne's iron gate stiffened as Karl approached; and when he was close enough for the old man to see Karl's boyish face in his father's military coat, the guard relaxed and smiled.

"God's greetings, Karli," the old sentry said in the local dialect.

"God's greetings."

Karl stopped at the rusty gate. It had been four years since his father came by truck to be handed down on a stretcher and carried to Uncle Adi's farm where he died from mustard gas burns. Four years since the daily blood deluge ended. Four years since death came whistling on the night wind.

Staring through the wraught iron across the empty courtyard, Karl saw the concrete administration building, its yellow stucco peeling; and next to it, on the right, the infirmary, where his father, Doctor Captain Jacque Meister, had tended to the Franz-Joseph Light Artillery Group's medical needs. It was there that his mother had lain white with fever for six weeks after Billy's birth and finally died, while Karl held her thin fingers.

The two thousand men and officers of the artillery group were gone now, too. Karl was only nine years old on that grim day in December, 1915 when his father drove him and little Willi in an Army Damilier to Uncle Adi's farm. Then, after a hurried good-bye in the big hall, Karl followed his father into the snow-covered courtyard, and watched the gray sedan slide through the ruts, and wind its way down to the village below; and still watching, he saw it appear on the other side of the village and turn through the woods toward the caserne.

Karl's grandmother was American, the child of a French father and Chippewa Indian mother. Karl's grandfather had met and married her in Michigan. Then brought her home to Austria. When Karl's father was born, they'd named him Jacque, after her father.

Karl had learned that his grandfather wasn't Austrian either. "Our family came from Mittenwald, a small village in Bavaria near the Austrian border," Karl's grandfather had told him. And that was the reason the family home in Badenberg was called *Villa Bavaria.*

Although he had gone many times to see his grandparents at the *Villa Bavaria*, he always made a special trip at this time of year, not because it was the anniversary of the war's ending, but because it was the anniversary of his father's death. He knew that his grandparents were glad to see him at those sad times, just as he was happy to be in the warm comfort of their smiling faces.

Karl nodded good-bye to the old sentry and continued north along the Helenthal. He paused under the Roman aqueduct, pulled his coat tight about him, and glanced across the wide valley to the Fuerstengut castle ruins, high on a craggy hill; and then he turned his gaze south, where the Helenthal wandered along the river bank. High over the woods he could see the ruins of castle Schauenstein. This is home, he thought. And this is what I'll be leaving in the Spring, this land of sweeping beauty.

Turning west from under the aqueduct, Karl saw the tall cliffs behind the *Villa Bavaria.* The view up there was even better, he knew, one could see miles up and down the valley, all the way to Vienna and the Danube.

The *Villa Bavaria* was a three-story building divided into four large apartments. It's facade was covered with bass reliefs of angels. And a huge scroll rolled across the windows at each level. The third story was built of heavy timbers with a narrow balcony which ran the entire length of that floor and disappeared around each end. Below this was a second, shorter balcony which formed the roof over the columned entrance. A red and yellow awning, which normally stretched over the lower balcony, was now furled for the winter and covered with canvas.

The villa's main entrance, over which were carved the ornate words "*Villa Bavaria*," opened to a circular stairway, which led to the second floor, now occupied by Karl's older cousin, Eugene Meister, the building's current owner. "Uncle Eugene," Karl always called the tall, thin man with the wrinkled monkey's face.

An architect lived on the third floor with his wife and four children; and a widowed school teacher lived in the ground floor apartment on the north end, where Karl had spent his early childhood before his father was ordered to the Western Front.

Karl's Grandfather, whom he always called "Opa," and his Grandmother Grazie, whom he always called "Oma," lived in the other end of the ground floor, facing the apple orchard.

Opa was tall and thin with narrow shoulders and a long face. His beard had been white as long as Karl could remember. Karl remembered, too, that his clear, light blue eyes always sparkled.

Oma Grazie looked more Indian than French, with her large brown eyes, high cheekbones and straight black hair. She was about five feet ten inches: and she stood straight, not like the other tall women he'd seen who slumped their shoulders. His Oma and Opa had one thing in common, they both had very large, hooked noses.

Closing the gate behind him, Karl turned left on the flagstone walk and paused for a moment, facing the apple orchard. Then he went up the three stone steps, through the glassed-in porch, and twisted the mechanical clapper which sounded a loud ring on the other side of the heavy oak door.

"Karli!" his tall, lean grandfather cried out, pulling open the door and clasping him in both arms. "Come in. Come in. You must be freezing."

"And again no hat!" his Oma scolded, running her hand through his damp hair. "This time you must stay long enough for me to knit a nice cap," she said. "And you'd better promise to wear it, Karli."

"Yes, Oma. I promise."

Then Karl slid his backpack to the parquet floor and thrust in a hand. "Fresh bread for you, Oma," he said, pulling out a flat, round loaf and handing it to her. "From Aunt Theresa's oven, yesterday."

"And for you, Opa," he said, again reaching into the knapsack, "fresh cheese." He gave him a round, yellow, hard-crusted slab, almost as large as the bread.

His grandfather took the cheese with hands stained dark from years of rolling moist tobacco leaves into firm cigars at his workbench off the kitchen.

"Come, Karli. Sit and tell us your plans, his grandfather said, motioning to the walnut table next to the green-tiled stove in the living room where they had their meals.

"Ah, Heurige," said Karl, when his grandmother brought in the bottle of clear white wine, always pressed from the current year's grapes.

"To the future," his grandfather said with moist blue eyes as they stood at the walnut table and clinked glasses.

"To your future, Karli," his grandmother said.

"And to your good health," Karl replied. He felt the delicate sting of the dry wine. "Oh, it's as good as ever," he said to them. "I think I'll miss it almost as much as you."

Oma sliced bread and cheese onto supper boards, which was followed by big bowls of lentil soup from the iron pot on the tile stove; and looking at Karl with pain in her brown eyes, she said, "So, Karli. You're going to America in the Spring."

Karl shook with excitement. "Yes, Oma. "April. I sail from Bremen."

Karl sipped his second glass of Heurigen, thinking of the letter he'd sent to Dewing & Sons of Kalamazoo. If his master would attest to his woodworking skills, they'd hire him and advance the fare, the reply stated.

Karl was sixteen. He'd finished his carpentry apprenticeship. But there was no work in Austria. He thought that if his grandfather had gone to America, he could too. He'd go to Michigan. The land of the tall Indians. And if he got homesick, why, he'd go back to Austria—maybe with an Indian bride.

"We visited the Chippewa," his grandfather said, interrupting Karl's thoughts. "Went by paddle-wheel steamer to the very north of Lake Michigan. From there, we traveled by canoe."

The old man paused, and lit one of his black cigars; and as the smoke curled around his narrow face, continued with his narrative. "Wilderness surrounded us," he said, leaning back in his chair and drawing again on the cigar. "Lowlands, with seas of marsh grasses, reeds, and brush on the banks above, melting into wooded hills. We paddled up the Green River. Then along the Hendrie, until it merged with the Tahquamenon River at Frenchman's Lake. From there the river flowed through marshlands."

"We weren't able to stop anywhere," his grandmother interrupted.

"No. There wasn't a dry spot. Many times I stuck the paddle into soft ground and my arm disappeared in the muck. Sometimes up to my elbow.

"But we knew that," Oma said. "My mother made us a map. And she told us we'd have to sleep in the canoe along that stretch. But there was no keeping us back."

"After many miles in the canoe," his grandfather continued, "we were in nothing but reeds, tall and dark green. And they waved in the wind, like rolling seas in a strong breeze." The old man's eyes closed, as he tipped his head back and blew smoke toward the ceiling.

Karl felt the stove's radiant heat on his back and the warm Heurigen within.

"Yes," the old man said, and his eyes opened wide with a start. "We camped three nights in an area where the banks were higher and drier. And—"

"But the mosquitoes," said Oma. "They were awful!"

"Yes. Terrible," Opa said. "Paradise has the world's biggest and thirstiest mosquitoes."

"Always got under the netting somehow," she said.

"But we never got lost," Opa said. "Your grandmother watched for the water's flow against the Pike Weeds, which reached almost to the surface. She was very good at it." He smiled at her, and after a long pause, continued. "That's how we followed the current through the larger lakes and marshes, and always reached the main river branch on the other side."

Karl's grandfather turned and stared at the wall. "Farther along," he said, "we reached the upper Tahquamenon. The lands of the Chippewa. Red-winged Blackbirds were everywhere. Great Blue Heron, cranes, and the most beautiful ducks. Some common only to that area, with iridescent green, blue and purple plumage." The old man's eyes blinked shut for a moment. "This was the land of the Chippewa, Karl. Of the Tahquamenon Falls. Where the water, red with iron deposits, cascades hundreds of feet."

Oma broke in. "Everyday living wasn't very pleasant. The Chippewa weren't warrior people. But when fighting broke out, they responded. Sometimes, too well."

"More than half the men were over six feet," Opa said. "That's where your father got his height—and you too."

"Now," said Oma, "what bothered my mother most was the torture. Our tribe was no better than the others, she told me. If a battle went bad and left hostile feelings, and they usually did, there was torture—burning at the stake—but first, probing with sharp sticks. Indescribable pain. But nevertheless, Karl, the Chippewa considered themselves to be the ultimate human beings—a superior race. 'Anishinabe!' they called themselves. And it means 'Original Man.' They lived in comfortable ignorance, thinking they would never die, and would live as champions of all peoples in the hereafter. And believing this, they committed terrible atrocities, fearful only of death with dishonor at the hands of revengeful tribes."

She paused and looked at Karl with a smile in her eyes. "But you, Karli," she said. "You'd have nothing to fear from them."

"No?"

"Because," the old man broke in with a wide grin, "there were always widowed women, or women whose prospective husbands had been killed or died—"

"Those women," Oma said, "always had first choice of prisoners, Karli. That's how my mother caught my father." She rocked with laughter. "The French grew bolder. A raiding party killed Chippewa and stole fur stock. And when the trappers started poaching on Indian lands, the Chippewa took their revenge. But my mother took my father to her tent." She smiled. "And I was born the following spring."

They talked long into the night, sipping the tangy Heurige. At last, Karl's grandmother made up his bed behind the stove and kissed him goodnight.

Then there came the last Christmas in Austria. Karl and Billy lived on the farm with Uncle Adi, Aunt Theresa, and their two children.

Leaving the *Villa Bavaria*, where he'd spent Christmas Eve with his Oma and Opa, Karl walked through clean snow which took him past the deserted caserne and into the little village of Eisenkreutz.

Warm candlelight from every window fell upon the fresh snow in the village square. Several people crowded around the Christmas tree in the parlor of the big house across the way. Suddenly, the door opened and a band of children brushed snow from their clothes, stamped their feet, and went in.

"Ah," he heard the father say, "back so late from Oma's house. But you were playing on the hill, right?" The father laughed and closed the door.

It's nearly midnight. Bright stars overhead are mirrored by many sparkling lights on the mountain sides. These are the pitch torches and lanterns of farmers and shepherds, making their way down winding paths for Christmas mass in the village church.

Karl waits in the village square, now. Soon he sees the family Gunst. First, Uncle Adi, his mother's brother, comes into view. He's short and strong as a bull. His limbs are so short and thick that Karl thinks of him as a muscular dwarf, with a curling white mustache, and bushy white hair sticking out from under his green hat.

In his left hand, Uncle Adi swings a lantern. Aunt Theresa hangs on to his right arm. She is no shorter than Uncle Adi, but still must run to keep up with his long strides. She has a small and youthful face, which beams at Karl as they approach.

And the children follow behind. They are Karl's two cousins and his brother, little Willi. First comes Seppi, lanky, with light brown hair, blue eyes, and his mother's cheerful, oval face. He is two years older than Karl. And his real name is Joseph, but everyone calls him by his nickname.

Next to Seppi is Karl's brother, Willi, now eight years old, smiling his big teddy-bear grin.

Behind the two boys is Hannelore, a plain and simple girl, blue-eyed and freckled, with her blonde hair woven into pig tails. She is one year younger than Karl, and he has called her little sister as long as he can remember.

"Hurry Hanna," Karl calls out. "Come along now, little sister, or you'll be left behind for the goats," he teases with a laugh.

The church bells ring out as they hurry through the village square. The doors stand open, and it seems to Karl that the church shimmers from a thousand candles. There will be no other lights tonight, he knows.

They kneel at the door and make the sign of the cross; and as they slide into pews, the old priest sings out in a loud voice, *"Gloria!"* Then louder than Karl has ever heard him sing, the priest continues, *"Gloria in excelsio Deo!"*

At the end of the sermon, the choir, high in back, sings out the mellow verses of "Silent Night," and the congregation joins in, each holding a lighted candle.

When mass ends, everyone turns to his neighbor, and those in front and behind, and shakes hands, wishing all a Merry Christmas. The handshaking and wishing continue down the aisles and spill out into the village square, where the men and women slap arms and rub hands to keep warm, and talk with people they haven't seen since Easter.

Then family groups drift off in different directions, pulled along by tugging children, anxious to be home and see what the Christ Child has brought them while they were gone.

Karl, too, is anxious to be out of the cold—at home, on the Gunst farm, where he knows there will be hot wine, spiced with cinnamon, and a warm fire in the parlor stove, presents under the tree to be exchanged, and after more of the hot wine, a warm bed under goose-down under the attic.

And in the morning, he knows, the bell in the loft will be rung by a string coming on pulleys from the kitchen. He, Willi and Seppi will stumble down, wash their faces and brush their teeth in the cold water trough in the hall, and sit down to a breakfast of sliced ham and hot rolls with Uncle Adi and Aunt Theresa.

The Gunst farm buildings are all housed under one roof. In the lower level, built of stone, and stuccoed inside and out, is the large parlor, with its huge, tiled stove, which heats the entire house. On the first floor is also the kitchen and a storage area, where slabs of bacon and ham hang above bread racks.

The parlor, where the family eats, opens onto the large hall with the water trough and pump over the well. Stairs at the end of the hall lead to the second floor. A door under those stairs opens to the privy, a narrow, tall room with high shuttered windows. Outside the house, Karl has seen the small door at the bottom of the privy; providing access for removal of waste, which is mixed with manure from the barn, thinned with water, and sprayed over the fields.

Across the wide hall, next to the altar, is a heavy door, which opens to the first barn. In it are four cows, two horses and the chickens. On the opposite wall of this barn is another door, which leads to a longer, lower barn with shuttered windows to ventilate the hay and grain stored within.

The second floor of the main house was built from large, square timbers which rest on the stone walls. All the second-floor windows face southeast, overlooking a wooden balcony. This floor holds two bedrooms and a small sitting room for the sole use of Uncle Adi and Aunt Theresa.

In the middle of the narrow hall on the second floor, steep stairs lead to a garret under the roof. This third floor has three smaller windows, which overlook a smaller balcony.

Access to the loft is by a trap door at the top of the stairs. In the cold winter, the trap door is left open to gather heat which flows from the tile stove through the open parlor door, and wafts up the stairs.

The loft is left open and unfinished, and contains the boys bunks.

They hurry now along the twisting road from the village, up the steep path to the house, and into the wide hall where they hang their heavy coats. The children wait anxiously in the dark hall, while Karl's aunt and uncle slip into the dim parlor and close the door behind them.

Suddenly the door is opened by smiling Aunt Theresa, whose milk-smooth face glistens in white light from many candles: on the Christmas tree, on windowsills, on the table, and on each small space throughout the parlor which will support a holder.

The Christmas tree sits in the parlor center, candles burning brightly, and splendid with glittering angel's hair hanging from all its branches, high and low. At the very top of the tree, suspended by a string from an overhead beam, a sparkling glass star, with pointed spines, turns slowly in the candle heat.

Under the tree, pastries and presents stand among animal figures. In front of those, rests a small nativity scene from past Gunst generations.

Uncle Adi stands next to the tree, his eyes sparkling with merriment, puffing on a long pipe.

"Happy Christmas, children," say his aunt and uncle in unison.

"Happy Christmas," the children answer.

Karl steps forward and shakes his uncle's thick hand. "Happy Christmas, Uncle Adi."

Turning quickly, he hugs his aunt and wishes her a happy Christmas. Everyone is hugging and laughing.

Then standing around the Christmas tree, with Aunt Theresa leading, they sing Christmas carols, ending with "O Tannebaum," and Uncle Adi passes out presents.

With presents, pastries and steaming wine glasses in front of them, the family sits on curved benches around the huge circular parlor table.

They open presents, starting with the youngest, and Karl brings Willi the skis he had so carefully carved and hidden in the storage room.

When Karl's turn comes, he opens the big wooden box in front of him. The top is packed tight with wood shavings and he sees nothing but the wood curls. Pressing his fingers into the springy material, he feels odd shapes below, but he can not guess the contents. Giving up and admitting defeat to the satisfaction of all, is told by Uncle Adi to dig in.

He tears into the packing. First, a hammer, chisel and rasp. Below, a plane, small bow saw and hand drill, all shiny and brand new.

Karl is quiet and sits there with a handful of wood shavings in each hand. He can't speak. He knows the enormous cost of the new tools.

"For a new beginning, Karli," his uncle says with a smile.

"The tools of our Lord," his aunt says. "Weapons for peace."

At last, Karl answers. "Thank you . . . Thank you very much. I'll be the best equipped carpenter in America."

Then nuts and sweet bread are eaten; and Uncle Adi leaves to sit on a stool before the oven door. Behind the small glass window, apples are baking. No one but Uncle Adi is allowed to supervise the apples. It is his specialty.

"They must be taut," he tells Karl, taking a long puff on his pipe. "With skins just ready to burst. And juicy. And baked softly to the core."

When Uncle Adi says the apples are done, they are placed on small plates, and the family returns to the round table. Glasses are refilled with yet stronger-smelling wine, for the liquid is slowly evaporating in the kettle on the parlor stove, leaving a brew thicker with cinnamon and spices.

Outside, a heavy snow falls in the window light to join high drifts around the house.

Inside, the air is warmed by the kitchen oven and the parlor stove. The aroma is overwhelming; there are a dozen familiar smells, as well as those special to Christmas; the smell of stucco walls, the overhead timbers, the hot porcelain tiles of the parlor stove, and above it all, the pine scent of the tree, honey-wax candles, wine, cinnamon, baked apples, roasting chestnuts, incense from the hall altar, the faint smell of hay and cows from the barn, Uncle Adi's sweet tobacco; the smell of people in a warm room, clothes from storage, and shirts washed for the holiday.

It is long past midnight, and the parlor clock chimes two. Over a distance of three miles from the valley below, Karl hears the high pitch of a steam whistle near the river. It is the holiday train from the south, with its cargo of Christmas relatives on their way to Vienna.

Karl realizes that in the spring he will drive with Uncle Adi behind the horse, through the sleepy village of Eisenkreutz, with its small wagon factory where Karl had carved Willi's skis, and past the village school over the post office where Willi still studies, and leaving the village behind, travel to Badenberg, where he will say goodbye to Oma and Opa at the train Station. From there he will ride the train to Vienna, and from there north to Bremen where he will board a ship for America and the Dewing Window Factory at Kalamazoo.

***

"So," Mr. Dewing had said from behind his desk at the window factory, "you're leaving us, Karl."

Karl nodded and thanked the vested man for giving him a start.

"Well," Mr. Dewing said with a chuckle, "we shouldn't have sent our best man to Southport. But you've been a good worker, Karl. And I wish you success."

"Thank you, sir. Thank you very much."

"You can always come back," Mr. Dewing said, waving his cigar and smiling broadly. "Perhaps we won't lose you to the lake steamers yet. You may change your mind."

"Well, it's really for the Coast Guard that I'm doing it, sir. The cutter service. They're taking on new men. There's heavy traffic in rum runners on the lakes now."

"Ah, yes. Prohibition."

"But I need the navigation school first."

"Well, Karl," Mr. Dewing said with a wink. "Do me a favor."

"Yes, sir?"

"Let one or two slip through."

Karl laughed and shook Mr. Dewing's hand. "Sir," he said, "when prohibition's lifted, I'll escort the first shipment to your door."

Early the next spring, Karl wrote to his brother in Austria.

"Dear Willi: Good news. I have completed my studies and entered the Coast Guard Service. I live with twelve men in a large loft over the boathouse.

"Our Captain, John McKenzie, is a good man. And he helps me with my manuals. He told me that with hard study, I could become a captain too some day.

"I wanted to be on the ships, but they were all full, and I was assigned to the old life saving service. These are the men who go out in small boats to rescue seamen in distress.

"My rank is surfman. And all the men have the same rank, except the most experienced man, Timothy Bennett, is called the Number One surfman. Usually, we just say Number One.

"The station commander, Captain McKenzie, is a warrant officer, and that is what I would like to be. But first, I must be the Number One surfman for a few years.

"I have no problems with any of the men, and they are a good bunch, except for Bennett, the Number One man. He conducts the boat drills and is in charge when we are out. But he isn't a very good leader, and loses his temper when things go wrong.

"You'll like this little town. It is just like a sea port. And Lake Michigan is very large, like an ocean. But it isn't salty. Many ships come here. They are all sizes, and bring in lumber, coal, finished goods of all kinds, and a great amount of paper pulp for the Kalamazoo mills.

"Some of these ships are from Europe. And one came last week from Bremen with a cargo of Swedish paper pulp. I talked to the crew and they were surprised to hear German. But they spoke low-land German, and understood our Austrian about as well as English, which wasn't very good.

"Large steamboats come here from Chicago in the summer, carrying as many as 2,500 people in one boat. Most of them have side wheels and look like the river boats in Mark Twain's books. When the Chicago boats come in, the town is crowded with people. Long carriages and big automobiles are everywhere, and take the boat people to many resorts around the city.

"Lake Michigan is well stocked with fish, and many men fish the lakes with nets. In one month an Indian fisherman I met at the dance pavilion, earned $600.00. He bought a new Ford automobile with $350.00, and this is a good example of what the fishermen can earn, while I get by on $80.00 a month.

"I like the Coast Guard. But I think I will be saving my money for two things: your passage, and a big fishing boat. And we can call the new boat *Two Brothers*. And it will be the strongest fishing tug made, with the best equipment and a big, diesel engine.

"Warmest greeting to Uncle Adi and Aunt Theresa, and our cousins. Tell them I keep the wood-working tools well oiled.

"Give my best and warmest greetings to Oma and Opa and tell them I will write them too.

***

Mending his nets now in the fish shanty, Karl thought about the letter he had written to his grandparents, and then about the time Sylvia cut him an extra-thick smoked whitefish at her father's market. He remembered gathering his courage and asking her to the pavilion dance. After they were married and her father went down with the *Merry B.*, he finally left the Coast Guard and made a down payment on a tug. It was then that Captain McKenzie sponsored his membership in the Southport Brotherhood of Grand Turtles. Captain McKenzie was the Exalted Ruler that year. Smiling broadly, he turned to Karl and said, "Just imagine, the State Covention will be held right here, in Southport, at the Pirate's Cove." Well it was the only place in the city which could hold five hundred people. Captain McKenzie grinned. "And Karl, you'll be there."

Karl knew the old man was disappointed to see him leave the Coast Guard. But he could never serve under Bennett. He thought the old man knew it too, and knew something had gone wrong with the *Merry B*. But since no one talked about the incident, there was no inquiry; and Bennett received his promotion to warrant officer. "The replacement," Captain McKenzie always referred to him, abstractly.

Under the old captain's sponsorhip, Karl was accepted by the Grand Turtles. He went through indoctrination, learned the secret handshake and the secret sign, and in October picked up a pen to sign the long document by which he pledged eternal fealty to the brotherhood.

"The Grand Turtles are a community asset," Captain McKenzie said, "with their support of the crippled children's fund, and many other social activities." It was time, he told Karl, for the young Austrian immigrant to become a member of the community, in name and spirit.

Humbled by association with Germany, there was little sense of patriotism in that small segment of the earth which remained Austrian following the loss of the World War. The Austrian's hero was more likely Wilhelm Tell, the fabled archer who wrested Switzerland's freedom from the early Austrian rulers.

But, here in America, in Southport, patriotism flourished at the Grand Turtle Lodge No. 102.

Karl's eyes raced down the long page, drinking in line after line, while the big clerk with short hair shaved high over his ears, beamed at him. Karl froze when he came to the words at the bottom. Then he read the words again. "This can't be," he said to the stout man in front of him at the table.

"What is it, Karl?" the man asked, with stern eyes and a short, quick smile.

"Why, it says here . . . Wait a minute. I'll read it: 'I hereby affirm that my blood is pure and entirely of the Caucasion race.'"

"Yes?" The man nodded impatiently.

"Well," Karl paused, with a blank look on his face, "I'm not pure Caucasian."

"You . . . must be," the big man stammered, and pulled Karl's application to his face. "It says here—race, background—Austrian. That's sworn to by Captain McKenzie, the Exalted Ruler."

"But, I'm part American Indian."

"I see," the clerk said with a serious and business-like face. "But that's a different matter. This problem first came up in Hawaii. And it was determined then, after careful study, that all members of the Mongolian tribes were truly Caucasians. I mean scientifically proven, you understand. I don't have all the details, of course. But common origins were traced. And from there to the Indians—they, you know, are a Mongolian tribe, and, therefore, Caucasian. So—there's no problem, Karl."

"And Jews?"

"Oh, I'm glad you asked, Karl. Absolutely no problem. We have several Jewish members."

"Well," Karl asked, "would there be a problem if I sponsored your cook someday?" He pointed to the kitchen doors.

"The colored?"

"Yes. Your cook."

"Well . . . that's not the same," the clerk said with a nervous laugh. "We even had an Indian Vice-President of the U.S. Harding's administration, I think. Or was it Coolidge? Just shows what one can become in this country, don't it? And one of our best Jews was Exalted Ruler about ten years ago. But the colored? Why, that's why we wrote this in here, you know?"

"My good friend," Karl said somberly. "I must give this serious thought." He rose very slowly and stiffly with a deep frown across his forehead. "I can't remember for sure. It may be that my Chippewa grandmother was part Negro—or was it my French great-grandfather—but I really think I should be certain before I sign such an important document as this. It wouldn't be honest, would it?"

"No," the clerk replied with an icy voice. "It wouldn't be honest."

"Well," Karl asked. "If it turned out to be true, would it cause problems?"

"I don't care to answer you, Mr. Meister," the clerk said. "And I suggest you leave our hall. I think you're mocking this great lodge."

Karl went quickly, holding a smile in check; and shaking his head, he walked down to the river where his new fishing tug sat in the quiet water.

White wings swooped down and landed on a piling at the boat's stern. It was a red-billed tern, and Karl thought it was a good omen for the new tug. "Name it *Three Sisters,*" Willi had written back, "after the girls in the neighboring village who saw the vision of the Blessed Virgin."

"And so I named it the *Three Sisters*," Karl said to himself, sitting there in the fish shanty on the Black River, watching the glowing stove and listening to the snoring of the half-breed Indian behind it and Corky's labored breathing along the wall.

***

In the galley of the stricken *Tres Belle*, three men hauled the cook stove up the canted deck and reconnected the stove pipe. Other men huddled around the chief engineer. His peajacket and trousers were hard with ice, his face was ashen, his breathing was shallow, and he'd long since stopped shivering.

Surging waves slammed against the cabin sides and spurted through broken portholes. "It's no use," the second engineer said and shook his head. "Everything's wet—the coal, the kindling, even the matches."

Seven

In the drafty fish shanty, Corky sat up and rubbed sleep from his eyes.

Karl paused with the flat needle with which he mended the net's frayed twine. He spoke quietly and nodded to where Joe Bear lay huddled behind the coal stove. "Let him sleep," he said. "We'll not be be going out today."

Joe stirred behind the stove. "Any news of the ship?" he said in a groggy voice.

"No," Karl replied.

"Any news of Billy?" Joe's voice was stronger.

"No. Nothing new," Karl said.

"What's Bennett doing?" Joe struggled to his feet and leaned against the wall.

"Not a damned thing," Karl muttered, and poured black coffee into a cracked mug. "I just came from the station." He sipped his coffee. "Bennett's bringing in Calhorn's bloodhounds. Said they can smell out a ten-year old bone six feet deep."

Corky shook his head. "Damned idiot! That weren't a good thing to say in front of those poor souls at the boat house."

Karl stood and dropped the gill net into the wooden box at his feet. "Bennett said he'll have Calhorn search the rocks for bodies from the *Tres Belle*."

"We can't just stand around here, Karl," Corky said. "Let's go down and take another look at that ship."

***

"My God!" Karl gasped, as the old pickup ground to a halt on the bluff over Deer Point. Through the leaping, boiling spray, he saw the *Tres Belle*. "She's settled in," he said. "And her back's broken."

The freighter lay parallel to the beach, leaning toward shore, as if trying to hide her face from the fearful waves which pounded her. She was broken near the stern; and the aft cabin, which carried her lone smoke stack, rocked under the force of each mountain of water which slammed against it.

"God help any men in that part of the ship," Karl said. "If the stern breaks free, it's certain to roll into deep water. And it's pointed that way already."

Wind blew freezing spray to the top of the two loading masts at each end of the hold. The guy wires supporting the masts had grown a foot thick with ice.

The long, twisted deck was awash to her iron rails at her low mid-section. The ship's hatch planks lay strewn along the beach with the tarpaulin covers. Clouds of dark water spilled from the open ship, carrying away its cargo of powdered coke.

At the bow of the twisted freighter, the forward deck house stood almost erect, as if still voyaging on.

On the beach, groups of men huddled around three fires.

Karl stumbled through loose sand, leaning against the hard-driven sleet to the middle fire.

"See it?" Tall Jim Poindexter said to Karl, holding out his field glasses. "A face—there—in the forward deckhouse!"

Karl focused the glasses. "Yes," he said. "I see it." And a white spot appeared in the round black window and then the window went dark again.

Moving the binoculars along the forward deckhouse, he saw another white spot in a black porthole. Adjusting the lenses, he saw darker dots on the white. The dots were eyes. They were faces. And they were alive.

"Men are still aboard the ship!" he shouted out. And grabbing Poindexter's coat, he asked him, "What did Bennett say?"

"He said to wait."

"Hell, they'll freeze to death," Karl said in disgust. "They've been out there fourteen hours already. No heat. No light."

"I know," Poindexter said, lowering his head. "I'm only a surfman, Karl. Bennett says its too dangerous."

Down the beach, Karl saw dark blue jackets struggling toward the fires, led by an old man and three slim dogs on teathers. Behind them, two men carried a blanket-covered stretcher.

"A seaman from the wrecked ship," said Poindexter. "Name's Lyton. The cook's helper. Calhorn's bloodhounds found him wedged in the rocks about a mile up the beach."

As the struggling group came closer, Karl saw that one of the men in dark coats was a priest.

"The dead man's French-Canadian," Poindexter said. "Father Malloy gave him his last rites."

But the priest could not have heard his last confession, Karl knew. Whatever sins were unforgiven when the man went into the water were frozen with him. Karl thought how long it had been since he had gone to confession—four—yes—four years, it was.

"Forgive me father, for I have sinned," he had said the standard phrase as he stepped into the confessional. Behind the walnut-framed screen, he could see Father Malloy's shadowy figure.

"It's been many years," the priest said, "to make it easier, Karl, start with last week. And if you're not comfortable with that, we'll cover a little more ground."

"I've killed a man. And I've been unfaithful, Father."

"What?"

"I've been unfaithful to Sylvia, and I've killed a man."

The screen flew open. Father Malloy stared at him. "Good God, Karl! Come in here!"

He followed the priest to his study, where Father Malloy closed the heavy door behind him and motioned Karl to a seat on the couch. Karl settled quietly onto the cold leather, wondering what he should say to the little priest with the receding hair line, who peered at him from the corner of his eye.

"Father Malloy opened a cabinet. "It's not church wine," he said over his shoulder. "It's good Irish whiskey." He poured amber liquid into two, thick glasses. "Killed someone, you said?"

"Yes, Father."

The priest added more whiskey to each glass. "And unfaithful?"

"Yes, father."

Father Malloy paused with the bottle in his hand. Then filled the short glasses to the brim, and reaching one glass to Karl, stood before him. "Take it," the priest said, and downed his glass.

Then sitting at a small stool he'd pulled from his desk, the priest folded his arms and looked at Karl. "When were you unfaithful?"

"This summer, earlier."

"Why do you come now?"

"I wasn't ready, I guess—it's been bothering me for a long time. But I wasn't ready."

"And when did you . . ." The priest gulped twice. "When did you kill someone?"

"More than ten years ago, Father."

"A man? A woman?"

"A man, father."

"And why do you come to me now?"

"Well—that hasn't really bothered me, Father. But I thought I should get everything out."

"Doesn't bother you! Karl, how the hell did it happen?"

Karl explained how he had killed Big Mike Curla and buried him on the beach.

The priest nodded. "The car in the river. I remember reading about it in the paper." Then the priest shook his head. "But, Karl, I can tell you feel no true remorse . . ." He looked at Karl for a long time and shook his head again. "There are times, sure, when killing can be justified. Certainly in defense of family, or one's own life, and in defense of another life. And God help us, I think that madman, Hitler, will start a war yet. And killing the enemy in defense of country is justified."

The priest leaned forward on the stool, put his elbows on his knees, and rested his chin in his hands. "What would have happened, Karl, if you'd yelled before you struck with the shovel?"

"I don't know, Father."

"Would he have stopped?"

"Maybe."

"Could you have defended yourself, Karl?"

"I think so. He had a razor. But I had the shovel."

"You see, Karl, we're all God's children. I know nothing of the man. But it's likely his heart wasn't all black. And one could say you'd decided to be his executioner. I'm sure God knows your heart and your intentions at the time."

The priest leaned back on the stool and slapped his small hands on his knees. "You know we don't judge, Karl. It's for God to judge. Understand?"

"Yes. I understand." Karl looked intently at Father Malloy, remembering he'd been taught it was the priest who had the power, given by God through Peter, to forgive sins; but still not really believing it and wondering why the hell he'd come to confession after all.

Father Malloy wondered the same. "Another whiskey, Karl?"

"No thanks, Father." Karl held up his glass, still half full.

"I'll have just a wee," the priest said, going to the cabinet, where he poured his glass full. "Now what's this you're saying about being unfaithful?" he said as he returned to the stool with his glass.

Karl told Father Malloy about the bright day in June that year. He was standing on the tug's stern platform. A gold and brown Essex, with a long hood and broad white-walled tires, slowed on the bridge and caught his attention. A woman in a red hat leaned from the driver's seat and threw him a kiss. Karl grinned and waved as the big car moved slowly across the bridge and out of sight behind the fish shanty. Then he walked carefully down the gangplank, balancing two heavy wooden boxes of torn fish nets on his shoulders. "Get your needles and start sewing," he said to Joe and Corky.

He placed the heavy boxes on the floor; and while bending over, pulling nets from the boxes, he saw black silk stockings come into his view. Then straightening slowly, he saw a slim hand holding a red purse. The dress was buff or tan, he remembered. Large black eyes met his from under a broad red hat.

"Hello, soldier boy," the woman said.

"Flora! What are you doing in Southport."

"I'm staying at the Pirate's Cove," she said, winking at Karl in that same disconnected fashion she had done many years earlier. "Dutch Schultz owns it now."

She stepped close and placed her long fingers lightly on Karl's beard. "Soft," she murmurred; and then stepping back again, a hand on one hip, she looked at him askance. "Take a bath. Get rid of that fish smell. Meet me at the Blue Lagoon." She looked at her watch. "One hour. We'll have a drink and talk. Remember?" she said and winked again. "It's at the Pirate's Cove. Where we have something in common."

Flora turned and walked briskly from the shed without waiting for a reply.

Karl stood in the sun, watching the sleek car backing down the drive, and scratching his beard.

Behind him, Joe and Corky stretched a torn net on a long table. Fumbling for a flat wooden sewing needle under the net, Joe said, "Not bad. Not bad, Karl."

"Now men," Karl said, cocking his head and looking at the men with a slight smile, "it's strictly business. That's the gal who used to send us those big, fat orders from Chicago."

"Sure, Karl. Sure," Corky said with a grin. "Strictly business."

"Did you hear that, though," Karl said. "Fish smell. What fish smell? Corky, she must have got a whiff of you."

Now what could she want, Karl wondered? And he walked farther down the sunny drive, away from the two fishermen at the table, who laughed and joked, and said together, "Sure, Karl. Business."

He looked at his watch. "One hour," he muttered to himself, and scratched his beard again. "That would be about four o'clock. And damn. She said something in common." Big Mike Curla, he wondered?

At four o'clock, Karl swung his long legs into his old Ford roadster and mashed the starter button. The engine fired, and the car's four cylinders began their muffled bark as he turned up the gravel drive to the Dunckley Street Bridge. "Damned if I'll take a bath," he said in the car, as he turned into the Pirates Cove and drove through the iron gates.

He found Flora at a small round table near the big window at the rear of the Blue Lagoon. "Sit down, soldier boy," she said cheerfully as he walked up.

Leaning back in the rattan chair, Karl looked through the open window at the silver lake beyond the bluff. "You wanted to talk to me?" he said nervously.

"Yes." She smiled. "And I don't bite, Karl. Pull up your chair."

Karl slid his chair closer and met her eyes across the table. "Is it about Big Mike?" he said very low. "You said something in common."

She raised an ivory cigarette holder to her lips, and Karl leaned forward and snapped open his lighter. She took the hand holding the lighter in hers, lit her cigarette, and leaned back. "Would you like a cigarette?" she asked.

"No. Thank you."

"Fish." She blew smoke past his face.

"I know. I smell like fish."

"Yes. You do. But we wanted to talk to you about fish. A new contract."

"Why?"

"Because I owe you, Karl," she said quietly, and leaned forward again. "I like to pay my debts." She ran a soft finger over his tanned hand. "In full—understand?"

"We do fine," Karl said awkwardly and pulled his hand from the table.

"It's not a gift," she said. "We won't pay more than market price, F.O.B. Chicago." She leaned back and took a long puff through her cigarette holder. "But we can give you a production contract. Guarantee purchase of everything you catch."

"Any strings?"

"One," she said firmly. "You must be exclusive with us. Dutch wants to corner the market."

"Is it legal?"

"Yeah. It's legal."

"Okay," Karl said. "When do I sign?"

"You don't sign with me," Flora said. "Herman Shansky runs that business. We meet him at six." She rose from her seat and continued. "Come along. I've got clothes for you. I knew you'd smell like fish."

Karl followed her down the sidewalk and up the stairs to the second floor of the Parrot's Beak. He entered the suite behind her and stood in the foyer.

"Come in, Karl. Come on in," she called to him from the living room.

Flora let the venetian blinds fly, and they fluttered down the double window, as Karl walked into the bright room.

He felt strangely warm and uneasy as she sat down on the couch, drawing her legs under her. "We have almost two hours," he said to her. "I could use the clothes, if that's all right. But I need to get home—and take that bath."

"There's no hurry," she said, rising and walking to the bathroom. Karl heard water running in the tub. "Your bath," she said, passing him on her way to the bedroom. Returning, she held out a tan suit. "Size forty," she said. "I bought it in Chicago." She folded the suit onto the couch. "Size fifteen shirt," she said, returning once more from the bedroom and placing a white shirt next to the suit. "And I picked out a tie. Like it?"

"Yes. It—it's very nice," Karl said, taking the brown striped tie in his hand.

"Shoes," she said, placing wing tips on the floor next to the sofa. "I guessed at the size. You'll have to wear your own if they don't fit." She tossed a package on the suit. "Clean underwear—and socks."

Karl said nothing, and she walked up and took his hand. "Don't you like them?"

"Yes, Flora. They're all very nice. But, look, I don't think—"

"No one's going to bother you. I'll go downstairs and have a drink. Go ahead. The bathroom door has a lock. I said before, I'm not going to bite you, Karl." Flora looked up at him with her large black eyes. "The only thing Herman said was, 'If he smells like fish, I ain't buying.'" She stepped back and looked at Karl demurely. "Hey, soldier boy, I don't own the company."

Karl entered the bathroom, locked the door behind him, and slipped into the tub. The warm water closed around, and he breathed a familiar fragrance in the lather. "Lilac," he said to himself.

Looking up, he saw the door open slowly. And Flora stood before him in a white silk robe. She let it fall from her shoulders—and then to the floor. "I have a key," she said softly, smiled, and climbed into the big tub.

All of this Karl then confessed to Father Malloy in his study. After Karl had completed his confession, the priest rose quietly and paced back and forth. Then turning to Karl, he said again, in a quiet and subdued voice, "And why do you come to me now, Karl?"

Before Karl could answer, the priest continued. "Do you think it's like when you were a child? Do you think I will set penance of ten 'Hail Marys' and ten 'Our Fathers' and say 'your sins are forgiven, go my son and sin no more?'"

"No," Karl replied. "I didn't think that would be it." He remembered being uncomfortable on the couch, for he hadn't considered what the priest might require for penance.

"Jesus said from the cross," Father Malloy looked intently at Karl as he spoke, "'forgive them, for they know not what they do.' Is that what you ask of God, Karl? Forgiveness because you didn't know what you were doing?"

"No, Father."

"Well good. Nothing would be gained by that—and God may see it as a further sin—an attempt to relieve your guilt without seeking true forgiveness. Do you understand, Karl?"

"Yes, Father." Karl was growing very warm under his wool sweater. He'd thought of telling Sylvia—he should be open and honest, he had thought then—seek her forgiveness. But now Father Malloy was talking about other sins. "You killed a man without thinking," the priest continued. "That's understandable at the time. But it's been ten years." He paused again, leaning against his desk. "I'm not so sure you've thought about it much since. Have you?"

"No, Father. I haven't," Karl replied. But it wasn't true. He'd lived through that terrible scene in the resorts's basement many, many nights, when he'd awake with a start, sweating cold. Over and over he'd told himself, killing that son-of-bitch from Chicago, who called him a Hun and beat up on women, was no sin. Yes—he'd suffered remorse, just as Father Malloy was indicating he should. But now all he could think about was escape from those accusing eyes.

"You haven't been to mass in over five years, Karl."

"No, Father. I haven't." Karl's glance drifted to the door, and he was no longer listening to the priest.

". . . fish contract?" he heard the priest say.

"I'm sorry, Father," he said, embarrassed at his lapse of attention.

"Did you get your fish contract?"

"No, Father—I left."

Father Malloy smiled; and after a long pause, returned to the stool and sat before Karl, his face again in his hands. Then the priest lifted his head, and Karl saw a tried look in his gray eyes.

"Karl," said the priest, "when you went to the Blue Lagoon, what thoughts were on your mind?"

"I don't really know, Father. I was thinking she wanted to talk about Big Mike. That's what I remember."

"Well, what did you think she would say to you."

"About Big Mike?"

"Yes. If that's what was on your mind. What did you think she would say? And what did you think you would do?"

"I don't know," Karl lied, realizing he had gone to the Blue Lagoon knowing that Big Mike's death was not the reason.

"Karl, my son." The priest continued, and Karl waited, thinking he would, at last, state his penance; but Father Malloy paused and fixed his eyes upon Karl. He felt as though the priest were peering into the very depths of his soul. "Think," the priest went on. "It's also a form of prayer, and perhaps better suited to your nature than reciting 'Hail Marys' and 'Our Fathers.' Reflect upon the reasons for your actions. Search for the answers. And I'm talking about three things. One, why you gave the man no warning. Two, why you never mentioned in confession killing the man. And three, why you went to the Blue Lagoon."

Father Malloy rose slowly. "I'll pray for you, Karl," he said quietly. "Will you pray for me?"

"Yes, Father."

"You see," Father Malloy said, ushering him to the door, "we're all sinners. We must remember that we're mortals. We need prayer. We need reflection. And we're most in danger when we forget to be humble." The priest opened the door. "Come back, Karl—when your heart aches for God's forgiveness."

Later, while the weather was still warm that year, Karl had taken Sylvia to mass. When mass was over, he returned to the church overlooking the lake. Many times Father Malloy held open the heavy door; and then he helped ease the wheelchair down the steep steps. "Peace be with you, Karl," the priest said often. "And also with you," Karl would reply.

***

Now the stretcher stopped on the wind-whipped beach. Father Malloy stood before Karl and reached out his hand.

Karl clasped the cold hand firmly.

"Peace be with you, Karl," Father Gregory said.

"And also with you," Karl answered.

Later that afternoon, Karl went to the Coast Guard Station to confront Captain Bennett. "We saw them!" He stood in the door of the captain's office and shouted between clenched teeth.

The officer swiveled in his chair to face the intruder. "Close the door!" Bennett commanded in a high-pitched voice.

Slamming the door on the noisy crowd in the boat house, Karl stood stiffly before Captain Bennett. His eyes scanned the cluttered desk where the officer had been working.

The captain's lip curled. "What are you doing here, Meister?" he asked with a swift sneer.

Karl stepped forward and planted himself firmly before Bennett. "We saw faces in the windows," he said slowly and methodically, studying the officer's gray face. "It's been too damned long, Bennett. The ship's breaking up. Those men are freezing to death!"

"What are you saying, Meister?" Bennett was on his feet now, with a look of disdain in his eyes.

"Shoot a line, Bennett."

"And the bodies. The cook and his helper. How'd they get to the beach?" The officer's voice rose to yet a higher pitch. "They were washed off the deck, Meister! That's how. And what would happen," Bennett paused and stood straighter, "to any man on the deck when a ton of water crashed down as he secured the line?" Bennett glowered, and quickly went on before Karl could answer. "He'd be carried into the water, Meister! And he wouldn't live to reach shore."

"My God, Bennett. It's worth a try. We've gotta do something. It's twenty degrees and dropping. No heat on the ship. They won't last another night.

Karl saw the muscles in Bennett's neck tense, and the officer's body seemed to coil, as if ready to spring.

"No! No! No!" Bennett screamed. "Get out of my station!" Turning and leaning heavily on his desk, he looked over his shoulder at Karl sullenly. "What do you think I'm doing here? Your brother's out with the powerboat. Probably lost. I know the ship's breaking up. I haven't slept." Bennett sank slowly into his chair. "What do you want from me, Meister?"

"The surfboat—launch it. The ship's only two hundred yards out. Shoot a line for the boat to follow. It'll catch on something. If anyone slips into the water, the lifeboat can pick them up."

"We tried," was the quiet reply. "Last night. We couldn't get past the breakers—the undertow was fierce. And I won't shoot a line—that's just too risky."

"My tug." Karl stepped closer. "I'm offering you my boat. I'll handle the wheel."

"How?" Bennett said, and Karl could feel the sting of a sneer in his voice. "You couldn't get out the channel."

There was a sudden rapping on the door behind Karl.

"Come in!" Captain Bennett barked.

"Sir!—" Poindexter's tall figure stood in the door.

"Close the door!" Bennett interrupted.

"They found wreakage!" Poindexter went on as he slammed the door behind him. "On the beach. North of Holland."

Eight

Conservation Corps workers patrolling the beach found the wreckage," Karl told Corky in the battered truck as they drove north in the gray light on highway 31.

"Any idea what it is Karl? Any bodies?"

Karl shook his head. "Just pieces of wood so far. These storms will churn up anything—sometimes wrecks that've been on the bottom for years."

"Well, it's not likely they'd find any survivors now. Not if a boat's broken up," said Corky, peering ahead into the dimming light as the clanking Chevrolet raced along the curving road.

"Slow down, Corky! You'll miss the damned turn. It's along here somewhere."

It was dusk when they reached Little Pigeon creek, ten miles north of Holland. Ahead, they spotted tail lights of the Coast Guard Plymouth winding along a narrow dirt road to where the creek emptied into Lake Michigan. Several cars and trucks were parked along the bank, and Karl could see thirty or forty men and some women along the beach.

They parked the truck on a grassy knoll where old cars and rusted pickups had slid to a stop. Karl followed Corky across the wet sand to the muddy creek outlet. Reporters flashed pictures of a large box-shaped object floating in the surf at the creek's mouth. On the other side of the creek, wedged against sharp-bladed beach grasses, Karl saw a red-stripped funnel. "Oh, God—look," he cried out. "It's the *Chief's* smokestack."

"Make way here! Make way!" Karl turned and saw two men, dressed in dark green rain gear and wearing high black boots, leading a Farmall tractor onto the beach. The men carried grappling hooks tied to coiled ropes slung over their shoulders. High behind the wide tractor's bright lights, was a third man wearing the red pocket patch of the the Ottawa County Sheriff's Department, steering the machine through the loose sand.

When the throbbing tractor reached the surf, the two deputies in the lead tossed the grappling irons in an arc over the white box floating in the water and jerked the ropes hard, setting the hooks. Then they tied the lines to the tractor's frame just below its lights.

Upon a signal from the bigger deputy, the tractor backed away. The ropes tightened, pulling the large box through the surf. When it struck bottom near the water's edge, the big object tipped forward, showing portholes along its sides, paused there for a moment as the tractor's wheels spun in the sand, then fell over on its roof on the beach.

Karl ran forward with the crowd. Stopping between the bigger deputy and Captain Bennett, he said, "It's the *Chief's* pilothouse. This is the manufacturer's imprint here, over the forward windows." Stamped deep into the white wood of the overturned pilothouse were large letters, and Karl read them in the lantern light. "The Berger Boat Company. That's it," Karl said. "That's who made the *Sioux Chief.* I've been in her before." He looked up at the deputy. "Her smokestack's on the other side of the creek."

The big deputy turned to Bennett and shook his head. "Captain, with her pilothouse ripped off, that boat's gone to the bottom for sure."

Bennett's face twitched in the lantern light. Then he glanced nervously at Karl and stared out over the water. "Maybe the *Bradley's* still out there," he stammered. "The wind's gone down some and those waves are runnin' a little easier . . ." His voice trailed off. Then his face brightened and he took a step closer to the deputy. "I've got a powerboat out," he said louder. "Good men. There's a chance they took off the *Chief's* crew—and the *Bradley*, too."

The deputy's mouth opened, and for a long time he said nothing. Then he looked at Karl out of the corner of his eye, and said to Captain Bennett, "Yes. There's always hope. Men from our department have already searched north from Holland. And the weather's letting up a bit. But another gale's been forecast—"

"But it won't hit here until around noon tomorrow," Bennett interrupted. "My boys will be in by then!"

The deputy looked at Karl long and hard with a question on his face. Then he spun around and cupped his big hands to his mouth. "Men!" he shouted down the beach, "secure any wreckage you find. Put the small stuff in the truck. Pull high and anchor anything too big to carry." Turning back to Bennett, he put a hand on the captain's shoulder and said to the gaunt man. "Yes. With a bit of luck, I'm sure they'll make it."

Both men stared at each other for a moment. Then Bennett said, "Let me know if you find anything else." Turning on his heel and motioning to the three surfmen with him, the Coast Guard captain said over his shoulder, "I'll take my crew and search the beach north from Southport. Captain Johnson from the Holland station will take over here. He should be along shortly."

Bennett took three steps, stopped and turned back to the deputy. "Ask Johnson to send a party south from Holland. We'll be coming north with bloodhounds."

The deputy glanced at his watch, then looked up at Karl with a heavy frown on his face, and turned and walked silently away.

Karl stood near the pilothouse and stared into the pounding surf. "Forty miles," he wondered aloud. "How could the *Chief* be so far north, with the wind from the southwest?"

"Well, Karl," Corky said, walking up behind him. "It means they ran far out."

"No. The *Chief* didn't have enough power to turn into those waves. And even if she got lucky, and swung in a trough, she wouldn't be able to hold her heading."

"Then how did she get here?"

"I don't know. That old steam engine would have gone out with the first water over the boat."

"Karl! The Coast Guard boat. Do you think . . ." Corky paused, "they tried to tow the *Chief*?"

Karl rubbed his beard with his gloved hand. "The boat's too light for that. Much too light. And it was too damned rough for a tow."

"Maybe it was the current."

"The *Bradley*!" Karl pounded Corky's shoulder.

"Do you think the *Bradley* towed her, Karl?"

"No. Lashed her alongside. Stem to stem and stern to stern," Karl said excitedly. "The *Bradley's* a strong boat—and she has a good engine."

Corky pulled at his wind-blown mustache. "I know," he grunted. "Took it from an old thirty-six Buick last year. Eight cylinders. I helped put it in. But—"

"Lashed, Corky. Side to side. Not to bring her in, but to take off the crew. And they'd have run off with the seas-to keep the boats from smashing while they transferred the men." Karl waved his arm north. "Maybe tried a run for Muskegon, thinking they could make that channel. Hell, it's five times as wide as Southport—yes, that's it. They took off the crew and ran with her toward Muskegon. They did it quick." Karl's eyes danced. "Pulled alongside in a trough. Snapped out lines and cleated down. The *Bradley* took the crew off and held to the *Chief* as long as she could."

Karl plunged his hands into his pockets and rocked back on his heels, staring out onto the turbulent lake. "Two—three hours, I'd say. The *Bradley's* engine couldn't hold both boats into the wind. But like this," and Karl formed an angle with his hands, "ten—fifteen miles out, with the waves on their quarter." He drew a line through the air. "Wind and waves from the southwest. The *Chief* would come in, right here!"

"But the *Bradley* never made Muskegon, Karl."

"Out there," Karl waved his right hand to the foaming waters under the dark, western sky. "Or north." He paused and frowned. "Corky," he said, pointing northward across the small creek, "let's take a walk."

Karl led the way across the stony creek bed, and they walked for twenty minutes, swinging their arms for warmth. Over and over, Karl said to himself, "At least I know the surfboat didn't tow the *Chief*. No, it couldn't have. Too light. Too much rough water. But, damn, it sure scared me to see the *Chief* here—thinking Billy might have tried to tow her to Muskegon. But no. He couldn't have got her this far. It had to be the *Bradley*. And Billy's still plowing into it."

"The wind's gone down some," Corky said. "But it's still cold as hell. And my feet are freezing. Let's head back."

Karl stopped suddenly and pointed along the shore. "Shine your light along there!"

They followed the bouncing light beam along the hard sand near the water, running past white-sided planking, past bits and pieces of framing timbers, and then they came upon a body. It was lying face down, and the water washed over it, coating it with ice. Below the ice coating, Karl saw a dark jacket, cork and canvas life preserver, and a wool, knit cap, pulled down low.

Karl dropped to his knees and made the sign of the cross. Then he rolled the man over. The lifeless eyes of John McKay, Jr. stared up at him. "Oh, God!" Karl cried out, "I thought it was Billy!" Then he hid his face in his hands and wept.

"Karl!" Corky was shaking his shoulder. "Get hold of yourself, Karl."

"Oh, Christ Jesus!" Karl could not stop now. The storm's turmoil had run his emotions high. He was tired. And he could not think, only weep. Weep for Billy, lost on the lake. And weep for the cold body of young John McKay.

"Look Karl!" He heard Corky's voice over the wind and waves. "His watch. It stopped a little before nine. They must have gone down last night."

Karl looked at the ice-encrusted watch. "Or this morning. Poor soul."

"Seems to be wound tight, Karl."

Karl rose slowly and looked out over the raging water. "He'd wind it when he got up, or in the evening." Karl looked down at the body on the beach. "That means he went into the water at nine last night, or nine o'clock this morning." Karl's voice grew stronger. "Either way, the *Bradley* must have had a line on his tug. And she may be afloat."

"Karl, we've only come a few miles. Don't you think he was probably still on the *Chief* when she broke up? The current could have carried him a little farther north."

"No," said Karl. "Look, Corky. The current wouldn't do it. Not this far. My guess is the *Bradley* brought 'em here. And if the *Bradley* survived that long, there's a good chance for Billy too!"

Karl looked again out on the lake, facing into the wind. He could see a huge sea still running far out on the water, and the wind was cold down his collar. Over his head, the moon suddenly broke through scudding clouds, casting a pale glow over the desolate scene.

As far as he could see, smashed planks littered the beach and washed in the surf. Then, farther out, glistening in the moonlight, he saw a large, black hull bottom, washed by the waves, and rocking with the swells.

His throat knotted. He couldn't talk. And then he pointed. Corky was pointing too and shouting, "It's the *Henry Bradley,* Karl! See! There! Look! See that spoon-shaped stern. That's the *Bradley* !"

***

When they drove up to the Southport station, Karl heard loud, excited voices coming from the boat house.

"It's Billy," Muriel said, rushing at him as he stepped through the door. "My God, Karl," she said, tears streaming down her white face, "he just called—from Chicago. They made it!"

"Billy?" asked Karl, frowning. "Billy in Chicago?" His senses had been numbed by the brutal scene north of Holland, and his mind climbed slowly from a dark abyss. The fire lighted deep in his soul by Muriel's rushed greeting glowed within him. A sweet, choked sensation pressed down hard on his heart. The picture of Billy on shore, perceived dimly by his clouded mind, took shape in a gray fog—and then he understood. Yes. Billy was safe. On shore. In Chicago. Alive. "Billy made it!" he cried out.

The full awareness of it all—his brother now beyond the reach of grasping waves and warm on the Chicago shore—burst upon Karl. "Holy Mary—Mother of God!" he said, lifting Muriel high. He put her down quickly and hugged her tight. Tears rolled down his cheeks. Then he glimpsed the smiling face of old John McKay, moving steadily toward him through the crowd. What would he say to the old man, he wondered? And to Muriel? Billy had escaped from an icy death at the hands of the man-eating sea. Karl had just been lifted from the depths of despair by the good news. But for Muriel and her father, it would be different. Their souls must travel from the welcome shock of salvation to the cold acceptance of a brother and a son lost forever to the family embrace.

"Billy called?" he asked, while his mind raced for the words to tell Muriel her brother was found dead on the beach north of Holland.

"Yes. Oh, yes. Thank God!"

"When! When!"

"Not ten minutes ago, Karl."

"And the crew?" Corky asked over Karl's shoulder.

"All safe," Muriel said through tears. "They fought the waves all the way, Karl. Twenty-seven hours. Billy said they had only three gallons of fuel left in the tanks."

"Yes," old man McKay's commanding voice with its pronounced Scottish burr broke in at Karl's shoulder. "From the two hundred gallons they started with. Another hour and they wouldn't have made it."

"Mr. McKay—" Karl said stiffly, avoiding the eyes of the old man.

"They're putting out tomorrow," Muriel said, interrupting him. "Billy told me, if the wind continues to drop they'll launch tomorrow and come as far as they can. He wants to search for Johnny and the missing tug crews." Muriel continued rapidly in an excited and nervous voice. "I know it's a lot to expect." She drew a deep breath. "But, Karl. Honestly. I didn't think I'd hear from Billy again. So it may be a time of miracles. What do you think, Karl? I know they found the pilothouse. But no men. If they'd gone down with the tug, they'd have been found—on the beach, wouldn't they? Some say they were picked up by the *Bradley*. And that she's headed for Chicago too."

Karl saw panic in Muriel's face and quiet despair in the face of Mr. McKay beside her.

"What do you think, Karl?" Muriel asked again.

Still Karl did not reply. Then, after a long pause, he said, "Muriel . . . Mr. McKay . . ." His voice was thick and he paused again.

"Captain Bennett told us you were at Holland," Mr. McKay said quickly. "Where they found the pilothouse. Was it north of Holland?" he asked.

"Yes. It was north of Holland, Mr. McKay," Karl said slowly.

"Look, Karl," John McKay was intent, in front of Karl now, "this is the only time my boat's gone out without me. And now she's broken up with my boy at the wheel." The old man's face was oddly rigid, as if held together by sheer strength of will alone, which, from time to time, waned, permitting a quiver of lip, a twitch of eyebrow, and threatened momentarily to give up the fight and let fear and sorrow take command; and then the old man asked the question Karl feared. "You were there," he said. "Does he have a chance?"

Karl didn't answer.

The old man's chin pressed forward. "Do you think Johnny and my men were taken off by the Bradley? I thought the Coast Guard might reach them. But Billy's in Chicago." The old man paused and looked at Karl, waiting for a reply. Then he said, "The Bradley's a mighty strong boat. She could survive that storm. And they wouldn't leave the old *Chief* without trying to take the men off, you know."

Still Karl said nothing. The silence grew.

"Dad," Muriel said, stepping forward and placing an arm around the old man. "As long as the *Bradley's* unreported—and until we hear different—there's hope. Of course the *Bradley* took them off. Now, truthfully," she said, "no one had much hope for Billy, did they?" She reached forward and chucked the old man's chin. "The impossible just happened. It'll happen again."

She turned to Karl. "Karl's too tired and worn out to talk much now. Aren't you, Karl?'

Karl knew the time had come; and he knew he was the one to say something. Tell Muriel and the old man, he thought, before the official news reaches the station and Bennett blurts out something stupid.

"Corky and me," he said deliberately and slowly, turning to the broad Irish net puller behind him, "went farther north, after the pilothouse was dragged up on the beach." He paused and looked firmly at Muriel, and then at Mr. McKay.

"Muriel," he began again, slowly, "I . . . It's bad news." He reached out and took Muriel's hand in his black glove, and put his right hand on the old man's shoulder. His tongue was thick, and he scarcely recognized his own voice as he continued. "We found the *Bradley*. Wrecked. A couple of miles farther north."

"Oh, no!" Mr. McKay gasped.

Muriel remained silent and squeezed Karl's hand.

Karl looked at her and she nodded very slowly, letting him know she was prepared, and understood what would follow.

"And Johnny?" asked Mr. McKay. "You found Johnny, didn't you?" the old man asked stoically.

"Yes," Karl answered. "His watch had stopped a little before nine."

"He always wound his watch in the evening," the old man said. "It was a superstition with him, you know—well—I knew it would come to this. It's been too long. But we can thank God for one miracle today. We have Billy." He paused and smiled at Muriel. Then turned to Karl. "Where is my boy now?" Where have they taken him?"

"To Holland," Karl answered. "They're waiting for your call."

"First," the old man said, "someone should tell Bennett. I know the lake. There's no sense searching the beach here. They're all north of Holland now."

The door behind Karl opened suddenly and three lean dogs burst into the boat house, followed by Mr. Calhorn and Captain Bennett. Behind them were three excited surfmen. "Bones!" one of the surfmen called out. "Human bones. By the key post, on the north beach."

"I told you," Calhorn said clapping Bennett on the shoulder as they strode through the boat house and into the captain's office. "Them dogs can find anything. Hell, you never know when you take 'em out just what they'll come up with."

"Human bones," the other surfman said. "And buried. Not more than four feet deep."

With a trembling hand, Karl motioned Corky aside. "Look after Muriel and old McKay," he said with a shaken voice. "Don't let them drive. Take them home. There's nothing more to be done here tonight."

"Sure, Karl."

"I'll walk." With those words, Karl turned and stumbled out the door.

Corky's voice trailed behind him as he turned his collar up against the wind. "My God," Corky said as the door closed. "Did you hear, Karl? Bones. Human bones."

Karl walked briskly along the station road with the cold wind at his back. When he reached the hilltop, he turned down Michigan Avenue toward his house. The sweet smell of burning hardwoods came to him on the downdraft from fireplaces along the shore. He shook the thoughts of Big Mike Curla's bones found on the beach from his head. Sylvia will be sitting before the fire, he said to himself. And at last, I have good news for her. Billy's safe.

In the yellow light behind the bay window's lace curtains, he saw Sylvia sitting at the open desk. Has she heard the mixed news? he wondered. Billy and the Coast Guard crew alive—and young John McKay drowned—with all hope for the other fishermen now given up. He paused before the bay window. Overhead, the wind hummed a low, mournful song in the oak branches. The exhilaration he'd experienced in the storm's early stages had passed. Billy had landed, safe and solid, across the wild waters. The seas had spit up the cold body of young John McKay. The *Bradley's* battered hulk had blown aground. The *Chief's* pilot-house was a silent witness to the big steam tug's fate; and Karl knew the debris north of Holland meant little hope for the remaining men.

His thoughts flashed briefly to the white faces pressed against the cold cabin glass of the *Tres Belle*. Would they survive another night, he wondered? And how many had already frozen to the core, breathing a final sigh in their steel tomb?

Standing in front of the house, listening to the pounding surf over the wind's roar, the startling news of bones found on the beach came back to him. I should have expected it, he thought. Once the fence was taken down, something like this would happen, sooner or later. He cupped his hand and lit a cigarette. Then ground it under his heel. What the hell, he thought, they'll figure out I killed Big Mike, or they won't. There's nothing I can do about it now.

Inside the bungalow, Sylvia whirled in her chair. "I heard it on the radio!" she said with a sparkle long gone from her blue eyes. "Billy—he's in Chicago!"

She pulled a scribbled paper from the desk. "They interviewed him, Karl. I heard his voice." Sylvia pushed her glasses farther up her nose and read from her notes: "We came in under our own power." She looked up at Karl. "He was so humble," she said. "Not really nervous, but a little shy. Just like when he first came on the train from New York." And glancing at the paper in her hand, read further: "Twenty-seven hours on the lake. Less fear than the folks at home. A stout boat, and a good motor . . ."

Karl was smiling broadly now. "That's wonderful news, Sylvia," he said when she paused from her reading. "What else did he say?"

"I couldn't get it all down, Karl." And looking at her watch, she said, "But they're broadcasting it again. At nine-thirty. Ten more minutes."

Sitting down in the wicker chair next to the desk, Karl waited with Sylvia and they listened to soft music until the nine-thirty newscast; and then they heard Billy's voice from Chicago.

"After leaving Southport yesterday," he said, "we went after the tugs. But we ran into some pretty big waves—and we sighted nothing. And we almost capsized—lost a man over the side. And we knew we couldn't stay in that area. We came in under our own power, after twenty-seven hours on the lake." Billy continued. "We probably had less fear than the folks at home. Every now and then, a wave'd reach almost thirty feet. But we knew we had a stout boat and a good motor and a capable crew.

"But we couldn't get back to Southport in those seas. Couldn't turn at all. During the next few hours, we tried it twice, and came near capsizing again. Lost Elmer Swain over the side that time. But we just fished him in by his line.

"We didn't have time to worry about anything. We just set about getting ourselves out of trouble. So we pointed southwest for Chicago and plowed away about two or three miles an hour. Well, we made it all right."

When the recording finished, Sylvia turned down the radio and beamed at Karl. "Billy's starting back in the morning," she said.

"I know. I just came from the station."

"Billy knows the tugs are lost. But he said he wants to help with the freighter, and search for the missing fishermen." She looked at Karl thoughtfully. "They're coming back with the boat." Her voice was strained. "Will they be all right, Karl?"

"Billy?" Karl said. "He's a good seaman. A fresh gale is forecast. But he'll hug the shore and put in if there's trouble."

By this time Karl was looking at the wall, not thinking about Billy, or the *Tres Belle*, or the crushed tugs on the beach. He saw on the blank wall a vision of Calhorn's bloodhounds, digging down through the packed sand and dragging out Big Mike Curla's white bones.

"Yes. Billy's a good seaman," he said again, absentmindedly. "He knows when to point in. And he'll take the long route, along the shore."

He turned to Sylvia, his beard in his hands. "We found young McKay," he said quietly.

"Yes. I know. It was on the news. Poor Muriel."

"Was there any other news?" asked Karl, leaning back in his chair.

"Many ships were lost, Karl. I don't remember how many. And many, many men. It's a sad night for their families."

Karl stretched and walked to the radio. "We've been lucky, haven't we?" he said, looking down at her. "And we've had a good life."

"Lucky—yes. With Billy."

Karl watched as she wheeled toward the kitchen; and it was then that he first noticed the weakness in her left arm. The wheelchair stopped at the dining room rug, and she pushed first the right wheel over the small rise, and moving her right arm to the other wheel, pushed it forward.

He sank heavily into the chair, closed his eyes, and listened to the soft music.

"Pea soup, Karl?" He heard at his elbow. Sylvia's low voice came to him through a fog now, and he opened his eyes and realized he'd dozed off. She was at his side, leaning forward, with a shallow bowl of green soup and steaming potatoes in her hands.

"Eat something," she said with a smile. "And go to bed."

He took the warm bowl from her hands and his eyes closed a few seconds, then opened steadily to hers. "Thanks, Sylvia. You go to bed now. I'll wait for the late news."

Karl forced his mind from thoughts of the old bones laid one by one on the beach, as they were pulled from the cold sand by the slim dogs, and managed a weak smile as Sylvia blew him a kiss and closed the bedroom door behind her.

With the living room quietly his, Karl put three new logs on the dying fire and returned to the radio.

". . . snow flurries with temperatures in the low twenties tonight, and worse to come," the announcer said. "Captain Bennett reports that the *Escanaba* is disabled in Muskegon, and will not be available for a rescue of the *Tres Belle*. But the Coast Guard will keep a vigil through the night and take the men from the wreck tomorrow, when the power boat, commanded by William Meister, returns from Chicago, Bennett told us.

"Captain Bennett has come under heavy criticism for his handling of the wrecked freighter. And local fishermen have said an attempt with a breeches buoy or surfboat could be made. The captain refused further comment when we asked about such rescue efforts.

"Nor would he comment on rumors that officers from the Chicago District were enroute to relieve him of his Southport command. However, anonymous Coast Guard authorities in Chicago stated that Captain Bennett appeared to be obsessed with the ancient grave found at Southport, to the neglect of his duties. 'The integrity of the Service is at stake here,' the undisclosed source said.

"Captain Bennett refused to give the media any details on the shallow grave, but claimed he was working with the Sheriff's Department and that he thought he knew who the body might be.

"We talked with Deputy Steward, who informed us that the investigation was under way and that no further statements would be made until the mystery of the shallow grave was solved."

Karl's face went stiff and he felt his heart beating hard. "Bennett knows nothing," he said under his breath. "The blithering idiot."

He turned and stared at the unfinished painting of his father-in-law on the short easel. Bennett should be relieved of command, he thought. He would have been discharged then, if the truth had been told when the *Merry B.* went down. If only we had come up from the lee side, he thought, the old man would be alive today. And Sylvia would be walking.

"The barge tug *Calico Ray*," the radio continued, "last reported off Southport with a broken rudder cable, is safe in East Chicago. Emergency steering gear brought the old ship into port late today. She had been badly buffeted by heavy waves, and lost her pilothouse with all communications. A lookout posted on deck shouted orders relayed down the companionway to emergency steering apparatus in the engine room.

"And the grim search for fifty-one missing seamen continued into the night today. Except for the body of John McKay, Jr., discovered earlier this evening, there has been no trace of the seven Southport fishermen lost in yesterday's storm.

"Vessels which weathered the heavy seas continue arriving at ports along the lake, to add their tales to those of others who survived. But reported as definitely lost, with all crew, were the *Anna Minch* and *W.B.*

Davock. Apparently, both ships went down south of Ludington Monday afternoon. Eighteen bodies and documented wreckage from both ships washed ashore throughout today."

Karl went to the kitchen, poured black coffee into a sauce pan, and heated it over the gas flame. Two more ships lost, he thought. And fifty-one men, now. If Bennett doesn't act soon, it'll be many more.

When he returned to the living room with his hot coffee, the radio continued with storm news.

"Two men are being held at Milwaukee today, pending federal charges for looting the abandoned freighter *Sinaloa*, which ran aground at Sac Bay in the storm yesterday. Authorities said the men had in their possession a direction finder, pilot wheel, compass and personal effects of seamen on the *Sinaloa*."

Fools, Karl thought. Risk their necks in choppy seas for a few stolen trophys. But he knew the waves were smaller on the lee shore off Wisconsin, and wasn't surprised to learn that many small boats had recklessly explored several grounded ships.

If only the *Tres Belle's* captain had gone up the Wisconsin side, he thought, he would have had a grounding at the most, and in protected waters. And now having made the wrong decision, the freighter's captain waits, while Bennett decides his fate.

The radio shifted to war news. "The German Luftwaffe," the announcer said, "raided Coventry, England again last night in attacks by wave after wave of bombers, which lasted over ten hours without let up. Hospitals, churches, hotels, theaters, banks, stores and complete blocks of homes and apartment buildings are in ruins. Thousands are dead or wounded and a large part of the city was destroyed.

"German officials in Berlin said the raid was in retaliation for the British raid on Munich during the Nazi party celebration last Friday. Hitler was speaking in Munich at the time of the daring raid deep into Germany, and furiously promised quick revenge."

Just a damned excuse, Karl thought. Our Austrian friend probably planned that attack for a long time.

"It is now," the announcer said, "a little after four, London time. And we have received information of new Nazi bombings. These are only preliminary reports, but it appears an estimated five hundred German warplanes swarmed over the English capitol within the last few hours, systematically hammering the city with millions of tons of high explosive bombs.

"Other targets were also attacked. The industrial city of Coventry was hit again. It is now assumed this is an all effort to knock out Britian's war base and air power, before aid from the U.S. becomes fully effective.

"High sources fear an imminent invasion by Nazi ground forces. And many say the end for Britian's ill-prepared island troops will come quickly, bringing total victory for the Nazis."

See, Karl thought to himself, the little corporal did have it planned all along.

"Nazi officials met with Soviet counterparts in Berlin last night, according to the German newspaper *National Zeitung*. The purpose, that paper reported, was to lay the ground work for a 'world coalition' with Germany, Italy, Russia and Japan in dominant roles. Work was begun, the paper said, on formation of an 'inter-continental peace system' after the war, which is expected to end shortly, with the four powers leading. The program was completed with a banquet at the Russian embassy."

Yes, Karl thought. The Russian bear joins with the Nazis. But how long do the Reds think they can keep the wolves at bay? And the Americans? The Germans alienated them in the first war, and they came in on the French and English side. They'll do it again, too. Hitler will make the same mistake.

"On the national scene," the radio continued, "Jesse Owens, once the world's fastest human, and the only triple winner in Olympic history, has completed bankruptcy proceedings in New York. The Alabama Negro who started picking cotton at age six plans to build a new life for his wife and child in complete obscurity, and refused to disclose his current residence.

"President Roosevelt completed a five-night cruise on the Potomac this morning, recovering from the election campaign strain. The ship cruised all through the night, lulling our president to sleep with the cradle song of its engines."

Rubbing his aching hand under the black glove, Karl muttered to himself, "Sometimes I think the entire country is asleep." Just as Austria slept while the Nazis organized and silently stole the country. And here I am, Karl laughed quietly, worrying about a few bones found on the beach. I can't do anything about it now. And I can't do anything about Austria. He sighed deeply and reflected for a moment. But I can do something for those poor souls on the wreck. Another gale's blowing in for sure. I feel it in my hand. Billy won't make it in time. Hell, I'll take them off myself in the morning. And he rose, stretched, and feeling himself again, reached for the radio.

"The eleven o'clock news has been brought to you by your friendly Kroger store, which will remain open tomorrow evening for your convenience. Chuck Appleton, the manager, says to remind you folks that everything in the store is a special—everyday. He's featuring a two-pound roll of Michigan Maid butter for sixty-nine cents. And all popular brands of cigarettes are just one-dollar-twenty per carton . . ."

Karl clicked off the radio, checked to see that Sylvia was sleeping soundly, and walked to the Antler Bar, where he found Corky and Joe.

"If Bennett sits on his ass tonight," Karl said to them, "I want to take the tug out for a look at that freighter in the morning. Maybe we can do some good—maybe even try a rescue—I'll need a crew."

"Count me in, Karl," Joe said, and looked at him squarely. "I know how you feel."

"Thanks boys. We'll give Bennett one more night. And if he doesn't act, we will."

Corky leaned back and thumped both hands on the wooden table. "Hell yes," he said, "we'll go out. Just let me know when you want me at the shanty."

***

The boilers on the *Tres Belle* had flooded soon after she grounded; and during that first night, the stern settled farther into the cold waves, and water in the firehold rose to a depth of fifteen feet. Shortly after midnight, when the water reached the gasoline-powered auxiliary generator mounted over the boilers, it sputtered to a stop. In the captain's office, the last of the emergency lights winked out.

After the cook and his helper washed overboard, one more man from the after house tried making his way along the railing toward the forward cabin, icy seas breaking over him at each step. Captain DuPays watched out the rear porthole from his office, and said a silent prayer for the man. Three times he saw the seaman wash over the rail, nothing between him and sudden death but the cold wire clutched in his frozen hands. The seaman tried a fourth time, and again had to pull himself back from the water. Then Captain DuPays recognized the man as the chief engineer, as he braced himself against the railing cables for a moment, standing there erect while a great swell rolled over him. It was a moment of decision; and then the chief engineer had turned and hurried back through the steel door of the aft cabin.

Captain DuPays no longer knew whether they were dead or alive back there. But he'd seen the fires on the beach, and the crowd on the shore during the day. Now the seven men of the forward crew were facing another night, huddled together for warmth in the captain's cabin. They'd gone almost twenty-four hours without food, heat, water, or lights. Water spurted through cracked portholes, and it was getting colder by the minute.

Nine

Holy Christ!" Karl cried out, as he sat straight up in bed. "What time is it?" The living room clock sounded five dull chimes. His bare feet slapped the cold wood floor. "Damn," he muttered to himself, "it's late."

The aroma of strong coffee came to him from the kitchen and pulled his senses from a hard sleep. He could hear Sylvia sliding pans on the stove, then the sweet crackle of bacon frying.

"Toast, Karl?" Sylvia's voice came loud from the kitchen, followed by a whistled melody.

"Sure!" he replied, struggling into dark wool pants and a red flannel shirt. Then, still barefoot, he padded to the kitchen.

"Shoes, Karl!" Sylvia pointed at his feet. "I won't have you coming down with pneumonia."

Karl grinned at her, happy to see her in good spirits. It had been a long time since she'd barked such an order. And his grin widened.

"Slippers, Karl." She waived a wooden spatula. "At least put on slippers. There's no heat in the house. And the linoleum is ice."

Yes, Karl thought as he turned toward the bedroom. It's damned cold. And he saw his breath in the air and frost on the windows.

"Now stoke the furnace, Karl!" she hollered after him. "Billy's coming home today. Muriel's worn out. I'll be cooking supper for them. If they won't come," Sylvia paused, "we'll take it to them. Even if I have to wheel it down there myself. Did you hear, Karl? We'll burn coal today, Karl. I want a warm house."

"Yes," was the loud reply from the bedroom. "I hear you, Sylvia." Karl whistled a childhood tune from Austria. Then he stopped and listened. It was blowing harder; and then sleet beat against the window.

Karl started the furnace, then called Corky, and then Joe. "Meet me at the tug," he told each of them. I'll be down there warming up the engine. We're going out for the *Tres Belle*!"

***

With the big diesel engine rolling over slowly with its rhythmic whoosh-boom-whoosh, Karl turned his attention to the tug's pot-bellied heating stove. With a bent poker, he stirred the cold gray ashes from its last burn; and when the cast-iron grate was almost cleared, he shook the remaining fluff into the stove's ash box below, pushed the few remaining clinkers through the grate, and emptied the box onto the smooth, black ice between the boat and the dock, where the ashes swirled and scattered in the wind.

Sliding closed the boat's side hatch, he returned to the stove and took old newspapers from a wooden locker on the floor. These he crumpled into the stove's firebox. Then he sprinkled sweet-smelling wood shavings over the papers, added kindling, then small slices of hard coal. He struck a large match against the rusty stove and lit the paper. Yellow flames curled, caught a fresh hold in the wood shavings, and lept through the kindling. When the black coal snapped and sparked, Karl closed the iron door and watched the fire glowing through the small mica windows.

The dancing light from the stove cast a feeble glow over the throbbing cylinders. This is really my home, Karl thought, as he smelled the burning wood and coal and the sweet diesel oil and the kerosene from the gimbled lantern and the ever-present fish odor.

These were the quiet moments before a day's run, and he enjoyed being alone, feeling the boat grow warm from stove and engine heat, and listening to the wind moan overhead. But this was a strong wind, stronger than it should be. It won't be easy getting out, he thought. And a lot harder getting in, if we can make the channel at all. But today we'll be netting men. Frozen men from the *Tres Belle*, God willing. And he added coal to the orange-glowing stove.

The dented pot on the stove hissed, and Karl poured old coffee into a dirty mug, added whiskey from his pocket flask, and lifted the cup to his lips. He felt the drink warm his chest. "Ah," he said. "That's the way to start a day."

Karl turned a box on its side and sat upon it. He lit a cigarette, sipped from his mug, and watched the gray morning through the shutters of the rear hatch. Below the boat's rounded stern, he saw a thin crest of black ice among the pilings, rising and falling in the slight swell that reached this part of the river from the lake. Snow and sleet swirled along the slippery surface. Ripples from the river, formed by the curling wind, lapped the ice edges.

Karl finished his cigarette and opened the rear hatch, startling a red-billed tern where it sat on a piling. The large bird rose, flapping its white wings against the wind, banked left, and without further effort glided across the wide river. When it reached the other side, it turned along the Williams Company warehouse and disappeared over the Dunckley Street Bridge.

A few minutes later, the tern glided in from the west and settled on the same perch. A good omen, Karl thought and smiled at the winter fowl, which cocked an eye in an inquisitive manner. "Yes," he said to the bird. "We're going out."

Then Karl ran ropes, criss-crossing the boat from stem to stern, high and low, making a secure hand hold every five feet for the *Tres Belle*'s crew as they came aboard. When he reached the hot stove, he wove a mesh from the iron loops in the workroom deck to steel rings overhead. "We don't want anyone burned on that thing," he said to himself.

These were Karl's standard procedures for heavy weather; and that morning, he streached the lines until they vibrated like violin strings when he snapped them. "Well, that should do it," he said to himself, "just room enough to duck under and strong enough to take the weight of those poor souls bouncing against them." He'd already made his plans. They'd run a stern line to the freighter; and the shipwrecked crew would make a slide for life down that line to land on the tug's rear platform. As soon as they hit, Corky and Joe would each take an arm and fling them through the hatch. There wouldn't be time for niceties, because they'd be coming fast, one after the other. So the ropes had to be damned tight.

Next, Karl went to the radio direction finder, mounted by wire straps over the pilothouse bunk, and tested it. He reached over his head and cranked the directional antenna. When he turned the crank, the loop above the pilothouse rotated broadside to the incoming signal. With the loop antenna in this position, the radio was loudest. Turning the loop parallel to the incoming signal make it disappear. When he reached this null, he would read the direction to the transmitter on the dial above the crank.

Many times, Karl brought the tug through thick fog to the channel entrance by fixing on the Southport radio station. He'd line the loop antenna up with the boat's keel and steer the tug until the signal hit its low. When that happened, he knew the boat was lined up with the transmitter, but he wouldn't know whether he was headed toward it, or away from it. So he'd run slow ahead, while Joe tossed a lead line from the bow. If the water got deeper, they were headed away from the station. If it got shallower as they went, they were headed toward the station.

If they were coming in, Joe would mark off the depth on the line. When they hit twenty feet, they should see the lighthouse, which was at that depth. If they couldn't see the red lighthouse, they would swing north if they were in green water, and south if the water were brown, for they knew the muddy river emptying into the lake flowed north with the current.

The Southport station was broadcasting the morning news, as Karl tested the direction finder; and he heard that his brother, Billy, had left Chicago early that morning. However, he'd run into a blinding snow storm and huge waves soon after leaving shore.

"The feisty Guardsman told us they'd planned to run straight for Southport. But visibility was zero and the waves were still running dangerously high. 'We would have made it without that snow,' Boatswain's Mate Meister said. 'It wasn't the size of the waves, so much as not being able to see,' he told us. Well folks, what can I say. It's been a tragic two days. But we have a real Southport hero in William Meister."

Karl smiled. "Billy deserves a lot of credit," he said to himself. "It took guts to put out again in that small boat."

***

And now Corky and Injun Joe had stomped aboard, they'd made the decision to go at the river's bend, they'd passed the irate Captain Bennett at the station on the channel, and the tug had survived a grounding on the muddy river bottom.

With the engine vibrating beneath Karl's feet, the tug churned forward in the rampaging waters. Ahead, he saw big waves cascading over the south pier. "Hang on boys!" he yelled below. "This is where it gets rough!"

"Damn!" Karl cried out, when the first wave slammed against the side of the boat, setting it on its beam ends and sending him sliding. He pulled himself back to the wheel and glanced along the thin planks of the pilothouse. No cracks.

"Any damage down there!"

"We took a little water through the hatch, Karl!" Joe yelled back. "But that's all!"

Just as the tug climbed from a deep trough, they were hit a second time, with the great force of water falling on the flat deck. The boat shuddered and rolled to the right.

Karl fought the wheel, as the *Three Sisters* pushed to within ten feet of the north pier.

Again they were hit by a side wave; and this time Karl felt a second shudder as the tug's stern scraped the concrete pier.

"More power! Give it more power, Karl!" Corky shouted from below. "Push it right into the red!"

Karl shoved the pilothouse throttle forward, and the big engine ran faster, and the boat surged away from the concrete wall. She's running damned hard, Karl said to himself.

Then a screaming buzzer sounded from below and a red light behind the wheel flashed on.

"She's overheating!" Corky shouted. "Karl! Do you hear the warning buzzer!"

"I hear it!" Karl shouted back. "But it's the engine or the boat now!"

The boat was out of control, yawing and pitching, and sliding dangerously to one side of the concrete channel, and then the other. Karl worked the wheel furiously, spinning it left, then right.

The fishing tug plowed on, buzzer screaming and red light flashing. He felt the boat shudder, as she smashed into each new curling monster from the lake; and then a breaker flung itself over the gray concrete and seized the hull, pressing the tug over on its side. Slowly, the heavy boat rolled upright, to be met by another one-two punch, and the process of struggling to its feet began anew.

At last, the red lighthouse crawled past the pilothouse window, and then the tug settled into a deeper, longer trough. They were clear of the channel. Karl spun the wheel to the left, and the boat turned to face the advancing seas.

Karl checked down the engine to full speed. The roaring engine slowed to a steady roll; and by the time they topped the third crest, the red light went out. The buzzer stopped.

Corky came up from below and stood by Karl in the pilothouse, grinning broadly with his thick lips. The boat was going like a train through the hissing seas and spray, lifted bodily in the air on a wave crest, and then she went down. Down, down and slammed into the bottom, and then rose once more on the next wave.

"Can you imagine," Corky said, "what it was like for Billy? These waves aren't more than twenty-five feet now."

Karl nodded. The *Three Sisters* shuddered and shook, pausing for a moment as she struck each gray wall.

The tug staggered up the next wave, and hung there on the crest, the prop vibrating clear of water. "We're running too fast!" Karl said to Corky, as the boat raced into the trough and plowed deep into a wave. He fought the wheel as the tug surged in the water. Then the boat paused again, lifted her huge deck house out of the sea and rushed over the crest. The boat shook again as the prop spun freely; and Karl reached forward and checked the throttle down to half speed.

"It's a big prop," he said to Corky. "A nice slow engine roll is all we need. See, she's running at a good speed now. Any faster and she'd shake the shaft right out when the prop breaks free."

He glanced at Corky. "How's Joe?"

"He's doin' fine." Corky gripped the handrail as Karl turned south and the boat rolled on the next wave. "But he's got some infection in his legs. You'd better make him see the doctor when we get in."

"Damn," said Karl and slapped the wheel, "I forgot about those burns."

"Wouldn't of done no good, tellin' him to stay home, Karl. He'd come anyway."

"Can he swim?" Karl asked.

"I dunno. I think so."

"Can you?"

"Yes." Corky gulped and took a firmer grip on the rail. "What do ya mean, Karl? Swim."

"Break out the life preservers and put 'em on. Pass mine up."

As the tug swung out of a trough, Corky went below for the life preservers.

Karl stared ahead. The whole western sky was filled with black towering clouds which moved slowly down upon them.

As Karl buckled his life preserver, he saw specks of sleet strike the window and slide slowly down the glass. Snow storm coming for sure, he said to himself.

It was about seven miles to the wreck; and at half speed, they were making slow headway against the driving seas. Karl glanced at his watch. Another hour, he said to himself. But I sure as hell don't like the looks of those clouds. Knowing they must beat the snow storm to the *Tres Belle*, he leaned to his left and shoved the throttle two marks into the red.

Now running at an angle to the waves, with the diesel churning faster, the boat slid along in the rough seas. "That's it," he said to himself. "Hold it right there. If she heats up, check her down a notch."

When they reached the wreck, the black snow clouds were rolling closer. Maybe fifteen or twenty minutes, Karl thought. That's time enough.

Glancing over his shoulder as they surged past the freighter, Karl studied the ship quickly. The stern section had cracked further and canted more steeply toward the sea.

Spinning the wheel to the right, he pointed the tug's nose into the waves. "We're there!" he shouted below. "Corky, take over the throttle! Go to half speed!"

In the engine room, Corky reached up and pulled back the handle of the dual controls. "Half speed it is!"

Now, Karl thought as he held the tug steady into the waves, we'll drift down on her. "Quarter forward!" he shouted to Corky.

Karl spun the brass knobs on the stern port and opened the window. About forty yards, he muttered to himself as they drifted backward toward the wrecked freighter. Now thirty; and he reached into the locker below the bunk and pulled out the flare gun.

Slowly the tug closed the distance, stern first. When they were within twenty yards, he shouted below. "Stand by, Corky. I want full power in about a minute."

The tug rose from a deep trough. As his eye came level with the freighter's forward cabin, Karl released the wheel and rested the red flare gun in the open port. "One . . . Two," he counted slowly, and then fired.

The flaming missile sailed in an arc and landed against the ice-encrusted deck house.

The hit came to Karl as a faint tap above the roaring wind and waves. It'll be plenty loud inside, if anyone's still alive. "Full speed, Corky! And release the override." As Karl whirled back to the wheel, he glanced over his shoulder through the open port. A young face popped into the middle cabin window. Then another, and another, until all the black windows were white with faces.

"Joe!" Karl called below; and the Indian's big face appeared at his knee, calmly smoking a black cigar. Karl laughed; who could say whether they'd smash to pieces against the *Tres Belle*, or capsize in a wild broach, or God knows what, he thought, and here stands Joe Bear, legs firmly planted wide against the boat's roll, his life vest slung over his shoulder, slowly puffing on that damned cigar.

"Put that vest on!" Karl said sternly. "Now!"

"Okay, Karl."

"And buckle it up, tight!"

"Sure, Karl." Joe cinched the belt tight around his chest.

"Now go back and take the heavy tow line, coil it down, just inside the stern hatch, ready to fly, see. And tie it to a quarter line with a monkey's fist," said Karl, referring to the balled throwing rope which looked like a monkey's hand.

Joe nodded.

There isn't a man on the lake who makes a monkey's fist faster than Joe, Karl thought. Tight and hard. And when he throws, he rarely misses.

"All set," said Joe, returning from below.

"Okay. Get Corky up here."

"Here's the plan," he told them in the pilothouse, as he turned the tug around. "We're going to drop in behind her bow, run along between the freighter and the shore, then ease up on her."

Karl turned to Joe. "We'll be inside her—bow on. And when we run up in the lee, no closer than fifty feet, let fly with the line. Don't look for anyone on deck. Just throw it. If you can, land the ball smack at the foot of the forward cabin door. Okay?"

"Sure, Karl. Just like that." Joe pulled the cigar from his mouth and grinned.

"Give me a puff on that damned thing."

Indian Joe wiped the cigar stem on his shirt sleeve and handed it to Karl.

"For luck," Karl said, taking a puff. His head swam. "God! That's awful."

He handed the cigar back to Joe. "You'll be throwing from the stern platform, port side, as I turn. And I'll be blasting away on the horn. Now, I should be able to see when they take the line." Karl shook his head. "Let's hope they're strong enough to pull in the lead."

"And what if I miss?" asked Joe.

"Then we'll do it again. Just haul in the line and wait for me to go around. Now, when I see they've got the hawser in and cleated down, I'm going to run off. Understand?"

"I got it, Karl," Joe said.

"I'm not sure how long I can hold position, Joe. So give them about sixty feet of hawser. And cleat it down tight as we turn. Tight as hell, Joe, 'cause we'll be puttin' quite a strain on it."

Turning now to Corky, Karl said, "There's a fire axe by the stove. Take it back and sink it into the deck at the stern. We'll need it later. Make sure it's in solid. We don't want it loose to go over the side."

"We gonna cut and run?"

"Right. As soon as the men are aboard."

Karl eased the boat over a wave. "Joe, don't leave any slack in that line. Pay it out as we go. I don't want it fouling the prop."

"And now we're goin' for the wreck," Karl said and spun the wheel to starboard.

Ten

Drifting sideways in a white surge, Karl brought the *Three Sisters* into the wrecked freighter's lee. There, the waters swirled and eddied in the waves which poured over the freighter's low midsection like a waterfall.

He moved the diesel's controls into neutral. Now the tug was slipping quietly forward in the protected waters, rising and falling with each huge wave which crashed against the stranded freighter and tumbled across its deck.

When the tug was carried high, Karl looked down on the wreck's white cabins. The swell passed through. The tug sank like a high-speed elevator. The freighter's black side rose high above him.

And when the tug closed to fifty feet of that steel side, it rose on the swell again. Karl pulled on the air horn. A rope ball whipped out from the stern as he turned, trailed by a light line. The big brown ball struck the ship's ice-encrusted rail and fell into the water. Joe had missed.

The tug wallowed in the big swells as Joe furiously reeled in the line for another throw.

"Hold it Joe," Karl shouted. "I'm going around!" And Karl opened the throttle and shoved the big shift lever to forward. A sharp snap came from below and the engine raced.

"The shaft broke, Karl!" Corky shouted up.

Karl slid the shift bar to neutral, checked down the engine, and raced below. "Toss the anchor! Cleat it down at the stern!"

Corky dashed to the stern with the big Northhill anchor and handed it out to Joe, who tossed it in an arc and cleated down the line. The tug rolled steadily toward the crowd around the fires on the beach, dragging the anchor through the sandy bottom. Then the Northill dug in and held. The line went taunt. The tug quivered and stopped.

Held fast, stern to the waves, the tug started taking on water, as the wind-whipped curlers smashed against the boat's rear platform. They closed and braced the rear hatch. But still the water spurted in, gallons at a time, faster than the pump could clear the bilge.

Now Karl had two choices: cut the anchor line and hope they survived a beaching through the surf, or fix the shaft before the tug filled and sank; and he knew there wasn't much time.

"I think we'd better cut the line and beach it, boys," he finally said.

If you're askin' for a vote," Joe said, "count me out, Karl. I can't swim."

"Corky?"

"I can make it, Karl. And I'll take Joe with me."

"Joe?"

"Shit, Karl. We didn't come all this way to wash up on the beach. Let's take a look at that shaft."

Karl slid open the bilge access. "Give me a light."

As he lowered the oil lamp, Karl saw the break, just forward of the stuffing box. "She's broken at an angle. Looks pretty rough. But if we can get something around it, and clamp it tight—"

"How much time we got, Karl."

"I'd say about ten minutes, Joe. But the longer we wait, the farther from shore we'll be when she hits bottom."

"How many hose clamps we got?" Joe asked.

"Hell, we've got plenty of those. What we haven't got is something to wrap around it."

"Well, we got leather, Karl," Joe said, pulling off a long boot. "And if we wrap it tight, and clamp it six or seven places, it might just hold. It's worth a try."

Karl looked at Corky. "What do you think?"

Corky shook his head. "Too much torque, Karl. It won't work. I'm for goin' in."

"Look, Karl," Joe said. "I've seen it done before, and it's held. Now what we gotta do is run that anchor line off the bow. Swing the boat around. We'll stop takin' in water that way. And then we can test it. It the tug moves out, and the splice holds, we've done it. If the leather tears, we can cut the anchor line then. At least that'll give us a chance to get ahead of the water in the bilge."

"You for that, Corky?"

Corky nodded. "It's worth a try, Karl."

They ran a second line from the bow to the stern anchor rope, and let the boat swing around.

"Now take the hacksaw and cut off the barrel of that flare gun," Karl said to Joe.

When Joe returned with the cut off barrel, they sawed it lenghtwise and split the barrel open with two screwdrivers. Then Karl slid the barrel over the broken end of the shaft, aligned the shaft, and slipped the piece over the break. Taking seven hose clamps, he put those over the splint and tightened them, leaving no spaces in between; and while he worked, he watched the water level go down in the bilge. I should have thought of turning the boat, he said to himself; and then to Joe, "You're a good man, Joe Bear, a damned good man."

Karl went to the pilothouse and shifted forward, while Joe watched the splint.

"It's holdin'," Joe shouted. "Give it a little more."

And when Karl eased the throttle forward, Corky shouted, "She's moving, Karl. I've got slack in the anchor line and I'm taking it in," and then after a moment, "The anchor's in, Karl. By God it's working!"

They slipped slowly forward and when the black side of the freighter loomed ahead, Karl sounded the whistle again and made his turn. This time the monkey's fist arched higher, landed on the icy deck, and bounced against the forward cabin door.

With the tug sinking again into a trough, Karl saw a dark figure spring to the rail above him and take the line in, hand over hand. Then three other men joined the lone figure, and the heavy hawser was flying across the water as the tug rose on the next swell; and before the tug sank into the next trough, one of the Canadian seamen snubbed the big rope tight on a bollard, and waved him off.

He shifted to reverse and spun the tug's wheel to the right; and spinning the wheel back again, he shifted into forward at quarter speed. The tug backed, and then lurched forward, turning slowly on its axis, as he repeated the procedure.

When the tug had swung completely around, he looked over his shoulder and through the rear port saw the heavy line rise from the water, snap tight, and vibrate as it took the full weight of the *Three Sisters*. "Thank God," he said to himself, "the splice is holding."

With three short blasts of the tug's horn, he signaled the freighter's men to start their slide. As he watched over his shoulder for the first man to appear at the rail, the tug struck bottom with a hard thud which knocked him to his knees in the pilothouse. "Damn," he cried out. "We're right over the sandbar."

Struggling to his feet, he thought, if she breaks up, we'll have to cut the line and beach her after all.

Looking over his shoulder again as the tug wallowed upward on a wave, he saw the first man on the line, coming down quickly. But the line slackend at the swell's peak, and the seaman on the rope dangled into the water. Then as the tug fell away in the next trough, the hawser snapped tight like a whip, throwing the seaman high on the line, his arms flaying through the air, as he held desperately to the rope with his legs.

The seaman completed a circle around the line, his legs clamped tight, ending with his head toward the water, and slid down the hawser until he disappeared from Karl's view at the tug's stern.

"I've got 'em!" He heard Joe cry out from below.

"More power!" Joe yelled. "Take the slack out of the line!"

The tug sat down hard again, shaking the pilothouse all around Karl. "Just give us five minutes, Lord!" he cried out. "That's all we need. Just five minutes!"

When the huge waves poured over the broken freighter's deck, the men on the ship clung to the bent rail, waiting for their turn on the line.

Behind Karl, the hawser was now rod tight. One man after another slipped over the wreck's icy rail, and slid down the rope, feet first, to be followed by slower moving figures from the old freighter's aft cabins.

God help anyone who slips off the hawser, Karl thought as he watched the swift descent. Our prop wash will drown 'em for sure, if they don't get sucked into the blades first.

Below, Joe caught the seamen as they landed, just as Karl had instructed, and passed them off to Corky as soon as they touched, neither man waiting for any word or reaction from the dazed survivors. "Don't waste a second," Karl had told them. And Corky was throwing them through the rear hatch, to slide along the floor, or if they were still standing, to careen against a rope.

Each time the swell passed through, Karl felt the tug crack her hull hard against the sand bottom.

Suddenly, there were no more men on the line. Karl wished he had counted. At least a dozen, or more, he thought. Then Joe's hoarse voice boomed from below. "We got 'em all, Karl! Every damned one!"

"Cut it!" Karl yelled. And as Corky's axe hit true and parted the line, the tug jumped forward, slammed down on the bottom, and lurched around in a sharp turn on the next wave, not to touch again.

"All buttoned up below!" Joe yelled out, as Karl inched the tug past the freighter's black bow and into open water.

Below, the frozen seamen huddled against the ropes around the pot-bellied stove and mumbled their thanks to Corky and Joe. Three men lay on the floor where they had fallen, crying out in pain.

A raw face looked up at Karl in the pilothouse. "I'm the captain. And thanks to you and your fine crew we're off. We've one broken leg, and a few cuts—but, by God, we made it." The excited face went solemn. "All but the two cooks and one man froze to death."

So young, Karl thought. Not as old as me, and the captain of a freighter. And Karl wanted to ask the red-haired Canadian why he hadn't turned into the waves sooner and run from shore before the seas and wind grew too strong. But he thought better of it. There'd be time later.

"Your name, sir?" the captain asked.

"Karl Meister."

"Well God praise you, Captain Meister. You're a brave man, indeed."

"And your name, Captain?"

"Jacque DuPays. Do you have a first-aid kit?"

"Yes." Karl turned quickly and pulled a small white box from the bunk locker and passed it down.

"*Mon Dieu*!" the white-faced man continued. "We wouldn't have lasted much longer. The men could hardly move. I started working them the minute you hit the ship." Jacque DuPays paused, looking up at Karl from the engine room steps. "What did you throw?"

"Fired a flare gun," Karl replied.

"Ah! *Mon Ami*. Very clever. But now I must see to my men. Thank you. And God bless you."

Karl nodded. He was glad to have the man gone just then, because the wind was rising rapidly and the air was thick with driving snow. Can't see a damned thing, he said to himself. Forward, it had become so dark he could scarcely tell where sea left off and sky began. But he knew he was running north, toward Southport, taking the waves on the rear quarter, and sliding down steep slopes ahead of breaking crests, running the engine as lightly as he dared and keeping the strain off the splinted propeller shaft.

After twenty minutes, he eased the bow until ten degrees swung across the gimbled compass, and lashed down the wheel. Then going quickly down the steps to the engine room, he glanced around. Several men from the freighter sprawled silently along the floor on each side of the big engine. "Take the controls!" he yelled to Corky crouching near the tug's stern. "We're about a mile off. And I'm going to have my hands full steering when we go in."

Returning to the pilothouse, Karl peered into the thrashing seas. Suddenly, the red lighthouse came into view, less than a quarter mile off the starboard bow. He could see waves breaking all around it, and spray flying to the top. He leaned back against the high bunk in the pilothouse, both hands on the spoked wheel, legs spread wide on the rolling deck.

Should we chance it, he wondered? Looking over his shoulder through the rear portholes, he saw nothing but rolling, boiling, black storm clouds above the raging waves behind them, and not a break in the dark sky.

Then he whispered to himself what he had known all along. "We can't stay out here. And we can't make the channel." It was impossible. It would be a wild ride down the steep slopes, with the tug washing left, then right, and careening more than the channel's width, before he could bring her under control.

It's one thing to run out on the lake, he knew. Keep the bow into the waves and power through. And quite another coming back with those curlers. As long as the waves were high and traveling faster than the boat, they lifted her stern and sent her broaching, with no way of knowing which way she might turn first. And then, too, if he ran faster, he could tear out that splice in the shaft and go out of control, crashing against the concrete piers, No. We can't chance it. Not with those waves washing completely over the pier to smash the bow about.

The channel entrance was all white fury as they rolled past, with spray blowing around the lighthouse, dancing higher than the light itself, and swirling and foaming everywhere, with waves criss-crossing and leaping to the sky.

"Corky! Come up here!"

"Yes, Karl."

"Douse the stove and cool it down. Careful. Don't crack it." Karl spun the wheel and the tug cleared the far side of the two piers and pointed toward shore. "Then get everything secured and everyone braced on the floor. And give me full throttle. Just keep easing it out and hope that splice holds. We're going to beach her!"

Karl heard a hissing noise and then saw steam rise from below as Corky poured water on the fire.

The tug seemed to hesitate, then churned forward in the smoother waters sheltered by the piers. He ran close to the concrete wall where channel spray leaped and water streamed down.

"Stand by!" he shouted below. "Thirty seconds. It'll be a hard grounding boys!"

The boat surged along on the swells.

"Here it is!" he shouted, as the boat rose and the long wave below it broke into a curl at the beach, carrying the boat high on the sand. The tug plowed on under its heavy momentum and slid to a stop.

"Kill the engine!" Karl yelled, struggling to his feet. And then suddenly, everything was quiet in the boat.

He glanced over his shoulder. Out on the lake, huge seas were still running and a stiff wind blowing spray. But in that dark chaotic world, high above the tumbling water, he saw a thin, blue crescent. The storm was at last waning. The man-eating lake had been denied another meal.

Karl stepped down from the pilothouse as Corky slid open the side hatch. "My God, Karl. You drove her high and dry!"

Leaning against the pilothouse bulkhead in the warm engine room, Karl lit a cigarette, as Joe ran the boarding plank to the wet sand. The exhausted seaman from the *Tres Belle* stumbled to their feet, peacoats buttoned tight, and slid down the smooth plank, ducking spray which broke around the tug's stern.

Captain DuPays lowered a young blond seaman to the inclined plank. The tug's old straw broom and a fish box slat were spliced to his broken leg. Cautiously the captain let the sailor slide, holding his right hand fast, while the seaman slipped along the plank until he reached the arms of his comrades below.

The captain turned to Karl and shook his hand. "Thank you," he said quietly. "If only the cooks had waited. We were in the forward cabins." The boyish-looking officer grimaced. "Shortly after we grounded, the stern section sagged suddenly. They became panic-stricken and made a wild dash forward over the broken deck. Through the porthole, I saw Rene clinging to the rail in waist deep water. Then a big sea broke over the ship. And when the water cleared, both Rene and the rail were gone. Seconds later, a big dark object, probably a hatch cover, struck the cook's helper farther back, and he went over the side. The chief engineer tried it later. He couldn't make it and turned back. But not before that icy water soaked him to the skin."

The captain paused, leaned out the tug's hatch, and peered for a moment over the lake. "Have they found the bodies?" he asked.

"Yes, Captain."

"God rest their souls—and the soul of the chief engineer—he froze to death in the aft cabin." And saying that, the captain slid down the plank and stepped off onto the spray swept sand. He turned and looked silently at Karl for a moment, then gave a slight nod, and disappeared up the beach, where a crowd gathered around the bedraggled seamen.

Karl lit the tug's kerosene lamp and lowered it into the bilge by its wire handle. The shaft had parted again on the last power surge. Leaning through the trap door, he saw a few inches of oily water around the engine base. Forward of the motor, the yellow lantern light revealed three breaks in the main beam. As far as he could see in the dim light, every rib of the heavy tug was broken, and the normal hull shape had gone flat. He shook his head. Only the metal fastenings along the wooden ribs and the metal skin over the planked hull had kept the boat together while it pounded on the sandbar. They were fortunate, indeed, he thought.

Now he realized it was the boat's flattened bottom that caused them to plane so high on the beach. But she was still watertight. And they could trench around her and float her off in calm weather. After that, he'd pull the tug up on the river bank next to the shanty. There, he'd jack her up in a collar, replace the broken beam, repair the ribs, and the tug would be ready for fishing again by spring. But for now, the season was over. And he'd look for other work to pay the bills.

"Meister! You in there, Meister!" A raging voice came to Karl in the tug. He closed the trap door, ducked under the safety ropes, and shuffled to the open hatch.

Captain Bennett's dark figure stood at the foot of the gangplank, leaning back against the howling wind, a hunting knife clenched in his right hand, his legs planted wide and firm in the sand. "You'll pay for this Meister!" he snarled. "Damn you! Make a fool of me!"

Bennett seemed to tense, as if ready to spring. Then, after pausing with the knife held high, he charged up the plank.

Karl met him with a boot square to the chest, and sent him sprawling backward onto the snow-streaked sand.

Bennett scrambled to his feet. His face was white with rage, and he was weeping uncontrollably. "You bastard!" he cried in a high-pitched voice.

Karl could see no sanity in his eyes, only a hate-filled glare.

And then Karl snatched a flat wrecking bar from its holder on the bulkhead.

Still snarling, crying, and glaring more hatefully than Karl had ever seen, Bennett stepped forward.

"Bennett!" Karl shouted, brandishing the big, flat bar. "You come up here again, and you'll meet this!"

The captain backed from the gangplank. His face went pale, and his voice became a whimper, as Karl banged the flat iron against his palm.

Bennett turned and ran, stumbling and falling, scrambling to his feet and storming away up the beach. "You'll pay, Meister!" he shouted over his shoulder. "You'll pay for this!"

Karl watched the flaying figure rush headlong toward Corky and Joe in the crowd around the *Tres Belle* survivors at the road, where a half dozen cars parked at angles to the beach in the drifting snow.

Suddenly, Bennett was down in the crowd, and two surfmen were on top of him. They pulled him, kicking and screaming, into the back of the gray Coast Guard sedan. The car backed quickly onto the road, turned, and disappeared down the winding road along the river bank.

One by one, an ambulance and the other cars, all packed with huddled, frozen men from the *Tres Belle,* left the beach and roared away down the river toward the Dunckley Street Bridge.

When the last car had gone, Corky and Joe turned and ran toward Karl in the tug.

"Did you see that?" Corky asked breathlessly, when they reached the gangplank. "The crazy son-of-a-bitch tried to kill me!" He held out his left arm to show Karl where the knife had ripped his coat sleeve. "Joe kicked 'em! Right in the balls!"

"Dropped like a stone." Joe grinned, with a stubby cigar clamped in his stained teeth. "An old white man's trick," he said, with a look of mock apology on his face.

Across the seething channel from where the tug lay beached, Karl saw the rescue cars pull up to the boat house, led by the official sedan. He watched as two Coast Guard men dragged Captain Bennett from the rear seat of the gray Plymouth, still struggling against the surfmen, who held his arms behind him.

"It's been one hell of a day," Karl muttered, and ran down the gangplank. He slid the plank into the tug, reached high, and closed the hatch.

Turning toward the road, he slapped Joe on the back and grabbed Corky's arm. "Let's go home boys."

Sylvia was waiting at the door, and opened it from her wheelchair as he came up the walk. "Billy called," she said. "He's laid-over in Michigan City."

"I know," Karl said, closing the door. "I heard it on the radio."

"He wanted to talk to you, Karl. Something's wrong at the station. Billy couldn't reach Bennett. He wants you to see him. And he asked me . . . Just a minute." Sylvia wheeled to the desk. "I wrote it down. The number is 9-486, Michigan City. He wanted you to call as soon as you came in."

"When did he call?"

"Not five minutes after you left. And, Karl—they want Billy to take command of the Southport station—but he refused. He couldn't do that to Bennett, he told me. Karl, you know he idolizes the man."

Sylvia twisted the message in her hands. "Karl, he wants you to stand by Bennett. Help him launch a lifeboat when the weather clears. He said the waves are already going down fast there." She looked anxiously at Karl. "Billy thought it might work. He told me he'd drive up, but State Police report all roads still blocked by fallen trees."

She looked up at Karl with tears in her eyes. "Billy was so upset," she said after a short pause, and wheeled closer to Karl. "Can you do it? For Billy? I know you never liked Bennett, but Billy told me it's for the honor of the Coast Guard. And then he said Bennett's career is over if he doesn't act fast. Can you do it, Karl?"

"They're in," said Karl wearily, collapsing into the rocker by the fireplace and closing his eyes.

"What, Karl?"

"They're all in."

"Who?"

"The men from the freighter."

"Oh, good. Billy will be so happy."

Karl opened his eyes and studied Sylvia, searching for the right words. Low music played on the radio and the fire crackled warmly behind him; and now he felt how tired he was, and how exhausting the rescue had been. But what would he say to her?

"Call Billy," she said. "He's so worried, Karl." Her face beamed. "Isn't it wonderful? Call your brother, Karl. It would mean so much more to him, coming from you."

"Bennett didn't bring them in," Karl said quietly. "I did. With Corky and Joe on the *Three Sisters*."

Sylvia stiffened. "And Bennett?" she asked.

"I don't think he's in control of his senses. He threatened me, and swung a knife at Corky, his own brother-in-law."

"Karl," Sylvia gasped. "You don't mean what you're saying."

"Yes, Sylvia." Karl shrugged his shoulders and leaned forward. "It's true." I don't know what came over the man."

"We have a special bulletin," the radio interrupted. "The seamen of the *Tres Belle* were taken from the wrecked freighter aground off Dear Point about one hour ago. Karl Meister, brother of Boatswain William Meister, played a major role in the rescue.

"Timothy Bennett, captain of the Southport station, was not available for comment. But it is believed he took part in the heroic effort.

"Several of the freighter's men sustained injuries and one seaman is reported to have broken a leg. All are at the Southport hospital undergoing treatment for exposure.

"The freighter's captain, Jacque DuPays, told us his men wouldn't have lasted another hour. They were frozen stiff and barely had the strength to slide to safety, he reported.

"The captain had the highest praise for his rescuers. 'We were without heat for thirty-six hours,' he said. 'And all blankets were in the stern quarters. Without water, some men ate ice, but that made matters worse' the captain said. He believes this resulted in the death of the chief engineer, who's body remains on the wrecked ship.

"The four Coast Guard men laying over at Michigan City were overjoyed upon learning of the rescue. Boatswain's Mate William Meister stated they would remain there for the night and make a fast run for Southport in the morning.

"When asked about the controversy surrounding the delayed rescue, Boatswain Meister told reporters he felt Captain Bennett had been vindicated, and he expected an apology would be forthcoming from unnamed local fishermen who had been critical. He told reporters that prudence is sometimes the better policy, and that he was quoting his older brother, Karl, owner of the fishing tug *Three Sisters*.

"Captain Bennett knew better than to yield to pressure, he told reporters. And he praised Bennett for not risking the safety of his men in a premature rescue attempt as some had urged.

"Captain Bennett was not available for comment. And Dr. William Keith told this station that Bennett remains in the hospital under heavy sedation. The nature of the captain's injuries were not disclosed.

"Bennett," Sylvia asked, "was he badly hurt, Karl?"

"He wasn't with us," Karl replied after a long pause. "He tried to stop us from going out." Karl paused and watched the horror spread across Sylvia's face. "When we came back, I couldn't make the channel—so I beached the boat. Bennett was there—he tried to knife me and Corky. Two guardsmen overpowered him. That's why he's in the hospital. Sylvia, he's gone mad."

"But, Karl . . . the radio—"

"The report's wrong, Sylvia. Bennett wasn't with us. I don't know what's wrong with him—he's out of his head."

"Poor Billy," Sylvia cried. "He has no idea. Will you call him, Karl?"

"I think," Karl said, rubbing his beard and leaning back in the rocking chair, "it would be better if I wait until he comes in. It's too touchy to handle over the phone. He'll understand."

Eleven

Number One surfman Nesmith rested his elbows on the tower window and scanned the horizon with binoculars; and when he sighted the Coast Guard powerboat he cranked the field phone and shouted the good news. The surfman below who took the message, dropped the phone on the desk and ran through the sand to the town's coal-fired electric generating building next door. Five long blasts sounded on the power plant whistle.

Hearing the the pre-arranged signal, members of the American Legion, Veterans of Foreign Wars, and the Southport Yacht Club, along with fifteen hundred citizens of the the small city, swarmed to the Coast Guard station on that bright afternoon in November to welcome home Boatswain's Mate William Meister and his heroic crew.

Pushing Sylvia along in the bouncing wheelchair, Karl raced down the sidewalk toward the lake. "Slow down," she cried, as they bumped off the curb and onto the asphalt road leading to the boat house.

Down the long hill ahead of them, Karl could see a large crowd pushing and shoving around the station. Then he heard the school song coming from behind the boat house; it was the high school band, playing in honor of its most famous football center, Karl's brother, Billy.

And looking up from the black road which now steamed in the hot sun, Karl saw the small lifeboat enter the channel, plowing smooth brown water. Billy stood at the wheel, waving to the cheering throng which crowded the piers on each side. The surfmen in the boat also stood tall, waving to the left and then right, as the boat came up the river.

When the launch was about one hundred yards from the boat house, the band paused, and then struck up the "Star Spangled Banner." Karl saw Billy, standing with one hand on the wheel, salute the flag, which stirred in the soft breeze on its pole behind the station. The boat crew stiffened and also saluted. The crowd went quiet while uniformed men saluted, other men pressed hats to their chests, and women held hands to their hearts.

The boat sailed serenely past the station, made a wide turn, passed in review again, and then a third time. Karl chuckled. He knew the crew couldn't stop saluting to take a line as long as the national anthem played.

Then the band finished and the crowd broke into a wild cheer as the last note trailed off. Billy brought the boat smartly to the pier, stepped off and saluted the flag again.

Karl saw Muriel fly into Billy's arms, and then heard him ask, "Where's Captain Bennett?"

Threading the wheelchair through the crowd with Sylvia urging him on, Karl shouted, "Billy! Billy!" Sylvia, now leaning forward in the chair, also cried out. Billy turned and waved at them as they pushed forward in the throng. Still clutching Muriel to his side, Billy's face suddenly went dark as a surfman whispered in his ear.

"Speech! Speech!" the swirling crowd roared, pressing forward against the musicians who now tottered on the dock's edge.

"For Christ's sake!" the paunchy band leader cried out. "Stop shovin'" With a scream he tilted back at the water's edge, swayed for a moment, and then splashed into the muddy river. He surfaced quickly and thrashed about, while his hat floated away in the current. "I can't swim!" he shouted, and disappeared beneath the dark water.

A thrown line struck the band leader's bald head as he rose again near his floating hat; and when he sank a third time without grasping the rope, two surfmen dove as one, and pulled him to the iron ladder near the boat ramp.

Eager hands reached down and lifted the dripping man straight up the side and down on the flat concrete. He sat there, his mustache a brown streak, his face pale green, his blue eyes cold and staring. His long brown hair which had been carefully combed forward to hide his shiny pate, now dangled from the back of his head to below his shoulders. "My hat," he gasped, pointing to the river.

Karl followed his stretched arm and saw the visor point skyward and then slowly slide beneath the surface, as if the hat were some great ship going down by the bow.

A man behind Karl laughed; and then the crowd roared as the band leader struggled to his feet. "My hat!" he shouted above the din again, pushing his wet hair forward. "My lucky hat!"

A surfman wrapped the shivering band leader in a blanket and led him toward the boat house. Billy followed, then stopped, and turned to the crowd from the station porch. With Muriel at his side and one hand on the low, white rail, he waved to the crowd and said, "We're glad to be back!"

A hoarse cheer rose from the crowd around the station, rolled up and down the throng along the channel, and echoed back from those assembled across the river.

"We were fortunate," Billy said, raising both arms to quiet the crowd. "But others were not. The *Bradley's* crew hasn't been found. And only young McKay's body has been recovered from the *Chief.*" Billy leaned forward against the rail. "There's little hope of more survivors," he said. "But until the bodies are all counted, we have a duty to search."

Billy glanced at the bright blue sky and then his watch. "We have good weather now," he said, looking down at the crowd. "We'll leave in an hour. Thank you for the fine reception."

And turning quickly to the surfman at his elbow, Billy said, "Top off the tanks, Ed." Then he turned on his heel, and with Muriel in hand, strode through the station door, followed by the boat's crew and two reporters.

Shortly after the station door closed, it burst suddenly open again, and the reporters backed onto the porch. A burly surfman pushed them hard from inside, then stepped back into the building and closed the door.

"No pictures, no interview, no statements," Karl heard the tall reporter wearing a gray trenchcoat say.

The second reporter clutched a large camera. "You'd think he was Julius Caesar," he said, "returning to a Roman welcome. Stuff it I say."

The two men turned from the door. "We'll get the goods on Bennett yet," Karl heard the tall reporter say; and then the men ran through the crowd, climbed into a Ford coupe parked at the road and roared off.

The band leader left the boat house, wrapped in a blanket, and walked to a black Chrysler station wagon where a blonde woman sat behind the wheel. Opening the passenger door, he turned and shouted to the high school musicians, who then marched onto the road and up the river, followed by the big car.

As the band marched silently away, the crowd went to cars and pick-up trucks. And those on foot spread along the river bank and spilled across the road, mixing with the vehicles leaving the station.

Karl and Sylvia waited on the concrete dock behind the boat house and watched the surfman filling the motorboat's tanks.

Then Billy's beefy frame burst through the door, followed by three Coast Guard men.

Karl stepped forward. "Billy!"

But there was no reply as his younger brother brushed quickly by, reaching down and squeezing Sylvia's arm as he passed.

Billy and the surfmen jumped into the power boat; its motor coughed and fired; a Coast Guard man shoved the bow and the boat swung into the river, roared down the channel, and turned north on the lake as Muriel waved from the station porch.

"Billy?" Karl said again as the power boat became a speck on the horizon; and turning to the station door, he saw it close quickly behind Muriel.

"Billy," Karl said a third time, spinning the wheelchair abruptly and pushing off across the parking lot. "Damn," he muttered. "Billy should've let me explain."

"Karl, please slow down," Sylvia said feebly as the wheelchair bumped through the rutted gravel in the parking lot. She was holding her left arm.

"What is it, Sylvia?"

Karl stopped the wheelchair and bent forward. She turned her head and her eyes darted up to him. She took a quick breath. "Nothing, Karl."

"Your arm, Sylvia." Karl was knealing in front of the wheelchair now and took her left arm. "What's wrong?"

"Nothing," she answered in a stronger voice. "It's better now." She shrugged her shoulders. "The excitement, I guess . . ."

"Is it your heart?"

"No, Karl. I just get a strange twiching now and then. Doctor Keith says it's nothing serious."

"Nothing serious?" Karl looked at her tense face. "Are you sure, Sylvia?"

"Yes, Karl."

"We can go back to Grand Rapids," Karl said, studying her face. "To the clinic."

"In the spring," she said, leaning wearily back in the chair. "If there's no improvement, I'll go back then."

"I can borrow the money. We don't need to wait until spring."

Sylvia's eyes closed for a few seconds. Then they opened steady on him. "We'll know by spring," she said, taking a deep breath. "See. Twitching's stopped. Let's go home." And when they reached the top of the hill, she was breathing easier.

"Karl, why do you think Billy's so upset?"

"Bennett," he replied, and turned the wheelchair onto the sidewalk along the lake bluff.

"No . . . I don't think so," Sylvia said after a pause. "It's more than that. Do you realize," she said, twisting up at Karl, "that no one from the Southport station made the rescue? And Billy—"

"Billy's a hero," said Karl, finishing her sentence.

"A hero, yes. But how does he see it?"

"I don't know what you mean, Sylvia."

"Well, he went out after the two tugs. But he didn't find them."

"Sure. The storm hit. He didn't have a chance. Billy knows that."

"Knowing it may not be feeling it, Karl."

"He couldn't turn—waves were too big. He had to run to Chicago."

"Had to, Karl?" she asked as he crossed the street and eased the wheelchair up the curb and onto the sidewalk toward their house.

"Well, Billy's no coward, Sylvia. Of course he had to."

"That's just it. I raised the question—you became defensive, Karl. Perhaps Billy's doing the same thing."

"Maybe. But that's not like Billy. It's the honor of the Coast Guard—and he sees me as Bennett's downfall."

"But how many questions does Billy raise and answer?" she asked as they reached the house door and squeezed through. "He said on the radio they'd gone north. Isn't that where the tugs were?"

Karl hung his coat on the door and lifted a thick quilt from Sylvia's lap. The living room was warm from the stoked furnace and the sun streamed through the bay window. "Visibility was way down," Karl finally answered. "And the waves were high. He couldn't have found them."

Sylvia backed her chair to the lace curtains. "Karl, there's been no rescue at Southport since the 1913 storm. And the whole town knows why Dad died." She stared at the unfinished painting of her father on the *Merry B*. "Billy must have heard the rumors. And how long has it been, Karl, since anyone said good things about the Coast Guard? I've heard jokes." She shook her head. "Not very funny."

"But, Sylvia. No one knows what happened out there with the *Merry B*. Nesmith's the only man left. And he never said a thing."

"You knew, Karl." She looked at him quietly. "Bennett probably thinks you talked. I've heard he accuses you of spreading false rumors, of maligning his good name. Billy told me so."

Karl turned to her angrily. "I never said a word."

"Bennett likes Billy," she said. "Helped him with his manuals and examinations. Saw that he was promoted. There's a lot of good feeling between them."

"I know," he said. "But—"

"And if someone asks Billy why he went all the way to Chicago instead of beaching the surfboat, like you did, Karl—" she paused for moment "—what does he say?"

"Well, that was different. The wind was down some when I went out, and the waves a lot smaller. I don't think Billy could turn around."

"Maybe so, Karl. But Muriel's brother, John Jr., is dead. What does he tell her?"

"He made a prudent decision," Karl said angrily.

"Prudent?"

"Yes. Prudent!"

"And you—you're prudence itself, Karl. But you went out and took the freighter's crew off."

"There wasn't any choice. Billy wasn't here," Karl said defiantly.

"Karl," she said calmly. "Look at yourself. Steaming mad. Do you understand?" She paused. "Do you understand now how Billy must feel?"

Stunned, Karl rocked uneasily on his feet.

"John McKay wasn't there to greet Billy, Karl. What must Billy think?"

"Think! Why . . . he—"

"He's angry, Karl. He loves the service. You've embarassed Billy—and made Bennett look like a dunce."

"Those men on the ship were freezing."

"But the weather was getting better. How much later could a surfboat have gone out?"

"Look, Sylvia." Karl was tense in front of her, jaw thrust out. "The other surfboat could have gone when I did. Right off the beach. Or Bennett could have shot a line. It was only two hundred yards. He didn't do a damn thing!"

"I realize that," she replied. "Karl, you're still angry. Now calm down. I was only trying to explain Billy's feelings."

"One man died from exposure. How long could they have lasted? One hour? Two? They barely made it down the line, Sylvia. Two men were tied on, hands and feet, and eased down with a teather."

"And that's what you wanted to explain to Billy?"

"Yes. Certainly."

"I understand, Karl. But Billy doesn't. You've got to talk to him." Sylvia sighed and rested her head on her hand.

"You need to rest," he said softly, stroking her thinning hair.

"I'll talk to Muriel," she said. "In the morning. I'll feel better then. Billy must be very tired, too," she continued. "He looked tired, Karl. Didn't you think so?"

"Yes, Sylvia. He looked very tired."

In the bedroom, Karl spread the covers over Sylvia and gave her the rosary and white prayer book from the stand. He watched quietly until he saw her breathing deeply—she was asleep.

Karl pulled his chair closer to the mahogany Grundig in the living room and leaned forward. "The sun sets today at five-thirteen and rises tomorrow at seven-twenty-one," the announcer said, concluding the weather program; and then the radio reported that an investigation was underway concerning the recent activities of Captain Bennett, citing his failure to effect a rescue from the *Tres Belle*.

Leaning back in his chair, Karl smiled. Well, the son-of-bitch has finally been dismissed for incompetence.

The radio droned on. ". . . a complete tabulation," the announcer continued, "of Michigan's record-breaking ballots, cast a week ago yesterday, confirms that Wendell Willkie won Michigan's nineteen electoral votes by a slim margin of less than one percent.

Thank God for Roosevelt, Karl thought. At least he doesn't have his head in the sand. If only we could do more to stop the Nazis. But he knew that anything more than destroyers and Lend-Lease to the English was beyond the President's power.

"Dr. Preston Huxley," the announcer's rich voice boomed, "minister of the People's Church of Chicago, and well know writer and radio commentator, paid tribute to our four Coast Guardsmen earlier today. Dr. Huxley compared the men to world heroes, and said, 'none were more gallant than the four who put out in the raging storm Monday afternoon to aid their fellow townsmen.'"

"Sylvia!" Karl cried out. "Billy's a national hero!" And hearing no reply from the bedroom, he turned again to the radio. "I'll tell her in the morning," he said to himself.

Then the radio announced that a naval reserve officer would be at the Southport Post Office next Tuesday, recruiting for the Benton Woods station. "Since the national emergency," the broadcaster said, "the Benton Woods unit has sent forty men and officers on active duty with the U.S. Navy. Most of the men are serving on the Arizona in Hawaii."

Ah, Karl thought, now that would be good duty. Billy should do that.

"A 'white paper' published by the House Un-American Activities Committee," the announcer said, "charges that Nazi agents are seeking control of the American economy. The Nazis hope to tie American business into the German Reich, after what they anticipate will be a successful and imminent conclusion of the war.

"The German documents accumulated by the committee center chiefly around Dr. Heinrich A. Grauenhaft. Dr. Grauenhaft, an American citizen, is head of the Haemisch Chemical Company of New York."

"What!" Karl cried out, leaning close to the radio. "Not Dr. Grauenhaft."

"The committee claims that records of his activities, as well as other German organizations, indicate that Nazi efforts in this country were not devoted solely to propaganda and espionage, but that the German government has over a period of years systematically infiltrated all levels of American business and government."

"Sylvia!" Karl shouted again, jumping from his chair. "This is unbelievable. Dr. Grauenhaft, in New York. I know him." He stood there, thinking back to those malignant eyes across the dining table at the *Villa Bavaria*. The dark and brooding eyes of Heinrich Grauenhaft.

Karl opened the bedroom door as the setting sun slanted through the window and shone upon Sylvia's peaceful face. Her eyes were closed behind her glasses, and a thin smile was on her lips. The open prayer-book lay on her lap. She held her rosary loosely in her right hand.

"Sylvia," Karl said, as he walked to the bed. "You won't believe this. The radio is talking about Dr. Grauenhaft. A Nazi. And I know him from Austria . . . Sylvia . . ."

Karl touched her white hand. "Sylvia," he said again, quietly. "Sylvia, do you hear me?" He lifted her hand from the prayer-book, and it was cool to his touch. "Sylvia!"

***

The afternoon of the funeral was dark and dismal, a bitterly cold and cheerless November day. Karl stood in the falling snow and watched the long line of cars wind down the gravel road from the cemetery. Alone now by Sylvia's grave, he began the rosary in his native Austrian dialect. First he recited the "Apostle's Creed." Then one "Our Father," three "Hail Marys," and one "Glory Be To The Father," struggling to recapture the comforting faith he had known as a child.

After a short pause, he continued again, saying the "Our Fathers" on the large beads and the "Hail Marys" on the smaller beads. Always one "Our Father," followed by ten "Hail Marys," and closing with a "Glory Be To The Father;" starting again with one "Our Father," and followed by the "Hail Marys," as he worked through the rosary.

Karl knew he should meditate while he chanted the dusty words. That was the way he was taught to say the rosary. But he could only think how alone and empty he felt, standing before Sylvia's fresh grave. And he struggled to comprehend whether the child-like feeling which overcame him was because of the ancient chant, or whether he had become in his mind a child, begging for something; what it was, he did not know.

Thoughts raced confused at several levels of his consciousness. He heard his voice, chanting the mysteries of the rosary; and on a different level in his mind, he followed Jesus through the Agony in the Garden, the

Scourging, the Crown of Thorns, the Carrying of the Cross, and finally, the Crucifixion. Still another part of his thoughts were remembering his childhood and searching for the simple truths he had accepted so easily and without question long ago. And above all, he thought it was a dark, cruel, and unfair day, both for him and for Sylvia, who was so naive in her goodness that she failed to notice the uncalled for harshness in his voice whenever he was tired or frustrated.

Pausing now, with the snow falling softly on his shoulders, and having finished the rosary, Karl kissed the cross, and slipped the beaded string into his overcoat pocket. Then leaving the cemetery, he walked first to the river, where he stood on the bank, watching the snow melt as it struck the water. "Perhaps," Karl said to himself, "life is no more a mystery than the snow—returning to water."

As he approached the Dunckley Street Bridge, he saw the red-billed tern lift from its perch on the piling, flap three times, and rise slowly in the wind over the bridge. The bird swooped down to Karl on the river bank, circled three times over his head, and silently disappeared in the direction of the cemetery

At home, Karl started a fire with the last of the fireplace wood. It was cold in the room. The furnace had gone out long ago. I should stoke the furnace, he said to himself, before the pipes freeze. But he could only sit before the fire, smoking cigarettes and thinking of Sylvia.

He'd gone to the cemetery with Sylvia's mother and her brother; and he knew it was wrong to refuse the invitation for a wake at their house, where he had proposed to Sylvia long ago. But he wanted to be alone with his thoughts, harvesting memories of good years, and storing them carefully away.

And this is what he did before the fire, while he wept quietly, and sometimes smiled, remembering his life with Sylvia. All the while, he knew, too, that his life was also running out, like the sands in the hour glass.

But Karl realized he must deal with practical matters. The matter of coal, which the chilly room reminded him was running low in the basement. He was out of money now, and needed work.

Sam Decker, he thought. I worked for him before. I can harvest ice again.

It was a hard and early winter at Southport that year. But he'd read that the southern states were hot, building up a great demand for ice. He'd seen Decker's men packing the frozen blocks in railroad cars and trucks, to be covered with sawdust and shipped to the Gulf Coast. Other shipments, he'd read, went as far as South America and Africa, to cool plantation owner's drinks, where electricity was expensive and the new refrigeration plants hadn't taken over.

***

"With the war and all," Sam Decker told Karl at the ice plant on the river, "this will probably be our last year for export. But," Decker said, thrusting his thumbs under the suspenders he wore over his plaid flannel shirt, "we're goin' like hell. Paying good wages and working long hours."

Decker puffed on a curved pipe and squinted at Karl from behind an old plank desk in his small office. "Corky Reiley is here, ya know. Well . . . he's a good man. And that Injun—Joe Bear—he's a good worker too."

Sam Decker leaned across the old desk and pushed aside wrinkled papers. "Now, Karl," he said, "I don't want no trouble, understand?"

"Yes, sir?"

"You'll get my meanin'," he leaned back in his chair, "when I tell ya Bennett signed on yesterday."

Karl sat silently. He thought Bennett had left town after his dismissal. After a long pause, he said, "Well, sir, you won't have a problem with me."

"Now Tim Bennett is a good man." Decker continued. "His nerves are 'bout gone, though. I'd like to use him as a foreman—but for now, he'll just work alongside the other men. He has a family to feed too, ya know."

"Yes, sir. I understand."

"And when he's recovered—his nerves, I mean . . ." Decker paused. "Well, hell, Karl. Just work with him. But—what do you seamen say—give him a wide berth, okay?"

"Sure." Karl rose and shook the small man's hand.

Sam Decker ran two crews that year. Karl was put in charge of Corky and Joe; and Captain Bennett worked with two farmers. Whenever possible, Karl did give Bennett a wide berth, always working at the opposite end of the ice field, timing his operations to avoid the Captain at the conveyor. First, they chopped a large hole to the water two feet below, then sawed twenty-inch strips with an eight-foot cross-cut. Then they took the big saws, which ran three inches from tooth to sharp tooth, and cut twenty-inch blocks from the long strips. When they had cut several blocks, they all stopped and slid the ice across the lake to a conveyor.

The conveyor was powered by an old Dodge engine, and was used to load the ice onto three trucks. By noon, the three trucks were usually packed, and they would tow the conveyor to the ice-house, where the blocks were piled high and packed with sawdust for insulation; and sometimes the ice was loaded directly into trucks or freight cars for an urgent shipment south.

At the ice-house, Bennett and the farmers unloaded, while Karl and his crew worked the other end of the conveyor.

But there were times when a lake was fully harvested and both crews cut the thinner blocks along the shore; and that was when Karl noticed Bennett becoming more agitated each day, sometimes gesturing with his fist and mumbling as Karl passed near.

By February, the river had frozen over; and at the end of the month, when the ice was a foot and a half thick, they worked the river bend below Sam Decker's plant, where they harvested for industrial use.

It was about six o'clock on a cold Tuesday afternoon when Sam Decker shuffled onto the ice and announced a special phone order for Cuba. "Can't be river ice, fellas," he said with hands in pockets and round belly thrust forward in his plaid shirt. "We'll need that clear ice from Silver Lake. Now our old stock is pretty well back against the wall, so we'll cut tonight. Any volunteers?"

Karl stepped forward, followed by Corky, Joe and Bennett.

"How late?" asked the tall blond farmer.

"We can be back and unloaded by midnight," Sam Decker replied. "If we work right along."

"Well," the farmer said, "count me out. I've got chores."

"Me too," the other farmer said.

"Joe," Decker asked, "can ya work with the Captain, here?"

"Sure," Joe replied, trailing cigar smoke from his thick lips.

"Captain," Decker asked, turning now to Bennett, "you see any problem workin' with the Injun?"

"I've no problem working with a good man," Bennett said with a sneer and rubbed a glove across his face. "But I won't work with this glory-seeking son-of-a-bitch." He waved his hand defiantly at Karl.

"Now, Captain," Sam Decker said. "Don't be stirrin' things up. You take the big Ford stake. I'll follow you in the Chevy. We'll be pullin' the conveyor. So don't go too fast, in case we have a problem. And take Joe with you, okay?"

"Sure," Bennett replied. "And who's boss?"

"Well, there are only two of ya. But I guess you are."

"Okay then. I'll go," Bennett said, turned on his heel, and marched to the Ford truck. "Come along, Joe," he said over his shoulder.

Joe spat, bit off the end of his black cigar, chewed twice, looked at Karl with a knowing smile, and turned to follow the captain.

The two trucks stopped on the thick ice at Silver Lake, where the men cleared a large area with snow shovels. Then they placed a white-gas lantern at each of the four corners, first pumping up the round, flat-bottomed tanks and lighting the delicate mantles. The lanterns hissed brightly, casting a sharp cold light over the black ice. By midnight, the field was littered with crystal ice blocks and Mr. Decker started the conveyor motor. "Bring the lanterns in," he said to Karl. "Move 'em closer, so we can see here." Sam

Decker pulled the conveyor lever, and the belt jumped forward. "Joe," he said, "And you, Corky. You two fellas start loading." Then he turned to Bennett. "Captain, you rest and stand by. Step in when one of these men tires, 'cause we're gonna run fast. I'll be up in the truck, packing. Karl, you come up and help me when you come back."

Karl slid two lanterns along the ice by their wire handles, picked them up in the heavier snow, and carefully sat one on each side of the conveyor. Then he went for the other lanterns farther out on the ice. As he bent to pick up the first glowing lantern, he heard a hoarse voice behind him.

"I know. I know all about it, Meister."

Karl whirled to see Bennett in the white lantern light. The captain was half bending and dancing from side to side with a wild look in his eyes. "I know you did it," Bennett whispered louder. "You glory-seeking bastard! I know you killed Mike Curla!"

Karl froze with the lantern in his hand.

"You did it!" Bennett said louder yet, bouncing around Karl and waving a fist. "I can see it on your face." Then he stopped and leaned closer and whispered hoarsly, "You're the one, Meister. You killed him."

Bennett danced quickly back, waving his arms and running in half circles. Then he stopped, crouched, and moved slowly forward. "Look here Meister," and so saying he held out his right hand.

In Bennett's palm, Karl saw a shiny brass disk. The captain moved closer now, waving the bright object before Karl's face. Then he suddenly snapped shut his fist and sneered at Karl. "Your brass button, Meister," he snarled in a hoarse whisper. "Yes. It's from your chauffeur's coat—and I can prove it!"

"Bennett! Meister!" Sam Decker shouted across the open water. "What's goin' on out there!"

Karl raised the lantern slowly. "We're coming!" he shouted; and holding the lantern high and turning to Bennett, Karl said, "What do you have there Bennett? Let me see it."

The captain jumped back, balancing first on one foot and then the other and laughing hysterically all the while. "I know what it is, Meister," he said, springing quickly to the side. "I had it traced—to Chicago."

"Traced? Chicago?"

"Yes! Yes!" Bennett said. He was running from side to side again, thrashing about, half crouched, both arms flaying. "I've got you now, Meister."

"Bennett!" Karl shouted, stepping forward with the lantern, as the frenzied Captain backed toward the open ice cut. At that shout and sudden movement, Bennett too, stepped quickly back and spinning on the icy edge lost his balance and fell sideways into the black water.

Karl rushed forward as Bennett splashed in. Decker, Joe and Corky came running as Karl reached for the Captain's heavy wool coat. "No!" Bennett shouted. "You'll never get it!"

"What the hell!" Decker said as he ran up to Karl on the ice. "Bennett! For Christ's sake! Get over here!"

"Get 'em away!" Bennett screamed, fighting the water's pull on his heavy clothing.

"Run," Decker said to Joe. "Get a pole from the truck. Quick!"

Karl knelt on the ice with Decker and Corky, watching Bennett sinking lower in the cold water. "This way!" Decker shouted. "Bennett! Try to come this way! You're going the wrong way!" Joe ran to the other side with the long pole and stretched it far out over the open water. Bennett reached out a feeble hand and grasped the pole.

"Both hands, Bennett!" Joe shouted. "Grab on, quick!"

And then the Captain sank beneath the dark surface, letting the pole slide from his fingers. Joe jumped after him, and surfacing a moment later, said, "He's gone! I can't find him!"

"Get out of there Joe!" Decker shouted. "That cold will take you in a minute."

Running around the open water, Karl caught Joe's arms and pulled him onto the ice.

"Corky, start the Chevy! Get the heater on!" Decker said at Karl's side. "Karl, get Joe into the truck."

"I'm okay," Joe said in the truck, and Karl ran to the water's edge. Decker lashed an ice hook to the long pole and plunged it into the water. "It's no use," Decker said. "It's deeper than hell here. I've dragged as far as I can reach. He's gone." Stepping back from the open ice cut, Decker turned to Karl. "What was that all about? I heard him calling you something—"

"A glory-seeking—"

"Yes—well, he's done for now. Poor soul." Turning to where Corky crawled along the ice's edge, Decker said, "Do you see anything?"

"Not a trace. Not a thing."

Sam Decker called the Sheriff's Office from a farm house down the road and deputies came and dragged the lake with grappling hooks while Decker and the two men finished loading the trucks.

"We're calling it off for tonight, Mr. Decker," the Sheriff said, walking up to where the men watched from the conveyor. "I'll get statements from you fellows tomorrow."

It was ten o'clock the next morning when Karl returned to Silver Lake with Joe and Corky in the pick up, after making statements at the Sheriff's Office.

They parked the old truck behind the two black-and-white patrol cars and walked out on the ice to where a group of men stood near the open water cut.

"Calm down, Ned. It's only a body." Karl heard the Sheriff say to a deputy, as they walked up. In the circle of men, he saw a dark figure and white face below the clear ice. It was Bennett, lying on his back, arms outstretched, and staring directly at him.

***

Karl was summoned to the coroner's inquest, which was held at City Hall the following week. The tall, frail and balding coroner stood up and looked around the men seated at the long table in the hall. A few women sat with other men in rows of folding chairs in front of the table, and Billy Meister sat by himself against the far wall near the entrance. Karl sat quietly in the first row of chairs and listened nervously to the coroner. "Most of you know me," the coroner said. "My name is Ivan Jessup, and I'm the County Medical Examiner. We don't call them coroner any more, but it's the same thing. And this isn't a formal hearing. My job is to investigate and determine the cause of death. Sheriff Steward here," he pointed to the pudgy sheriff at the end of the table, "and I then make out a report for the prosecutor if we feel there's some evidence of foul play."

The Medical Examiner paused, pulled off his glasses and wiped them with a handkerchief; and sliding the lenses again on his long nose, continued. "I live here in Southport, and there's been a lot of talk. This is a small town, and we have to live together. So I called this meeting, sort of a press conference you could call it," he glanced quickly at the reporters in the front row next to Karl, "because I think it's important to clear the air."

Then the Medical Examiner sat down quietly, turned to the man on his right, and said quickly, "This is Dr. Sam Becker from the Kalamazoo Regional Psychiatric Hospital." Nodding to the small, prune-faced man with large ears, the County Medical Examiner said, "Go ahead, Sam."

"The little doctor coughed nervously, opened a manila folder in front of him, looked timidly around the room, and began, "Captain Timothy Bennett was referred to me for consultation some time ago by his personal physician, Dr. Keith—it doesn't matter when that was, precisely—and I don't seem to find it in my notes here. Anyway, it was evident that the captain suffered from a nervous disorder." The psychiatrist paused and shifted nervously in his chair, and then turned to the Medical Examiner and asked, "Are you certain it's proper for me to disclose this?"

"Quite certain," the coroner scowled and answered, "You're under subpoena—you have judicial immunity."

"Well it seems a bit unethical—"

"Believe me," the Medical Examiner interrupted, "everything's perfectly legal and proper. Good God, Sam, you should've talked to me about this before. Now get on with it."

"Well," the psychiatrist continued in a squeaky voice, "the captain appeared aloof and withdrawn, as if he were preoccupied with some problem, and hung his head forward and stared at the floor." The doctor paused and fumbled through his notes.

When it became obvious the Kalamazoo psychiatrist had lost his train of thought, the the Medical Examiner turned to him and asked, "Did you ask him about any problem that might account for this preoccupation?"

"Yes." The psychiatrist looked up and nodded. "He complained that his bowels were gangrenous and were causing his stomach to rot away. Food eaten by him turned to poison in his stomach, and the gnawing pain made it difficult for him to sleep or rest—but he didn't actually suffer from any such physical condition—it was a delusion."

The prune-faced doctor looked around the room, as if he felt quite satisfied with his pronouncement.

The Medical Examiner tapped fingers on the table, waiting for the psychiatrist to continue, and when the little doctor still sat there smiling, the coroner asked, "Was there anything else, Sam, about Captain Bennett's condition?"

"Yes," Dr. Becker continued, "He heard voices—those voices were real as far as he was concerned—and he imagined that the voices came from many different sources: trees, different people he passed on the street, and finally, Mr. Calhorn's blood hounds." The psychiatrist looked at Karl Meister. "He believed the blood hounds told him Karl Meister had killed a man and buried him on the beach—that would be the old bones found near the key post during the storm—and he had this fantasy that he'd prove it some day. But what was more important is that he believed Karl Meister was the devil incarnate, and that he was out to destroy him. Under such conditions, it became my opinion that Captain Bennett might react with violence against Mr. Meister. He felt the devil within Mr. Meister called the captain bad names, and that he should do something about it."

A hushed murmur went through the crowd.

"Was there anything else you can tell us, Sam," the Medical Examiner asked, "which would explain the captain's conduct at the time of his death?"

"Yes—whenever he talked about Karl Meister, Captain Bennett became quite excited, waving his arms about and speaking in a loud voice. His breathing became rapid and noisy. And then he said that someone was making accusations against him, and the author of the accusations was a person from outer space and had thus far succeeded in making himself invisible, but that he would not escape. That when he discovered him he would kill him. And it was becoming apparent to him that this someone from outer space was Karl Meister."

The people all around Karl were talking louder now, and then Karl felt a heavy hand on his shoulder; and Billy said to the reporter, "Would you mind moving over one seat, I want to sit next to my brother." And as Billy sat next to him, he said to Karl, "I'm sorry—I had no idea."

Karl only half listened to the remainder of the proceedings, and the next words which entered his consciousness were: "A brass button." The sheriff was speaking from the other end of the low table. "'Zilco Company, Chicago,' was stamped on the back. We had it traced," the Sheriff continued. "It was a limited run, made up for the old Life Saving Service in 1914. Most of them were rejected because of a stamping defect," the sheriff said, holding up a small brass disk. "But this one seems to be okay. The defect was in this little triangle, right here." And he pointed to the brass button. "The old Service accepted some." The square-jawed, heavy sheriff took a deep breath. "And those that were sent back were discounted to a Chicago uniform company." He paused and took a notebook from his shirt pocket. "Yes. Cooke Uniform Company. They made chauffeur's coats and other domestic uniforms."

The sheriff rose and placed the brass button on the table before the coroner. "We suspect," he said looking around the room, "that Captain Bennett kept it as a souvenir when the old Life Saving Service was merged with the Coast Guard. That was before your time, Karl," he said looking to where Karl sat next to Billy.

"Any idea," the coroner asked, as the sheriff walked from the table, "why he'd pull it from his pocket while drowning? It was clutched tightly in his hand, ya know."

"Not the slightest," the sheriff said, shaking his head.

Part Two

The Schildwache

The Schildwache

For the Angel of Death spread his wings on the blast

And breathed in the face of the foe as he pass'd;

And the eyes of the sleepers wax'd deadly and chill;

And their hearts but once heaved, and forever grew still

Lord Byron

FORWARD TO THE SCHILDWACHE

In 1939 the German military rolled through Poland in a matter of days. England and France declared war immediately; and for seven long months did absolutely nothing.

"I shall spread terror by employing all my resources without warning," Hitler had promised the world. "The sudden, dreadful shock of mortal terror—that's what counts!"

Then the Wehrmacht moved again, storming Denmark in a few hours and invading Norway. Four weeks later, Hitler's army attacked Holland, Belgium and Luxembourg. The Dutch army was beaten in five days, and the Belgian in nineteen, driving theAllies to the Dunkirk beaches. Seventeen days later, Paris fell, and by June 1940 the Wehrmacht had gained complete control of Europe for the Nazis.

There followed fifty-seven devastating night raids on London. The American ambassador, Joseph P. Kennedy, advised President Roosevelt that Britian could survive no longer than a few weeks. World War II was over.

But England held.

And then Germany attacked its Russian ally. "Yes," Hitler declared, "we are barbarians! We choose to be barbarians! It's an honorable title." And he kept his word.

Inside Germany a shadow government grew, supported by three thousand military men in key positions, ready to take over the minute Hitler was killed. The center of the military opposition to the Nazi regime was Admiral Canaris, head of the Abwehr, the office in charge of Germany's intelligence, sabotage, and counter-espionage activities.

Canaris was a strange man who played his dangerous double role quietly. He slipped warnings to the Dutch. He cautioned Denmark and Norway of coming attacks. But he was opposed to overt resistance to Hitler, and was content to thwart the Fuehrer's plans by quiet and determined sabotage, and he served as a cover for the more active spirits and supplied them with efficient intelligence information.

TheAllies ignored his warnings. They didn't believe Canaris. They didn't believe in a German underground. Not even Churchill, who never fully realized the source of his German information, could believe that the head of Hitler's central intelligence was an anti-Nazi, plotting Hitler's death.

America was still at peace. But Roosevelt saw war coming. "The time has come," he told Colonel "Wild Bill" Donovan. Around the world, Donovan's "moles" recruited over the years, began to report to OSS, the new central intelligence organization. But they were not enough, and he scoured America for immigrants. "Let me say a word about these men," Donovan said after the war, "they were French, Italian, Austrian, German . . . but they were all Americans."

Karl Meister was one of those Americans.

One

On a bright August afternoon in 1941, Karl Meister paced the rosewood-panelled waiting room of the Haemisch Chemical Company offices in New York. He glanced nervously at the brunette receptionist, who smiled back a teethy, red-lipped grin, wondering what business brought this tall man in his early thirties, with such black hair and black eyes and a hard face which still showed lighter where he had shaved his beard, to Nazi headquarters.

I must look like an ass, Karl said to himself, and pulled at his shirt collar. Coat's too small. Hat's too big. Pants are baggy.

"Mr. Meister." A small man peering through tiny glasses held open a heavy door. "We take only written orders. We don't receive personal callers."

"I understand," Karl answered in German. "And I have one." He pulled an Olson Company purchase order from his thin case.

"Are you a relative?" the clerk asked.

"No, sir," Karl answered, and they were both speaking German now.

"Ah! A friend?"

"No, sir."

"Then . . . an acquaintance?"

"No. Sorry."

"Yes. I see," the small clerk said in a soft voice and reached for the purchase order.

"But my cousin is a business associate," Karl said quickly.

"Business associate!" the clerk replied. "You should have told me, Herr Meister. Dr. Grauenhaft will see you at once."

The clerk whispered to the receptionist; and then turning to Karl, said, "Follow me, sir."

Karl walked behind the little clerk down a long hall, up a flight of stairs, and then the clerk stopped and motioned him through an open door. Behind a polished desk sat a short, stout man Karl had not seen in many years, but recognized at once as Dr. Grauenhaft. "It's good to see you again, sir," Karl said and stretched out a hand as the man heaved his bulk from his chair.

"And you're Karl Meister. Alex's cousin."

"Yes, sir."

"The last time I saw you . . . it was Karli, then." The stout man paused and scratched his bulging stomach with a fat hand. "And we sang 'Silent Night.' Very beautiful."

"Yes, it was," Karl replied. "But, sir. I don't mean to impose. I work for the Olson Match Company, now—in Ohio. And we're desperate. We need phosphorus. The war, you know. So I made a trip here to deliver our order. I don't mean to take up your valuable time."

"Sit down, son. Sit down. Time's not a problem today, Karl. Today I have other problems. Reporters hound me. They give me no peace. And the police. Spies everywhere, let me tell you." The stout man settled into his swivel chair. "That's why I have an office on two floors. I can slip out and down the elevator while they watch the entrance below." He laughed, pulled a black cigar from a desk drawer and lit it, blowing a big smoke cloud. "No one's figured that out yet," he said, and laughed again.

"Karl, do you know what this is?" He rolled the cigar between his finger and wide thumb.

"No, sir."

"It's your grandfather's," he said. "Alex sends them to me. Would you like one?"

"Thank you, sir. But no. I don't smoke cigars. Opa still sends them to me at Christmas," Karl said, using the familiar German name for grandfather. "But I don't smoke them. I'll save them for you."

"Well thank you, Karl. That's very nice."

"If you don't mind," Karl said, "I'll smoke one of these." And he took a Chesterfield from his shirt pocket.

"Oh, certainly, Karl. Certainly." And then leaning across the desk, Dr. Grauenhaft said, "Your purchase order, Karl, let me see it." Karl handed him the typed order. "Hmmmm," the portly man said. "This much phosphorus?"

"We have a good business. And with the war in Europe, we feel we need to stock up. Supplies are getting short. And we're running very low now,

Herr Doctor. I thought you could help."

The fat man slowly tapped his cigar until a thick ash fell to the glass of a salamander ash tray. "Karl, how long is it since you've been home."

"Well," Karl replied, "Michigan's my home now. I'm a citizen. I haven't been back."

Dr. Grauenhaft leaned forward quickly. "I too am a citizen, Karl. For many years now. Since long before you were born. Yes. I was here during the first war. And it wasn't a comfortable time for us, believe me."

"I thought you lived in Berlin then, Herr Doctor."

"Oh, no. Berlin was my second home. I've always lived here in America. Out on Long Island." Dr. Grauenhaft paused and his broad face smiled. "You'll come home with me, yes? It's no problem, Karl. We have many servants."

Karl nodded. "Thank you, sir. Yes. I would like that."

"And Karl, you should go home sometime, soon."

***

Karl waited in the lobby until the clerk motioned from the hall. Then he walked to the elevator and took it to the garage under the building, where he found Dr. Grauenhaft waiting in the rear of a black Packard limousine.

"One must be very careful," Dr. Grauenhaft said in the dark car. "Trust no one. Not even my chauffeur." He nodded toward the uniformed driver on the other side of the dark glass partition. "We have a new social order. But Hitler is a reckless man. Very popular with the people. But reckless and dangerous. He moves too fast."

"Too fast?"

"Yes. And I fear he'll have America in the war before Germany's ready. He's given the order to torpedo neutral shipping, you know. And this time the U-boats won't surface and warn off passengers." Then turning to Karl and puffing rapidly on his cigar, he continued, "Unless we have another two years to develop our weapons before America comes in, Karl, Germany will lose the war."

Dr. Grauenhaft turned to Karl. "America is a sleeping giant. When its factories convert to war production, tanks and aircraft will come rolling off the Detroit assembly lines like countless birds in the air." He wrung his hands and sighed. "Germany is still recovering from the last war—and the devastating depression that followed. We need more time."

***

The heavy Packard filled with cigar smoke and Karl thought he would suffocate before they turned into a large estate on Long Island. They passed through an iron gate, which was opened smartly by a young man wearing a black uniform. The car rolled down a long seashell-paved drive, overhung by large oak trees. A three-story building with two wings and a columned porch stood at the end of the long drive.

As they drove up, Karl saw three antennae rising high behind the house. One was beamed northeast to Germany. A second to the south. And a third to the southwest. Mexico and Latin America, he said to himself. They must be very busy here; and he remembered the radio newscasts, warning of Nazi operatives and naming Dr. Grauenhaft as the suspected head of German activities.

In the clearing west of the mansion, he saw other high poles with wires running to the ground in huge Vs. These, he knew from his briefing by Captain Harding, were directional receiving antennae, capable of intercepting the weakest shortwave signal over thousands of miles; and they also pointed to Germany, Mexico, and South America.

Dr. Grauenhaft had not overstated the number of servants. There were indeed, he noticed, a very large number on the grounds, assuming they were actually servants; and going through the entrance, he saw many more inside the mansion.

"Unfortunately," Dr. Grauenhaft said as they walked along polished marble to a brightly lit room, "my family is in Berlin. The war, you know. Travel arrangements are getting difficult. And I don't think a sea passage is safe now. Not with our U-boats prowling these shores."

Karl nodded.

"And now," Grauenhaft said, patting Karl on the shoulder, "we'll sit here by the fireplace and have our cognac. They'll call us when dinner's served. Until then, we smoke a little, and we drink a little, and—yes—we'll have some coffee, too. And they can take as long as they want." He laughed and lit another cigar. "Let me think now. Yes—Karl, you came to America in 1922. Correct?"

"Yes, sir. 1922."

"Eighteen years, Karl . . . A long time."

Karl studied the broad face. Well now, he said to himself, I believe he's about to take the bait.

"Yes, sir. It is."

"You should go back, you know. For a visit. Before the war comes here."

"Here? I think it'll be a long time before that happens. The Germans are talking about an early consolidation of their gains."

"Yes. I've heard that. But I feel it coming." Dr. Grauenhaft took a quick breath. "You know," he said, "we hoped America would come in our side."

"Our side?"

"Yes—of course. You're right, Karl. I mean the German side. We're Americans now. Me much longer than you." He shook his head. "To think you'd have to correct me, Karl. But there was a time when I thought Colonel Lindberg would use his influence, and swing America our . . ." Dr. Grauenhaft paused and smiled. "The German way. But he let us down."

"Yes. And Roosevelt's for the English."

"Of course he is," Dr. Grauenhaft snapped. "America isn't neutral. This country is simply not neutral!" His voice rose to a higher pitch. "To send trucks, to give destroyers, to promise war planes. These things are aimed at the heart of Germany." He pounded the chair vigorously and cigar ashes flew. "Of course," he continued with a lower voice now, "Austria is part of the Reich. So these weapons are aimed at your homeland too, Karl."

"Yes," Karl answered; and following Captain Harding's instructions, he said. "It's too late for any effective measures here. Our lobby no longer has a voice in Congress."

"Our lobby? Our lobby?" Dr. Grauenhaft laughed loudly.

"Now I'm doing it," Karl laughed. "Of course, I mean the German lobby." He raised his glass in salute. "To a good future and your health, Herr Doctor."

"Thank you, Karl. And to your health. And to the German-speaking people of the world."

"Prosit!"

"And to the new social order."

"Prosit, Herr Doctor."

When the dinner gong sounded, Karl rose and followed Dr. Grauenhaft to a high-ceilinged room, where a long table, surrounded by high-backed chairs with blue velvet coverings, stood on a polished parquet floor. At the far end of the room was a massive fireplace, with a copper-sheathed hood leading up to a black eagle on the wall. The eagle was made of hammered iron. It was an ancient Germanic symbol, with sharp gothic talons and a large head, narrow eyes and open beak.

A red-and-black flag hung on each side of the eagle. At first, Karl thought it was the Nazi Swastika. But there was no white circle and the familiar hash-marked cross in the center was missing. In its place was a black shield with a yellow line running diagonally across it; and scrolled underneath were the words *Siempere Schildwache.*

On the other walls were stuffed animal heads: deer, moose and elk; and as Karl looked back over his shoulder toward the door they had just entered, he saw above it, huge elephant tusks and a full Bengal tiger with splendid white stripes mounted on the wall.

"I hunt," Dr. Grauenhaft said quietly. "And I'm a very good shot." He said the words so calmly and methodically that Karl felt he was not really bragging, only making a statement, such as one might announce his occupation, or address, offending no one.

Several young men stood behind the blue chairs waiting for their employer; and when they reached the table, Dr. Grauenhaft motioned Karl to a chair on the left. He stood and waited until the German took his seat at the head of the table. Then all of the men pulled out their chairs and sat down in a precise, military movement.

At that moment, a tall blonde woman, whom Karl guessed to be about twenty-five, walked up to the table and laid a slender hand on Dr. Grauenhaft's shoulder. "Uncle Heinrich, she said with teasing blue eyes, "you must introduce me to your friend." She smiled at Karl.

"My niece," Dr. Grauenhaft said, rising then from his chair, as Karl and all the other men also rose. "Elska Banghardt. My sister's child." Grauenhaft smiled and took her hand. "We wait for her, but she makes a point of being late. To test us, I think. Now sit down, my dear, before you make us all uncomfortable, and I'll tell you the man's name."

The woman slid gracefully into a chair across from Karl and smoothed out her white satin evening gown.

"Our guest's name is Karl Meister," Dr. Grauenhaft said.

"How do you do, Miss Banghardt." Karl reached over the table, feeling awkward.

"You needn't do that," the stout German said. "She's quite American. Born in Boston. And American women no longer shake hands, you know.

"But I like to shake hands," Elska said. "Especially strong ones." And she squeezed Karl's fingers.

If she were not so albino, Karl thought, this tall slender woman could be part Indian. She had very high cheek bones, almond-shaped eyes, a straight nose, large full lips which always looked moist, and smoothest skin Karl had seen. Her hair was more white than blonde and flowed down over her bare shoulders.

They all sat. The German leaned back in his chair and cocked his head toward the slender woman. "My niece tends to overdress," he said. "But we have no objection. She is a stunning child. Don't you agree, Karl?"

"Yes, sir. I do agree."

"Uncle, you flatter me. But I love it," she said, smiling at the German. And Karl realized she talked with a lisp. She was so strikingly beautiful, he'd heard only the mellowness in her voice; and then the lisp was there again as she said, "Uncle Heinrich, please ring for the food. I'm starving."

The conversation remained with those three at the end of the table. They were separated from the eight young men farther down by two empty chairs on each side; and that stern-looking group, all wearing dark uniforms with the Schildwache emblem he'd seen over the fireplace, ate in silence.

And when coffee was finished, those stone-faced young men rose as one upon a wave from Dr. Grauenhaft's hand. First bowing to the German at the head of the table, who nodded acknowledgment, they then turned on their heels, and marched silently from the room. Then Elska, too, rose quietly, squeezed her uncle's arm, and with a wave at Karl, left the dining hall.

Dr. Grauenhaft puffed steadily on a black cigar and watched three young girls clear the table.

"I don't like to look at dirty dishes," he said. "And I always drink three coffees—then a cognac. Bad habits, yes? But I've lived a long time with my habits." He chuckled and winked at Karl. "And you, my friend. No bad habits?"

Karl tapped a Chesterfield on his watch. "I smoke. And I drink a little."

"And you're never drunk?"

Karl shook his head.

"But perhaps you drink a little too much now and then, eh?"

"Not for many years."

"I see . . . And women?"

"My wife died last year."

"Yes. I know, my friend. And I was sorry to hear that. But are you involved with any women?"

"No, sir. Why the questions?"

"Well, we've had a file on you for some time now—"

"Me, sir? Why?"

"The Schildwachc, Karl—wc'vc watched you long before your rescue of that Canadian ship. Yes, you were quite the hero. I recognized the name. And now that you've shaved off the beard, I can see a little of the Karli again." He laughed, and then turned silent; and after a pause, said, "Why did you?"

"What, sir?"

"Shave the beard?"

"There aren't many businessmen with beards these days."

"Well that's a handsome scar on your face—Heidelberg?"

"No, sir. I never went to a university. I got it the same time this happened—an accident." And Karl held up his gloved hand.

"Too bad. It's a noble scar." Dr. Graunehaft scratched his fat stomach. "But why the Olson Match Company?"

"I needed the job, sir."

The German pulled on his ear. "And how did you get that job, Karl? That's what bothers us."

Karl knew the question would be asked. "Well, it was in all the papers. 'Small town fisherman down and out after losing boat in rescue,' is what they said." And Karl remembered Captain Harding carefully drafting that news release at Fort Wayne.

The German nodded again. "Karl, we don't have the best intelligence system. Good. But not the best. Not yet. Certainly not as good as the British. That's our weakness. Too many high-spirited amateurs." He leaned back in his chair and fixed his deep black eyes on Karl. "As I said, we've had your file for a long time. And naturally I've watched it, since you're Alex's cousin. But I have one final question."

Karl swallowed hard. "Yes, sir?"

"The Grand Turtles—why did you turn them down in 1924?"

"I think you mean 1929, sir."

"Yes, I see. 1929, then. Why?"

This was a question Karl had not anticipated. What was his reason for not joining the Southport lodge of the Grand Turtles? "The Jews," he said, leaning forward in his chair. "It was an organization of Jews."

"Yes. That's true, but—"

"They took in Jews," Karl said quickly. "A Jew had been Exalted Ruler." Karl smiled inwardly when he remembered telling the sober-faced registrar his grandmother was part Indian and he couldn't sign the application.

"The organization is our front." Dr. Grauenhaft laughed. "That idiot—the registrar. Stupid man." Laughing again and puffing on his cigar, he leaned forward. "Yes, Karl," he said. "The Jews are the cover for our organization—but you wouldn't know that—they don't even know it."

"A front?"

"Oh, yes. We've been around for a long time. Long before Hitler came to power." Dr. Grauenhaft leaned toward Karl, "I think we have a place for you, once you understand."

"But I'm not a Nazi, Herr Doctor."

"Very well," the German said. "Neither am I. And as I said, Hitler's a reckless man, a dangerous man." He grabbed Karl's arm. "He's obsessed with the Jew. Yes. And there are rumors that his own great-grandfather was a Vienna Jew. Can you imagine that, Karl. Can you imagine what madness pulses in his distorted brain?"

Dr. Grauenhaft leaned back in his chair and sipped cognac, his eyes half closed; and then setting his glass on the low table, said to Karl. "Did you know the Romans once occupied Vienna?"

"Yes. We learned that in school."

Then lighting another black cigar and jabbing it vigorously at Karl, the stout German said quickly, "But can you imagine Hitler now claiming his

Austrian birth as Germanic purity? That mad dog may be descended from some drunken Roman corporal—probably a Jew!" With that statement, Dr. Grauenhaft roared with laughter.

Karl smiled a little behind his glass.

"We must stop him!" Dr. Grauenhaft banged the table. "Hitler is utterly mad! But first, we will use him—and all the Nazis—and then we will destroy him, and the true order will take power. A new Germany will rise from the Nazi ashes. Not a Roman imitation with hand salutes. But a social order based upon intellectual reason." Dr. Grauenhaft sighed, as if a great burden had been lifted by his explanation. "Does that shock you, Karl?"

"No, sir. It doesn't," he lied. "It fits my beliefs, sir. Yes—I think I feel the same."

Rising slowly from his chair, his eyes blazing with excitement, Dr. Grauenhaft said, "We'll keep some of the Nazi programs. Breeding—but on a purely scientific basis." Then he smiled at Karl. "As the registrar tried to explain, we researched the question. American Indians are descended from the Mongolian, who is descended from the Caucasion. That's why you were chosen, Karl. It's not the best blending, but acceptable." The German paused and smiled at Karl. Then his face went dark. "And," he said, "the Nazis waste some of our best talent. Yet they let a Negro become mayor of a German city. Essenbach, Karl, a small city near Cologne, took a Negro as mayor last year."

Then Dr. Grauenhaft said, "Karl, you look a little pale. Too much cognac?"

"It's been a long day, sir," Karl rubbed his face and forced a smile, "I was on the train all night."

The German laughed and his thick body shook. "And I talk too much. Of course you're tired. I should have realized. But you understand our thinking now, Karl?"

"Yes, sir. I understand."

"You see, Hitler is our puppet. And when the time is ripe, we'll cut the string." Dr. Grauenhaft drew a finger across his throat and smiled. "You're an intelligent man, Karl. You understand our position. And I think you can make a choice now. Are you with us?"

Stretching out a hand and smiling, Karl said, "Without reservation, sir."

"Good, Karl, good," the German said, shaking Karl's hand. "Welcome to the Schildwache. Now we go to my study where we'll have another coffee—cognac too if you'd like—and listen to Wagner for a while. And then your room will be ready."

***

"I'm your orientation officer," Elska said to Karl with cold formality in the breakfast room overlooking the Atlantic Ocean. "My job is to explain our political structure and determine whether you're acceptable."

Karl took a long sip of black coffee. "Acceptable? For what?"

They were the only ones in the spacious room at that hour and already the sun was high in the east and sparkled on the rolling waves in the picture window behind Elska. She was leaning on one elbow now and stirring her coffee, and she looked up at Karl and smiled. "For service with the SFD."

"SFD?"

"Yes, Karl. The *Schildwache Freies Deutschlands*, 'Sentinels for a Free Germany.'" She paused and smiled again at Karl. Then she lit a cigarette as she talked. "Uncle Heinrich likes you. Your cousin, Alex Meister is second in command."

Karl nodded and said nothing.

"So you'll go far—if you accept your assignment."

"What is my assignment?" He asked casually and smiled at her, but his heart was pounding.

A frown passed over her face. "We'll cover that after your briefing, in my office after breakfast, Karl."

When they finished breakfast, Karl followed Elska's trim figure down a long hall covered with thick red carpeting, up a winding staircase, and into a large room in the mansion's east wing.

"This," Elska said with a sweeping gesture as they entered the room, "is my office."

"Very nice," Karl replied. Her lisp was barely noticeable.

Looking around the room, Karl saw blue walls with painted gold trim, and a large map of Europe hanging on the wall.

Elska took a seat at a large desk before French doors which opened to a balcony overlooking the ocean. "Please," she said, "sit down, Karl."

Sitting across the desk, Karl turned for a moment to several large portraits on the wall behind him. "That's Bismark. The Iron Chancellor," he said to her. And the others are General Staff officers, aren't they?"

"Yes—and the the civilian is Fokker, the Dutchman, the father of German aviation. I put him up there as a reminder when the Luftwaffe destroyed Rotterdam."

Elska took a red folder with the familiar black-and-yellow shield from her desk and fixed her eyes hard on Karl. "Now listen carefully. Our party differs from the National Socialists, the Nazis, on fundamental issues. The Jews, for example, we don't seek them out. But we're not blinded by anti-semitism, either." Glancing at her notes, she smiled and looked up at Karl. "Apparently, Uncle Heinrich is satisfied with your feelings on the Jewish question."

Following the manual before her, Elska traced the origins of the Schildwache, explained the party's goals for a world dominated by German culture, and read to him the party creed.

She opened a gold cigarette case and offered one to Karl.

"I have my own," he said, "thank you." And then he leaned back in his chair and lit a Chesterfield.

"Now," she asked in a solemn voice, "do you understand what we've covered?"

Karl nodded. "Yes. I understand."

While he was lost in thought, Elska suddenly leaned forward and brushed white hair from her eyes. "The glove," she asked, motioning to Karl's left hand, "how did it happen?"

He shrugged his shoulders, explained as he had so many times how they approached the sinking trawler from windward, and how his hand was crushed between the Coast Guard launch and the capsized boat.

"I see you hold a cigarette," she said, "do you have much use of the fingers?"

"No. But I get by. I grasp things," he said, opening and closing the black glove.

"People will remember you, Karl, because of that hand, and your beautiful scar." Elska closed the manual and replaced it in the desk drawer. "We're about finished." She folded her arms on the table and studied him for a moment. "You haven't heard of Strasser's group, have you, Karl?"

He shook his head.

"We work with them." She leaned forward and looked seriously at Karl across the desk. "But you must have no contact with them." She leaned back again and took a long puff on her Turkish cigarette. "There'll be no room for Catholics in our government."

"I'm Catholic."

"You haven't been to mass in years," Elska said coldly. "You're no more Catholic than your cousin Alex, who openly renounced the Church."

When Karl said nothing, Elska continued with a short laugh, "Hitler signed a concordat with the Vatican. A simple understanding. He'll leave the Catholics alone, and they'll leave him alone." She paused and her cold smile faded. "And Hitler will deal with the Catholic question later—after he's finished with the Jews."

Karl looked at her. "A third of the Germans are Catholic. I don't think Hitler'd have much success against those kind of numbers."

She turned and gazed out on the balcony for a moment, and then looked quickly at him. "Karl, you're a very naive man."

He swallowed hard. Perhaps he was naive, he thought. But he'd let her little insult go for now. The mission was all that counted. He forced the words out, "You told me at breakfast there were three organizations."

"Yes." Her voice was mellow again, as it had been when she came to the dinner table the evening before. "We covered Strasser's group working out of Montreal. The third is the Black Square."

Karl watched her closely as she again brushed away a light blonde lock which continually fell across her pale blue eyes. There was again a humbleness about her that he hadn't seen all morning.

"George Viereck," Elska said, looking at Karl intently, "is the founder of the Black Square. George was brought to New York when he was eleven, and automatically became an American when his father was naturalized. But now he's one of our major problems here."

Karl said nothing and waited for the explanation.

"George Viereck is a monarchist. He wants to bring back the Kaiser. And he's already received over five hundred thousand dollars." And rising slowly from her chair, she said, "And a lot of the money Viereck receives would go to us if he weren't around." She paused and took three quick puffs on her cigarette and ground it out in the ashtray.

"And the Nazis?"

"We work with them the way a fakir works with his cobra. Never take our eyes off them. And when Hitler is dead, they'll come to us." She opened the French doors and walked out onto the balcony. Come here, please, Karl."

He followed her into the sunlight, where she pointed to the eastern horizon.

"Across that silent water, Karl, lies a nation of silent people. Uncle Heinrich told me long ago, that ten percent of the Germans are pro-Nazi, ten percent are anti-Nazi, and the remaining eighty percent will blindly support whatever party is in power."

She looked at him with a strange light in her eyes. Then she paused and stepped closer. "And, Karl, I have learned that Uncle Heinrich is right. And I've learned something else about the German people."

He stood his ground as she moved closer with a tense smile on her lips. "And what's that?"

"The great silent majority will also follow the last person to speak."

Elska's smile widened. And brushing past Karl through the French doors, she said, "Now, you will have your medical examination. And this afternoon, we'll complete our little discussion, and then we will talk about you."

***

At a long wooden table off the kitchen, Karl sat with a group of ten silent young men, and finished his lunch of vegatable soup and cold meat cuts. As he smoked a cigarette with his second cup of coffee, a tall man dressed all in black, walked up behind him, and tapping him on the shoulder, said, "Herr Meister, come with me."

He followed the man to Elska's office, where she waited at her desk with a manila folder in her hand.

"Karl," she said as he was ushered into the room, "you have an excellent medical report." Dropping the folder on her desk, Elska motioned him to a chair, moistened her lips and lit a cigarette. "Uncle Heinrich is sending you to Germany."

"I see," Karl replied, his mind churning. "And what does that mean?"

"That you'll be officially recruited by Admiral Canaris of the Abwehr—German Intelligence. He works with us."

"Canaris—German Intelligence?" Karl stammered. This could be something—if I worked for German Intelligence, Donovan would have the ultimate mole. "Is Canaris a member of the Schildwache?"

"No, Karl. But he's sympathetic to our cause. He keeps us informed. And he helps place our agents." Elska looked at him with steady eyes. "And he's taken a great many risks. He warned the Dutch, but they ingnored him. And later, he warned the Danes—and Norway too." She paused. "My father's Norwegian." And then continuing in an icy rage, she said, "But each time they failed to act. They couldn't believe the head of German intelligence was giving them Hitler's plans."

She rose from the desk. "And that has been our problem with the free world. No one believes us. No one believes there is a German underground, Karl. We have no outside support. For years we furnished the English Military Attachee in Berlin with documented war production plans. No one listened except Churchill. And he was powerless." She walked to the portraits behind Karl. "Now Churchill thinks every German is a Nazi."

Turning in his chair to face Elska behind him, Karl asked, ""Will I work for Canaris, then?"

"No. He'll recruit you. And then he'll reassign you to the SS."

"The SS?" Karl said with a puzzled look, rising quickly from his chair. The idea of working as a mole in German intelligence had intrigued him. But marching with Hitler's elite storm troopers had no appeal, and there didn't seem much chance of learning anything helpful.

"Yes, Karl, the SS. Himmler operates a full intelligence network too—and Himmler's much closer to Hitler. Uncle Heinrich wants you in the SS. Understand?"

Karl sat down in the chair before the desk, and for the first time, seriously thought about what he was doing and where Captain Harding was leading him. After thinking some time, he got up, lit a cigarette, and paced the room.

"Well, Karl?" asked Elska at last. "What's your decision?"

"I understand," he said, stopping and facing her. "But does it have to be the SS? I—"

Before he could continue, she blurted out with a heavy lisp and stern tone, "The Fatherland is at war—we're fighting for Germany's life—we must win." She jumped to her feet. "And at the same time, we must defeat Hitler's thugs. We're fighting for survival of German culture, Karl, on the military front and on the home front. Hitler pushed us into the war we didn't want. A war we must now win, because no one will accept anything less than a total German defeat and total destruction of our heritage." She scooped the manila folder up from the desk. "Read this and sign it!" She handed Karl a two-page, printed document.

Karl read the small print. Below the words he saw the same certification he had rejected at the Grand Turtle Lodge in Southport years earlier: "I hereby affirm that I am of pure blood and the Caucasion race." He quickly signed his name and the date, August 21, 1941. This time, he raised no objections.

Taking the document and smiling at Karl, Elska said, "Now you're enrolled." She made an entry in the folder. "September fifteenth. Report to Uncle Heinrich's office in New York."

Then she walked around Karl and closed and locked the door; and going to a liquor cabinet in the corner behind the desk, she asked, "How about a drink?"

Karl nodded. "Whiskey."

"On the rocks?"

"On the rocks would be fine."

She slid into the chair next to him. "How is it?"

He nodded again. "Good."

"I drink for the taste," she was holding her glass high to him. "Gin and tonic." She smiled at him over her glass. "And I'm very careful. I never get drunk. Getting drunk is like making love and getting pregnant." She raised the glass higher. "Prosit!"

"Prosit, Elska," he said smiling back at her and emptying his glass.

Elska left the chair and returned with more drinks, saying, "Drinking harms no one. The doctor's, I suppose don't agree. But it's a comfortable feeling, the glow, the warmth inside. Don't you agree?"

Karl nodded. "And there's no commitment—except to the bottle."

"But it's a cold commitment, Karl. There's no lasting warmth in it."

"Yes. But it's safe enough, isn't it?"

"You drink as a substitute for love? Is that what you are saying?"

Karl smiled and didn't answer.

Elska lowered her eyes. "Love is never simple."

"Oh, I think love can be simple," Karl said. "One only needs confidence in himself. And confidence in the special person he finds. That's simple enough. And from that, everything flows naturally."

"Perhaps for you life is that simple, Karl. But then you're a man. You don't sit and wait for that special person." She straightened in the chair. "And you are a romantic, Karl. And like all romantics, you are naive."

Rising slowly from her chair and unlocking the door, she then turned to Karl. "A toast," she said. "To September 15th. And Karl, you must report, you know. Or I'm afraid Uncle Heinrich will have you shot."

Two

Captain Harding, a man in his early forties with sandy hair thinning on top, struck a match, lit his pipe, and leaned back in a smoke cloud behind his oak desk at Fort Wayne. His blue eyes, set in a pallid face, studied Karl Meister for a moment. "We're new to this game," he said dryly. "And we're entirely dependent on the British. But September 15th! My God! We'll have damned little time to train you!"

"They're quite serious," Karl said. "She told me to report on the 15th or I'd be shot. Grauenhaft says I already know too much."

"Yes. That's true, Karl. It's happened before."

Karl stared at the Army officer in silence. That was one thing he had neglected to tell Karl.

"We'll put together something, Karl. Perhaps we can get some help from the British on a crash program. Are you still with us?"

"Captain, I've gone through their indoctrination. It doesn't look like I have a choice." He pulled at his shirt collar. "And I have no family, no commitments. I guess I'm ready for this."

Captain Harding made a quick call to Canada. His face beamed. "Karl, you start training immediately."

"Now?"

"In the morning," the captain answered. "We start with radio procedure. Then you're off to Canada."

Hurrying down the hall behind the Captain, Karl asked, "What about my things in Cincinnati?"

"We'll take care of them," Harding said over his shoulder. Then he stopped in the hall and turned back to Karl. "Give me your apartment keys. I'll have everything brought here." Taking the keys, and slapping Karl on the shoulder as they went along toward the adjutant's office, Captain Harding said, "Damn, Karl. This is it. We'll make your September 15th deadline!"

Karl was assigned bachelor officer quarters, and started radio training the next morning. By eleven o'clock, he'd reached his old sending speed at the navigation school and started on a general course in radio components and theory. For the remainder of the week, he studied weapons handling and worked on his code skills, until he no longer heard the individual dots and dashes and each character took on its own special sound.

On the following Monday, Karl was driven to a secret British training camp on the shores of Lake Ontario near Oshawa, where he was introduced to H. William Harvey of Lancaster, England, a squat man with sunken eyes and endless energy. "We're bloody well going to do it," Harvey said. "Not because of you, Lieutenant Meister, but because of me. I have it from the top, and that's our man Hyde, to push you through this program—and that's what I'm going to do—from six in the morning until midnight. And if you fall asleep, I'll wake you up."

Startled by the verbal onslaught, which started with the first handshake and continued uninterrupted until the short Englishman finished, Karl stood and looked at Harvey. "I'll do my best. That's all I can say."

The Englishman looked at him with a blank face and shook his head. Then taking Karl's arm and rushing him down the hall, Harvey said, "We start right now, sir. Unless you have some strong objection."

"I don't object. It's my life on the line, you know."

"Now there's a sensible man," Harvey said as they strode out the door and across the courtyard to the training room. "Anything you don't pick up, could be the very thing you need to get out of a tight situation some day."

***

I just hope to God I haven't made a mistake, Karl thought to himself. And all this started with a late knock on the door at Southport. Karl had opened the door to see two army men standing in the dim light. "We're Army Intelligence," Captain Harding said simply. "I'm Captain Roy Harding. My driver is Sergeant Bill Dean. We're from the Fort Wayne post—Detroit, and we want to talk to you. Can we come in?"

When they had taken chairs, the Captain leaned forward and said, "this is why we want to talk to you." He pulled a newspaper from his trench coat and spread a November issue of the *Detroit Free Press* on the coffee table. It was the story of the *Tres Belle* rescue.

Captain Harding unzipped a leather pouch and began to read from a file: "Karl Konrad Meister. American citizen. Born December 10, 1906 at Badenberg, Austria. Speaks German as well as the Austrian dialect." The captain paused and looked up at Karl then. "Your father was a doctor. He served in the war as a captain with an artillery unit on the Western Front.

Returning again to the file, he continued: "Father died from combat wounds. Mother also deceased. Grandparents reside Badenberg. Grandmother an American citizen. Only brother," the officer turned a page, "serves with the U.S. Coast Guard at Southport, Michigan. No other close relatives."

The army officer then closed the file and leaned back in his chair. "There's more," he said. "Information on your uncles and aunts, cousins and so on. But what's important is that you speak German, are a U.S. citizen, know code—"

"I passed the examination," Karl said. "But I'm not that good."

"And this," the captain tapped a finger on the newspaper, "is what caught our attention. Quite simply, Mr. Meister, we're looking for brave men who will serve their country."

"We're not at war," Karl replied. "And I'm not a brave man."

"But we will be at war, Mr. Meister. And you're what we want." The captain took a deep breath and fixed his eyes directly on Karl. "You know Dr. Grauenhaft!"

"Dr. Grauenhaft!"

"Your cousin, Alex Meister, is the man's Berlin lawyer. And Dr. Grauenhaft is the head of all Nazis in America."

"I heard some of it on the radio."

"There's quite a bit that didn't reach the press," Captain Harding said.

"And Alex?"

"He played a major role in the assassination of the Austrian Chancellor...." Captain Harding paused and glanced at the sergeant. "What's his name?"

"Dollfuss, sir."

"Yes, Dollfuss. He outlawed the Nazi party and blocked Hitler's efforts to take over Austria. Your cousin Alex had him killed—on Hitler's orders."

"And how do you know I'm not a Nazi?"

"Well, we never know anything for sure," Captain Harding answered. "But nothing suggests that you—how shall I put it?—would become the Devil's partner."

Karl smiled and leaned back in his chair. "What is it you want from me?"

"We want you to work for your country, Mr. Meister."

Captain Harding lit a cigarette and cocked his head at Karl. "We're forming a new intelligence service. And we'll be taking the best men from the Navy as well as Army G2. And we want you as an agent."

"A spy, you mean."

"A spy. Our eyes and ears. Someday Germany will be our enemy, and that day isn't very far away."

"You think the Nazis will go that far?"

"Sure. Who do you think is next?"

Karl crumpled an empty Chesterfield pack in his hand. "May I have one of your Camels, Captain?"

The captain tapped a cigarette out of his pack and reached it to Karl. Then he handed him a white card. "This is my number."

Karl turned the card over in his hand. "Olson Match Company," he read. "Roy Harding, Export Sales."

"And it's obviously our front," Captain Harding said. You'll be an Olson man too. For a while, anyway. And we're offering you a commission in the Army. Second lieutenant?"

Karl nodded. "And who is to know?"

"No one. Not even your brother." The captain rose slowly. "You'll be sworn in at my office, in Detroit." Captain Harding reached out and shook Karl's hand. "And the beard, of course. That'll have to go," he said with a laugh.

***

On the second day at the British training camp, the Englishman, Harvey, stood in front of Karl's desk in the training room and held out a flat brown object. "What does this look like?"

"I don't know. But if I had to guess, I'd say it looks like—"

"Shit."

"What?"

"Camel dung!" Harvey beamed. "It's a disguised landmine. ForAfrican operations. Smells like it too." And he held the brown object under Karl's nose.

"Christ," Karl said. "That's awful."

"Smells like the real thing, doesn't it?"

"I'll take your word for it."

"It's a chemical agent in glassfibre. Plastic is what you Yanks call it."

"Now, Mr. Harvey—"

"Call me Bill. Only use last names when necessary. Get into the habit."

"Okay. Bill, then. May I ask you something?"

"Sure, Lieutenant. That's my job."

"How will I use a landmine disguised as camel dung in Germany?"

"Germany?"

"Yes. Germany."

"I thought you were slotted for North Africa. Sorry Yank. Bloody stupid of me."

They both laughed; and Harvey collapsed onto a chair, clutching the plastic camel dung to his chest. "Yank, for that blunder I owe you a drink."

"You're on."

When they returned from the officer's club, Harvey pulled a bottle from his pocket and held it out to Karl. "Do you know what this is?"

Karl took the bottle and read the label. "Pyramidon . . . Sure. For pain and headaches. You can buy it in most any drug store. Even in Austria. Same thing as aspirin."

"Well, Yank, It's not quite the same as aspirin. But you're right. It's a common pain reliever," Harvey said. "And it doesn't mix well with heavy drinking. That combination can produce shock, coma, and sudden death."

"I understand."

"And from now on, this will be your constant companion," Harvey said, taking the bottle from Karl's hand and holding it up to him.

"Now I don't understand."

"You will." The Englishman took a sheet of plain white paper and placed it on the table. From his pants pocket, he took a second bottle, and holding that up for Karl to see, said, "Pyramidon in solution. Tablets ground and dissolved in water."

Then Harvey took a toothpick from his vest pocket. "Any sharp object will do," he said. "But these are the least conspicuous." And he dipped the toothpick in the solution and scrached on the paper.

He blew on the sheet, and when the solution had dried he handed it to Karl and said, "Read it."

"It's blank."

Harvey took a third bottle from his pocket. "Now look carefully at the paper. "Do you see anything at all? Anything that might cause you to think there's a message on it?"

"No. I can't even see where the solution dried."

"And you wouldn't see anything under a microscope, either, Karl. But this is an iodine re-agent," he said; and he spread the re-agent on the paper with a toothpick. "Give me your cigarette lighter."

Then taking Karl's cigarette lighter, and running it back and forth with the flame lightly touching the paper, Harvey said, "Be careful not to burn the damned thing."

He handed the paper to Karl. "Now read it."

"Your code name is Peter."

"Now these are simple items you can buy anywhere, Lieutenant. And they won't arose suspicion. But as you might expect, the Germans use it, too. So, you wouldn't pass a message this way if you were under suspicion."

"I see," Karl said. "Can I try it?"

"That's what we're here for."

Karl took the pyramidon solution and wrote several messages. But each time he brought out the letters with the lighter, he found the sentences running into each other, and words overlapping.

"It takes practice," the Englishman said. "Something like writing in the dark. But you'll get it soon enough."

Then Harvey showed him how to write with with ammonium chloride. "We don't need a re-agent with this," he said. "Just run the lighter over the blank paper, and see. There it is."

Karl looked at the brown writing and nodded.

"Now this is a little more dangerous," Harvey said. "First, you wouldn't want to be caught carrying the solution, because you wouldn't have an explanation for it. And any good intelligence man would know you were up to something. But all it needs is heat. Sometimes the sun is enough. And that's it's greatest weakness. Any heat exposure may bring it out."

Finishing with the writing, Harvey said, "There are other methods, of course. But the important thing is to keep it simple. That's why these are the best. And remember, Karl," he said gravely, and placed a hand on his shoulder, "if the Germans suspect you, they'll test every scrap you touch. So don't send anything. Not even in code. That's rule number two."

"And rule number one?"

"Get the hell out!"

On Sunday afternoon the Englishman placed four drinks on the table before Karl. "Take a sip from each one and tell me what it is," he said. "Just a small sip."

Tasting the first glass, which he immediately recognized, Karl smiled, and said, "Hell, that's my apricot brandy."

"And the next one?"

Karl sipped and paused. Then he took a second drink. "I don't know. What is it?"

"It's a White Lady. Try the next one."

"Bourbon—straight."

"Good. And the next?"

"Oh, that's great stuff," Karl said and smiled. "Whiskey again. But a distinct peppermint flavor."

Harvey looked at him with a faint smile. "Now, Karl, you may finish one of these drinks. Which one would you like?"

"Is this a test, or something?"

"Sure. Which one do you want?"

"Well, I'll take my apricot, here."

"Go ahead. Drink up."

Karl emptied the glass and turned to the Englishman, saying, "Now what?"

"Good night, Karl."

"Good night?" Karl looked at his watch. "Why it's only a little after five."

"I know. But you're about to learn a hard lesson."

"I am?"

"Yes. In less than fifteen minutes, you'll be fast asleep, and you'll stay that way for twelve hours."

"What?"

Nodding and smiling at Karl, Harvey said, "You've just been slipped a Mickey Finn. A bigger dose could put you under for more than twenty-four hours. And during that time, anyone could search your room, your luggage—do most anything—you wouldn't wake up. And if you didn't know the symptoms, you might not be the wiser."

"Which one was it?"

"Three, actually. The bourbon you said tasted like peppermint, the White Lady, and your lovely apricot brandy, the one you finished. And Karl," he said with a smile, "Never drink Creme de Menthe—and do switch to straight whiskey."

Harvey rose and took Karl's arm. "Now," he said, "I'd better rush you off to quarters, before it's too late."

By the time Karl reached his room and staggered through the door, his legs were rubber and heavy. He felt dizzy and sat down on the bed. "It's stuffy in here," he said. "And I don't think I can get up to open the window. Would you get it for me?"

"No, Karl. It isn't stuffy. That's one of the symptoms. Remember it."

Going then to the door, the Englishman turned and said, "Just lie down. I'll come back and throw a cover over you. And in the morning, you tell me whether you remember me doing that."

Karl felt his muscles relaxing and fought for strength. He still heard Harvey's voice through a fog. "Better lie back now, before it's too late and you fall over on the floor."

Then the room began to swirl around Karl, and he rolled a shoulder onto the bed.

He awoke, feeling very weak and groggy, at eleven the next morning, and sat up on his bunk. Sure enough, he said to himself, Harvey came back and covered me up. And I never noticed it.

Looking around the room, he slowly became aware that the radio pounded out loud music, a dixieland tune with a fast beat.

Staggering to turn off the radio, he saw a note taped to the dial. It read: "Did you have a nice sleep, Karl? Where is your wallet?"

Karl's hand went to his coat pocket. "Damn," he muttered. "Now where did that go."

And feeling something hard in the pocket, he pulled out a small cardboard note, which read: "Your wallet is in the dresser. You have been searched and your identity papers exchanged, copied, or destroyed, perhaps even switched. What would you do now?"

"You see," Harvey said at lunch, "Drink straight whiskey. That way you'll pick up the mint flavor and know it's a Mickey."

Leaning back and looking at Karl with a small smile on his thin lips, the Englishman asked, "How do you feel?"

"My God," Karl said, staring at his vegetable soup, "this is worse than any hangover."

"Yes. But it could be mistaken for a hangover, or a touch of the flu. Now you know. And for the next day or so, I'm afraid you're going to have a rather bad time of it." The Englishman grinned. "I wouldn't wander too far from the crapper, if I were you, Karl."

"Thanks a lot."

Now noticing a sour-bitterness in his mouth, Karl said, "Nothing tastes right."

"That's expected, Lieutenant. But the more you eat and drink, the quicker you'll get over it."

"Our instructons are sent to Germany in packages of cocoa," Harvey told Karl when they returned to the training room. "These are packed by Leineweber in Buenos Aires, a German grocery firm." He pulled a small packet from his black case, opened it, unfolded the envelope on his knee, and handed it to Karl.

"Take your lighter," he said, "and pass the flame under the printed side."

Doing as the Englishman instructed, Karl saw letters and numbers appear in brown on the white paper.

"These are what you chaps will be using."

Looking at the brown printing, Karl said, "How do you do it . . . In Buenos Aires?"

"Karl, we operate on a need-to-know basis." The Englishman said, taking the envelope and turning it over in his hand. "How we get the frequencies to you isn't important."

"And what happens when these frequencies are discovered?"

"We switch every six months. But we monitor the old frequencies too—for the duration. Because there'll be some operatives we can't reach."

Then handing the envelope to Karl, Harvey said, "Always burn it. And then mix the ashes in water and flush them down the drain. Keep nothing."

At the table in the officer's club, Harvey lit a thin black cigar. Then leaning back and blowing cigar smoke at the ceiling, he said, "It takes a full minute to zero in on a transmitter. That's a lot of time. Now, no message should ever be over thirty seconds. Break them up if necessary. And always remember, the next time you go on the air, there'll be a German listening for you. And when he hears that signal, which he'll recognize, he'll come a little closer to pin-pointing your location. So keep moving. By then, they could have one line of position. And sometimes, that's all they need. Say, for example, if you're on a coast. Well, they know you can't be too far up the line. And all they do is run along it until they find you. Now you could be in a building. On a boat, perhaps. Or in a car. But there you'd be. And they'd know it couldn't be anyone but you."

Karl put down his coffee and looked at the Englishman. "That's a tough order," he said. "I've got to keep down to thirty seconds, but I can't send too fast, or it won't be received."

"Omit all unnecessary words and characters. The transmitter is sending only when the key is pressed. Otherwise, you're off the air. Not like voice, where the signal is constant and the words are imprinted on it." Harvey sipped his coffee, and putting down the cup, said, "Do you understand that, Karl? Never transmit from the same location twice. Keep your messages short."

After the break, Karl learned to build a low-powered transmitter from common German radio supplies; and after he transmitted his first message over the hand-made radio, Harvey held up fingers in a victory sign and beamed at Karl. Then he rose and walked to where Karl was sending. "The big danger is lugging around the sending crystals. Since each is cut to a specific frequency, the Germans will have no doubt what you're up to if they're found. And if you chuck them and look for a replacement later, some smart clerk may report the purchase." Pulling a wire loop from his case, the Englishman said, "And here's the answer to that problem." He held up the wire loop and pulled it tight. "Just drop it over his head from behind. And make sure the clerk's dead before you leave."

Three

On the afternoon of September 15, 1941, Karl Meister stood on the afterdeck of the *Vulgo Alonso*, an Argentine cargo ship bound for Lisbon, and watched the Statue of Liberty disappear over the taffrail. He had reported to the Haemish Chemical Company office in New York that morning. The clerk with the small glasses told him Dr. Grauenhaft was out, but everything was in order, and then handed him a Spanish passport and ordered a taxi to the ship.

So much for fanfare, Karl thought, watching Miss Liberty grow faint in a blue haze. His only instructions were to report at the Hotel de Parque in Estoril, Portugal. And Dr. Grauenhaft's soft-spoken clerk, who's expression never changed, handed him a voucher for the hotel, saying, "In no event, Herr Meister, are you to go near the Hotel Palacio across the promenade—remember that."

There was no further explanation, and when Karl looked at the little man quizically and demanded an explanation, the clerk's eyes narrowed behind his small glasses, and he said again, "You are not to go near the Palacio. Those are your instructions, Herr Meister." The clerk waved a finger at Karl and shook his head. "No questions, Mr. Meister—those are your instructions. And when you report to the Hotel de Parque, Mr. Meister, you will receive a further voucher and a train ticket to Madrid. The hotel clerk will give you those when you check out. And if there are no changes in our plans, the hotel clerk will tell you to meet a Senor Manuel Ortega at the tourist information desk in the Madrid station. When you arrive in Madrid, just ask for Senor Ortega," the small clerk had told him. "Remain at the information desk, and you'll be contacted."

Looking around him now at the old tramp steamer, Karl's worst fears were confirmed. He'd seen peeling paint and streaking rust down the sides as he walked up the steep gangway. The *Vulgo Alonso* was a dirty ship. Accumulated dirt, grease and grime lay everywhere, making the iron deck slippery and dangerous. No true seaman would permit this, he thought to himself. One bad roll on a stormy night and someone will break a leg.

Forward of the cargo deck, he saw cabin ports and pilothouse windows dirty and streaked. Inside, thick paint flaked from the walls of his small stateroom. His mattress was lumpy and sweat-stained, and smelled of old tobacco and former occupants. Cockroaches crawled the walls everywhere, and seemed to hold a secure position on the ship. They even appeared at the Captain's table, and the greasy vessel's master flicked a roach aside with a thick finger when it climbed the side of his plate.

Four dark passengers, all silent young men, ate with him at the Captain's table, which was the custom on tramp steamers. But the dinner talk Karl had hoped might enlighten him was absent. The Captain responded to neither English nor German, and what little conversation took place was in Spanish or Portuguese, Karl wasn't sure which. But he was almost certain from the expression on his face, that the Captain understood English.

It was hot at the Captain's table. Sweat ran down Karl's face. Karl had hung his suit coat on the back of his chair when he saw the men in shirt sleeves at the table. But even so, the heat was unbearable, and the cotton cloth stuck to his back.

The other men all smelled strongly of hard sweat and chewing tobacco and soiled clothing. No one's had a bath on this ship for months, he thought, watching the Captain push piles of a thick, pasty goulash into his mouth.

Once more Karl spoke to the dark men around the table. "A good start," he said, "and the weather looks like it'll hold for a few days."

But each attempt at conversation was met by a confused look on young faces about him and a firm, hostile glance from the Captain. So we're to remain silent, he said to himself.

After the evening meal was finished, the Captain rose and abruptly left the hot room. Karl went on deck. From watching the wake and the speed of the waves passing, he estimated they were making about ten knots. Not bad for an old ship, he thought. We should make Lisbon in about twelve days.

On the second night, as he tossed on his bunk in the stuffy cabin, Karl heard the engines go silent. He sat up in the moonlight filtering through his dirty porthole and looked at his watch. It was a little after midnight. Soon the ship rolled in the swells. Engine trouble, he wondered? Calculating quickly, he estimated they were about four hundred miles out of New York. "Yes, engine trouble," he said to himself, pulling on his trousers and looking out the small port at the black, oily sea; and then he slipped into his dark peacoat and went on deck.

As he closed the steel door behind him, he saw a searchlight coming from the water off the port bow; and as he watched, the light's beam bounced off the old ship's pilothouse and played along the deck, blinding him momentarily as it passed.

Karl went to the rail and leaned out. He could see the cigar shape of a submarine lying low in black water under the full moon. He searched for markings. "Too dark," he muttered to himself. "But it's German for sure."

Then there was a noise ahead of him on the old freighter, and a cargo net suspended from a short boom swung over the side. Out on the water, moonlight flashed on wet paddles as four men rowed a black rubber boat to the ship. There was a fifth white face in the rubber boat. What have we here, he wondered? A new passenger? He stepped back into the shadows. Just then, the ship's high loading lights snapped on, illuminating the deck and the water around.

Waiting quietly there in the shadows, Karl heard a voice coming over the water from the rubber boat. "Ahoy the ship." The voice was speaking English with a heavy German accent. From forward, near the pilothouse, came the clear reply, "The cargo net's over the side. We'll take your man aboard on your signal."

Karl stepped quickly to the rail and looked down, as the rubber boat slid on a swell and stopped at the cargo net. The four men with paddles wore dark sweaters and dark wool caps. The man in the middle, who rolled into the cargo net as Karl watched, was also dressed in black, except for a white officer's cap. Interesting, Karl said to himself and stepped back once again into the shadows. From there, he watched the net rise high and swing out of view along the freighter's cargo deck. As it swung, Karl saw the stout man again, standing in the webbing, gripping the sides.

With his back to the wall, Karl inched forward; and when he reached the corner, he peered around, and saw the man step from the cargo net and follow the ship's captain into the pilothouse.

As he hurried back along the rail, Karl saw flashing signals from the submarine and the rubber boat moving swiftly away. Then the freighter's engines started.

Pausing at the iron passage door, he watched until the rubber raft reached the submarine, where the four men scrambled out and hauled the black boat on deck; and then he felt the vibration of the freighter's motors under his feet and heard her propellers churning water. As he closed the passage door behind him, he saw the submarine running on the surface toward the west. It's headed for New York, he thought. Probably on a surveillance mission. And from there it will follow some unsuspecting merchant ship, or radio ahead to comrades on U-Boats in the Atlantic, and another freighter will slide to the bottom.

The new man wasn't at the Captain's breakfast table, nor did he appear at any of the meals that day, or anywhere on the ship. Later that next night, as Karl walked from his cabin down the narrow corridor to the communal head, he had an uneasy feeling and was positive he was being watched. There's no reason for it, he thought, but you get these feelings and somehow you know. Standing in the foul-smelling bathroom, he quickly cracked the steel door and peered down the passageway. In the dim light cast by a mesh-covered bulb in the hallway ceiling, he saw his stateroom door close.

Karl waited in the lavatory. And when he'd given the intruder enough time to search and get out, went to his room. His sea bag was undisturbed The fine thread, always laced into the draw string so that it was invisible, was still there. No one had opened the bag. Well now, he thought, rubbing his chin. I couldn't be mistaken. I saw the door close. Someone was here. Then pondering this mystery, he took his glass from the corner sink and poured his evening bourbon; and lifting the drink to his mouth, he detected a faint taste of peppermint. He stood there, smiling and remembering the Englishman's advice. "Oh yes! Drink it straight." He sniffed the glass. I wouldn't have tasted that peppermint in my apricot brandy. And now we'll play the game, he said to himself. Just about a fourth should do. He drank from the glass and poured the remainder of the spiked whiskey into the sink. Then went to his bunk. After a few minutes, he laid back and felt his muscles relaxing. Suddenly, he was fighting to stay awake.

Damn! I've overdone it. Well, I guess these are things you learn the hard way.

Lying there, Karl checked his watch. Only fifteen minutes had passed since he drank the knock-out drops. Now is when it will hit hard, he thought; and reaching over to his crippled left hand, he squeezed hard. Pain shot up his arm. It's working, he said to himself. When he checked his watch again, another five minutes had passed and he was still awake. So squeezing harder now, he let the intense pain push the fog from his head. But soon he knew he was losing. He glanced at his watch again. Hell, only ten seconds had gone by—he'd thought it was ten minutes.

Suddenly, he heard a metallic click, the door latch, sounding as if it were coming from far away. He closed his eyes and breathed deeply, pretending sleep. Then he heard footsteps on the metal floor and a rustling next to his bunk. Lying there quietly now, his face feeling stiff like an iron mask, his right hand pressing painfully on his left, fighting the drug with that pain,

Karl waited.

And when he saw orange glowing through his closed lids, he knew a light had been flashed in his face. Thank God I drank enough, Karl thought. Otherwise I'd have flinched, and the game would be up.

A paler orange, now steady behind his closed eyes, told Karl that the overhead light was on and that the intruder was satisfied he was out cold from the drops. It's not that hard to pretend, he said to himself. Hell, I am almost out.

Hearing now sounds of glass, metal, and a heavier thud, he realized his sea bag was emptied on the small table next to the sink; and listening to boots shuffling on the steel floor, he was certain there was only one man in the room.

The orange glow disappeared from his closed lids, and he knew the light was off now. But he could still hear the man's boots scrape the floor and his heavy breathing. Opening his eyes carefully, Karl waited until his vision adjusted to the darkness, then looked about the room. Just then he saw a dark figure moving closer and quickly shut his eyes.

When he heard the feet move away again, Karl opened his eyes and saw a face in the moonlight at the window. The man wore a white cap with a dark visor; and Karl saw a broad nose, thick lips, and a heavy mustache.

A light flashed again in his face.

Lying still, and breathing slowly and deeply, Karl waited for the light to go out. Then he felt cold sharp steel on his throat. Don't panic. Don't panic, he kept saying to him self. Who'd want to kill me? If he's German, there's no reason. And if he's American, there's no reason. But what if he's American, and doesn't know about Captain Harding? And my God, that was *Mein Kampf* in my sea bag, Hitler's book. But what the hell. We aren't killing people for carrying the book. And I couldn't do anything anyway. I'm half out. And if I jump, he'll kill me for sure. Just don't sweat. Just don't sweat, he kept saying now. Nothing's happened yet. He hasn't cut yet. He must be testing me. He's not sure.

Karl felt the knife go away; and then the light left his face and he heard the feet on the steel deck and the door slam.

Well, he thought, lying there and breathing hard. I must be pretty important if they go to these extremes. Christ, you never know what you're getting into in these things. At least I didn't have anything to make him suspicious.

Sitting up, he reached over and pulled his sea bag across the floor. Down at the bottom, he found the other bourbon bottle, sniffed it quickly for peppermint, and took a cautious taste. Then he gulped heavily from the bottle, put in on the floor, and fell back in his bunk; and he was sweating now.

When he awoke in the morning, he looked at his watch. It was nine o'clock. This is one time you miss breakfast, he said to himself. They wouldn't expect to see me. Not this early. So I'll wait and show up for lunch.

Sitting in his bunk, he opened Hitler's big book and read from *Mein Kampf* until noon, when he walked slowly to the ship's mess.

Karl apologized to the Captain for having missed breakfast and told him he felt a little dizzy and seasick.

"Yes," the Captain answered in English. "But you'll get better soon, my friend." And for the first time, the Captain smiled at him.

***

On Karl's second day in Portugal, the small oily-haired clerk at the Hotel de Parque slid a white envelope across the desk and said, "Your ticket to Madrid, Herr Meister. Ask for Senor Manuel Ortega at the tourist information desk when you reach the station."

Karl nodded and walked onto the sunlit veranda. In front of the veranda, high palm trees looked down upon well trimmed semi-tropical shrubbery and neat hedges shaped in geometric designs. Flagstone walks curved throughout the garden, leading to a fountain in the center; and on the other side of the garden, stood the Hotel Palacio, a six-story ultra-modern structure with tall columns in the center. The forbidden city, Karl mused to himself.

He walked down the steps and into the garden, smelling the summer flowers; and while he stood in the garden, watching the Hotel Palacio through the fountain's thin spray, he heard a voice at his side. "Don't look around, Mr. Meister. Pretend you don't hear me—and listen carefully. Someone is watching you from the veranda, a broad muscular man with a mustache. And your first assignment, Karl, is to kill that man. Now I'm going up to the fountain, and on the other side, out of his view, I'll leave a weapon on the fountain ledge. It's a single shot thirty-eight disguised as a cigarette lighter. Hold it in your palm—and when the time is right, press it to his head and snap the cover—that's the trigger. It'll make a helluva noise, so make sure you have an escape route when you do it. And don't try it around here. It's not worth blowing your cover. Now, Karl," the voice continued in a dry monotone, "If you run into a problem, get in touch with one of the clerks at the Hotel de Parque. They're on our side. Now circle wide to the left. I'll go straight for the other side of the fountain and disappear from there. The gun will be on the ledge. Good luck."

Karl walked slowly to his left, and as he did so, he glanced over his shoulder and saw the man who had searched his room on the *Vulgo Alonzo* watching him from the veranda of the Hotel de Parque. When Karl passed the far side of the fountain, he reached out quickly and picked up a black cigarette lighter. It was unusually heavy in his pocket. And while still hidden from the veranda, he paused and saw a tall man, dressed in a white suit, emerge from the other side of the botanical garden and stride swiftly up the steps of the Hotel Palacio, never once turning his head.

After walking awhile in the long garden which lay between the two hotels that faced each other in stone silence, Karl turned and strode casually to the Hotel de Parque. "Shit," he mumbled to himself. "I can't kill this guy. Hell, I don't know a damn about him. What the hell do they expect from me." When he stepped onto the veranda, a large man walked out from behind a column where Karl had not seen him. It was the man with the broad face and the thick mustache. "Do you have a light?" The man's big hand brought a cigar to his face."

"Sure, Karl answered, taking a matchbook from his pants pocket. He struck the match and lit the man's cigar. Their eyes met for a moment over Karl's shaking hands. "*Danke,*" the man muttered through a smoke cloud. "*Bitte,*" Karl answered, and his voice was shrill and strange. Then the man turned and walked into the lobby. Karl glanced at the matches in his hand. Olson Match Company. "Oh—good God, he mumbled under his breath."

He walked into the dark lobby and turned toward the bar, passing the big man again who settled into a leather chair and unfolded a newspaper; and as Karl sat at the bar, drinking straight bourbon, he studied the man in the mirror. He sat there in that leather chair, the newspaper resting in his lap, and when their eyes met in the mirror, Karl was the first to look away. Damn, he thought, that man knows something. And I'm supposed to kill him? Christ, he's cold as steel. And he's smart. Sits in the corner with his back to the wall.

Karl drank two quick bourbons. Then the big man rose from the wicker chair and strode out of view in the mirror. Karl followed to the veranda. But he was nowhere to be seen. And while he stood there in the sunlight, he heard the man's deep voice at his elbow. "What did the man from the Hotel Palacio want?"

Swallowing hard and turning to the broad face of the mustached man, Karl answered quickly, "He told me to kill you."

"That's what I thought," the powerful man said with his eyes steady on Karl. "Give me the gun."

Karl reached in his pocket and handed over the black cigarette lighter. Standing there close to Karl and rolling the heavy lighter between his thick thumb and forefinger, the man said, “Interesting, Karl. Thank you.” The man walked down into the garden, whistling to himself.

Four

At the tourist information center in Madrid, Karl asked for Senor Ortega; and after standing there for half an hour, heard a deep voice behind him say in German, "Herr Meister, I'm Senor Ortega."

Turning to the voice, he looked up to a blond young man in a white suit who stood a full head taller than Karl.

"Hans Boelle. Welcome to Madrid," the tall man said with a laugh, and stretched out a hand. "Follow me."

They walked into the sunlight, crossed the boulevard and entered a small cafe on a side street. Inside the cafe it was dark, and Karl followed the tall man through a sliding door and into a smaller room, where Hans Boelle motioned Karl to a table under a shuttered window.

A waiter appeared in the doorway as they each lit cigarettes. Karl asked for a beer while the tall man ordered coffee and cognac. After they were served, the waiter nodded to Boelle and slid the door closed.

The blond man in the white suit leaned back with a cigarette in his hand and said, "He's been eliminated."

"What?"

"The man in Portugal. The man you were supposed to kill. You see, the cigarette lighter was also a bomb, which we detonated by remote radio. Of course it didn't kill him. But it put him down; and one of our operatives finished him with a stiletto. It was done in the market place—quite crowded at the time." Hans Boelle took a long puff on his cigarette and smiled at Karl.

"We think you're safe now." Boelle paused and looked at Karl. "You blew your cover, Mr. Meister."

"I . . ."

"Well, makes no difference now. But remember, if you're given a mission, Mr. Meister, carry it out. You're damned lucky we took care of him before he reported you."

"Who . . . Who are you?"

"Hans Boelle." The blond man finished his cognac and took a sip of coffee. Then drawing slowly again on his cigarette, continued, "Kupschmidt Shoe Company, Berne, Switzerland. Since we're neutral, we travel quite freely throughout Europe, including Germany and the occupied countries. And our shoes are quite popular. You've heard of them, of course?"

"No . . . I hadn't"

"It's really a very good shoe," Boelle said dryly, "It's Goodyear stitched. And you haven't heard of it?"

"No," Karl answered, shaking his head very slowly, and finding the smiling man now quite irritating. "Should I?"

"Yes," the blond man said quickly, and he was no longer smiling. "The Kupschmidt shoe is our link to inside Germany. Didn't they teach you anything?" And not waiting for an answer, continued rapidly, "The man you were supposed to take out was a double agent. He'd just returned from England. And we believe he stole radar information—enough for the Germans to set up their own system." Then Boelle stopped and stubbed out his cigarette. "Radar, Mr. Meister, is the key to the air war. Knowing when and where the enemy will strike makes it possible to intercept him, and saves both gasoline and aircraft."

"I never agreed to assassination," Karl said angrily. "If that's what you want, get another boy. I'm not the type."

Boelle straightened suddenly and looked at Karl with a startled look.

"Just what is my mission?" Karl asked, his voice still angry. "And who are you—where do you fit in?"

"I work for OSS. Our chief in Europe is Allen Dulles in Berne. Boelle was leaning forward now and he tapped another cigarette on the table and shoved it into his mouth. Then striking a match, smiled again and said, "I never use lighters." Then he leaned back and continued. "You know we've got to help the English hold out. At least until we're officially in the war. Well, the submarine is the problem now—Britian's winning the battle in the air, and a German invasion's no longer the threat." Boelle pointed a finger at Karl. "That's where you come in. The U-Boats operate out of Northern France, choking off vital supplies. It's been impossible to hit them in their concrete bays. And from there, they slip into deep water and disappear. But most of them are built in Northern Germany—and they go back home for retro-fits, understand?"

Karl shook his head.

"The North Sea is shallow along the German coast. So if we can spot them coming out to sea, there's a good chance the British can pick them up in open water and finish them off. So if at all possible, Mr. Meister, your job is to get to the German north coast; Kiel, Hamburg, or Wesermuende."

Karl nodded.

"Now Wesermuende you may remember, Karl, was the central headquarters of the German U-Boat fleet in the first war. It's right at the mouth of the river. And Bremen, the major German submarine construction center, is about forty miles upstream. And all the subs going to and from there sail right past Wesermuende. So Wesermuende is your priority. Get there, get a radio, and spot the subs for the British."

Hans Boelle laid a map of Berlin flat on the table, and explained to Karl the route he was to take and where to report when he reached that city. With a wistful smile, Boelle described the German capital as he remembered it before the war. He paused looked up, and smiled. "I envy you." And saying that, the tall blond man folded the map, rose and motioned Karl out the door.

Karl followed him to a black Mercedes sedan, and they drove to the German embassy, where a uniformed guard waved them through iron gates after a cursory inspection.

***

It was three o'clock the next afternoon, when Karl climbed aboard a Lufthansa Fokker Tri-Motor at the Madrid airport.

The big, square-bodied plane, with its huge overhead wing, lumbered down the concrete runway and lifted off toward Berlin.

Sitting at the big window under the wing, as they flew northeast, Karl watched the landscape turn from golden brown to dark green below the supporting strut.

After three short refueling stops, the young co-pilot poked his head into the cabin and announced that they were making an approach to the Berlin field. "We'll have cloud cover down to three thousand feet," he said. "And it may be a little rough going in."

The engine's roar quieted, and Karl felt the vibration in his seat lessen when the pilot throttled back. Now Karl heard the wind whistling past the window as they descended through milky clouds. Now and then, the plane dropped in air pockets, and he felt himself float in his seat, and then go heavy again. The boxy plane started to sway and bounce, and the old man beside him reached for a paper bag on the seat ahead. If I weren't a seaman, I'd probably be getting sick too, Karl said to himself.

Then they broke out over a dull gray landscape below the clouds where it rained. The old man next to him glanced nervously at Karl and folded the paper bag into its holder. Well, Karl thought, smiling to himself, I'm glad the old man made it.

He held his breath as the plane went into a tight turn, straightened, and glided toward a canyon of concrete structures; and as they descended, Karl gripped his seat, thinking he'd take a good sea storm any day over this. It looked as though the plane would hardly fit between the buildings.

Short bursts came from the three engines, as the plane leveled, and then sank quickly down between apartment houses, where Karl saw housewives hanging clothes on balcony lines, while children played at their feet.

They were down, bumping and jolting along gray, wet concrete, with the engines screaming and the cabin shaking, as the pilot reversed pitch and brought the big plane to a stop.

Then following a map on which Hans Boelle had sketched his route, Karl took a street car to the city's center. There, he exited at the Kaiser's old palace, a brown sandstone building facing Unter-den-Linden.

The famous boulevard was lined on each side with tall linden trees, just as Boelle had said. But even in good weather, the sun would never reach the tables at the outside cafes. They were hidden in the shadows of brown-and-green camouflage suspended on high poles over the street.

Turning his trenchcoat collar up against the raw mist, Karl carried his heavy bags west along the boulevard, past the Russian Embassy, the University of Berlin, the library, the huge and ornate opera house, and the finest hotels and most elegant shops in the world. Over all was a pervailing sense of gloom, not so much from the dark and wet sky, but from the flapping netting over his head.

Having walked a distance of less than a mile, Karl looked up to the imposing Brandenburg Gate. On the columned structure's top, he saw the chariot of victory from Napoleon's time, over which was now mounted the Nazi Swastika.

Passing through the big arch, he saw the burned-out Reichstag, where the former German Parliment, now disbanded, had given Hitler full powers.

Turning down Wilhelmstrasse, he walked to a guadrangle of government buildings, where he presented the papers Boelle had given him to a sentry at the Abwehr entrance. Receiving a sharp "Heil Hitler," with its stiff hand salute which he did not return, he followed the sentry into the musty building.

Inside, the sentry motioned to a clerk sitting at a polished wood desk, and clicked his heels, again saying, "Heil Hitler," and turned on his heel.

The sallow-faced clerk, with thin blue lips, rose slowly, glancing at the papers the sentry had handed him; and frowning at Karl, gave the Nazi salute.

Karl raised his right hand weakly. You'd think they'd get tired of this, he thought, and he said meekly, "Heil Hitler." Hell, I should have practiced this damn thing. Obviously I'm not showing the right amount of gusto, here. Otherwise this damned clerk wouldn't be shaking his head.

He followed the thin clerk up two flights of stone steps, along a marble hall, and through oak-framed glass doors, to a large waiting room, where everything was dark paneling and brown leather.

Karl sat in the waiting room, while the clerk spoke to an equally thin and pale woman behind a small desk. When the clerk left, the woman walked over to Karl. "Come with me, sir," she said, as he rose from his chair.

He followed her down a red-carpeted corridor to a dark walnut door. She knocked. Received a response, and opened the door. Karl nodded to her as she motioned him inside and closed the door behind him.

A tall slender woman, wearing a black uniform, with the familiar red arm band which displayed the Nazi Swastika in a white circle, stepped from behind a desk at the high windows. She was young, with very white-blonde hair swept back and pale blue eyes; and then he recognized the lisp, as she said, "Hello, Karl. Welcome to Berlin."

"Hello, Elska," he stammered, his throat feeling tight and dry. "I didn't expect to find you here."

"Like it?" She turned to display her SS uniform, which consisted of a black jacket trimmed in white, with white lightening bolts on the lapels, a black skirt, and high black boots.

"Very stunning."

"Karl," she was walking closer to him, "I've had you reassigned to our group. Waffen SS Intelligence Service."

Reaching out and taking his hand and pulling him closer, Elska said, "Now you'll be wearing the SS uniform, Karl."

She walked quickly to the desk and picked up a folder. "You've been assigned to radio communications. Intercept operator, with rank of signal-sergeant." She paused, and looking up from the folder, with her chin slightly elevated, said, "I'm a lieutenant."

"A lieutenant. That's good, Elska. Very good." He stood there, thinking, now what? "I'd like to be assigned to the North Sea coast," he stammered. "Can you do that?"

Striding quickly across the room, Elska stopped before him and said, "And we will make one thing clear from the start."

"What's that?"

"I make the decisions here, Karl. If we need you on the North Sea, that's where I'll send you. Now why is it you want to go north?"

"Well . . . I . . . Why not. It's the only seacoast in Germany. Why not? I want to be near the sea. That's my life."

She was in front of him suddenly and pulled him close and kissed him. Well, he thought, it's in the line of duty now, isn't it? And God knows I'm not going to say no. What is it? A woman scorned is what? Anyway, I'm not taking chances. So if this is what she wants . . ."

She stepped suddenly back and smiled at him. "You don't want to be that much closer to England, do you, Karl? To make contact with the British? Or to spy on our shipping?"

His face went white and his heart froze. Damn! That statement was for someone else. Someone in the building with earphones scribbling down everything they said. She's covering her ass. "Now Elska, if I weren't absolutely trustworty, your Uncle Heinrich wouldn't have sent me here." He paused and watched a smile grow on her face. "And if I weren't loyal to the Third Reich, I'd assume you'd be the first to know."

She nodded approval.

Christ, he said to himself, she hits me with that and I'm supposed to act natural. But the damn thing is, she got it right. Exactly right. But it's impossible. She couldn't know anything about Captain Harding. It's just a stupid coincidence.

Then still reeling in shock, Karl said quickly, "Did you know I was coming?"

"Certainly. I knew when you left New York. That's why all the paperwork's done."

Now he knew it was just a coincidence. She wasn't in New York when he left. She'd already gone to Germany. And she didn't even suspect Karl played a double role. All she knew was that he wanted to go north. She might even think Dr. Grauenhaft had given him an assignment up on the coast.

"And now here you are," she said with a smile.

"Yes, here I am." He laughed. "Now what do we do?"

"We continue where we left off." She returned to her chair on the other side of the desk and lifted the phone. "But first we'll get you quarters. Then you rest for the day. And report back here tomorrow at seven-thirty." She motioned Karl to a seat and spoke crisply into the phone.

Putting down the phone, she said without a trace of the lisp, "In a few minutes my clerk will escort you to your quarters on Bendlerstrasse."

"Did you say seven-thirty?" Karl asked— "in the morning?"

"Oh, yes, Karl. Our days start early here. But we finish by six. And we always take long lunch hours." She rose again and walked around the desk to him. "And tomorrow, when you've rested, we'll take a very long lunch hour—in my apartment."

***

Karl appeared at Elska's office promptly at seven-thirty the next morning, still wearing the gray suit in which he left New York, and which by now was very badly wrinkled.

"Never mind the suit," Elska said. "You'll get your uniform today, and then we can have your suit cleaned and pressed." She paused and looked at him seriously. "I suggest, however, that you throw it away. It's obviously American and not very much in style. You won't have much use for civilian clothes. But if you'd like, I'll help you find something."

She lit a cigarette from her gold case, and smiled at Karl from behind her desk. "We have some very good shops in Berlin. I can dress you most elegantly." She looked at him with sparkling eyes. "I think you'll be most handsome in your uniform, Karl. Try it. And then see if you have any real need for a suit?"

She paused and looked at him coolly. "I think you'll like your assignment, Karl. Radio interception."

Karl nodded.

"And it's on the North Sea coast. That's what you wanted. And today we'll complete your political indoctrination. After that, you'll start training with Captain Blautisch."

"Where?"

"In Berlin, Karl. In this building. But I have you for the week. We can cover what I have in a few days. And then we'll take a little vacation, if you agree."

"Oh, I agree. I'm not all that anxious to get started."

"I assume you remember Morse code from your Navigation School?"

"Yes. I was never very good. But I remember it."

***

Karl was fitted for a uniform later that morning and for lunch they ate at an outside cafe overlooking the Havel river. When they finished, they took a street car to Elska's flat on Bucherstrasse.

"You must always be careful," she whispered to Karl on the streetcar.

Everyone's an informer. It's an honor in the Third Reich. Children inform on parents and receive medals. Trust no one." She bent close and brushed her lips across his cheek. "Yes, Karl, I belong to the Schildwache, and our time will come."

It had been a long time since Karl held a woman. Elska was a beautiful girl, marred only by her unfortunate lisp. But that wasn't all of it. No. And it seemed to Karl, in her flat, as he held her in his arms, that he was holding something he might yet lose, his sanity perhaps, and even his respect for human dignity. This was a mad world. Full of pomp and comic majesty—Berlin—could this be the world of the future, a life where ordinary and rational men were pushed into darkness, and you watched silently, while psychotics took command and pushed toward total destruction. And then he could think of nothing but the full, moist lips against his, demanding, and her supple body which trembled in his arms and the firm breasts against his naked chest, and her arms locked around his neck and the soft, gasping noises she was making in his ear.

They lay there for a long time in each other's arms; and when he left her warm bed, he put on his Waffen-SS uniform, the gray wool trousers, the gray tunic with white lightening on the contrasting black collar; and the gray military cap with the German eagle on its high peak and the skull and cross bones, the SS death-head, embroidered on its black bill.

***

Karl completed his training to the satisfaction of his commander, a lieutenant ten years his junior who once was a concert violinist in Vienna, and who now followed Hitler with blind enthusiasm. Having received his orders and said good-bye to Elska at the central Berlin station, Karl rode the night express to Wesermuende on the North Sea coast. It was Sunday when he arrived, November 9, 1941, just four weeks before the Japanese attack on Pearl Harbor.

At that time, America and Germany were still at peace. But nevertheless, Karl didn't know what to expect when he reported to his duty station with the Waffen SS. Although he was born an Austrian, he'd lived most of his life in America. There's bound to be a lot of suspicion, that he knew. Certainly not everyone will buy this story of a sudden love for the Third Reich. But then again, maybe they will believe it. He'd gotten this far, thanks to Dr. Grauenhaft and the Abwehr.

The Waffen SS were so thoroughly indoctrinated in Nazi propaganda, Karl felt they'd follow Hitler to hell. And why not the same for a young

Austrian? Why couldn't he become a loyal Nazi? Sure, the question answers itself, he thought. Whenever anyone asks me, I counter with the statement questioning their loyalty. Yes—what do they think Hitler is? Why shouldn't I support him and the Nazis? Is there some reason I shouldn't follow his grand plan? Do they think Hitler is someone to be scoffed at? And only if one doesn't believe in Hitler could he reject the Third Reich. Pure logic says anyone with any sense believes in Hitler, doesn't it? Therefore, to question my loyalty is to question one's belief in Hitler's power of persuasion. And with those thoughts, he went to see his commander, SS Lieutenant Christian Kirsh.

"The SS are an elite group," Lieutenant Kirsh said to him from behind his walnut desk on the second floor of radio operations. He pawed at the black collar of his field-gray tunic. "We're not the tools of the Gestapo, those civilans who arrest in the dark morning hours. We're a military unit. The best. And we interceptors are the best of the best. Now, my friend," he said, fixing his watery blue eyes intently upon Karl, "you have special qualifications. You're fast on code, and you understand English. I have a special mission for you—succeed and our unit will receive a commendation; I'll be promoted, and I'll see that you're justly rewarded."

"Sir?"

"On May 10th, Rudolf Hess, Hitler's Deputy, flew to England in a light plane. My job, Sergeant Meister, is to find out whether he made it and what the English did with him. That's your assignment. I want Hess!" The chubby officer slapped a hand on the desk and then jumped to his feet. "Heil Hitler!"

Karl sprang from his chair and returned the stiff-armed salute. "Yes, sir. Understood. Heil Hitler." And then he followed a lance-corporal to his station where the corporal handed him earphones and gestured to a booth with a small table upon which sat an Olympia typewriter in front of a rack containing two short-wave receivers. The corporal smiled wyrly. "Welcome aboard, Sergeant." And as Karl slid onto the wooden chair at the table and adjusted his headsets, the corporal leaned close. "Gave you the old Hess witch-hunt talk, did he. Well good luck. The frequencies we're searching now are on the pad there—Herman's pad." And as the corporal turned to leave, he said over his shoulder. "Herman failed on the Hess mission—he's now at the Russian front."

So there's humor with the SS, Karl said to himself. But it's not very damned funny. And flipping through the dog-eared note pad, Karl frowned. God, he thought, I have no idea what I'm doing. It looks like Herman didn't either. And plugging in his phone jack, he spun the dials to the frequencies jotted down by his predecessor, thinking it's damned unlikely the English will take to the air and tell all they know about Hess. Then he felt a hand on his shoulder, and looking up saw the corporal smiling at him again. "I forgot to tell you," the corporal said through his smile, "the British code is in the drawer."

And when Karl pulled open the drawer he found a spiral bound document with the Abwehr imprint. German Central Intelligence had broken the English code.

***

Karl's quarters were in a two-story brick building overlooking the Weser River. He decided to act quickly. At the end of the midnight shift, he signed out a portable transmitter, and taped the antenna to his barracks window. It was a perfect transmission site, a straight line to England over open water beyond the river dyke.

He worked feverishly, practicing the message with the transmitter key disconnected, until he achieved maximum sending speed. He decided to transmit in plain English on the priority frequency he knew was monitored by the best British agents at Dover. He could send only once, and his transmission had to be brief. He decided to send at high speed and hope for the best. You fool, he thought, as he wired up the transmitter key. Idiot. Sending messages from the backyard of the Waffen SS.

Pausing and taking a deep breath, he seized the key and hammered out the message: "Peter. Need credibility. Info Hess, please. Your code." And he gave the frequency and time he would monitor. Then having finished the transmission, Karl returned the radio to storage and destroyed the sign-out sheet. Looking at his watch, he calculated he had the radio in his possession for twenty-one minutes; and having returned it without being discovered and destroyed the record, no one would know he had taken it.

Three nights later, Karl sat before his receivers in the intercept building at the far side of the quadrangle. He had copied reams of British communications since sending his message, and now, on the assigned frequency and at the time specified, he picked up call signs he had not previously heard. He adjusted his ear phones, and his good right hand raced over the typewriter while his left forefinger tapped keys in rhythm to it.

Damn, he thought, this is it, this is it, and those fellows have someone who can send faster than me. Then when the transmission ended he opened his cyrptographic book and decoded the message. As the words took form, he rang for Lt. Kirsh, who came to the center, rubbing sleep from his eyes.

"Lieutenant," Karl said. "We have it." He read the intercepted message: "Rudolf Hess arrived Scotland night of May 10th. Aircraft landed safely under escort. Hess working with British for separate peace. Supports anti-Nazi elements in Germany." Karl put down his notes. "That's it, sir."

"Sergeant," Kirsh said, "this is wonderful. "Unbelieveable."

"It could be a ruse, sir. But it's an authentic transmission. Central London Admiralty to all ships at sea."

"We've done it, Sergeant. We've beat Canaris this time."

"Sir," Karl asked innocently, smiling inwardly, "why would they transmit such a message with routine traffic?"

"I don't know the answer to that, Sergeant. But this goes straight to Berlin."

"May I suggest caution, sir. I don't know. There's something about the message—and it was transmitted at very high speed—much too high for ship traffic." And all the time Karl was thinking, I'm going to cover my ass, just in case.

"Very well, Sergeant. I'll forward this with your comments. But my God we did it, Sergeant. I'd love to see that red-faced Canaris when this hits Berlin."

Karl watched as the fat lieutenant bounced on his heels, and then rushed off to the security cable room.

The following Monday, Karl saw a shadow fall over his typewriter while he worked his receivers, and turned to see the beaming face of Lt. Kirsh.

"Sergeant," Kirsh said as Karl removed his headset, "we did it. Canaris confirmed the report."

"Congratulations, sir."

"Thank you, Sergeant. Thank you." And Kirsh again bobbed up and down on his heels and left the room, whistling a tune from the *Three Penny Opera*.

As signal-sergeant, it was Karl's job to assemble the non-priority interceptions at the close of the midnight shift each Monday. As he sorted the British communications, he stopped short and took a deep breath when his eyes fell upon a message copied by Private Engelhass. The interception time was 0011 hours the previous Thursday. He knew it was his transmission to Dover.

But the message was garbled. No one will be able to decipher this, Karl said to himself, as he read the characters: "Pe-t—. Need cr———t—y. Info 5ss." He smiled, when he saw that the new recruit had run all the dots of H and E together and mistook them for the number 5. But then his throat tightened. The bastard picked off the reply frequency. Of all the dumb luck, he thought. Below the copied message the Private had typed: "Strong signal. High speed transmission. Do not recognize sender."

Karl's phony message on Hess had gone straight to Berlin as top priority. Engelhass' interception would go by courier in the morning. The cryptographer in Berlin would connect the two messages; and since all intercepted communications were numbered sequentially, he couldn't destroy Engelhass' work without raising suspicion.

With sweating palms and fear knotting his stomach, Karl sat at his desk and studied his Dover transmission. It won't be hard for them to fill in the blanks. They'll figure out the word "Peter" for sure. And the frequency is right there—the frequency I asked for. My God, my God, he said to himself over and over. Then overwhelmed by the realization his one and only transmission had ended his career, he closed his eyes and thought about those peaceful years fishing for lake trout and whitefish on Lake Michigan. And why had it come to this—all because of one stupid mistake—an ego trip. He wanted to scoop the Abwehr on Hess—make a fast name for himself. And now they would scoop him—his body that is, after the firing squad. They'd just scoop it up and throw it into an unmarked grave.

***

On Long Island, it was a little after three o'clock in the morning. Dark-clothed, grim-faced and silent young men hurried about the Grauenhaft mansion. Three men stuffed documents into the basement incinerator. Others packed radio equipment into concealed luggage compartments. In groups of two and three, they piled into cars and station wagons and drove down the long tree-lined drive and out the iron gate for the last time.

Under the slate roof in the attic, Dr. Grauenhaft puffed on a cigar and nervously paced behind a radio operator intent on glowing dials. "Any word from the sub?" he asked the radioman.

The operator raised his hand for silence and pressed the headset tighter to his ear. Then he swiviled in his chair and said, "It's on the surface." And swinging quickly back to his transmitting key, hammered out a short message. He waited for a moment, and when the high pitched dashes and dots in his earphones stopped, he said without turning his head, "Message received and confirmed."

"Good."

Dr. Grauenhaft nodded to the young man seated near the door, who then raised a .45 and squeezed off three rounds into the radioman's back.

The man with the gun switched off the light and followed Grauenhaft from the room, locking the door behind him. As they went quickly down the stairs, Dr. Grauenhaft said to the man with the gun, "Damned double agent. And I'm the one responsible for sending Meister to Germany." He paused on the second floor landing. "Is the launch ready?"

"Yes, Herr Doctor. Everything's in order."

"Good." Heinrich Grauenhaft looked at his watch. "Meet me on the beach at three-thirty." Then he turned and went to his study where he picked up a photograph of his niece, Elska Banghardt, and slipped it into a leather case.

In the dark radio room, the operator raised his head slowly. He saw the orange dials glowing through a fog, reached out and turned the knob on the transmitter. Using the last of his strength, he pushed his right hand forward, found the transmitting key, and tapped out his last message.

Five

In Wesermuende, it was already nine-thirty that morning. Having faced what he now considered the inevitable, Signal Sergeant Karl Meister was much calmer. He'd thought it all through. Well, I'll just meet it head-on, and see what happens.

So that morning he handed Engelhass' interception to Lt. Kirsh, saying, "Herr Lieutenant, look at this. We can't send in this sloppy work, especially when we've done so well on Hess. The Abwehr will be looking critically at everything. And this is abominable," Karl shook his head. "Very poor work, sir—he's missed characters—what he does have is wrong—I don't think you want this waved about Berlin when you're up for promotion."

"Sergeant, you're right. Very bad work."

"And look here, sir, he says it's a very strong signal. So Berlin will find no excuse. And, no doubt the bungler's copied the local Luftwaffe."

"Yes—yes, Sergeant. I think you're right."

"Sir, I don't have authority to delete sequential numbers, otherwise I wouldn't bother you with this trash. But I've taken the liberty of noting on the transmittal sheet that this item was destroyed—on your order—erroneous interception of local traffic."

"Yes, Sergeant." The Lieutenant puffed out his chest and smiled broadly. "I have that authority, you know."

On the graveyard shift that night, Karl walked up behind Private Engelhass and said, "A word of caution my young friend. Strong signals mean a local military unit. You won't make corporal by sending Berlin garbled Luftwaffe transmissions."

***

During that week, Karl sent three more messages from his room overlooking the Weser River. Each time, he waited until after midnight, and took the storage room key from Kirsh's desk. Then he unlocked the security area door, and took the black-cased telefunken transmitter from its shelf. After he sent his message, Karl returned the transmitter, destroyed the sign-out sheet to which he had forged Kirsh's name, and returned the key.

Finally, he thought, I'm sending something useful. From his room overlooking the dyke, he could see far out the wide Weser entrance to the North Sea. It was from the sea that the U-Boats came, some battle-scarred and running rough, as they plowed the river's surface past his window. You know it's a major overhaul when they come in here, he remembered. The submarines operate from bases on the French coast. But this is where they come for the big jobs. They come back to where they were built—forty miles up the river at the Bremen shipyards. They all came to Bremen. Even the ones that had been made in Wesermuende, just south of his barracks. And a few of the earlier ones which were built in the Navy shipyards across the river at Wilhelmshaven for the first World War.

So he watched the subs go up the river for repairs. Never very many. Just a few now and then. Those battered boats didn't interest Karl. But the reconditioned U-Boats and the new submarines coming down the river was something important. If he'd let the British know they were coming, they'd catch them in the shallow North Sea, or in the English channel, or when they tried a run around England's north coast.

He copied down the U-Boat numbers as they motored past below his window. At night he sent his messages, using the simple code he'd learned from Harvey; where he translated everything into digits, added the year of his birth, subtracted his age, and added the days from September 15th, the start of his mission.

***

"It's an easy system to remember, Karl," Harvey had told him over coffee at the officer's club on Lake Ontario. "Your code will always be different from any other agent. And on the fifth block you start with a clear 'P.' That tells us what we need to know for your code." Harvey looked at him for a long time and smiled. "Sure," he said, "You're wondering if it'll take the Germans long to figure that out. Well, the answer is—it won't." Harvey paused and smiled again. "But by the time you've sent enough messages for them to get a handle on your code, you'll probably be spotted and located by direction-finding equipment." Taking a long drag on his black cigar, the Englishman smiled at Karl over his coffee and said, "And then it's all over. So remember, Karl the important thing isn't the code. Hell, you could send in plain English and it wouldn't make any difference. We're the ones that'll use the information. But it does slow the Germans down a bit. Now what's really important—"

"Is to keep moving. Never send from the same spot twice," Karl interrupted.

"You're damned right. Remember that and you'll be okay. And Karl, don't stay more than six months. Get out. No matter how important you think you are, get out. Nothing justifies the risk. Don't try to be a hero. Hell, no one will know what you did anyway."

***

But Karl had now sent eight messages from the antenna tapped to his barracks window, and he knew he could be in trouble. It had happened once. His broadcasts fed off onto the local SS collecting antennae, spilling over a wide range of frequencies. What else is there to do, he wondered? You don't just sit here and let this pass.

Disregarding Harvey's warnings, Karl sent again. He continued sending, night after night. He was sending fast, hoping the interceptors couldn't copy his speed. But then bits and pieces of his messages started showing up in the daily traffic.

Then, when he looked at the night operations log on Thursday, and saw the graveyard shift had called for a fix on one of his transmissions, he realized no more messages could be sent from his barracks window. It had been a short transmission, completed before the operator finished his call. However, the German DF unit was certain to be monitoring the frequency—and the next time his signal went out, they'd draw lines on a map which criss-crossed within ten feet of his radio.

He replaced the operations log on its peg, stole a transmitting key and three cyrstals from the maintenance room, and in the morning took a train to Hamburg wearing his SS Uniform. It was time to build his own transmitter, using crystals, rather than the Telefunken unit with its unreliable coil which spread the signal over such a wide range of frequencies.

The clerk at Radio Suhr in Hamburg snapped to attention with a crisp "Heil Hitler," as Karl entered the small shop. "Heil Hitler," Karl replied;. and when the only other customer left the shop, Karl pointed to a transceiver in the glass case behind the bald clerk. "I'll take that."

The clerk looked at Karl's black-gloved hand and surveyed his uniform. "Ya," the clerk said nervously and opened a thick ledger, "my last Peilwinkel. Is this an offical purchase?"

Karl pointed to the white SS lighting bolts on his tunic, and said, "You're not to make any entries, understand?"

"Ya, ya."

"And I'll make no report. It's fortunate for you, my friend, that this is your last transceiver," he said to the shaking shopkeeper, "You must know this unit is on the restricted list!"

"Ya! No! Herr Sergeant. I had no idea—"

"They're in short supply." Karl pulled a small notebook from his vest pocket and entered the name and serial number of the transceiver, then the date and the words "purchased at Radio Suhr, 11 Wiesmuelerstrasse, Hamburg, proprieter . . ."

"You own this shop?" Karl asked.

"Yes, sir."

"Your name?"

"Suhr, Otto Suhr."

"Very good," Karl said and entered the shopkeeper's name. "Sign here, please Herr Suhr."

Karl counted out the purchase price in Reichsmarks. "No receipt," he said. "But please wrap this in brown paper."

Karl smiled to himself as he closed the door behind him and heard the shopkeeper say for the third time, "Heil Hitler—Seig Heil—and victory to the Third Reich, Herr Sergeant."

Upon his return to Wesermuende, Karl stopped at a small shop across the street from the main train station and purchased a block of Leineweber chocolate imported from Buenos Aires. He opened it in his room on the second floor of the barracks; and when he heated the label with his cigarette lighter, brown numbers and code letters appeared inside the label—the new British frequencies and transmission priority codes, under date of October 4, 1941.

After having memorized the new frequencies, Karl Meister took a bus to the military motor pool at the foot of Hafenstrasse where he signed out a Mercedes SS staff sedan—the privilege Kirsh, now promoted to Captain, had promised him as a result of the Hess scoop. Leaving the motor pool early that clear and sunny afternoon, he drove with the black Mercedes to Cuxhaven, a small city at the mouth of the Elbe River, twenty-five miles to the north.

There, he turned west along a narrow road, drove through the village of Sahlenburg to where the road ended at the white sandy beach overlooking the North Sea, stopped the car, and lit a cigarette. Then he walked first north, then south along the beach. The coast there was deserted—no buildings or signs of habitation. He returned to the car, clipped a power cord to its battery, inserted the other end into a voltage converter, and connected the transceiver. Then he strung the antenna along the top of the windshield, and opened the transmitter case. Now, he said to himself, I earn my keep.

Karl made contact with the British at Dover, and when he received his acknowledgement, he started his messages, pounding the code key mounted inside the transmitter case. He told Dover his SS unit had the British codes, as well as the call signs used to alert fighters which intercepted the Nazi bombers.

All during the previous week, Karl had copied several German military networks while on duty. He ran everything through Enigma, the German cipher machine, while he was the ranking man in charge of operations on the night shift. Now he sent the British everything he'd learned about the Nazi war machine: troop movements, aircraft deployments, General Staff assignments, and weapons production schedules.

When these communications were acknowledged, Karl switched the Peilwinkel to monitor. He knew he'd transmitted long enough for the German DF units to obtain a general location fix. Even the new man, Engelhass, would have picked me up, he thought. And I'm not there to stop him from calling DF. It's time to get the hell out of here.

Backing the sedan onto the dirt road, he returned to Sahlenburg and followed a small road along the deserted seacoast, receiving further messages from British Intelligence as he drove south past low dunes and marshes. It was during this drive that Karl received a request for any information concerning new weapons development.

He'd seen reports of rocket and jet engine testing at the Heinkel plant in Rostock, and he stopped briefly, hammered out that message, took down the antenna and slid the transceiver under the driver's seat.

Turning east again at the small village of Spieka, Karl drove three miles to Route 6, the main highway from Cuxhaven to Wesermuende. Except for an occassional bicycle on the path along the road, there was no vehicle traffic on the broad asphalt highway.

Karl heard the shrill warble of what sounded like a police siren, and slowed the Mercedes. He realized it was a German mobile direction finding vehicle when he saw a blue-gray communications van round the curve ahead, coming at high speed, with a loop antenna rotating slowly above its roof.

"Too late." Karl smiled to himself as the truck roared past in the direction of Cuxhaven. But that was too damned close.

On the next day, as Karl sifted the routine traffic interceptions, he noted that Private Engelhass had taken down parts of his messages. The man was getting better—and the private had ordered direction finding.

"I see you've copied some local transmitter," Karl said to Engelhass, joining the thin blond man at a table in the coffee shop below the radio rooms.

"Yes," the private answered curtly. "And this time I know it's not the Luftwaffe. We have no Luftwaffe at Cuxhaven."

"Cuxhaven?"

"Yes, Sergeant. I checked with DF. The direction was north—that's Cuxhaven."

Karl leaned forward itently, "Engelhass, you may have found a spy ship."

"Spy ship?"

"Certainly. It doesn't have to be a land-based transmission."

"Well . . . I don't know . . . Do you think it could be a boat?"

"It could be anything, private," Karl said, sipping his coffee. "But keep your eyes open. If you find him, you could receive a Hitler Medal, you know."

"But, sergeant . . . I don't think it was a boat."

"And why's that, Private?"

"Because, Sergeant, there was a change of location—about ten degrees."

"Ah," Karl said. "You mean a change in direction."

"Yes. Ten degrees. But that's movement. Much too far for a ship at sea, nothing could be that fast."

"No," Karl replied. "Not a ship at sea. But a small boat, close in. A fishing boat out of Cuxhaven. That could be the answer."

"But look here, Sergeant," the private said and took a map from his pocket, "it was low tide. If a boat transmitted from this direction north," the private pointed to a line he had drawn on the map from the Wesermuende DF station to the coast near Sahlenburg, "and then four minutes later from a point along this line," and he pointed to a second line which intercepted the coast southwest of Sahlenburg, "and this was a boat—at least thirty miles miles out—that's how far shallow water runs at low tide there—that vessel," the private paused and produced a notebook upon which he made several quick computations, "would be doing fifty knots. No fishing boat run that fast!"

"Private," Karl said calmly, "you should report these findings to Captain Kirsh. He'll be most interested."

"Well, sir . . . I did—and he didn't look at them—just screamed and said I had almost cost him a promotion by copying our Luftwaffe. Do you think, Sergeant, you could talk to him?"

"Yes, private. I will," Karl nodded sympathetically.

"It's very important to me, sir. I've been a private for a year. And already passed over for corporal before I came here." Engelhass lit a cigarette with shaking hands. "And," the private continued with a fearful look now in his eyes, "if I'm passed over once more . . . it means . . . the Russian Front."

"I see. I see," Karl said and paused, lighting his cigarette and turning to the young man. "Well, private, I'll do what I can."

"Thank you, sir. Thank you." And the private took Karl's hand and shook it vigorously. "I was a Hitler Youth commander. I must advance. It's expected."

"Yes," Karl said. "I understand." But you're too eager for me, Karl thought. And I know what you did in the Hitler Youth. You did what they all did. Informed on your neighbors, maybe even your parents. And you'll do anything to advance in the SS. Leaning back then in his chair and drawing on his cigarette, Karl said to himself, and I think it'd be much better if you were sent to the Russian Front.

That evening Karl sat in the stuffy communications center, monitoring Dover radar. Damn, he said to himself, the English haven't changed call signs or frequencies. And when British radar passed the word to inland fighter bases, Karl intercepted the message, using the old cipher book, and gave it to the man in operations, who then radioed the German bombers, telling them the English would have planes aloft in minutes, and giving the German pilots the precise airfields from which the fighter planes would take off.

Hell, Karl thought, there's no excuse for this, I risk my neck, and they ignore the message. Warn the British. Tell them everything we have. And what do they do with it? Nothing. Harvey knew it was me. He knows I'm reliable.

The next morning, Karl learned all English transmissions had gone silent on the graveyard shift, during the time Private Engelhass was intercepting the radar stations.

"That bungling idiot," Captain Kirsh screamed.

"Sir?" Karl had just greeted the Captain with his customary, "Heil Hitler," and he was startled by the fierce tone in the Captain's voice. "What's happened?"

"Engelhass. He's screwed up again, Sergeant. Must have been sleeping. The English changed call signs—frequencies too —and Engelhass missed it all."

"Do you mean, sir, he didn't get the new call signs?"

"Nothing. He claims all transmissions just went dead. Now that's never happened. They always give the new frequency in code, and the call signs, and it's a matter of minutes before we have them again." Captain Kirsh's face had gone bright red and he paced up and down the room, then whirled suddenly to face Karl. "Goering called me this morning. Wanted to know what the hell had happened. Tremendous losses, Sergeant. He said the English came from nowhere—and no warning from us. What could I tell him. Nothing. Nothing at all!"

"Maybe I can find out what happened," Karl said to Captain Kirsh, who was jumping up and down on his toes and twisting his hands. "Where's Engelhass, sir?"

"That . . . That . . . I'll never see his face again, Sergeant. He's gone. I shipped him to the Russian front ten minutes ago."

***

Five hundred miles southeast of New York, a German submarine broke the dark surface and signaled a freighter rolling slowly on the night swells. The forward hatch opened on the U-Boat and four seaman scrambled onto the iron deck and inflated a black rubber boat. They slid the boat into the water and motioned to Dr. Grauenhaft, who climbed out the open hatch.

Then the two seamen on the sub handed the big German down to waiting hands in the rubber boat, and jumped in after him. A few minutes later, Dr. Grauenhaft swung in a cargo net and was hoisted aboard the old freighter, bound for Lisbon.

***

The third week in November came cold and wet, with low black clouds rolling in on the wind from the North Sea. These were bleak and cheerless days, but nevertheless Karl's heart sang. Each night, he worked the dials of his two receivers, searching for the missing Dover network lost by Private Engelhass. He would like to lose them forever—but that couldn't be. Luftwaffe pressure on the Wesermuende SS contingent mounted daily. And when he tuned in to the BBC nightly broadcasts on his lower receiver and heard the mounting toll of German bombers lost to the RAF, he knew there'd be another call from Goering in the morning.

Karl recognized the peculiar rhythm of the unseen but familiar hand, which tapped out warnings of approaching bombers. You still drag the key a little too much on your "Es," he said to himself. And I'd know your little singsong anywhere. No, you can't hide from me. Not the way you send. He had found the British radar network. Now what, he wondered? If I turn this in, a lot of German pilots will turn and run for home. If I do nothing, they'll go down in flames over the English coast. And how many of those men are Austrians?

There wasn't really any choice, and Karl knew that. Sooner or later another German unit would recognize the sending pattern and pick up the Dover network. Or maybe one of the other operators on his shift, or the graveyard shift, would make the discovery. Right now his entire unit was in jeopardy—they could all be shipped to the Russian front—the Nazi answer to any military failure. And Captain Kirsh was desperate. Goering had made a personal plea to Hitler, advising that the battle for the air over Britian would be lost without radar interceptions. "And Hitler issued a directive to Himmler," Captain Kirsh had told Karl earlier that day from behind his desk.

"Yes Captain?" Karl asked, when after a long pause the captain said nothing further, but only grew paler and chewed on his fat lip.

"Yes . . . " Kirsh was sweating and wringing his hands, "and Himmler called me. Me—personally. He told me I wasn't immune to SD." And Karl remembered SD stood for the liquidation detachment of the SS; those men responsible for exterminating the Polish intelligensia. This fat officer looking at him from behind his desk had taken great pleasure in relating his exploits in Poland. And now Karl was inwardly amused to see the terror on Kirsh's face—the captain was threatened by his old unit. It was a far different look from the wide rubbery grin through which Kirsh had recounted his court -martial. "We were acting under orders of the Governor General," Kirsh said. "And his orders came directly from Hitler. That fool General Blaskowitz had us arrested. And then tried under Army Court-Martial," Kirsh explained, pressing a thick finger into his massive jowel. "And then the executions started," he continued. "Imagine, Sergeant, officers of the elite SS shot on charges of murder, arson, and rape. The Army simply didn't understand. Those were terrible, terrible times, Sergeant. I, too, was condemned to death—by the German Army!"

The fat man leaned back in his chair and roared with laughter. "There I was. Awaiting my fate, along with the best of the SS and the finest German policemen in the Polish districts." Kirsh paused again and then said, "Those were dark days, Sergeant. Dark days, indeed. But then the order for my release came. And the SS detachments were finally separated from Army command, as it should be, Sergeant, as it should be," he said and thumped his big fist on the desk. "And then there was a violent dispute between the Army and the SS," Kirsh went on. "Next, General Petzel joined with

Blaskowitz; the entire staff of the German Polish command plotted against us, constantly interfering with our handling of the Jews." Kirsh again smiled his big rubbery smile. "But then it all came to an end when Himmler came to Poland. He had brought a report sent by Blaskowitz directly to Hitler on 'The Persecution of the Jews.' Himmler burned that report," Kirsh said gleefully, "right on Blaskowitz's desk—in front of his face, Sergeant. And from that day, we were free of Army interference." Kirsh let out a big howl when he finished. Then his face clouded. "But it was not without cost, Sergeant. We lost some of our finest men."

Kirsh's career was over. He faced a return to the Russian front. The heavy man sat there, sweating and pawing at the thick skin folds which protruded from his collar; and as Karl watched the pale man, smiling inwardly and enjoying the irony, he heard a knock on the door, which opened at Kirsh's command.

A thin clerk stepped in. "A call for Sergeant Meister, sir—Berlin."

Karl excused himself and followed the clerk to the Adjutant's Office, where the thin man handed him a field phone, saying, "I think it's a personal call." With a nod, the clerk turned on his heel and closed the door, leaving Karl alone in the dimly lit room.

"Elska," Karl replied to the mellow voice with the lisp, "it's good to hear from you."

She wanted to know why he hadn't answered her letters. "It's not the same as talking to you," he said. "I'm just not a letter writer. I'm sorry, Elska . . . Yes. Yes. I promise. I'll write, I really will."

"I understand your weather is bad up there," Elska said over the phone. And when Karl didn't respond, she said more slowly, "Heavy overcast, and no sun for five days."

"Yes," Karl answered. "It's been pretty gloomy here."

And then Elska said further, "But we have a brighter forecast. And to cheer you up, mother baked a special cake, from a new recipe." Now Karl was confused. Elska's mother lived in Norway with her father. But maybe she joined her daughter in Germany after the Nazi invasion. And why in the hell would she bake me a cake. I don't even know the woman. "Why that's great, Elska. But I'm here in Wesermuende . . . Is your mother with you now?"

"Don't worry, Karl. A special courier is coming your way tomorrow. I'll send it along with him. It's right out of the oven, Karl."

He understood, or at least he thought he did. This was her way of saying Berlin SS had the new English codes from the Abwehr. The code name for Admiral Canaris, the intelligence chief, was "mother."

As he thanked her for the information and hung up the phone, the Adjudant's clerk came in with a personal message from Captain Kirsh. "I don't understand it," the clerk shook his head, "Kirsh told me, 'Tell Sergeant Meister I'm not going alone.'" The clerk shrugged his shoulders. "I suppose you know what it means."

Knowing full well that it was now a matter of self preservation, Karl Meister, the Austrian immigrant who had sworn loyalty to the United States of America, set to work that night to solve the puzzle and save the Nazi bombers from destruction.

He spun his radio dials to the left and right of the frequency where he'd heard the familiar signal, and copied the new call signs and a long message. The English began sending short blocks of letters and numbers. He knew it was an alert to the fighter bases and picked up the phone and called Captain Kirsh in his quarters.

"I believe we have them, sir," Karl said to the Captain, who stumbled up to his desk, red-eyed and whiskey smelling. "This is an air alert. I think we should warn the Luftwaffe." Karl looked at his watch. "The English are scrambling now."

"Are you certain?"

"Yes, sir—I am."

"Then you call, Sergeant. I'll take full responsibility, you understand." Captain Kirsh was wringing his hands as he spoke. Karl knew what the man was thinking. If the warning turned out false, Signal-Sergeant Meister is the one who'll hang.

"Yes, sir," Karl replied, and issued a general warning over the Luftwaffe line, advising of the British scramble.

Throughout the night, Karl studied his intercepted Dover communications. He identified the call signs for three fighter bases.

Well, he thought, until the new codes get here, I'll see if I can't show up the Abwehr a bit. It won't hurt to let Berlin know we also have some good intelligence in the field at Wesermuende. Late in the night, Karl issued a positive interception warning, giving two of four bases scrambled, with flight directions and estimated time of arrival. Kirsh still refused to let the warnings go out under his name. You're a damned idiot, Kirsh, he thought. I know what I'm doing. And when confirmation comes, Berlin will know. They won't be fooled. They'll know you ducked your job. And it won't be long before you see the Russian front after all.

And then it came. For the second time that night now, the Enigma machine clanked out confirmation by the Luftwaffe. Karl's warning was accurate. The German bombers were intercepted. But they'd climbed and when the English fighters came, the bombers turned and ran for a secondary target and then for home. There were no serious losses.

Karl stared at the last last line of the message on the gray Enigma machine, which read: "Thank you Sergeant Meister."

***

Rubbing his face awake in the morning, Karl heard banging on his door. "Sergeant!" a high voice from the other side of the door said. "Wake up, Sergeant. You have a personal message from Himmler!"

Opening the door, Karl saw the smiling Adjutant's clerk, who handed him a folded paper with the familiar perforations of the Enigma machine. "Congratulations, Sergeant," the clerk said and saluted. "And there's a packet here for you too, sir. It just arrived by courier from Berlin." The clerk handed over a large manila envelope as Karl closed the door.

Sitting down on his bed, he scanned the document from from SS Chief Himmler: "Goebels was estatic, and the Fuehrer sends his congratulations," the message concluded.

Karl broke the seal on the manila envelope from Berlin SS. Inside the packet was an advance copy of the key words and instructions for deciphering the new English code.

He dressed quickly, stuffed the envelope in his vest pocket, put on his greatcoat, and walked down the stairs and along the stone path between tall aspen trees, whose bare limbs swayed in the cold wind from the North Sea.

The radio building was at the end of the long walk. There, a black staff car, with German war flags snapping from its fenders, came abruptly to a halt. The uniformed driver stepped briskly around the car's long hood and opened the rear door.

A tall lieutenant in SS uniform emerged from the Mercedes limousine and strode up the three steps to the brick building, followed by the driver. The sentry at the door saluted with a stiff arm, stepped aside, and the tall officer and his driver disappeared through the door.

When Karl came up on the landing, he gave the sentry his mumbled, "Heil Hitler," receiving a stiff hand salute in return, and said, "Well, Franzi, I see we have a visitor."

"Ya, Herr Sergeant."

Karl leaned close to the short, middle-aged man. "Franzi, I know Max is your drinking buddy," he said, referring to the Adjutant's clerk. "Now tell me, who's the new lieutenant."

The sentry stiffened. "Sergeant, I know nothing which isn't my official duty."

"But, Franzi, how many times did I give you a lift when you had too much to drink, or left your sweetheart's flat late? Come on now, Franzi, return the favor. Nothing gets past Max. Who is it?" Karl nodded to the staff car.

"Well Sergeant," the sentry said with a quick smile, "he's Kirsh's replacement."

"Replacement! Ah . . . Thank you, Franzi."

"Sergeant . . ."

"Yes Franzi?"

"Please don't call me Franzi. The men . . . Herr Sergeant . . . Address me as Private Rothfuss . . . The men think I have special favors."

"You do," Karl said, and poked a finger in the sentry's bulging stomach, "I give you rides in my staff car so you can linger over your girlfriend's strudel." Karl turned and strode swiftly through the big doors, where loud voices came from down the hall. Stopping and poking his head into the Adjutant's office, he said to Max, "Captain Kirsh seems to be unhappy with his new assignment."

The thin clerk looked at his watch, saying, "News travels fast, doesn't it? Just two hours ago, Captain Kirsh was reassigned for duty on the the Russian front—the Sixth Army, under General Blaskowitz. He's a regular Army man now."

Karl couldn't contain a smile. "I'm sure he'll find that a pleasant experience."

That afternoon Karl was summoned for a meeting with his new commander. Having greeted the lanky lieutenant with a military salute, he received a curt "Heil Hitler," and was told to take a seat before the wide desk behind which the new officer sat. Karl took a chair and waited. The new lieutenant, a man in his early forties, sat there, said nothing, tapped his pencil on the desk, and stared at Karl. "I came up through the ranks," the lieutenant finally said then, tossing his pencil on the polished desk. "I, too, was once a field sergeant," the officer said. "Do you play chess?"

"No, sir. Sorry."

"So am I. None of the other SS men seem to know the game. And I detest playing with the regular army officers or those cocky Luftwaffe pilots." The lieutenant leaned forward and fixed his dark, narrow eyes on Karl. "My name is Hans Streicher."

Karl nodded and looked at the lieutenant. He had a flat, triangular shaped nose, a long narrow neck, a pock-marked face, with two deep pits on each side of his nose, and his well-oiled black hair was combed back flat against his long, thin head. His voice seemed to hum at a high pitch, like a man who'd lost his vocal chords. His words were punctuated with great gasps of air, as if he were constantly out of breath. "I see you were wounded," the lieutenant said, pointing to Karl's gloved hand.

"No, sir," Karl said, remembering the Englishman had told him to tell the truth. The best road to credibility, Bill Harvey had said. Following that advice, Karl replied, "My hand was injured in an accident . . . when I was with the United States Coast Guard."

"I see," the lieutenant said, leaning quickly back in his chair. "And how did you get here?"

"Oh, I left the Coast Guard years ago. Bought a fishing boat. Had some bad luck. And was recruited in New York." Karl paused and studied the lieutenant's unmoving face. "Recruited by the SS."

"I see. Sergeant Meister, we don't seem to have a file on you here. It's been retained by Berlin. Is there any special reason for that?"

"Not that I know, sir."

"And you're an American then?"

"No. I'm Austrian. I went to the States in 1922. I was eighteen at the time."

"And now you're here. You'll have some fine tales for your grandchildren, Sergeant. Are you married?"

"My wife died, sir. We had no children."

The lieutenant leaned forward, placed his elbows on the desk, and rested his chin on folded hands. "I'm divorced," he said. "The marriage was annuled, actually. She was a Jew. There's no place for her in the New Germany."

Karl nodded slowly.

"We had no children. I turned her into the Gestapo." The lieutenant smiled, as he took a handful of peanuts from the bowl in front of him and stuffed his mouth. "But you, Sergeant, you were in America. That's interesting. Did you like it there?"

"Yes."

"You're an honest man, Sergeant. What you say could be misunderstood, you realize." And after a long pause, the lieutenant continued. "And I assume duty compelled your return?"

"Duty? No. I don't think so. This is Germany's war. And I'm Austrian. But I know there'll come a time when America will be in it. There'd be no place for me there then." Karl paused, thinking this was a story which the Nazi officer would find acceptable. "And, I suppose it was a way home. I had no money. And what better duty than the SS?"

"Very pragmatic, Sergeant. Very reasonable. The lieutenant paused and took another scoop of peanuts, and munching between words, said in his rasping voice, "I was in Ireland once. Not the north, but Erie. The true Irish." The lieutenant scratched his long neck and smiled at Karl with hard, thin lips. "I was in a pub. War had already broken out. And I'll be damned if they didn't all buy me a drink. 'An enemy of England is a true friend of the Irish,' they told me."

"Yes, Lieutenant," Karl said, remembering the words of his Irish net puller in Southport. "I've heard that before."

The new commander rose quickly from his chair. "But now, Sergeant, what I wanted to talk to you about was the staff car. Your privileges have been revoked." And opening the door, he said in his rasping, hissing voice, "That's all Sergeant. You're dismissed."

***

On the old freighter, now two hundred miles west of the Azores, Dr. Grauenhaft fell against the rail of the rolling ship and kept from sagging right down by hooking an elbow over the waist-high rail. The old ship plunged into another wave. He was soaked through by the spray. He hung there and was sick again—the interminable seasickness that plagued him throughout the voyage. He'd gone without supper again. It was only the drink that kept him going; and he drank because he was scared. He could remember only one other time when he'd been that frightened. It had been the same kind of threat—the Gestapo at his Berlin hotel in the early morning darkness—was he Dr. Grauenhaft? they demanded. Yes. Yes, he was. And then endless hours of interrogation. Was he loyal to the Third Reich? Yes, he insisted, he was a loyal Nazi. But they'd searched his papers—the ambiguous documents, all in his personal code, setting up the Schildwache organization in Germany. What were they, the Gestapo wanted to know. He gave his explanation again, an explanation that wasn't accepted. No, they didn't believe it was necessary to do business in code. Was he working for the British, or for the Americans, and why was he there? Again and again it went on, what was the Haemisch Chemical Company? Was it a New York front for British intelligence? And then Alex, Karl Meister's cousin, went to work and he was free again.

They were very, very sorry, the Gestapo said to him. They didn't know—they had no idea he was with the SS. But now he'd sent Karl to Germany—and Karl was an American agent. And he, Dr. Grauenhaft would pay for that mistake—no, they wouldn't want an explanation—perhaps it wasn't a mistake, they would say, and then they'd pull his old file, the Germans never destroyed a record, and it would start all over, and Alex couldn't save him this time, not if his cousin was a double agent. So he heaved himself up and staggered along the rail to the radio room. He must try again. He had to reach Madrid. Tell them about Karl before the Nazis found out. And then they'd get word to Alex in Berlin. Alex would know what to do—he'd see that Karl was eliminated—very efficiently, and without a hint of suspicion. That was Alex's speciality.

Grauenhaft's legs felt like he didn't have a muscle left in them. But fear, that paralyzing fear, now turned to panic gave him the strength he needed, and he pushed himself away from the rail and lurched along the rusty wall to the radio shack where he heaved open the door. The wireless operator, his visored cap pushed back on his blond head, swung around in his chair.

"My God, Herr Doctor, this is no time to be out on the ship. You'll be washed over the side."

Dr. Grauenhaft leaned back against the steel door he slammed behind him. "Did you get through?"

"Naw, we're still too far out, Doctor. This old set barely carries. They're not receiving me."

"Try again!" Grauenhaft held himself up by the door's handle as the ship rose from a trough.

The radio operator pulled on his earphones, turned to his set and hammered on the key. Then he glanced over his shoulder and smiled at Dr. Grauenhaft. "I've got 'em."

Grauenhaft's heart slowed from its trip-hammer race as the radioman pounded out the coded message. The old man waited, sucking short breaths, while the wireless operator paused for an answer.

"Message received and confirmed," the blond operator said.

Six

Cycling along the dreary road from Wesermuende, Karl bent low against the rain. It was five-thirty now, and already so dark he could see nothing but the feeble light dancing along the paving stones and the tall reed grasses rising from the ditches and occasional scraggly bushes which marked his progress against the cold wind. In Hawaii, it was December 7, 1941. The sun was rising on Pearl Harbor.

He knew it was impossible for an English plane to spot that weak light, but regulations were regulations, Streicher had warned, so he snapped off the lamp when he topped the small hill before the Fliegerhorst, coasted to the sentry at the command post, gave his name, rank and serial number, and pedaled into the dark compound, thinking the next thing they'll want is for us to show our SS tattoo.

His left hand was stiff and cold. In his room, he removed the black glove, rubbed the gnarled fingers warm, and drank a large whiskey. Then he walked to the NCO mess, where he ate slowly, savored his coffee, and smoked cigarettes, to kill time before his shift. He'd seen enough that day. The Germans were building in Wesermuende again, at the old Lloyd docks off Hafenstrasse, where two U-Boats of a new class stood on the ways under camouflage netting.

***

Taking the headsets from the swing man, Karl entered the time in his log—1944 hours—and switched the lower receiver to the BBC. "We continue our report on the Japanese attack at Pearl Harbor." And then the BBC announced that Japanese forces had inflicted heavy losses upon American ships in the Hawaiian Islands. "Just moments ago," the announcer continued, "the United States declared war upon Japan."

With that announcement, it was a different world. But around Karl, everything was the same. Men hunched over their Olympias. Paper rolled in continuous streams through the black machines. The soft glow of radio dials and the hum of receivers filled the room. No one had heard the news. It was as if the real world didn't exist.

Damn. No one expected this. The Abwehr reports were advising that no Japanese military action against the United States was likely until after the first of the year—now America was at war.

For three days Karl walked in a trance. He had to get out.

The nightly Abwehr reports disclosed heavy, devastating losses, and advised that a full disclosure of the disaster had been withheld from the American people. The German agent in Hawaii listed the names of the ships sunk and disabled, the terrible death toll, and the numberless casualties, all from official American Navy sources.

***

On December 11, 1941, Karl sat in the sergeant's lounge, drinking scotch and soda and listening to music on the radio in the corner, while he waited for the time his shift started. All he could think was that he had to get home. Maybe he could steal a boat and head for England—get out before Germany declared war on American—get out while there was still time. He could wire a boat and start the engine, he knew how to do that. He'd have to slip past the German patrol boats, thread his way through the mines. My God, it never occurred to him that the time for escape would come so soon. Six months, Harvey had said. Get out after six months. And Karl had been in Germany less than seven weeks.

The radio in the corner stopped playing music and went silent for a few moments. Then Karl heard the announcer say that Germany, followed by Italy, had declared war on the United States. He sat there, watching the four Army sergeants, who had stopped in the middle of a round of scat, and saw their faces go solemn.

Yes, he thought, watching those old soldiers, it isn't happy news for them either. They know it won't be a quick victory now. They remember the first war, when American men and equipment poured into France, turning the tide. Japan took out our Navy. But that won't last, he thought.

Not long. Soon American planes will roll off the Detroit assembly lines to thunder overhead—and already the Luftwaffe was losing the air war.

Taking a deep breath, and watching the old sergeants pack away their cards, Karl felt suddenly very alone and impotent. He'd sent nothing to the British since Streicher pulled his staff car privileges. I could send from my barracks window, he thought. But Streicher's no clown, and there'd be no destruction of garbled messages. The new intercept commander was shrewd. Hadn't he himself taken over the station next to Karl and supplemented the missing Dover call signs when no one else found them during yesterday's sudden change?

Well, Karl thought, trudging through the cold, damp air to the intercept station, I've got to take a chance. I'll see who's copying what tonight. Then I'll pick out a frequency no one's near, one of the old ones Harvey gave me. And then I'll tell the British their codes are blown again. After that, I'll just see what happens.

When he came up the long stairs to the radio rooms where a sentry in a wire cage pressed the buttton and opened the thick iron door, he saw Lieutenant Streicher inside leaning against the wall.

"Come with me," Streicher said.

The lieutenant closed his office door and motioned to a seat. Then sitting on the edge of his desk, and in in his rasping, hissing voice, said, "You have a dilemma, don't you, Sergeant?" Without waiting for an answer, Streicher continued, "You don't have a stone face, Meister. It's quite clear you have a problem."

"A problem, sir?"

"Ah, but rest assured, Sergeant. Your dilemma is solved." Streicher cocked his thin head, his heavy lids half closed, looking like a cobra about to strike—cold eyes—a faint smile on his thin lips—his nostrils quivering. "You're relieved from all further duty, Sergeant."

"But why, sir?"

"Don't play the simpleton, Sergeant. Germany's at war with America. You have a brother in the United States Military."

"I'm not my brother—"

"You, Meister, have access to confidential communications. Now the Americans may attempt to reach you through your brother."

"The Americans wouldn't do that."

"And why not?" Streicher bent forward and jammed his pencil on the desk. "We would!"

Streicher paused with an amused look on his face, "You're no longer a member of the SS." With those words Streicher rose and gave a stiff salute, "Heil Hitler, Sergeant. It's nothing personal, you understand. Report to Captain Baumwolle, Luftwaffe Air Weather Service. It's the best I could do, you see Sergeant. And it's only a short move. Just up the river. And I've given you three days leave."

Streicher handed Karl his orders and walked him to the exit. As the lieutenant closed the steel door behind Karl, his last words were: "It's a pity, Sergeant, that you don't play chess."

Walking toward his barracks through the dark mist Karl thought, well, Streicher's right, it could have been worse. It could have been the Russian Front.

After sleeping fitfully that night, Karl rose early and turned his collar up against the cold wind, now spitting snow. He followed the curving road along the antenna fields to the low dyke on the river.

Two miles down the dyke was a gray building with a tower facing the river.

When he reached the building, he descended narrow steps cut into the dyke, opened an iron gate, and walked around the tower and into a small courtyard, which was surrounded by a low fence. At the far end of the courtyard was an iron gate, from which a narrow drive led through flat, treeless fields toward the distant city.

Karl went up three steps to the oak door of the Luftwaffe Weather Service and knocked. And receiving no answer to his knock, he pushed open the door and stepped inside. The hall was empty. Karl walked slowly along the tile floor and stopped at a door which was slightly ajar. Pushing it open, he looked around. The long table in the middle of the room was cluttered with papers, clipboards and notebooks. A gray metal desk with a worn leather chair stood near the window. Papers scraps of all sizes and shapes, some wrinkled and wadded, lay everywhere—on the table among the notebooks, on the desk, in the chair, along the bookcase tops, and on the floor.

As he stepped back into the hall, he heard a typewriter coming from his right. He went to that door, pushed gently, and peering in, saw the back of a graying blond Luftwaffe captain seated at a desk in the corner.

Karl knocked. "Sir!"

The man waved over his shoulder without looking up from his typewriter.

Karl watched, while the officer typed, using only his index fingers; and then Karl noticed a wire leading from a small earphone up to an old radio on a wooden shelf above the captain.

At last the officer finished his typing, rolled the paper from the old machine, examined it, and muttered, "Yes, yes. Um hum, that will do." And turning in his swivel chair, dropped his jaw. "What . . . What the hell are you doing here?"

Karl gave the stiff hand salute. "Heil Hitler. Sergeant Meister reporting, sir."

"Reporting?"

"Sir, I'm the new man."

"New man? I have no . . . you're SS." The captain took the orders Karl held in his outstretched hand. "Sit down, Sergeant." The captain motioned to a chair near the window piled high with books and papers.

"This chair, sir?"

There was no response. When the captain finished reading the orders, he looked up at Karl suspiciously. "Why'd they kick you out?"

"My brother's in the American Coast Guard, sir. I'm a security risk." Karl told the small captain how he'd gone to the United States, that he brought his brother over, and that he'd returned to Germany before war broke out.

When the officer asked about the SS, Karl told him about Dr. Grauenhaft in New York, and explained how he'd been recruited by the Abwehr and assigned to the SS radio detachment in Wesermuende.

"Well, Sergeant, you're not due here for three days."

"I thought I might check in early, sir. I guess I was anxious to see my new duty station."

"Well, Sergeant, this is it. The entire Wesermuende Air Weather Service. A one-man operation." The officer rose and stretched out a hand to Karl. "Heinz Baumwolle."

The short, bow-legged officer told Karl he had been a pilot in the first war, that the weather service had been a civilian operation until 1936, and that his reserve commission was activated, and the weather station placed under the Luftwaffe.

"I've been to America," the officer explained. "And I have an aunt in Chicago, and an uncle in Brooklyn."

Karl learned that the captain's daughter was his clerical assistant. But she was on a trip through Bavaria, he said, her fiancé had just been killed in Africa.

Then the captain looked at him sharply. "Sergeant, I really should see some I.D."

"Yes, sir." Karl handed the officer his SS identification card, and on it was his photograph, overprinted with the Swastika and the double lightning bolts, which formed the letters "SS."

"Yes. Good. That'll do." The officer took a key ring from his pocket. "This is to the outer door, and this," he held up a small flat key, "is to your quarters. I'll show them to you." And Karl followed him through a narrow door and up circular stairs in the tower. Captain Baumwolle opened the door at the top. "My wife and I lived here for many years, until Ingrid was born. You can move your things in any time."

Captain Baumwolle frowned. "Get rid of that damned uniform. Take this to the Luftwaffe Quartermaster," he said, scribbling on a small pad. "It's just south of the main army post. They'll fit you out."

"Thank you, sir."

"Adieu, Sergeant."

"Heil Hitler," Karl said, and saw the captain wince when he gave him the traditional Nazi stiff arm instead of the standard military salute abolished by Hitler. Well, this is one man who hasn't knuckled under, perhaps there are others, Karl said to himself.

That evening, Karl placed the Peilwinkel transceiver in his service bag, and hurried along the dyke to the weather station. He went up the narrow stairs in the tower and unlocked the door at the top. Feeling along the inside wall, he found a switch and snapped on the light.

In the room, a rosewood coffee table stood between two leather chairs and a sleeping couch. Two smaller chairs and a mahogany cabinet were along the wall facing the window; and a small sink, two-burner gas stove and a refrigerator with a coil on top stood along the adjacent wall, next to a narrow bathroom with shower. Karl was the sole occupant of a suite, complete with kitchen.

He switched on a floor lamp next to the couch, removed his boots, and placed his feet on the coffee table. Southport was so very far away now. He half-wondered whether that part of his life had really existed, whether he had ever been a fisherman in that peaceful little town before the war.

Then he turned out the lights, opened the blackout curtains, lit a cigarette, and sat in the dark, smoking and watching the stars overhead in a clear sky.

When he finished his cigarette, he stored his transmitter in the closet and walked slowly down the dyke to his barracks, where he heard noises as he went up the stairs. Opening the door, he found Captain Streicher standing in the center of his old room. A second man in a dark suit searched the wall locker. Bedding was strewn about the floor and his bags lay opened on the mattress, with their contents spilled beside them.

"A simple formality," Captain Streicher said. "The Gestapo." He shrugged his shoulders and nodded to the man in black. The second man looked up, scowled, and said curtly, "Everything's in order. Goodnight, gentlemen." Captain Streicher again shrugged his thin shoulders and followed the man out the door.

Karl repacked his bags, smiling and thanking God a thousand times he'd taken the transmitter to his new quarters.

***

At the Wesermuende weather station on Monday morning, Karl heard typing from below as he came down the spiral stairs. He followed the sound to the front room where he knocked on the door. The typing stopped and the door swung open. Before him stood the slender blonde woman he'd watched from his barracks window as she rode her bicycle along the dyke with her skirt blowing high over long legs.

"Good morning," she said, reaching out and shaking his hand, "I'm Ingrid Baumwolle." She spoke in a calm, low voice, unhurried and with a softness in it. "And you're the new man."

"Karl Meister," he replied, feeling the warmth of her smooth hand in his. "Good morning. Yes, I'm the new man. I . . . I didn't expect anyone . . . It's only six o'clock. Do you always start so early?"

"Oh, no," she said, her blue eyes sparkling. "But there's so much to do. And Vati gets things in such a mess. Sometimes I think I shouldn't take a vacation." She laughed and motioned to Karl. "Come in, come in. Coffee's ready."

So this is the SS man, she thought. Well perhaps I was wrong. He doesn't look at all like Gestapo. "Vati told me you've lived in America...." She poured his coffee and handed it to him where he sat at the long table, which was now clean of all papers and materials.

"Thank you," he said, taking the coffee and nodding to the creamer she held in her hand. "Yes. I lived in Southport on Lake Michigan, north of Chicago."

Ingrid stood there, sipping her coffee and watching the stranger carefully. Was he an SS plant? And her father was so naive. He'd already told this stranger about Aunt Emma in Chicago and Uncle Harry in New York. Didn't he realize the sergeant's sudden appearance was too much of a coincidence? And the stranger was housed in the apartment over the weather offices, free to roam about at night. How many times had she found Black-Square messages lying openly on the table? The door was never locked. There wouldn't be time to dispose of the messages if the Gestapo walked in for a routine inspection, she had warned her father.

And what was worse, her father never knew where half the messages were. And his habit of drawing the square. "But Vati," she had told him, "It's ridiculous. Anyone can figure out that 'Viereck' means 'square.' If you must doodle, draw something else."

But her father only chuckled.

Now, on her first day back, she saw that her father had been doodling again. The penciled square was everywhere. She'd gathered up what she could find and was retyping them when she heard the knock.

Now drinking her hot coffee and peering intently at the new man, she said, "I understand you've been taking night readings?"

"Yes," he replied, smiling at her over his cup. "But I'm afraid they aren't very good. I walk out on the balcony, whirl the hydrometer the way your father showed me—some times it's raining," Karl said, laughing, "and I get a dry reading."

She smiled. "The hydrometer's quite a trick. But you'll get it." And then she added with a serious look, "I see you make the entries correctly." She scanned the night log with her finger. "Barometer, wind direction, wind speed, precipitation—what a chore this was." She shook her head. "Every four hours. First Vati, then me. Oh, Sergeant, I won't miss those nightly trips to the station."

That evening at the supper table, Ingrid turned to her father and said, "What do you know about this man?"

"Sergeant Meister? He seems to be a steady type."

"But he was with the SS."

"True. And he was transferred. Too much of a security risk. His brother, you understand."

"He could be a Himmler man."

"No, Ingrid. When Meister came to see me, he was wearing his SS uniform. If he were a plant, why, we wouldn't even know he had been in the SS." Captain Baumwolle paused, and then turned to Ingrid with a laugh and said, "My God, Ingrid, he scared the hell out of me when he walked in that day."

"But, Vati. Didn't you say the most obvious was the easiest to conceal?"

Captain Baumwolle laughed again. "Well, there you have me, Ingrid. But I have a feeling about the man. He's been to America, a simple fisherman, he's no danger."

"A simple fisherman, Heinz?" her mother said, leaning over the table. "Tell me then, why would a simple fisherman be in the SS?"

"Yes, Vati. How did this man end up in the SS?"

"That, my dear," Captain Baumwolle said to Ingrid, "is what you'll find out." Turning to Ingrid's mother, a pleasant woman with a broad face, he said, "Now, Mutti, some more of your delicious ox-tail soup."

When her mother left for the kitchen, Ingrid's father leaned toward her and said, "We'll discuss this later, and then you can tell me about your trip."

***

"You two night owls," Ingrid's mother said to them in the living room of the flat on Himmelstrasse after supper, "for hours you sit and listen to the news, play blackjack, and never get sleepy. But me," she stretched and covered a yawn, "I'm too old for your intrigues," and she kissed them both and left the room.

Captain Baumwolle lit his pipe, and after a pause said, "Well, Ingrid. How did it go?"

"Dr. Goerdler is ready to take over the government with a full staff."

"So, the Mayor of Leipzig is finally ready to move."

"Yes. And in Berlin, we have General Olbricht—and General Oster, Chief of the Secret Service. They're prepared to march on Berlin today with General Beck, arrest Hitler, and establish a separate peace with the British and Americans."

"And Admiral Canaris?" he asked, taking a long puff on his pipe. "Can we count on him?"

"No, Vati. He'll join us. But only after a successful coup. Nevertheless," she said, taking a cigarette from her silver case and lighting it, "we have almost three thousand field officers, high-ranking men, and everyone agrees the time has come. But . . ." She paused and drew on her cigarette.

"Yes, Ingrid?"

"But, when it comes down to treason—these men are torn between loyalty to their oath and a real, overt act."

"Ah, yes. The Prussian ethic." Her father banged his pipe in the ashtray, took a fresh scoop of tobacco from his leather pouch, relit his pipe, and shaking his head, said, "Such elaborate plans. We're at risk every day. Too many people involved, and there must be some action soon or there'll be a leak—and then we'll pay the price. Tell me," he said to Ingrid, "who are the other generals?"

"Vati," she said, and her face burned with excitement, "first, promise me, not one name is to be doodled about. We can't trust your SS man. And you know the rule, nothing in writing."

"Yes. Yes, Ingrid. I understand. Now, who are they?"

"All the major Berlin units. The weapons school, the tank command, the infantry school, the Signal Corps—"

"General Fellgiebel."

"Yes, Vati. And Helldorf, the Chief of Berlin Police. General von Hasse—"

"Berlin Army Command," her father interrupted.

"General Witzleben—"

"Yes. I remember," her father said. "He wanted to march on the Chancellery and arrest Hitler in 1938. Too bad we didn't listen to him then."

"He'll be the commander of all armed forces. And then," she continued, "we have the Commander-in-Chief, France . . ."

"Yes. Yes. Go on Ingrid."

"Oh, it would take hours, Vati."

"What about General Lindeman?"

"Yes, he came in, along with most of the Generals of the Central Army, East. And, Vati, there are many, many more who will join once a coup is clearly underway. But they want no part of the plan."

The captain puffed on his pipe. "They value their heads more than a commitment. But tell me, Ingrid. What's the situation with General Rommel."

"He's with us. Von Stauffenberg assures me of that."

"And the Luftwaffe?"

"It's too difficult to approach any one on Goering's staff. But," she smiled and put out her cigarette. "We have Colonel Gronau on our side."

"Hans is with us, Ingrid! That's wonderful. And is he still—?"

"Yes," she answered, "he's in charge of the Berlin Luftwaffe."

Her father shook his head and continued, "And at this very moment Hoepner's tanks are at the gates of Moscow—Hitler feels we've won the war—that he's invincible!" He paused and was silent for a long time. Then pouring brandy into two small glasses, he said, "Who'll take the first step?"

"Von Stauffenberg."

"Well then," her father said, rising slowly, "prosit!"

"Prosit, Vati."

Ingrid placed her brandy glass on the mahogany table. "Doesn't it seem odd that an SS man joins us just now. It's not good, Vati. Not at all good."

***

At the Hotel de Parque in Portugal, Dr. Grauenhaft slammed the receiver into its cradle with a bang. "Thank God for men like Boelle," he said to himself in his room. Then he checked his watch. Eight-thirty. He would shave after a quick shower, and drink cognac in the bar. This Karl Meister thing had taken its toll on his nerves; and it was a rough trip on that stinking old tub.

But outside, the warm night air beckoned. Yes, he would drink some cognac and take a stroll through the gardens.

Seven

Drinking his third cognac at the hotel bar, Dr. Grauenhaft smiled at the stocky bartender. Good men, he thought, all of them good men. He walked out on the veranda as the bartender picked up the phone and called the Hotel Palacio. The big German had been sitting there on the bench tossing small pebbles into the fountain for some time when the thin man in a white suit walked up behind him and shoved a stiletto into the base of his skull.

***

Christmas came and went—and still there was no signal from Berlin.

All during the long year of 1942, Karl Meister went about his duties at the weather station, stalemated, while the German underground plotted Hitler's death.

Three times the shadow government acted, and three times they failed. Twice, a bomb went unexploded. It went off the third time, killing the man who assembled it outside Hitler's headquarters at Rostock.

The Abwehr conducted a thorough investigation, and mysteriously turned up no suspects.

In Berlin, Alex Meister, Karl's cousin, proclaimed himself head of the Schildwache forces, and set about cementing his relationships with the anti-Hitler men willing to throttle the shadow government in its infancy and establish a new order upon the Nazi ashes.

***

The spring of 1943 came to Wesermuende with skies clear and blue and the snow along the roads melted quickly in the sun. War hadn't touched the city. Air raid shelters were marked and sand-bagged and emergency instructions posted everywhere, but the English bombers passed over the port city on their way to industrial targets deep in Germany. Submarines slipped down the river during the night now, and Karl watched the dark sillouettes from his rooms over the weather station. The U-Boats were safe, he'd sent nothing to the British since his transfer.

Karl saw the night-shift workers pouring into the old Lloyd yards, which now buzzed with activity, and knew German submarine production was escalating there. He'd hidden his transmitter under the circular stairs in the tower. Without mobility, he couldn't risk a DF fix, and he had little doubt he was under suspicion. He was followed every time he left the station during those first few months. That had stopped. But every now and then he would notice a dark van parked far down the road, a large loop antenna rotating slowly over its roof. They could be after somebody else. It was a good location for a fix on anyone in the harbor area, and there must be others, he told himself. But he couldn't take that chance.

So there was nothing to do but wait. Wait until he could steal a battery to power his radio. Wait until he found a safe place to transmit. And then the bombers would come in low, pick out the reference points he would give them, and churn the shipyard and all the submarines under construction there into steel splinters.

He sat at the long table and sipped coffee, watching the morning sun walk its bright rays across the courtyard while Ingrid typed out weather reports for the Luftwaffe. It was as if there were no war at all—just news of battles in far away Africa and Russia. The British jammed the new German radar systems. So now the Luftwaffe had pulled back into the interior, relying on visual reports of enemy bombers which were relayed to fighter planes there.

There was no air war over Wesermuende either. Just the bombers going over high in the night and coming back high, and the useless anti-aircraft guns which sometimes pounded away when a unit commander thought he saw something in a searchlight.

While he was sitting there and feeling impotent and wondering if he would ever do anything useful again, Karl saw a three-wheeled motor scooter with a square trunk over its front axle stop at the gate. An old man in a brown uniform with the yellow coach horn of the German Reichspost embroidered on a shoulder patch came through the gate carrying a package. "For Sergeant Karl Meister," he said to Ingrid at the door. "He must sign for it personally."

Karl stepped to the door, signed the form on the clipboard and took the package. He glanced quickly at the label. It was from the Kupschmidt Shoe Company, Berne, Switzerland. The package had been opened, inspected by German customs, and stamped and sealed for delivery. "It's been so long I'd forgotten all about it," Karl muttered half to himself, but for Ingrid's benefit. "My shoes," he said, shaking the package. He hadn't ordered any shoes, but he remembered Hans Boelle in Madrid, the tall blond German who told him about the Kupschmidt Shoe Company.

After lunch, Karl opened the package in his room. Inside the box were heavy hiking boots. And there's a message in here somewhere, Karl thought to himself. But how did they know I'm here? He removed the inner lining of the left boot, took it to the gas stove in the kitchen, and ran the flame over the smooth white surface. Nothing. He did the same with the right boot. Still no message. He took his cigarette lighter and carefully heated the wrapping paper and then the box and it's lid. There was no secret message.

The boots fit perfectly when he tried them on. Wondering if the message was the package itself, he put them in the closet and returned to work.

After work that evening, when he was alone at the weather station, he took the heavy boots from his closet. Keep it simple, the Englishman had told him. But to send me boots meaning take a hike, get out? That's not likely either. He turned the boot over in his hands. They were well made. Excellent quality. "Goodyear-stitched," Boelle had said. "Didn't you learn anything?" Karl took his pocketknife and cut into the tough, waxed stitching at the thick sole. Then peeling back the hard rubber he found sixty Swiss Francs wrapped in thin white paper. Brown letters appeared on the paper when he ran it over his cigarette lighter. It was a coded message.

Taking a sheet of paper, he laid out three rows of nine squares across for a total of twenty-seven squares. Then he blacked out the fifteenth square, the date he started his mission. That square would not be used, leaving twenty six squares on the page. Going then to the first square, he inserted the letter "P," the first initial of his code name, and in the second square he put the first letter of his full name, "K," and in each third square thereafter, the next initial, until he had used up the first nine letters. Then he circled the fifteenth character in the coded message. That was the number five, which gave him the clue to the remaining spaces. Putting into the blank squares each fifth character of the coded message, he completed the page. He now had twenty-six figures; and those he lettered from left to right with the alphabet. It was a simple code, easy to remember and required no code-book. So if this message was for Karl, and for Karl only, it would decipher quickly now.

Using the chart he'd made, Karl printed out the message: "Report Golden Swan Munich. Escape Berne if contact fails."

Darkness was falling and he closed the black drapes and lit a cigarette. He'd almost forgotten about escape. And now I have to get to Munich, he said to himself—to the Golden Swan—they'd get me out from there—of course his contact would recognize him—he'd been briefed, shown Karl's photograph—and told about the hand, the hand with the black glove, and the scar on his cheek. And all Karl had to do was sit there in the Golden Swan—probably a waiter was in on it—and then someone would come along and say his name, mutter a few pleasantries first, and then give him the escape route.

And if anything went wrong, he had the Swiss Francs. It would be up to him to find a way out. But how to get to Munich. He couldn't just leave. No, he needed a pass—he couldn't buy a train ticket without a pass.

He decided to ask Captain Baumwolle for a two-week leave, that's what he had earned now—and he hadn't used it—hadn't gone to Bavaria, to Herrn Chiemsee, the military recreation area on the big island in the lake south of Munich. It was still a little early, not that warm even in the South, but he wanted to avoid the crowded summer conditions there, that's what he'd tell the captain. And the captain would understand—Karl didn't mix—he was a loner—and that was because of all that time he'd spent in America. Yes, Captain Baumwolle understood, knew why Karl made no friends, he was a security risk, wasn't he? And sooner or later the conversation would get around to America and his feelings about the war.

But Captain Baumwolle had gone to Hannover for a briefing Ingrid told him in the morning. He'd be back the next day.

***

Ingrid was typing the morning weather report on the day her father was to return, when a tall blonde woman, wearing the uniform of an SS lieutenant, slamming the door behind her and marching up to the desk, interrupted her.

"Heil Hitler," the SS woman said, and gave a stiff salute.

"Heil Hitler," Ingrid answered automatically, rising from her desk. "Can I help you, Lieutenant."

"Yes, please. I'd like to speak with Sergeant Meister." The image of polished ruthlessness faded with Elska's lisp.

Ingrid watched from the window and saw Karl open the door for the SS woman; and then he slid behind the wheel. "Interesting," she said to herself, watching the black Mercedes drive out the iron gate and onto the narrow road toward the city.

When her father returned from Hannover latter that morning, she told him about the mysterious visitor with whom Karl was so friendly. "This time I'll be the one to say we shouldn't jump to any hasty conclusions."

Captain Baumwolle frowned. "Now, Ingrid, if you're telling me this is just a social call, I must say your intuition is . . ." he paused and fixing his eyes on her, continued, "somewhat questionable?"

"No, Vati. This time I'm right. There's something between the two, something more than business."

"Then you think they're friends?" he asked, pouring a cup of coffee.

She took the coffee from her father's outstretched hand. "More than friends."

"Lovers?"

"Perhaps, Vati. But that isn't what I meant."

"What then?"

"She looked worried—distressed."

"But isn't that natural? He's been booted from the SS—she's taking a risk—meeting him."

"Of course!" Ingrid exclaimed. "That's it." She put her coffee cup on the table and whirled to her father. "They're both taking a risk."

Laughing then, Captain Baumwolle said, "You see, Ingrid. Your father knows something of this world, too. People aren't made of wood."

"Vati, you don't understand. I searched his room."

"Ingrid—you should have asked—"

"The package made me suspicious—shoes from Switzerland?

Her father shook his head.

"Well I was curious," she continued. "And when he rode off on his bicycle yesterday, I took a chance. There was nothing in his room—nothing at all—you see, that's what's odd, the shoes weren't there. Then when I came down the stairs I heard a creak on the third step. Those oak steps don't creak, Vati. And when I looked closer, I saw the varnish around the nails was chipped. And I wedged a screwdriver under that step and lifted it. Under the step was a small case. And when I opened it, I found a short-wave transmitter, Vati—complete with sending key and five crystals for the ten-meter band."

"What frequencies?"

She handed him a slip of paper upon which she had scribbled the frequencies. He took it to his office, compared it it to a small card from under his desk blotter, and said, "British Intelligence."

***

At the Gasthaus Stortebeker Karl leaned over the mahogany table in the dark booth, and said to Elska, "Now what's this urgent message . . ."

"They shouldn't have transferred you, Karl. I read the reports. You were the best operator there." Elska lit a cigarette and also leaned forward, her voice quiet, and said, "That's why I've come, Karl."

Karl nodded to the waiter who set two coffee cups and a cognac on the table.

"Welcome to the Stortebeker," the red-faced waiter said. He turned to Elska, and stared blankly at her black SS uniform. "And Fraulein Lieutenant," the waiter bowed, "a special welcome to you."

"Thank you."

The waiter rose on his toes and then swooped in a low and exaggerated bow. "My name is Hans Stortebeker. This Gasthaus has been in my family for many generations. The original owner was my great-great grandfather," the man said proudly and smiled down at them. "He was a North Sea pirate."

And now looking at the waiter with an irritated smile, Karl said, "That's very interesting. Please tell us about it after I've finished talking with the young lady."

Except for an old seaman across the dance floor, who sipped beer between puffs on a large pipe, the gasthaus was empty.

The waiter stepped back and stood there, ready to pounce forward if anything was needed.

Karl turned to the stout man and said to him, "Do you have music?"

"Music. It's early, my friends. But, yes. I can play the accordian for you. In the old days, I played for the tourists, mostly English, then. Regular customers, they were. And always," he paused with a distant look in his eyes, "we played all night. We danced all night. Those were good times, I tell you. Stortebeker's was their first stop." He paused again with thumbs under the suspenders behind his short jacket.

"'*Wiener Blut,*'" Karl asked. "Could you play 'Vienna Blood?'"

"I knew it," the owner said, "you're Austrian. How could I miss that accent!"

The man took a large accordian from a shelf behind the bar, and nodding and smiling at them across the dance floor, struck up the familiar Strauss waltz; and when the song was finished, the owner bowed as Karl and Elska clapped, and then the old seaman clapped too, and the owner, grinning broadly, began to play the "Blue Danube."

Elska reached for Karl's hand. "We have a man in Norway and he must get out." Her eyes were serious. "He has with him plans for a new weapon.

A ground-to-air missile. Karl, its unbelievable," she said, leaning closer across the table, her coffee cup trembling in her hand. "The missile follows a directional beam, straight up, carrying over six-hundred pounds of explosives. And, Karl," she continued with a frightened look now in her eyes, "he's my uncle. We must get him out. He's on the run. There isn't much time."

"Does he belong to the Schildwache, Elska?"

She studied his face for a moment. "You haven't heard,—no, you'd have no way of knowing. Uncle Heinrich's dead, Karl. Killed in Portugal—on his way home—just after Pearl Harbor. Your cousin, Alex, runs the Schildwache now." She paused and pulled her hand away. "No, my uncle doesn't belong to the Schildwache, Karl."

"I'm sorry, Elska. I didn't know Dr. Grauenhaft was dead."

She nodded and bit her lip. "He was assassinated, Karl. First, we thought the Nazis did it. But now Alex thinks it must have been an American agent, because nothing else has happened."

"I don't understand, Elska, why is your uncle trying to smuggle out plans for a new weapon; and why are we—the Schildwache—supposed to help him?"

"Karl, I don't want you to do it for the Schildwache—do it for me, he's my uncle, Karl. And the plans are in his head, he developed the missile—he's the project engineer."

"And now he's no longer a loyal Nazi."

"Karl, he was just a misguided old man working with German scientists. But then, after what the Nazis did in Norway, Karl, he just couldn't work for them anymore." Looking Karl steadfastly in the eyes, she said, "I've been to Norway, Karl." She shook her head in silence for a moment. "And now I no longer want anything to do with the Schildwache. I'm not even sure I want Germany to win the war. I just want to get away from it all—it's so different—not what I expected. And Uncle Heinrich's great plan to use the Nazis—it just won't work, Karl. And now your cousin Alex . . . I don't think the Schildwache would be any different."

Karl sat looking at her and saying nothing. After sitting there for some time, sipping his cognac, he asked, "What would Alex do if he knew how you felt?"

"Karl, I think he'd shoot me."

He leaned back in the booth. "And that's what he'll do to me if he finds out I helped your uncle escape." But Karl was getting out of Germany now, and maybe the missile plans would help win the war. And so he said, "What do you want?"

"You know code, Karl. You know radio. I need you to transmit a message."

"From here? From Germany?"

"Yes. To the British."

"And how do you think I would do that?"

"I don't know, Karl. Can't you find a way? Can't you do it for me, Karl?"

Well, he thought, this is a hell of a mess, this business. And is this some kind of a trap? Sure, I go hauling out my transmitter, and some damned Gestapo follows me, and then it's all over.

"Elska, how do you know you can trust me—and how can I trust you? I thought everything was for Germany." And he was thinking, well, if it's a trap, and I don't turn her in, I'm dead. If I do turn her in, and she's telling me the truth, she's dead. This is one of those times when you'd better be right.

"Why would I lie to you, Karl?"

He decided to test her. "Can you get me a transmitter, Elska?"

"No, Karl. I can't just walk in off the street and order one."

"How about parts, crystals, a transmitter key, anything?"

"Karl, I couldn't . . . I just can't . . . no one would give them to me."

"All right, Elska. I'll see what I can do."

Karl listened as she gave him her uncle's code name and told him a fishing boat would establish a rendezvous in the North Sea a week from Sunday.

Then she gave him the latitude and longitude, which he jotted on a small paper strip, rolled it tight and slid it into a small tube on his watch band.

Across the dance floor, Mr. Stortebeker broke into a polka, and the old seaman banged the table in rhythm with the music, and Karl and Elska clapped to the beat.

Then the song was finished, and Karl ordered a beer and a glass of Steinhager.

When they left the gasthaus, the old seaman was staggering around the dance floor to a fast polka, and Mr. Stortebeker nodded goodbye to them while he swayed back and forth, punching out the lively tune on a black and white accordian.

Karl said *"aufwiedersehen"* to Elska at the weather station; and after watching her drive from the stone courtyard, he turned to see Ingrid looking from the window of the typing room. Her face disappeared from the glass as Karl's glance met hers.

And when he entered the building, Karl decided to wait until morning before asking the captain for leave. It was perfect. The captain would probably assume he was going off with Elska.

That evening, after Captain Baumwolle and Ingrid had left for the day, Karl took the transceiver from under the circular stairs. His heart froze when he saw that the thread he had carefully wound around the hasp was missing. He knew that someone had opened it—they hadn't seen the black thread against the black case. And how much time do I have before there's a knock on the door, or worse yet, no knock, with the door splintering and thrown wide, as Gestapo men rush in.

Well, he thought as he smoked a cigarette in the dark, sipping whiskey from a small flask, if the Gestapo had been tipped off, they'd have come for me long ago. Maybe it's just a coincidence, Elska being here. Hell, if the Gestapo knows, the games up anyway, isn't it? And if Elska is working with them all they would gain is evidence. But the Gestapo didn't need evidence. Not for anyone. They took them out and shot them, or sent them off to concentration camps, no questions asked.

He went to the window overlooking the dyke, and pulled the black curtain to one side. He could see no one in the soft moonlight. And going then to the other window, looked out. There was no one in the courtyard below.

Cautiously, Karl slipped out the station door. He climbed the stairs to the dyke, and walked around the building in ever wider circles. Now he was quite certain—no one was watching him. He wasn't under surveillance. Damn, he said to himself, I must have forgot the thread, that's all. And returning up the circular stairs to his room, Karl emptied his whiskey flask and fell asleep.

In the morning, he asked Captain Baumwolle for two weeks leave. "Starting the first of the week, sir, if possible. That'll give you time to find some one for the night readings."

Captain Baumwolle smiled from his chair. "I can take the night readings, Sergeant. And Ingrid will help out. It's no problem."

Karl asked for permission to go to the city. "I need some personal items."

"Certainly, Karl."

Ingrid smiled when Karl met her in the hall. A strange new smile that he first saw after Elska's visit, almost a mask now, that's what the smile was, he realized, a forced smile; and he smiled back and wished her a good morning. Then he pedaled through the iron gate and onto the narrow road leading to the city. Karl needed a battery for his transmitter. He'd decided to transmit Elska's message before he left.

As he rode along through the cool air, he heard the air raid siren, which everyone ignored since there had been no bombing attacks at Wesermuende. A few minutes later he saw a group of twenty-five Lancaster bombers sweeping low over the city toward military targets inside Germany.

He passed the Gasthaus Stortebeker on the city's outskirts and smiled at the tavern's big signboard with the owner's name under a tall square-rigged ship. The sign squeaked on its hinges as he passed, almost as if the wind were playing a Strauss waltz, he thought.

He turned the corner and rode past Speckenbuetel Park, where bare hedges and stone walks ran down to a large pond surrounded by naked oak trees. On the other side of the park were small apartment houses, two and three stories high, with high-peaked, red-tile roofs, some with skylights, indicating residences in the attics. On the other side of the street was the Metropol Cafe, with a huge bay window rising two stories to the roof. The buildings in this part of town were all concrete and stucco, and painted in pastel colors of yellow and pink, with some light gray and white. Cables stretched from high peaks across the narrow street, holding lights which swung in the wind. Here Karl was careful that the bicycle wheels didn't catch in the street car tracks, as sometimes happened when the streets were wet and he'd go sprawling along the cobblestones.

After riding for half an hour along the narrow, winding street, Karl came to Hafenstrasse, a wide boulevard, separated by a pedestrian island, where the yellow street cars stopped. Since it was a sunny day, there were many people in the street, enjoying that rare day in Northern Germany when the sun came out.

Karl passed the middle school, which sat far back from the street. There, children played war. The smaller boys wore dark pants, and the little girls skirts, mostly plaid of different colors, with matching wool stockings. This was the main section of the city where the buildings were taller, some as high as six stories, and all had several chimneys on their steep roofs. Gutters and down spouts ran at all angles, finally reaching the cobblestone sidewalk, where rivlets ran to the curb. Stores, once filled with appliances and consumer goods, occupied the lower level. Karl stopped at a small electrical shop next to the Karstadt Department store, locked his bicycle in the rack against the wall, and entered the narrow building.

An elderly clerk, with small steel-rimmed glasses, stood behind the high counter. "May I help you, Herr Sergeant," he said in a weak voice.

"Yes, I'd like a small battery, portable, twelve volts."

"I'm sure you understand, Sergeant, that—" The air-raid siren split the air. When it was quieter again, the clerk continued, "Herr Sergeant, the battery is a restricted item. You must have a permit."

Damn, Karl thought to himself, perhaps I can bluff the man. "There's no problem. I'll send it down by courier." Karl smiled and shrugged his shoulders. "No problem. My courier will be back in a matter of minutes."

"But it's a restricted item, Herr Sergeant." The shopkeeper squinted behind thick lenses, speaking the words slowly and with determination.

Karl saw the battery he needed on a shelf over the clerk's head, and he considered simply reaching over and taking it. He needed that battery. He was willing to pay for it, and this squeaky little clerk keeps talking about a permit.

Once more Karl told the clerk he would send a courier; and when the clerk again refused, Karl unfastened the leather flap over his service revolver. But he knew that if his bluff failed he couldn't shoot the little clerk, and he snapped the revolver flap shut, thankful for the high counter which blocked the clerk's view of that stupid move.

Old Harvey wouldn't be very happy with me, Karl thought. Hell, he would've killed the poor bastard with his wire loop so there wouldn't be any noise. Turning from the clerk toward the door, Karl said over his shoulder, "All right. I'll get a permit."

Opening the door he heard the roar of the Lancasters down the street.

"Home to England," the clerk's soft voice said behind him.

Looking down the street, Karl saw the planes were coming straight at him, barely above the roof tops, and less than half a mile away. Suddenly there was a shrill whistle in the distance, followed by a muffled roar and more whistling shrills and rolling thunder.

"Jesus Christ," he shouted. "They're bombing!" And he froze, as did the people in the street, watching the steel death curtain march steadily along Hafenstrasse, throwing bicyles, cars, dirt, paving stones, and people high in the air. Buildings shook, paused, suspended in distorted shapes, and slid slowly into the street. Still Karl couldn't move. He watched as a small boy, running with his rucksack flapping, and pulling a little girl by the hand, disappeared in a blinding flash.

Karl was blown back into the shop and along the floor, where everything swirled and glass shards flew through the air.

He stumbled to his feet and stood in a dust cloud. He could scarcely see; and as he struggled toward the light, he saw a large hole where the store front had been.

Outside, dust swirled everywhere in the wind. An acrid smell hung in the air. There were more sudden flashes with roaring blasts, which again knocked him to the ground.

Karl lay there, waiting, and when the flashing blasts finally stopped, he staggered to his feet. A huge crater marked the spot where the two children had been running.

His bicycle still stood in its rack. As he unfastened its lock, he looked through the blown-out store front. Rubble lay everywhere. Then stepping back into the shop and looking around in the debris, he called out for the clerk. There was no answer. Karl spotted the battery, sitting on the shelf above where the counter had been. Walking over the splintered wood and glass, he took the battery and quickly went to his bicycle where he strapped it on the luggage rack.

The street was full of screaming, milling, people; and across the street, he saw a geyser where a water main had broken.

His greatcoat was torn and flapped about him as he pedaled past a yellow streetcar lying on its side, with people climbing from its broken windows.

He buttoned his coat collar against the cold wind, and pressed on, passing several burning buildings. At the corner, where he turned down a side street leading to the weather station, he saw a bombed-out apartment building, sheared in half, and looking like a doll house with the front open. On the second floor, he saw a man sitting at a table, fork in hand, staring blankly into space.

Behind him, Karl heard the faint wail of sirens from police and ambulances rushing to the devastated scene.

Along the side street, windows were blown out everywhere. And now and then, Karl stopped and carried his bicycle over rubble which had slid into the street from the small apartment houses.

Pedaling faster now, he passed the Metropol Cafe. Its high bay windows were gone. It was then that Karl realized he could barely hear people who were shouting and screaming in the streets. He put a hand to his ear and felt sticky wetness—his ear was bleeding—the drum was ruptured. He stopped and wiped the blood, and pressed a handkerchief against his right ear to stop the bleeding.

Down the street, past Speckenbeutel Park, Karl saw that the Stortebeker sign was gone. When he came to the corner, he stopped and stared—the gasthaus had taken a direct hit, leaving only one wall holding the mahogany booths where he had talked with Elska. A small fire burned in the rubble.

Karl searched the debris, calling out for Mr. Stortebeker. There was nothing, only the silent flame licking timbers in the center of the flattened structure.

And as he rode through the iron gate to the weather station, he saw Captain Baumwolle standing with Ingrid on the steps. "Sergeant," the Captain called out, "thank God you're back." His voice came to Karl as a whisper.

Ingrid's lips were moving too, but Karl heard no sound. Tears streamed down her face. He realized her mouth was forming the words, "Mutti. Mutti." And turning on the steps, Karl saw three wide smoke pillars rising from the distant city.

Captain Baumwolle rushed past Karl and ran to his battered Opel in the courtyard. When he reached the old car, he turned and motioned, and Karl understood—he was telling him to take Ingrid inside.

In the building, Karl shook Ingrid, saying over and over, "Telephone."

Finally she understood, and dialed the phone. Ingrid punched the button and dialed again. Then three more times; and then her face beamed and her lips formed the familiar word, "Mutti."

Ingrid now talked excitedly into the phone, crying all the while. Karl left her and quickly went up the circular stairs to his quarters. When he returned with the short-wave transmitter, Ingrid was still on the phone, her back to the door, and he slipped past.

Karl felt strangely warm across his chest as he lifted the battery from the bicycle luggage rack; and the warm spot on his chest was growing larger as he ran quickly along the dyke toward the antenna field, where he slid down the small slope and crawled under the chain-link fence. The ground was damp and cold there, and he pushed the radio ahead of him through the wet grass, crawling on his stomach, until he reached the west arm of the tall 180 antenna.

Stretching a hand up past the insulator, Karl wrapped the short-wave lead tightly around the wire which formed one leg of an inverted "V." He smiled at the thought of using the SS field for his transmission. I may as well send both messages—let the British know about the submarines in the Lloyd yards. The grand finale. My swan song.

Karl knew his transmitter, feeding directly into the intercept antenna, would be amplified a thousand times before it blasted the earphones of the SS operators; and the resulting signal would be a screaming wail, which no ear could stand.

Pulling himself to a sitting position in the tall grass, Karl lifted the transmitter to his lap and tapped the sending key. "Dover," he sent in code, "this is Peter."

Pausing for an answer, and hearing none, he repeated the call. This message is too important to send blind, he thought—make contact first, and then have confirmation. Otherwise, someone will be risking their neck in a useless rendezvous.

"What the hell's the matter here?" he muttered, over and over; and still not receiving an answer, he checked all the connections, looking for a weakness in his system.

Then, very faintly, as if from worlds away, Karl heard the Dover reply. There was nothing wrong with the equipment. It was his ears! Good God, it must be blasting, and I can barely hear it.

"Waterfall," Karl tapped out the code name for the Norwegian operation, followed with the full message, and the grid coordinates for the rendezvous. Then he transmitted the information on the German U-Boats under construction at the Wesermeuende yards.

Karl waited. There was no response. Again, he sent the message and waited.

Faintly, he heard the answer: "Message confirmed. Get off the air. You have been transmitting too long!"

The SS operator working the inverted "V" that day, jumped from his seat, threw his earphones onto the desk and grabbed his ears in pain.

Lieutenant Streicher dashed out of his office and picked up the howling headsets. "Quiet!" he screamed at the startled operator. Then he reached over, turned down the gain control, pressed the headset to his ear, and listened to the last of Karl's message. When the earphones went silent, he turned up the gain control and heard the weak acknowledgment, warning Karl to get off the air. Then his hand went to his head, and with nostrils quivering, Streicher shouted out, "Of course. The antenna field!"

In the antenna field, Karl closed the transmitter case; and looking down then, saw his greatcoat soaked with red. He reached inside the coat, where all was wet and sticky. Now he knew what the warmth was he'd felt earlier—it was blood—oozing into the heavy wool coat, which absorbed it like a sponge.

He disconnected the antenna lead and crawled to the fence, squeezed under, and pulled the transmitter after him.

He paused at the top of the dyke and looked across the antenna field to the distant Intercept Building, where tiny figures ran to a half-track.

Sliding down the smooth stone surface, Karl stumbled to the river, where he swung the transmitter in an high arc, and watched it plunge into the black water and sink quickly.

He was light-headed now, and stumbling along the slippery rocks, he splashed south toward the weather station, reeling and falling in the water as he went along.

At the weather station, he crawled up the stone dyke, staggered down the concrete steps on the other side, hurried through the courtyard, and burst into the building.

"My God, Sergeant! What's happened?" Ingrid screamed as he stood swaying in the doorway.

Eight

Karl Meister opened his eyes. His stared at the ceiling over his bed, and he tried to bring into focus the halos he saw there. Slowly the lights took form; and as his eyes moved down the long room he recognized hospital beds.

Next to his bed sat an SS lieutenant with a pock-marked face and two large pits on either side of his nose. "Good morning, Sergeant," Streicher said, and looked at Karl with the piercing eyes of a cobra ready to strike.

"How did I get here?"

With the expression of an interrogator grown tired of useless discussions, Streicher shook his head and said, "You know very well how you got here, Sergeant."

"I remember going to town—on my bicycle. And then I remember standing on steps . . ." Karl told the truth, for at that moment, that was all he did remember. It was fortunate for him that Streicher had not waited with his questions. But then the lieutenant hadn't listened when the Doctor explained how scopolamine worked. He was intent on his prey and thinking only that the truth serum would finally expose this American spy, and that he would be promoted—perhaps receive his first Hitler medal.

"Go on. How did you get here—to the Army Lazarette?"

Karl felt this strange compulsion to tell the man everything. But through the fog in his head he understood Streicher wanted only to know how he got here, not about the battery or the transmitter.

"Sergeant, I think you understood the question. Now answer it!"

"My cigarettes," Karl said. "I think they're in my coat pocket."

Streicher opened the green locker. Karl saw a clean uniform hanging over polished boots. "There's nothing here, Sergeant," Streicher said feeling the pockets of Karl's service jacket.

"They must be in my other coat. The one I was wearing when . . ."

The pits on each side of Streicher's nose were deeper and darker now. "When what, Sergeant?"

"When the bombing started."

"Where were you then?"

"Hafenstrasse."

The lieutenant's face went dark, and his forehead wrinkled as he bent his long neck closer to Karl and in a voice which hissed from his thin lips said, "I should have you shot, Sergeant."

"Shot!"

"It was you—in the antenna field, damn it—I know it. We tracked you, Sergeant. To the dyke. You went into the river, and that's why the dogs lost the scent." Streicher leaned closer still and Karl could smell his foul breath. "Did you go north, Sergeant?" And hearing no response, "South? Damnit! You were in the antenna field!"

The lieutenant hadn't listened when the Doctor explained the procedure under scopolamine, and now he had violated the first rule, he had alarmed the patient.

"Antenna field, Sir?" A nurse walked by and Karl spoke quickly to her, "Nurse, where's my uniform? And my great coat? The one I was wearing."

"We burned them, Sergeant," the nurse said, stopping with a chart in her hand and smiling at Karl, and then at Streicher. "You were very lucky," she said. "They were torn to shreds."

Streicher rose quickly and turned to the nurse. "Were they wet?"

"Wet? Heavens no," she said over her shoulder as she walked away. "It wasn't raining, Lieutenant."

Karl sank back into his pillow. He was confused. He remembered his clothes being wet. And he could tell the lieutenant nothing about how he got to the hospital.

Karl turned to Streicher, who now stood over his bed, rubbing his chin. "The last thing I remember is standing on steps." And that was all Karl did remember.

The lieutenant's eyes narrowed. "Sergeant," Streicher said, "I say again, it's a shame . . . a shame that you don't play chess." He spun on his heel and strode quickly away down the long row of beds.

***

"Amateurs," the fat man in the black suit said to Karl at Gestapo headquarters. "Every SS man thinks he's a detective." He pulled round glasses from his face and wiped them on his tie. "Schmidt," the man said, shaking Karl's hand. "Don't worry about Streicher—what does that shithead know, huh?"

Pushing his glasses up on his nose, the fat man sat down at his desk, and licking his finger, flipped through a sheaf of papers. "Don't worry, Sergeant. If anyone's to be concerned it should be Streicher. My God. What nerve. Here, I see we recruit agents," he tapped the file with a stubby finger, "and this idiot transfers them to the Luftwaffe. I can't believe this—the weather service."

The Gestapo man rose from his chair, and slamming the report on the desk said rapidly, "Streicher. My God, what's the man done!" And then turning to Karl with a sigh, he said, "The last thing you remember is standing on stairs. Well the idiot should have looked at the admission sheet. That's where they found you, Sergeant. Your bicycle was on the landing. And you, my friend, were slumped against the hospital door."

Karl smiled and said to himself, that explains it. He shifted his toes in his large service boots. Captain Baumwolle has very big feet.

The Gestapo man shook his head. "And not to completely waste your trip down here, I'll show you something." Karl followed the short man to a large drum, which was six feet long and as high as his shoulders, where Karl saw several large cards arranged in rows. The cards flapped as Schmidt spun the cylinder. "Pick a name," the fat man said, "any name."

"Meyer," Karl replied.

"That's common enough." Spinning the middle section, Schmidt stopped at the letter "M," pulled a large card from the file, and said, "Franz. Franz Meyer. We'll take him."

The Gestapo man held the card up to the light. "Now what would you like to know about the man?"

"Oh, I don't know . . . Where was he born?"

"Wesermuende," Schmidt answered. He told Karl where Franz Meyer lived, where his parents were born, where his grandparents were born, Meyer's religion, and that of his parents, as well as his grandparents. "His pass number is 68743," the Gestapo man said. "He can't rent a hotel room without it. And he's registered to this address." He tapped the sheet. "Before he moves, he must first get permission from his local precinct. Then they'll issue moving papers. And without that permission slip," Schmidt continued, smiling and wiping his glasses a second time, "our friend Franz can't register at his new police precinct, wherever it is. It's a simple system. Each policeman knows his district. He knows everyone who lives in each house, each flat. Sooner or later, he'll know if some stranger comes to the house or apartment. And if they haven't registered at the station, he'll arrest them."

The Gestapo man showed him the back of the card, where Karl saw photographs of a smiling Franz Meyer, front view and profile.

"And his wife?" Karl asked.

"Same thing. But on a separate card. And the beauty of these things," the man said, smiling and waving the card, "is that, with one good clerk, we can put a pin on that map showing every person who has a grandparent with a drop of Jewish blood."

Karl's eyes followed the man's pointing finger to a large map hanging on the wall, covered with red, green and yellow pins.

"And what are those?" Karl asked, pointing to the pins.

"That much, my friend, you needn't know." His squinted eyes lifted and peered at Karl for a moment. Then he took the card to the file, and inserted it saying, "Every station, mind you Sergeant, each precinct, has a file like this. And that's how we control the people. That's why we have so little crime. They can't hide from us. Not like Chicago." He paused and looked over his glasses at Karl. "What a terrible city it must be. Full of gangsters. But I'd like to go there . . . after the war. They certainly could use our system."

After a while, Schmidt asked Karl if he'd like to return to the SS. "I couldn't work for Streicher," Karl replied.

"No. That's understandable, Sergeant. But in Berlin, perhaps?"

"Radio is all I know," Karl said, thinking all the time he had to get to Munich, to the Golden Swan, and then escape. This was no time for a transfer to Berlin. Smiling at the little man, he said, "And now, of course, a little bit about weather reporting. That's where I'd like to stay, sir."

"But surely, Sergeant, you can do better than that—really, weather work? Dr. Grauenhaft was a good man. He wouldn't have recruited you to do weather analysis."

Karl let his eyes roam over the short man who now sat at his desk looking at Karl quizzically. Karl wondered how far he could play his hand. Perhaps he could avoid a Berlin transfer. Leaning forward, he said quietly, "Can you arrange for Streicher's transfer?"

"Yes. That can be arranged," Schmidt said slowly and methodically, fixing his eyes on Karl, with a faint smile at the corner of his mouth. "Do you want the command?"

"The command?"

"Yes. You have friends in high places, Sergeant. My orders are to interview you, return you to the SS, and arrange for your promotion to lieutenant . . . Now we were thinking of Berlin, but—"

"But, sir, I'm only a sergeant."

"These orders come directly from your cousin, Colonel Alex Meister.

Berlin SS wants you as soon as I've cleared up this Streicher matter. And I assure you, I've done that. Now if you want to stay here, I'll see what I can do."

Karl nodded and Herr Schmidt picked up the telephone and called Berlin. The Gestapo man's face was without emotion as he explained Karl's reluctance to transfer to Berlin. Karl knew it could be done. Heinrich Himmler was the head of both the Gestapo and the SS. The two competing organizations shared some of the same Berlin staff.

Herr Schmidt hung up the phone, smiled at Karl, and said, "It's done. You have command of the Wesermuende Intercept Unit."

Karl said to the man who now watched him intently over his small glasses, "And Streicher?"

"He'll be reassigned to Berlin—staff work."

Two days later, Karl left the hospital still feeling weak, numbed by the strong pills he took against the pain in his chest. He carried with him the orders signed by SS Obergruppenfuehrer Ernst Kaltenbrunner which promoted him to lieutenant, assigned to him command of the intercept unit and granted a two-week recuperation leave.

"Vati," Ingrid Baumwolle cried out as she watched the black Mercedes enter the courtyard and roll slowly toward the weather station, "it's the Gestapo!"

"Keep calm, Ingrid. Keep calm!" Captain Baumwolle said to her as he stumbled into the typing room, dropping papers along the hall as he went.

Ingrid saw a man in the back of the car, and as the driver opened the door and saluted stiffly, she recognized the black uniform of the SS. "Its Karl Meister."

"Meister?" her father said over her shoulder, looking out the window. "By God, it is. And he's an SS lieutenant."

When Karl came through the door, he paused and looked at them both. Then he said to Captain Baumwolle, "Thank you sir." And he shook his hand, and said then to Ingrid. "Your father has awfully big feet."

Sitting around the table in the front room, drinking coffee, Karl asked, "Why did you do it?"

"Well," Captain Baumwolle said, "I'd just returned from the city. There you were, unconscious on the steps. And Ingrid was trying to pull you through the door. We checked for the transmitter. And when we didn't find it, we knew you'd been sending something. My God," Captain Baumwolle took a quick sip from his coffee cup, "we were scared. I won't deny that. I didn't know where you'd been. And there was a trail of blood and water leading from the dyke."

"I washed it down with a broom and lye," Ingrid said, interrupting her father, "while Vati changed your clothes. We couldn't find any boots."

"We used mine," Captain Baumwolle said. "And then we shredded your uniform, rubbed in dirt, and took you to the hospital.

"There was confusion everywhere. We just propped you against the door and left your cycle on the landing. You'd lost a lot of blood—we weren't certain you'd live."

"I don't understand, sir," Karl said, looking at the Captain intently, why didn't you turn me in?"

Ingrid turned to Karl. "We didn't know what to think when I found the transmitter. I wasn't certain about anything. You could have been an SS agent."

"SS?"

"Yes," she said. "That was my first thought, since you came from the SS. But I really didn't think you were working for them. And I decided to wait and see what would happen. Then the woman came, the SS Lieutenant. I could see she was your friend. There was something else there too. And then we realized you must be sending a message from her."

Captain Baumwolle leaned forward, nodding slowly, and handed Karl his sixty Swiss Francs. "At first we thought you were a spy, perhaps sending information to the British." He looked at Karl a long time. "This is a perfect location for spotting U-Boats putting out to sea. But then the transmitter was under the stair. Not a place you'd keep it if you were using it. So we knew you were up to something else. That's why we took you to the hospital."

There was a long silence. And then Captain Baumwolle continued, "If you and your friend were working for the SS, you wouldn't have been transferred. Nor would it be necessary for her to travel here from Berlin. So we knew her message was for ears outside Germany."

Now Karl nodded. They'd guessed that much. But that was all they knew, and they weren't sure of that. And why hadn't they turned him in? Were they Schildwache?

"While you were in the hospital, the Gestapo searched your rooms," Baumwolle said. "And then Lieutenant Streicher questioned us. So we knew we'd made the right decision. You weren't with the Secret Police, or they wouldn't have searched. You weren't with the SS, or Streicher wouldn't be asking about the transmitter. We could see there was some kind of game going on between the SS and the Gestapo, because they were asking about each other." The captain paused and sipped his coffee. "I guess that's life in Germany these days. But at least we knew you weren't one of them."

Captain Baumwolle put his cup down on the table and said, "We know only that you had the transmitter—and that you have some connection with the British."

Karl sat there, sipping his coffee and saying nothing, but thinking, he's guessed there's some connection with the English. But he's German—a Luftwaffe officer. But he can't be a Nazi. No. And he doesn't know anything for sure.

Then Captain Baumwolle looked up at Karl, and said, "Some times, Lieutenant, it's better not to know too much." Refilling his coffee cup from the pewter pot which sat before him, the Captain continued, "I don't know why you're here. And I don't want to know. But you have contacts, both within and without Germany, and now you're the commander of the intercept unit. Streicher's gone. But I must tell you, Lieutenant," and here the Captain paused, and fixed his deep, blue eyes steadily on Karl, and in a low, calm voice said, "if you are a British agent, please understand that you're the enemy. But there may come a time when you could be useful." Leaning back in his chair, he asked, "When that time comes, Lieutenant, could you get a message to the British government? Someone in authority?"

Karl studied the officer for a moment, and then said quietly, "Sir, if it's an important message, I can get it through for you."

Captain Baumwolle rose slowly, and walked to a cabinet near the window, "Schnapps, Lieutenant?"

"Yes, sir. Thank you."

"And you, Ingrid?" the Captain asked.

"Cherry liqueur please, Vati."

"Then prosit," the Captain said, turning to Karl and Ingrid. The three touched glasses. "To the future, Lieutenant. To the future, Ingrid."

"The future," Karl replied.

"Yes—to the future," Ingrid said.

"Now if you two will excuse me." And as Captain Baumwolle left the room, Karl turned to Ingrid, and said, "I'd like to take a little walk along the dyke. Will you join me?"

"Yes. That'd be nice." And now she would find out what she could about Karl Meister. Her father had told her to use her charm, "It's worked for centuries," he had said, "And I've seen the way he looks at you. Enemy agent or not, he's still a man. Find out what he's up to. And if we're wrong and he's nothing more than a spy, then we'll turn him over to the Gestapo."

***

"Your father's an unusual man," Karl said to Ingrid on the dyke.

"Oh, perhaps," she said. "But don't take him too seriously, Lieutenant." And looking up at Karl, she said, "And now I will tell you a little secret."

"Should you?"

"Oh, Lieutenant," she said, taking his arm as they walked along, "there's no harm in it." And stopping and turning to Karl with a smile, she said, "He copies his weather reports from Amsterdam. He has this little receiver on the shelf over his desk connected to an earphone. And then he copies the Netherlands report, projects the forecast ahead to our area, and adds local humidity, winds and barometric pressure. He thinks I don't know," she said with a laugh.

Karl suddenly found her warm hand in his, squeezed it and walked with her along the sunny dyke, watching three sea gulls sweep low over the gray river.

It's a strong hand, she thought as they walked along. And what will he do now in the SS? Is he an English agent, she wondered? Or American? He did take the transmitter. And he must have used it. So there's some connection with the woman SS officer. He didn't belong to the Black Square, that she did know. Then it came to her. The Schildwache! Perhaps the rumor was right, they had infiltrated the SS. But they were as bad as the Nazis, maybe even worse. In the end, Karl Meister would be an enemy after all. It would be better, she thought, if it turns out he's nothing more than a simple spy. She knew that if he belonged to the Schildwache, there would come a time when she'd have to kill him. That was something her father couldn't do. But the Black Square members were on the Schildwache death list. They were just waiting. And when that time came, it would be Karl or her father.

The next Saturday, late in the afternoon, Karl called for a staff car, and returning the driver to the motor pool, drove to the Baumwolle flat on Himmelstrasse. He rang the bell and waited for Ingrid. "See," he said to her, when she opened the door, "rank has its privileges, especially SS rank."

With Ingrid sitting beside him, Karl drove slowly through the narrow streets. At times he turned and took a side street, when the road was blocked where rubble hadn't been cleared.

At last they arrived at the Columbus Restaurant, a two-story, white stone building overlooking the river in the old harbor. The restaurant was on the second floor, with the lower floor being used for the bottling facilities of a soft drink company which distributed Ess, a popular beverage.

The waiter, dressed in a tuxedo, showed them to the table Karl had reserved at the front of the restaurant where a huge window, running from the floor to the ceiling, curved along the entire wall.

Ingrid ordered a cognac and Karl brandy. When they had finished their drinks and were sitting there, sipping strong Turkish coffee topped with whipped cream, the waiter brought thick, savory ox-tail soup, and then the main course of roast duck.

"We should feel guilty," Karl said to Ingrid. "But somehow I don't. Maybe it's just rationalization. Someone else will eat it if we don't." He smiled at her, thinking he may as well enjoy the privileges of his new status.

I didn't make the rules, he thought, and he wondered what the people would think, if they knew how the Gestapo and SS lived, while they went hungry now that war had come home and the store shelves were empty.

"This is the way it was before the war," Ingrid said. "We came here then."

"With your fiancé?"

"No, Karl. I wasn't engaged. Sure, I came here now and then. But there wasn't anyone special."

"Your father told me your fiancé was killed in Africa.

"He did? Well . . . that's Vati. But—no, Karl. There wasn't anyone. Perhaps he thought . . ." And she paused. Now what? Vati and his cover stories. He should at least let me know what he tells everyone. And then looking over and smiling at Karl, she said, "Well, you know fathers, always trying to marry me off. No. He just assumed, I guess, that we'd get married." Seeing that Karl had accepted the explanation, she smiled back at him, nodded out the window, and said, "Isn't it beautiful?"

Low clouds hung in the sky to the north along the river, and sunlight streamed through the clouds, casting silver beams over the rippling water. Small fishing boats chugged slowly up the river with the incoming tide, followed by sea gulls which circled overhead, waiting for scraps tossed from nets which the men flaked into big wooden boxes on the aft decks of the varnished boats passing under the window.

"I was once a fisherman," Karl said to Ingrid, and then he remembered he was going home. "I'm leaving for Herrn Chiemsee in the morning. Two weeks leave. I'll miss you, Ingrid." When he spoke it was with deep conviction because he had grown to care very much for the blonde woman and her father, and he was leaving them for good.

She smiled demurily and lowered her eyes. "I'll miss you, Karl," she said softly.

Karl felt the blood spread hot in his face, and said quietly, "And I . . . I you, Ingrid."

When she looked up, Karl reached across the table, and taking her soft white hand, stared into her large eyes. They sat quietly, neither talking, each thinking they understood, through the eyes, what the other was thinking. And all this time a quiet peace which Karl felt he had never known, settled over him, and for the first time in many years he relaxed, intoxicated by the moment.

And she was thinking, Vati was right, a little charm does wonders. And before long I'll know whether he belongs to the Schildwache. And then I must find some way to do it quietly and quickly. Vati has already talked too much. Asking him if he could get a message to the British. My God, to tell the Schildwache that—he's probably already relayed a message to Berlin:

watch out for Baumwolle, he wants to play cozy with the British.

Beyond the window, Karl saw the sun setting in a blood-red sky, streaming banners of gold and red through black and silver clouds, and reflecting in the now dark water below.

They sat silently, holding hands across the table, while the sky darkened, and then Karl realized the waiter was at his elbow. "An after-dinner drink, sir?"

"Yes. Bring us champagne. We're going to drink to the future."

"And more of the Turkish coffee, with plenty of cream," Ingrid said to the waiter.

It was dark outside when the waiter returned, with only a soft violet glow in the west where the sun had set. And candlelight, softer still, glowed from the back tables where they could burn without violating the blackout restrictions. Soon it was too dark for anyone to see, and all was black beyond the windows. The waiter closed the heavy curtains and lit the candle at their table. Candlelight danced in the champagne glasses and reflected from Ingrid's eyes. Eyes so soft, Karl thought he felt the softness touch his heart. Her face was radiant in the creamy light, and her blonde hair, resting lightly on her shoulders, glowed in the magic light. It was then, that a string quartet started with a Viennese waltz. Karl guided Ingrid to the parquet floor, where they swirled and spun with uniformed and elegantly dressed couples under a large chandelier.

After midnight, they left the Columbus Restaurant. Karl driving slowly, Ingrid nestled on his shoulder, picked his way carefully along the dark streets in the dim glow of the car's blackout lights.

He stopped in front of the apartment building on Himmelstrasse. Seeing Ingrid's mother peeking from behind dark curtains on the third floor, Karl pulled Ingrid into the shadows, where he kissed her goodnight. "Goodbye, Ingrid. Until we meet again."

"*Aufwiedersehen*, Karl. Until we meet again."

He stepped back and blew a kiss to her mother, who then disappeared from the window.

I'll come back, somehow, he thought as he drove away. When this is all over, and the world is at peace again, I'll come back to Wesermuende. If only I could tell her now, ask her to wait for me.

As Ingrid closed the door behind her, she sighed with relief. My God, she thought, the Schildwache. I've got to talk with Vati in the morning.

Nine

A red-faced old man with a close-cropped mustache, wearing a green suit and leather hat boarded the train at Bremen on its first stop, fifty miles south of Wesermuende. He stood with his bag in the compartment door, peering at Karl through thick glasses. "May I join you?" he asked. Karl nodded, and the old man lifted his big bag onto the seat next to Karl and slumped wearily into the seat across from it.

Turning to the window as the train left the station, Karl saw a graying dawn beyond his thin reflection. And now, as the train picked up speed through flat wheat fields, the old man asked, "Are you on leave, soldier?"

Karl nodded again.

"Streicher," the red-faced man in the corner said to Karl. "My name is Otto Streicher. And you?"

"Karl Meister. Lieutenant. Waffen SS."

"My son is in the SS," the old man continued. "Perhaps you know him? Hans Streicher?"

Karl nodded a third time.

"Hans is in Berlin now," the old man said. "And my oldest boy is in the hospital at Frankfurt. That's where I'm going now." The old man leaned forward, unzipped the side of his bag, removed a small package which he unwrapped on his lap, exposing a hard roll, which he then spread with liverwurst. This he washed down with a beer taken from another section of his big bag; and when he finished the beer, he put the empty bottle into his bag and turned to Karl, saying, "I live in Bremen. Do you know the city?"

Karl shook his head. "I've only passed through a couple of times."

"I thought you were probably Austrian from your accent," the old man said. "Bremen's a beautiful city. You should see it before it's gone!"

This sudden outburst so startled Karl that he was unable to answer. Statements like that were forbidden in the Third Reich.

"Bremen is our oldest port," the old man continued. "Far older than Hamburg. And it has the most famous Ratskeller in Germany."

"Yes. I've heard of the Bremen Ratskeller." Karl looked at the old man who sat there, smiling and staring straight ahead.

"And in the Ratskeller, Lieutenant, you may sample over five hundred different wines. Then opening his second bottle of beer, Otto Streicher told Karl there was a plaque in the Ratskeller before Hitler's time which read: "Happy is the man who has reached the harbor, for he has left the sea and its storms behind him, and now sits warm and quietly in the good Ratskeller of Bermen." And then Otto turned to Karl and said, " But the verse is from Heinrich Heine. And the plaque is stored away now—in exile, just like Heine, who fled to Paris many years ago."

Karl had read the newspaper accounts of the long prison terms for those who spoke out against the Third Reich and he was taking no chances with this old man who could be baiting him, so he said nothing and sat in silence as the train ran south through yellow fields, where winter wheat bent to a soft wind under the morning sun in a clear blue sky.

At last settling back into his seat, his face redder yet, the old man pulled a blue envelope from his coat pocket, and handing it to Karl, said, "Lieutenant, could you read me this letter. It's from my son. My eyes . . . And my wife, she couldn't finish it. Poor woman. And now she sits by the window, too crippled to travel, and cries for her son. But she couldn't finish the letter. Will you . . . please . . ."

Taking the letter from the old man, Karl opened it and began to read. He read where the son explained that he would look the part of a Bremen pirate, with eye-patch and wooden leg; and that he would be home soon. The son described the view from his window, and talked about many things from his childhood in Bremen.

"Yes. Yes. That's where she stopped," Otto said, "Go on, Lieutenant."

But Karl couldn't go on. A stranger's handwriting began where the son had stopped, explaining that Major Otto Streicher had died during the night.

Karl folded the letter, placed it in the envelope, and returned it to Otto, who sat silently, staring straight ahead.

And then Otto, after a long pause said quietly, "I see, Lieutenant. Thank you."

They talked no more of his son or of war; and when they reached Kassel, the old man took another train for Berlin.

The sun was going down when the train reached Coblenz; and since there would be an hour's delay for coupling to a leave train from the east, Karl walked to an old hotel across the square from the station, where he ordered a supper of ham and pumpernickel with beer, to be followed by a glass of Steinhaeger, a strong schnapps.

The waitress, a young girl of sixteen or seventeen, with braided blonde hair, told Karl she came from Assmannshausen. The town was near the famous "Lorelei Rocks," where, according to legend, many Rhine sailors had been lured to their deaths by the sweet voice of a young maid on the night air. She explained that the name "Lorelei" came from the old Frankish words: "Lure", meaning "Elf," and "Lei," meaning rock. But Karl wondered whether "Lure" wasn't closer to its English meaning. "What do you think?" he asked the young girl, hoping she would linger at his table.

Her smiling face went serious. Putting a dark beer down on the small table before Karl, she stiffened and said, "I don't think we should pollute our German heritage with senseless English meanings." She turned on her heel and left the room.

By late evening, the long train, now burdened with additional coaches carrying exhausted soldiers on leave from the Russian front, crawled slowly along the Neckar Valley past the ancient city of Heidelberg. Karl wanted to visit the famous university town since having read of the colorful student life as described by Mark Twain, who had lived in a small hotel above the city where he wrote most of *Huckleberry Finn.* But there was to be no stop at the student city; and he strained for a glimpse of the old castle on the hill across the river where students walked their dogs above the city, dipping their caps to passers-by and singing drinking songs to accordians played loudly.

Karl left the train at the Munich station late the next afternoon and hurried to the Golden Swan Cafe near the university, where he spent the evening drinking coffee and cognac at a table in the corner and waiting for his contact. When no one approached his table, he returned to the train station and checked into the little hotel across the street which was very neat and clean and run by Catholic nuns.

In the morning, he left the hotel and walked to the museum to pass the time until the cafe opened. It was a large, sprawling building with several rooms, displaying machines and inventions from the middle ages to modern times. None of them interested Karl. His mind was on the cafe where a waiter should have passed word to his contact by now; and his thoughts were on escape to Switzerland, probably a short flight to Lisbon, he thought, and then a ship home; and shortly before eleven, he left the museum and headed toward the Golden Swan.

On his way along the wide boulevard, Karl saw a pamphlet tacked to a tree over a wooden bench. He'd stopped there for only a moment, checking his directions, when his eyes fell upon the paper, and not believing what he saw, moved closer and read: "Hitler told us that he would not rest until every

German was a free and happy person. And now, no one dares risk a free word. More and more we hear from the secret police, who make their early visits between five and six in the morning, to do their 'duty.' The visited ones disappear into concentration camps, and most Germans do not even know they exist."

Karl looked around quickly. This was treason. Just reading the small pamphlet was a crime. But Karl was curious. Who would risk instant death by writing such things, he wondered? And seeing no one on the street who looked like Gestapo or police, Karl moved closer, rested a hand on the bench below the pamphlet, and lifted the top page.

"Will we wait until the war is over?" he read further. "And everyone will say we accepted this Nazi criminal government without resistance. The Hitler Regime is a dictatorship of evil. The Nazi powers must be brought down by military force."

Karl moved quickly away from the pamphlet and hurried across the street. He stopped there on the corner and lit a cigarette. Whoever wrote that won't live long, he said to himself. My God, the man must be awfully brave, or stupid, or both.

Standing there on the corner, he smoked his cigarette, watching the people stop when they saw the pamphlet above the bench. Then they would step closer, read a few lines, whirl around, faces turning white, and rush away, some making the sign of the cross as they went.

As he turned from the tree, and walked through the cool air, he passed students who looked at him in silence, not a word coming from their grim lips in response to his greeting. He shook his head. It was the damned uniform. They weren't at all like the Heidelberg students described by Mark Twain who walked their dogs, played music, and drank all night. Their faces were serious and their expressions sullen as they went by. Now darker thoughts ran through Karl's mind. He remembered the big file Schmidt had shown him in Wesermuende. He remembered, too, that every German police precinct had such a file. Yes, he thought. The police are very systematic. You know it won't be long before the poor fellow is arrested. And then he'll be shot. But by God, someone was speaking out. Who would take such risks? It wasn't just the one pamphlet. He passed three more, each containing a similar message; and as he walked closer to the university, more students passed him. They trod slowly, without talking, still and quiet, and looking determined. They must all be under suspicion, he thought. And they're waiting. Soon the Gestapo will sweep in, arresting and torturing. And someone will finally talk. And it'll be all over.

When he reached the Golden Swan Cafe, he took his same seat at the small table. Leaning back in the soft chair, he closed his eyes. This wasn't the place to be. Something was going to happen here. The Nazis wouldn't let this pass. And where the hell was his contact. What was he supposed to do? His pass was for recuperation at Herrn Chiemsee. If he sat around this town too long, the Gestapo would want to know why. Why so much time in Munich? And then a background check. And that would be it, he'd lived in America. And then he'd be detained for more questioning. What did he have to do with the pamphlets? they'd want to know. And then he would miss his contact. And then he panicked. The Swiss Francs. My God, they're in my bag. What if they search my room?

He opened his eyes and looked out the window, where wet snow started falling. The last snow of spring, he thought, and he watched for his contact as young people came through the door, shaking the soft flakes from their coats and hats.

Someone sat down at his table. It was a young man, quite handsome, with coal-black, well-oiled hair combed straight back.

"Good morning," the man said quietly, and nodded as Karl looked at him.

The man was dressed all in black, had an elegant mustache, and his long fingers were well manicured. This must be the man, Karl thought. But the tables were filling up and it was customary to take any empty chair, although one usually asked permission. So Karl knew he must be careful. And he felt uncomfortable about this stranger at his table.

"Are you here for a particular purpose?" the man asked.

"No," said Karl, curtly. "And you?" He saw the man blink, and thought, well, if that's the code word, I certainly missed it.

"Yes," the man replied. "I came to observe."

Now what? Karl wondered and glanced out the window. Maybe I should leave and try this later. Hell, I'm supposed to be recognized. And that shouldn't be too difficult. He took his gloved hand from his lap and put it on the table in plain view. Maybe this is what he's looking for, the man with a bad hand.

Still the man said nothing. Karl waited a few more minutes; and just as he was thinking again of leaving, the man bent across the table, and asked, "Do you have a mirror?"

At this moment, the swarthy waiter came with Karl's cognac and second coffee on a round, silver tray, and putting the tray on the table in front of Karl, took the stranger's order. "Also a cognac," the man said. "And coffee, too, with whipped cream."

Nothing further was said by the man. After the waiter left, Karl said at last, "No. I don't have a mirror."

"Ah, that's too bad," the stranger said. "I've just come from the barber. Would you believe that a few moments ago I had a full beard?" he said, rubbing his chin.

Karl watched the man, saying nothing. These curious statements must be the code words. I had a beard before I was recruited by the Shildwache. Captain Harding told me it had to go—another one of my sacrifices—and he's passed that information along. Sure, and he remembered Harvey saying the code would probably be something only he would know about, and Karl started to say, "Are you my contact?" But he paused for just a moment.

The stranger drank from his coffee cup and laughed quietly. Then turning to Karl, he said, "I apologize for laughing, Lieutenant. I thought you might be someone I was to meet."

Karl smiled broadly. "And who might that be?"

"An SS lieutenant," was the stranger's answer. "But I see you're Waffen SS. I should have recognized the difference."

"Perhaps you were to meet him at another cafe," Karl said, "or at another time." And all the time Karl was saying to himself, is this man testing me? What if it's true, and he really isn't my contact? But if he is, and I let this slip past, then what?

"Well, you're not the man, that's for sure," the stranger said. "You people don't get into this sort of thing. "It's all so terrible," the man continued, his narrow eyes closing slightly. "But I suppose if it was to happen, Munich would be the place."

"Happened? What's happened?"

"Treasonable pamphlets—and more. This morning we found the train station painted with very distressing messages. 'Down with Hitler,' they said. Can you imagine? And its never dark around the station. Someone has foolish courage."

Now Karl was positive the black-suited man was Gestapo, and he'd almost asked him for instuctions for an escape to Switzerland. "And what are you doing about it?"

"Oh, we know who they are. Most of them, anyway. And we're going to get them—all of them."

"And then what?"

"They'll have a trial," the man said calmly, taking a cigarette from an engraved gold case, and offering one to Karl. "And then we'll execute them."

Karl declined the stranger's cigarette and lit one of his own.

"Combat wound?" the stranger asked, looking at the black glove on Karl's left hand.

"Yes," Karl lied, "Tunis." And then he felt ashamed. There was no need to pretend bravado with the effeminate-looking man. Why, he wondered, are we always trying to please them.

The man stretched a limp hand to Karl. "Albert Hesse," he said, "and you are?"

Karl shook the man's hand, thinking for a moment he'd give him a false name. But then said, "Karl Meister," when he realized the next request would be for his identification, and he'd have enough problems explaining why he was in the Golden Swan when he was supposed to be on a train for Herrn Chiemsee.

Albert Hesse nodded slowly. "Karl Meister . . . You're Austrian, then. I thought I recognized the accent." Hesse told him the student ring leaders had already been arrested and tried after four days of interrogation. "Remarkable young people," Hesse said, "those leaders of the White Rose. Hans Scholl and his sister, Sophie. Never broke—remarkable. And they came from a good German family, too. Both had been in the Hitler youth." Hesse sipped his coffee and watched Karl over his cup, and then setting the cup on the table, continued, "They showed no appreciation for the education they received from the Third Reich, Lieutenant, while others sacrificed good German blood at the front . . . And someone's still nailing up those damned pamphlets."

Karl said nothing while Hesse fingered his mustache. Leaning forward in his chair and speaking quieter now, Hesse said, "They'd been distributing those damned pamphlets for over a year, they appeared in Berlin, and then Hamburg. We had to act. We watched them. Collected information." Looking slowly around, and continuing in a softer tone, Hesse said, "We wanted the others. But we couldn't wait any longer. Pressure from Berlin. So we arrested them. Got nothing out of them. Damn them." With those words, he slammed the table, and his face was red now.

"Finally," Hesse said, "we took them to trial before old Judge Freisler of the People's Court here in Munich. Freisler, I must say, is a fierce looking man. And he was in his best form that day. Sophie testified first. Admitted everything. And then she turned to Freisler and said, 'You all agree with what we've written, but you're afraid of saying so.' Her brother, Hans was just as stubborn." Hesse stirred in his seat, his voice now rising in agitation, so that people at other tables turned their heads, as he said, "They were taken to Stadelheim prison. The SS had strict orders. They were to be executed and buried. That was it. But their parents were allowed to see them. And then the guards took them out of their cells to meet one last time." Hesse paused with a thin smile on his lips. "And then we executed the guards." Hesse was leaning very close to Karl now and speaking in a whisper. "Those guards, SS men, were also members of some damned anti-Nazi group. That's why we were so ineffective here."

Karl went completely cold when Hesse showed him a Gestapo badge in a leather case and said, "And now I'd like to see your identification. Just hand it over—let's see who you are and where you're from."

Karl laid his military paybook on the table. Hesse picked it up, leafing through the pages which contained his identity photograph, his promotion to SS Lieutenant, and the abstract of his two-week leave to Herrn Chiemsee.

Albert Hesse made notes in a small book from his suit pocket. "What do you find so facinating about Munich?"

"I decided to stop here when it turned colder." Karl smiled at the dark-haired man in the black suit. "Snow at Herrn Chiemsee is not that appealing."

"So you visited the museum," Hesse said, "And why did you come here, to the Golden Swan?"

"I wanted a coffee, and a cognac," Karl said quickly.

"You walked all the way to the university for coffee? Come now, Lieutenant, you passed several cafes on the way."

"Well damn it, Herr Hesse, I just happen to like long walks. How in the hell was I to know where I was going, I don't know this city. And when I got this far, I stopped in."

Hesse tapped his fingers on the dark wood. A smile spread over his face. "All right, Lieutenant. All right. But this is no city to be wandering around in—not at this time. Where are you staying?"

"The Bahnhoff Hotel."

"Very well. Return to your hotel, Lieutenant. You're under house arrest." He closed Karl's paybook and stuffed it into his suit pocket. "You won't need this for a while. And if everything checks out, you'll get it back at the People's court tomorrow morning. I'll see you there, Lieutenant. At nine. And you can watch the second trial. Surely you have time . . . since you're on leave. Judge Freisler will be presiding. And you'll have something to tell your grandchildren some day."

The next morning, Karl walked from his hotel near the train station to the gray building housing the People's Court. There, he saw Hesse waiting for him at the top of the wide stairs.

Karl returned his Hitler greeting, received his paybook, and followed Hesse to the courtroom, where seats in the front were reserved for party members. Looking around the crowded courtroom, he could see that SS men and black-suited Gestapo outnumbered the white-faced civilians.

All stood and gave a stiff-armed, "Heil Hitler," as Judge Freisler entered and sat at a high bench under a huge eagle with swastika.

"The court is now open to Public Session," the clerk announced; and the reporter duly entered his words into the record. Then the clerk announced in a shrill high voice that this was the trial of a student named Schmorell, a university professor named Huber, and eleven other students.

Judge Freisler screamed out the charges, reading from a thick file before him on the bench, his face distorted, and scarlet red.

The older prisoner was the first to speak. They should never have permitted Professor Huber to testify, Karl thought as he listened to the quiet middle-aged man calmly claim he had done nothing illegal. Hesse, next to Karl, was restless, and constantly shifting in his seat, as Huber explained from the witness box that, on the contrary, they had stood by the rule of law. "We asked only for the return to clear moral principles," Huber said. "To the rule of law, to mutual trust among all men—this was not illegal, but a restoration of legality," he said. And then turning and looking directly at Karl, sitting among the SS and Gestapo men, the professor said, "Every morally responsible citizen should raise his voice against the threatening tyranny of might over right, of capriciousness over free will."

Karl braced himself, expecting an outcry from the assembled Nazis around him. But there was stunned silence. The courtroom was quiet—without a sound—as the professor continued his attack on Nazism. With a voice as calm and assured as if he were lecturing his students, he said, "During the past ten years the Nazi Party has destroyed every sense of moral obligation, as well as freedom."

Judge Freisler was on his feet, screaming at the professor, who sat quietly, with an amused look on his calm face.

"You will die for your actions against the Third Reich!" the judge shouted; and shaking his fist at the witness, the judge sat down, saying, "Now confess your crimes!"

Karl listened as the professor continued, recounting the acts of Hitler and the Nazis, calling them hideous crimes against the German people, while Judge Freisler sat, gripping the sides of his high bench, his face white with anger and the viens standing out on his knotted forehead.

When the clerk announced the noon recess, Hesse turned to Karl and said quietly, "I think you've seen enough for today."

"Yes," Karl answered. "I have seen enough for today."

"Now come with me," Hesse said. "We'll have lunch. And we'll go to the University to hear Geisler, the district party leader. Then you can catch your train to Herrn Chiemsee."

They drove to a restaurant on the street down from the Golden Swan, where Hesse showed his pass, and they were seated at a linen-covered table. "This restaurant is reserved for the SS and party members," Hesse said. "We must keep the government fed."

Now Karl understood why he had been so elegantly served everywhere he stopped, while others ate meager, non-meat meals and thin soup. It was the uniform which called for the best from the secret larders.

Hesse explained that the meeting would take place at the Museum of Technology Karl had visited earlier. It was one of the few halls big enough to hold the university's faculty and student body, Hesse told him.

***

At the museum auditorium, SS men stood guard at the exists, and there were dark-suited Gestapo agents everywhere. There must have be at least five thousand students and faculty crowded into the room, Karl thought. Geisler, a tall thin man with a yellow complexion, told the assembled throng that the German Sixth Army, surrounded at Stalingrad, where over a half million soldiers had already died from starvation and enemy action, was now gone. Over twenty-five generals and twenty-five hundred officers were lost—including the brother of Armaments Minister, Albert Speer.

And all this, Geisler shouted from the platform, was because of lack of support from the German people. "Hitler," Geisler said, "has no use for young men who bury their heads in books, using their studies as an excuse to evade military service. You are all malingering," he shouted, "and all who are physically able should go into the Army—and those that are not, must go to work in war industries." A wave of murmurs spread through the crowd.

"He's going too far," Hesse said to Karl, and looked nervously about him at the angry young faces. "These students are all children of party members—they have special exemptions."

Then Geisler said, "If you don't go voluntarily, you will be called up."

There was a general commotion all around, which suddenly stopped as the SS men at the exits drew revolvers.

Geisler stood, watching the now silent crowd. "As for the girls," he said, "they have a duty too. There's no reason why every healthy girl shouldn't present an annual testimonial to the Fuehrer in the form of a son." Geisler continued with a high laugh, "I realize this requires a certain amount of cooperation. And if some of you girls lack sufficient charm to find a mate, I can assign to each of you one of my adjutants, whose antecedents I can vouch for—and I can promise her a thoroughly enjoyable experience."

"My God," Hesse said, "that's too much. The idiot!"

From behind him, Karl heard a voice shout out. "We won't have our students insulted!" This was followed by shouts from other students. Karl was caught in a sudden uproar as students swirled and pushed around him. Then there was a rush for the exits.

He saw several SS men lifted high above the crowd; and then he, too, was grabbed from behind, lifted from his feet, and carried swiftly through the exit and thrown down the stairs, landing outside among a group of SS men, who had lost their drawn pistols to the crowd.

Karl struggled to his feet, and was swept into the street by a crush of students who pounded him and the other SS with closed fists and shouted,

"Free our comrades! Give us back our comrades!"

Karl broke free with a small group of SS men, and ran with them down a side street. When they turned left, he went right and ducked into a small shop. "Where's the back door!" he shouted to an old lady behind the counter. She pointed, mouth open and speechless. He rushed down the aisle, out a side door and into an alley. He could hear shouts of a noisy crowd in the streets, and then shots ringing out, and a heavy machine gun, and then more shots. When he reached the end of the alley he came out onto a wide boulevard. People were running everywhere, and farther down the street, in the direction of the museum, a car was burning. He ran with the crowd, away from there, and when he had gone several blocks, he ran faster and jumped aboard a moving street car which carried a sign reading: "Central Train Station."

When he reached his hotel, he grabbed up his bags, which were packed and ready, and hurried down the stairs. There, a policeman stopped him in the lobby. "A state of emergency has just been declared in Munich," the officer told him. "All telephone and radio service is cut off. No one is allowed on the street."

"I'm SS you idiot!" Karl screamed at the startled man and pushed his way out the door. He ran for the train station and through the wide double doors, as other policemen swung into place a heavy barricade. Again he shouted, "SS!" And again the bluff worked.

He ran along the lower level platform, and when he saw a train leaving for Salzburg, he grabbed the rail of a moving coach and swung aboard. The train was headed south, that's all that mattered now. He'd missed his contact in Munich and was on his own.

Karl pushed down the narrow aisle of the third class coach and took the first empty seat. Suddenly a conductor was standing over him. "Ticket please, sir."

"There wasn't time," Karl said, "I'm going to Chiemsee." He showed the conductor his pass.

"You'll have to take a bus from Rosenheim," the conductor said. "This isn't a leave train. We don't stop at Chiemsee."

Karl paid for a ticket to Rosenheim and settled back on the wooden bench. That will do fine, he thought. It's ten miles from the Austrian border.

And when he reached Rosenheim he bought hiking clothes and packed them into his bag. Then he set out down the road for the Austrian border and Innsbruck beyond. He'd gone less than a mile when he saw a small convoy coming up the long hill behind him. "Need a lift, Lieutenant?" the driver of the first lorry asked. "Thanks a lot," Karl answered. "Where ya headed, Corporal?"

"Italy, Lieutenant."

"Well fine. You can drop me off at Innsbruck. Missed the damned train."

"Anything for a fellow Austrian," the corporal said, "I'm from Graz, Lieutenant. And I'd say you were born not far from there with that accent."

"Badenberg, Corporal."

"That's what I thought, sir."

Karl took a seat in the open cab, and a few miles later they were in the foothills of the Alps and crossed the border into Austria.

They reached Innsbruck long after dark, and Karl thanked the corporal for the ride. He had no pass for a hotel this far south, and SS or not, he wasn't taking chances. So he put the small city behind him; and when he found a shephard's cabin high in the hills and now vacant until the summer grass season, he changed into his hiking gear and went to sleep in a straw bed.

The next day he traveled through Uppper Austria by bus from small town to small town, until he was in the area where the three countries of Austria, Liechtenstein and Switzerland met. His last meal in the Third Reich was near Bluwald, a small Austrian village, where he purchased a hard loaf of bread and cheese.

That night he moved silently through the pine forests, always hearing the German border patrols long before they were near. He raced across a small clearing in the clear moonlight, threw his bag over a high, barbed-wire fence, and scrambled over. On the other side, he picked up his bag and ran. He was in Switzerland; and when he was in the heavy forest again, he stopped and made a shelter from old pine boughs and rested there, too excited to sleep.

When it was light enough to see, he walked west ahead of the sun, until he found a small dirt road. He followed this road and shortly before noon found himself in the small Swiss village of Niederzell. The bright red flag with white cross flew from every attic. Everyone on the clean streets of the little town was smiling, and the spotless shops were full of foods Karl had long forgotten. Chocolates of all kinds. There were no shortages. And freedom was in the air.

He bought a huge chocolate bar and ate it with relish as he walked to the train station at the far end of the small town. There he spent twenty more of his Swiss Francs for a train ticket to Berne. Three other passengers waited for the train. An old peasant woman, probably going only a short distance, a man Karl took to be a local businessman, and another man who looked like he might be a district official of some type. The man who looked like a businessman asked Karl for a light, and he gladly reached in his pocket and pulled out his matches. He would have kissed the man at that point, and there wasn't anything he'd not do for these wonderful people. As the man opened the matches, Karl suddenly reached out and grabbed them. "I'll light it for you," he stammered. They were German matches!

The man was almost too polite. He smiled again after Karl lit his cigarette. Then he said, "May I see your identification, sir?" At the same time he opened a leather case and said again very politely and with his friendly smile, "Swiss Police, Aliens Department. These matches are quite common in Switzerland. But you just gave yourself away."

Karl found himself on a train. Not bound for Berne, as he had hoped, but on his way to internment near Zurich, and he was in handcuffs. The Swiss were intent on protecting their neutrality he learned, and they were especially nervous over German spies, and the Wehrmacht they expected to come crashing through on its way to Italy, when American bombers choked off the Austrian passes.

Ten

Allen Dulles was a wiry, gray-haired man with a rather broad face, a trim mustache and a flat forehead. His clear gray eyes were intent behind steel-rimmed glasses. "You certainly have a beautiful view of the mountains from your window," he said to U.S. Army Lieutenant Karl Meister in his Zurich cell. He explained that an agreement had been negotiated with Major Max Waibel, the head of Swiss Military Intelligence. In exchange for Karl's release, the OSS would supply the Swiss with information on any German intentions to violate the tiny country's neutrality.

They drove to Berne, and took a roundabout way to the Herrengasse where Dulles had his headquarters. "The city is a nest of German agents," he told Karl. "Be extremely cautious at all times." Since the one greatest danger was a sureptitious photograph taken with a telephoto lens to be shipped to Berlin and examined by the Gestapo, they never entered or left the building in daylight. Karl would be leaving again in the morning, long before sunrise—his destination was Vienna.

They poured over maps late into the night and Karl memorized names and code words and addresses. It would be a quick trip. And Karl was going as Wehrmacht Sergeant Hans Mueller, complete with pay book which contained his service record and the fictious medals he'd received in the African campaign where he'd received wounds to his left hand.

He wasn't going home after all. He was too valuable. It was difficult getting agents into Germany, Dulles told him; and after his mission in Vienna, he would be returning to Wesermuende as Lieutenant Karl Meister of the Waffen SS. There, if at all possible, he was to resume his transmissions. Many U-Boats had been intercepted by the British as a result of his work; and there were rumors of a new German aircraft carrier under construction somewhere along the north coast. "That ship would be a major problem if it gets loose in the North Sea," Dulles said. "And that will be your number one priority."

Karl left Switzerland at almost the same point he'd entered. He was wearing the same hiking outfit. But in his bag he carried two uniforms, those of a Waffen SS lieutenant and a German Army sergeant. He went from safe house to safe house in each little village, following the route of the Austrian underground, until he reached Innsbruck, where he boarded a leave train as Sergeant Hans Mueller of the Wehrmacht. He was on his way to Vienna where he would make contact with 05, the Austrian resistance movement. He was to meet a disabled soldier at the number 38 street car stop near the Schottentor. "It will be easy to recognize the man," Dulles told him, "he'll be wearing a Wehrmacht uniform, carrying a book on parrots . . . and he has no legs. Offer to help with his wheelchair. And then ask if he remembers Papagei." Karl grinned then, Papagei was a parrot in an old Austrian comic strip.

The disabled soldier would make final arrangements for Karl's meeting with Wehrmacht Major Stillfried. The major and several of his friends from the former Austrian officer corps were about to set up an active military resistance group in Vienna. Their Berlin contact was at the house of Hilda Krummbach in the suburb of Zehlendorf-West. Hilda Krummbach was the link to Colonel von Lahousen who had worked for Austrian Intelligence until 1938, when the country became part of the Third Reich. Colonel von Lahousen, Dulles had explained to Karl, now worked for Admiral Canaris, head of the Abwehr, in his Berlin headquarters. Karl's job was to deliver the key words, codes and frequencies for radio communication between Vienna and Dulles at Berne, and if at all possible, convince the Austrian underground that their only chance for success was through cooperation with the OSS. If Karl succeeded, Dulles would then have a network running from Berne to Vienna, from there to Berlin, and from Berlin to Karl on the North Sea at Wesermuende.

When Karl's work was done, he was to switch uniforms for a short visit to his grandparents at Badenberg, and then return to Wesermuende. If he kept to his time schedule, he would be back on the North Sea at the end of his two-week convalescent leave.

The train rattled on toward Vienna, Karl thinking of the big house in Badenberg, remembering how it was to awake to the sounds of Oma in the kitchen and the smell of coffee. It had rained hard that last night he was there; and when he awoke the next morning on the cot behind the green ceramic-tiled stove, the rain had stopped, and he saw yellow light playing on the dry oak leaves, which still clung to the tree beyond the glassed-in porch.

His grandparents had already eaten at the little table in the kitchen, and he heard Oma say, "I think our Karli drank a little too much of the Heurigen, Opa."

"Now, Karli. Awake at last?" Karl heard his grandfather say, as his feet touched the cold wood floor. "Come, have some hot coffee."

Karl ate a breakfast of hard rolls; and then he went through the porch into the morning sunlight, walked past the tin gazebo in the apple orchard, and turned into the backyard. This yard was quite narrow, less than forty feet deep from the house to where it ended at the foot of a huge granite rock which rose straight up a hundred feet high over the roof. At the top was a plateau, where grass and fir trees grew, with a table of heavy timbers near the iron railing.

From that high ridge, Karl could see every building in the small city; the tall spire of St. Stephen's Church, the blue water in the open mineral baths, and far off to the north in a light blue haze, the Danube, curving toward Vienna. He'd gone with his grandfather many times to that city, delivering the black homemade cigars for the shops to sell to tourists. But those were not good times, those first years after the war, food was short and workers rioted; and while they waited for the train home, Opa told him how it was before the war, when the city danced to waltzes. Those were the times, his grandfather told him, when the gigantic ferris wheel at the Prater, the world's largest, never stopped.

After all those years, Karl was now on his way back to Vienna. All he could think about were the sunshine days before the First World War, when his father and mother were alive and they lived at the villa in Badenberg next to his grandparents apartment. Those were days when he heard his mother singing from the open window while he practiced with the osage bow Opa had carved. He shot his arrows into thick straw hung on the door of the storeroom cut into that huge rock which rose behind the villa.

No one knew who had carved that room into the rock. Opa knew only that it was there when his father bought the land and built the villa. "I like to think it was a storage room for a Roman outpost," his grandfather had said, rubbing a hand across his heavy beard. One day Karl shot an arrow high over the stone peak, and found it later in the storage room behind an apple barrel. The room was high, at least fifteen feet. It was dark under the stone ceiling. But that had to be where the arrow came from; and he took a ladder and climbed, reaching a narrow ledge on the back wall. He slid carefully onto the ledge, and grasping the rough wall, moved along it until he saw a long, narrow cut in the stone. Peering inside, he saw a small room in dim light. He crawled through and found he could stand. Overhead was a narrow shaft with steps cut into the sides. At the top Karl saw light.

He took candles to his secret room and there he read volumes of American-Indian stories.

"What are you doing in there?" His cousin Alex surprised him one afternoon coming out of the storage area with a book under his arm and an apple clenched in his teeth. Alex stood tall in front of him. The orchard and all of the apples belonged to his family. Freckles danced below his green eyes, and he demanded again, "What are you doing in the storeroom, Karli?"

No explanation would satisfy Alex, and Karl kept his secret. "That's a stupid book," Alex said, tearing the volume Opa had lent Karl, from his hands. "And this is the reason you do so bad in school. You're just like your Opa. That's what my father says. They wouldn't take him. And you'll never get into the university either."

"And why should I go to your dumb university to be a greedy lawyer?"

Alex grabbed Karl by his woolen shirt. "Karl, one of these days I'm going to beat the hell out of you. My dad's not greedy. He does what's necessary—the important work. And he wouldn't steal apples."

He heard nothing further from Alex about the apples until Chirstmas Eve on the second floor, where all the Meister family gathered at Uncle Eugene's long table.

"See, Karli," Alex said as his mother placed a steaming apple on Karl's plate. "You need only ask. Right Mother?"

"Ask what, Alex?" Aunt Agnes said.

"Oh nothing, mother. It's just a little joke between Karli and me."

"Quiet Alex!" Uncle Eugene glowered at the table's head. "Speak only when spoken to."

"But it's Christmas Eve," Aunt Agnes said in her soft voice. "The boy's excited. And he has a little secret with Karli. Don't you Alex?"

"Yes mother. Just a little secret."

"And now you'll be quiet, won't you, Alex? Be a good boy like Karli."

"Yes, Mutti."

"And here's a nice hot apple for you, too," Aunt Agnes said, placing a baked apple on Alex's plate.

"None for me. Thank you," the stout man seated next to Alex said in a heavy Berlin accent. "Your cabbage soup, Agnes, ah, absolutely delicious. And never have I tasted such delicate carp, or such succulent eel. But an apple, now. Oh, no. That would be too much." And he patted his large stomach.

"Dr. Grauenhaft," Karl's father said with a chuckle, "I can prescribe the apple to ease your conscience if you like."

"Thank you for the kind offer, Herr Doctor," the German replied with a laugh. "But I'll pass, and your little Karli can have two."

"Karli would like that." Alex broke in. "Wouldn't you, my little apple-eater."

Karl sat silent and waited for the storm he knew would come from the head of the table.

"Alex!" his Uncle Eugene said, his dark wrinkled face now hard, "you're excused from the table. Now go!"

Karl smiled as Alex rose, bowed to the elders at the table and left the room.

"Dr. Grauenhaft, do they celebrate Christmas in America half so well?" Uncle Eugene's wrinkled face now smiled.

"Well," the German replied, "I can only speak for New York and Boston, but I must say our American friends do Christmas rather well. They have about the same customs, in a general nature of course. Nevertheless, something is missing." He leaned back in his chair. "Something is missing. It's not the spirit, but the traditions, I think, which are lacking. Of course," he waved a hand over the table, "they don't have this at all. No carp—and they shudder at the word. In America, carp is a garbage fish. They don't have our special carp beds and they have no eel—no, not really a Christmas Eve tradition at all. The clam chowder in Boston is rather delicious. But no substitutes for me, please." His broad face broke into a smile. "And they eat a lot. Sometimes more than I can eat. And on Christmas Day they have a tremendous feast. Uncles and aunts, the whole big family, gather around piles of food, and eat so much they can't rise from the table."

"Dr. Grauenhaft," Uncle Eugene spoke up, and his lips had gone hard and thin on his monkey-like face, "what about the Jews? I hear a lot of Jews live in New York."

"Quite a few, yes. But not any more than Vienna," the German answered.

"Or in Berlin," Uncle Eugene said with a laugh. "That's where the real problem lies."

"Problem?" the German replied. "We have no problem. Berlin has the best Jews in Europe. Good citizens. Most of them businessmen. Why, the arts are full of Jews."

"Yes. I see. At least the Jews here are loyal to Franz Joseph," Uncle Eugene said. "Not like some nationalities in the empire. The Magyars, for example. They'll bring down the Empire yet with their demands for an independant and separate Hungary."

"Well your Jews know when to be quiet," Dr. Grauenhaft said. "How long has it been? Not two hundred years, I believe, since you people drove them out? And I won't talk about what you did to those who didn't leave. So it's understandable, that when they finally came back it was to be different for them. They remember. They know not to make waves in Vienna. But in Berlin, a Jew can say what's on his mind as well as the next man."

"How they travel though—the Jews," Uncle Eugene said. "From country to country." He raised his chin and Karl saw an arrogant look in his eyes as he continued. "How can they have any loyalty—any nationality?"

"Ah," Karl's father said. "And we? Who are we to say? Our ancestors came from Bavaria. They didn't consider themselves German, and neither did the Austrians. Both countries were aligned against the Prussians at the time. And then came Bismark with his wars of German unification under Prussia. Hell, those people had nothing in common, not even a common language, why English was a lot closer to the Hannover German than many of the dialects."

"Now, now," the Berliner said, "Prussia united the German States by force, that's true—"

"And fought us to keep out Austrian influence," Karl's father said calmly.

"Yes, but we're all German brothers now. I feel no animosity in Vienna. Absolutely none. Never," Dr. Grauenhaft said, looking defensive.

"We meant no offense, Doctor Grauenhaft," Uncle Eugene said, and his black eyes flashed at Karl's father. "Cousin Jacque, here," he said quickly, "is part French and American Indian. Perhaps he doesn't feel our unity with the German people."

"My mother is part French and part Chippewa, the Michigan Indian," Karl's father said. "And they called themselves the Anishinabe—the ultimate human beings—and they tortured their prisoners until they died, believing all the time they were a superior race."

"I see," the German said quietly, and lowered his eyes.

"Gentlemen, it's Christmas Eve," Aunt Agnes interrupted from the other end of the table. "Let's not talk of nations and politics . . . Oh, you men." She laughed and her blue eyes shown in her fair face.

"Politics, Agnes?" Uncle Eugene said. "I thought we were talking about race." And he accented the word "race" and drew it out so that it seemed to Karl to hang heavy on the air, a challenge thrown down the long table.

"Sometimes I think it's all the same thing," Aunt Agnes said in a soft voice and laughed nervously. "But you know," she turned to Karl and winked, "it's getting late and the Christ Child will be waiting for all to sleep so he can slip in and lay presents under the tree."

Aunt Agnes rose from her chair and crossed to the Christmas tree. Lighting the candles on the branches, she said to the group, "Come. You here, Karli. And Jacque. And come now, Alex. Everyone. That's it. Make a circle around the tree." She turned off the lights and the candles glowed upon faces. "Now, please," she said, taking Dr. Grauenhaft's hand, "join hands and we'll sing a Christmas song whose words were written by a simple Austrian priest to music composed by his dear friend in a neighboring village, a music teacher."

Her voice sang out high and strong, "Silent night . . . holy night . . ."

One by one, they joined in. Finally, the strong voice of Dr. Grauenhaft came from the other side of the tree, surprising everyone. It was a powerful, vibrating tenor which filled the room.

When they finished with, " . . . sleep in heavenly peace," Karl peered around the candlelit tree and saw tears running down Dr. Grauenhaft's cheeks. Uncle Eugene's eyes were dry and cool, and he coughed, looking embarrassed.

"Off we go now," Aunt Agnes said. "Mass starts in ten minutes.

"And we'll have a brandy and wait for you," Uncle Eugene said, slapping Dr. Grauenhaft on the back. "You too, Jacque, if you'd like."

"Thank you," his father said. "But Christmas mass has always been a special time for us."

They went down the stairs and onto the street, where they waited for Oma and Opa, who hurried from their apartment and joined them in response to his father's long whistle.

Holding hands, they walked through the fresh snow under a thousand bright stars; and as they went along, they joined other people hurrying to church. Over the steeple ahead, Karl saw a star bigger and brighter than he'd remembered seeing in the black sky—and this bright star had a double meaning for Karl—it was his first Christmas without his mother.

***

The Vienna leave train pulled into the West Bahnhof station late in the afternoon. Karl, alias Sergeant Mueller, took a street car to the Schottentur in the central city, stopping at number 38. There he met the disabled soldier in the wooden wheel chair, asked about Papagei, and was given an address in the Universitatsstrasse, where he showed the German soldier who opened the door his pass, and was directed to an old hotel in the third district Fassangasse. The ancient inn reminded him of his uncle's farm, with its stables in the courtyard.

There he received ration cards and was introduced to Captain Slokolov of the military resistance, code named 05. The captain had heavy eyebrows and a bushy mustache. His family came from a line of Georgian noblemen before that country became part of the Soviet Union. He was a fierce anti-Communist and hated the Nazis with equal passion. To him, Karl handed over the OSS codes and frequencies.

The Austrian 05 underground had several hundred men and were building up resistance cells in German military units in Vienna and Lower Austria. Now Captain Slokolov wanted to know, "Will the Allies help? We can't assassinate Hitler without their support. And unless we have assurances that America and England will recognize the movement and make a separate peace—let us continue against the Russians, we can't win the support of major German commanders."

Karl took a long breath and gave him Dulle's answer. "The request was submitted to President Roosevelt with the recommendation of the U.S. Joint Chiefs of Staff; and Roosevelt turned it down. 'If the German people want to do away with their leader,' Roosevelt said, 'I wish them success. But we can't engage in a policy of assassination of heads of state. It's unthinkable. What would the world become if its greatest democracy adopted such a policy? No. There will be no help from America.'"

In answer to the question of a separate peace, the response was also negative. Roosevelt and Churchill had just concluded talks in Casablanca. Karl told the captain that the joint announcement made at that time was exactly what Roosevelt meant and he would stick by it. Nothing less than unconditional surrender was acceptable. The United States would never turn its back on its Russian friends. The British response to a request from the anti-Hitler groups was the same. There would be no negotiated peace. Quoting Anthony Eden, Karl gave Britian's answer, "The world had been mislead too often."

Slokolov's bushy eyebrows knotted. "They give us no reason to go on," the captain said angrily. "Why should we cooperate with the Allies?"

"I don't know." Karl shook his head. "I have no answer for you. But Dulles told me if 05 will produce, show the Americans they are a force worthy of consideration, then he'll see what can be done."

"Will he supply equipment?"

"I think so."

"But you don't know."

"No. I can't promise that."

"And we risk our lives while Dulles sits in Berne. We're supposed to feed him information on German troop movements . . . And, what else? Yes, let him know of German intentions to move on Switzerland. We get nothing in return. And our own men are in those German units. Tell me why we should do that?"

"To shorten the war, Captain."

The captain laughed, "To shorten the war. And when it's over Germany and Austria will be neatly divided and the Russian bear will sit in Vienna. Roosevelt seems to me an awfully naive man." The captain tugged at the corner of his bushy mustache. His black eyes stared into space for a long time. He turned to Karl across the table, "Well Sergeant Mueller, we'll go on without them. Our transmitter is in the university physics lab. Will you ask the Americans to be so kind as to concentrate on military targets? They damned near killed me last week."

Karl ate supper with the captain and two German Army corporals who never gave their names, and was given a small room overlooking the courtyard. He had sent a telegram to his grandparents in Badenberg, fifteen miles south of Vienna. That's where he would go by train in the morning. But that evening he wanted to see the city of music, and so he walked to the old town center.

Everywhere, the streets were empty of cars because of heavy gas rationing. A few trolleys and busses ran along the Ringstrasse, now dark and gloomy. Pale blue bulbs burned low in the streetcars, casting an eerie luminescence over gaunt passengers' faces inside. The whiteness of their faces in the blue light gave them the pallor of death itself, Karl thought, as the drawn faces rolled slowly past. Faces which looked as though they were living in a dream, staring questioningly from the streetcar windows at Karl as he walked through the streets, now deserted except for an occasional old man on a bicycle.

Karl saw ominous street posters everywhere, warning of crimes against the state. "Listening to foreign radio stations was punishable by a minimum of five years in prison," he read from a sign in front of the opera house. He noted that the punishment could be death for "aggravated" offenses, described as listening to such broadcasts in groups.

In Wesermuende, he had seen posters warning against hoarding. Here they were again, with further warnings against trading on the black market.

On the train to Vienna, he had read of trials of those involved in the illegal trade. Otto and Martha Schnellert of Erfurt were executed for trading old clothing for rationed food. Nothing was said about those restaurants so popular with the SS and Nazi elite, the ones which required no ration coupons. They served exotic foods and choice wines to their select guests, who then executed Otto and Martha Schnellert of Erfurt.

Karl went to the *Villa Bavaria* where his grandparents lived, wearing his Wehrmacht sergeant's uniform and knocked on the heavy oak door facing the apple orchard.

"Karli!" his grandmother exclaimed. "For God's sake, it's Karli!" His grandfather, tall and frail, his pale face as white as his long beard, stood behind the French-Chippewa woman from Michigan.

These old people were Karl's Oma and his Opa. They could be dead before the war was over. No, he was not a Nazi he told them inside. He showed them his paybook. They looked at the identification and his photograph. "Sergeant Hans Mueller?" His grandfather said slowly.

"Yes," Karl said. "I'm telling you that I've changed my name to Hans Mueller. I'm a sergeant, in the Wehrmacht. I changed my name to protect myself from discrimination in the Third Reich. It was my only choice. And it was done by Dr. Grauenhaft in New York. You remember him, he was at Uncle Eugene's. And he brought me to Germany just before Pearl Harbor."

"Karli, you'd do that?" his grandfather asked. "What discrimination, Karli?"

"Discrimination against the Anishinabe," Karl answered.

Then a wide smile spread over his grandmother's face. She nodded and chuckled. "So that's what you want us to believe."

"Now don't ask me any more questions."

They talked about America and how Austria was before the Germans came. The time before the *Anschluss* in 1938; and about the flowering of the so-called "March violets," Austrian lawyers, and doctors, and professors, and the ordinary people who overnight suddenly became conscious of their Nazi convictions and embraced the new Messiah, their liberator, Adolf Hitler.

His grandmother was suddenly quiet. "Karl, they read from a paper when they came. 'We are all Germans,' they said. 'And we Germans are heathens and want no more Jewish religion in the Reich. We no longer believe in the Holy Ghost. We believe in the Holy Blood,' they said."

His grandfather said in a strained voice, "Goebbels decreed that the right-hand, Hitler salute, should be regarded as the only salute to Jesus Christ," and continuing with a grave face, he said, "The Nazis ordered the removal of crucifixes from all schools, as symbols of superstition. Holy pictures were taken down from all over the country. Children were forbidden to make the sign of the cross. And now . . ." He paused for a long time, and at last said, "—none of them do."

That evening they sat in the light cast by the lantern hanging from the overhead beam—not talking for a long time. "No electricity—reserved for factories and offices. And coal is rationed," Opa said. "But applewood makes a fine fire." Rising and walking to the tile stove, he took two small logs from the wooden box on the floor, opened the door, and placed them on the glowing embers.

In response to his grandmother's question about his brother in the Coast Guard, Karl said, "Willi was just going into the Academy when I left in 1941, Oma. I'm sure he's all right."

Karl's cousin, Seppi, from Uncle Adi's farm, had been killed at

Stalingrad, his grandfather told him; and cousin Konrad, from the apartment upstairs, died of wounds in Africa.

"But your cousin Alex," Oma said, "Dr. Grauenhaft's lawyer. He's the smart one. Now a Colonel with the SS, in Berlin." Karl smiled. "He married Hannelore, you know," Oma said.

"Hannelore Gunst?" Karl asked, wondering why the blue-eyed girl, with long pig-tails, would marry the arrogant Alex from the University of Vienna; or he marry her, for that matter, the simple farm girl, with little education.

"Well," Karl said, and after a pause, "at least they both have freckles."

"Let's drink to the good times," Opa said. When he returned from the storage room in the tall granite cliff behind the house, they all drank big mugs of light green Heurigan. "You see," Opa said, smiling over his wine mug, "some things are worth hoarding."

"That's true," Oma laughed. "And no matter what happens, there'll always be a time for Heurigan!"

It had been twenty years, since Karl left Badenberg for America. Now, as he sat holding hands with his Grandmother across the low table in the *Villa Bavaria*, it almost seemed that nothing had changed. Oma Grazie, with her large brown eyes, large nose and straight back, was eighty-one now. A few more wrinkles on her high cheeks, and her straight white hair was thinner. But the voice was still full, rich, soft and confident. "All will pass soon enough," she said.

Karl said, turning to his grandfather, "Do you still carve bows from osage wood."

"Ah, Karl, it's been a long time since we could get osage." Pulling on his thick beard, his green eyes still showing a sparkle, he continued, "And I wouldn't trust these hands with a knife anymore." He chuckled. "But I still make good cigars. "Can't smoke 'em anymore. Doctor Oma's orders." He waved to the room off the kitchen where his work bench stood over the chest full of sweet-smelling tobacco. "Just special orders now. For SS people—and the party men."

His grandparents' faces were white, the palor of those suffering vitamin deficiency; and there were red rings around the eyes. The shops were half-empty now. People stumbled along in long lines with color-coded ration stamps: blue for meat, yellow for dairy products, orange for bread. As Karl moved along with his special ration card, he glanced at the posters on the wall. "Have you seen this man?" each read. Near the counter was a poster with yesterday's date. Karl recognized the grainy photograph of a man he'd seen in the Dulles headquarters at Berne. The printing below the photograph offered a reward for information leading to capture of the parachute spy, believed to be somewhere in the city of Badenberg. The clerk punched his card, and Karl left the shop with a whole chicken wrapped in cloth. Had a telephoto lens in Berne captured his image, he wondered?

They ate the chicken that night. His grandmother saved the bones. "It'll make good soup," she said, laughing, "to go with the potatoes."

"But at least you have plenty of apples," Karl said.

"Yes," his grandfather replied, "But hording is punishable by death, so we don't store them anymore. Not even Alex would risk that. We leave a few on the trees. And at night the young boys come, climbing the trees and stuffing their pockets. Well—the funniest thing, I asked little Hans down the street, 'did you like the apples, Hansi?' and quite forgetting himself, little Hans told me his mother baked a pie—which means of course they have sugar, which is something we went without, until you came. But then, his father is a party man."

They drank late into the night, and when they went to bed, they were all drunk.

The next day was Sunday. In the afternoon, they left the *Villa Bavaria* for a walk to the park where a band would be playing. Just like in the old days, Oma told Karl. "Except the musicians are all a little old, and not very good."

As they walked onto the street from the villa, Herr Stegel, one of Karl's teachers from the elementary school, stepped out from the yellow house across the street.

"He doesn't talk anymore," Oma whispered to Karl. "And he may not recognize you. Anyway, it's better if you say nothing."

The teacher was followed by his wife. She was tall and thin, and a bit awkward, Karl thought. Her legs seemed to go in different directions as she walked. But he saw there was always a friendly grin on her long face. He nodded and smiled at her.

She was talking, as she came onto the street with her red-faced husband. Her wide nostrils quivered, and her large, gray eyes swept over Karl, as he stood there, with Oma and Opa, waiting for the old couple to pass; and as she went by, she was still talking and grinning, words that had no meaning. Then Karl realized she was talking to herself.

"Both of their sons are dead," Oma whispered. "Killed on the Russian front. And neither one seems quite right in the head anymore. I think he's had a stroke. And she . . . she . . . well, I don't know. The shock of it all, I guess."

They followed the old teacher and his wife down the road; and as they neared the park, other people joined them in the narrow street, between the small houses and empty shops in the town's old section.

The band was playing in a white kiosk at the center of the park. Old people sat everywhere on the benches under the chestnut trees. Small children ran up and down, squealing as they went, while their grandfathers tapped canes on the stone walks in front of the benches, and shushed for quiet.

A thin old man with dyed red hair was leading the band in a Strauss waltz as Karl and his grandparents took seats on the white benches.

Then the band leader stopped. He looked at his watch and turned to the crowd. "It's a beautiful day," he said, looking up through the old trees where the sun streamed down through the fresh leaves and the chestnut blossoms. "And it's been a long time since we had such a big crowd." Laying his baton on the rail, he clapped, and then the players clapped. People all around answered by clapping.

The red-haired band leader bowed low and turned on his heel, his baton raised high; and when he brought it down, the band struck up the German national anthem, "*Deutschland Uber Alles.*"

The old people struggled to their feet. While the band was playing, Karl heard a loud voice behind him singing the old Austrian National anthem. Turning quickly, he saw his old teacher, Herr Stegel, shouting out the words: "God preserve them, God protect them, our Empire, our land ...."

The band stopped.

The old teacher's wife was singing too, her gray eyes blazing; other gray-haired old men and women joined in, and the song rolled through the crowd in the park.

Looking over his shoulder, Karl saw the red-haired band leader shaking his head. "No! No!" he was shouting at the crowd. The conductor whirled to the band, which then played louder and faster.

Suddenly, people were falling back across the park. Through the path they made, Karl saw young boys, dressed in brown uniforms with the Nazi armband, swinging clubs as they came.

"It's time to leave," he said to his grandparents, taking each by the arm; he rushed them down the stone path to the street, turned and saw a Hitler youth raise his club and knock the old teacher to the ground. The singing stopped. The band went silent.

***

Karl rose early the next morning and dressed in the dark. His bag was on the small cot behind the old ceramic heating stove. He packed away his Wehrmacht uniform, slipped into the SS gray with black and white trim, donned his death-head cap and went silently out the door.

Dawn was breaking, and when he opened the villa's gate, he saw a Kuebelwagen, the military version of the Volkswagen, at the end of the street. Another dark car blocked the other end. The street was sealed off, and SS men were going house-to-house.

Eleven

Karl closed the storage room door behind him and snapped on his lighter. The ladder was there, behind old apple barrels; and as he pushed his bag onto the stone ledge, he could hear the SS banging for his grandparents. "Security check! Open up!"

Then he was in the stone room high over the old barrels. The rusty lock had snapped with the first blow of his service revolver. They'd see it, lying there on the ground. He'd dropped the ladder behind the barrels when he was on the ledge. Maybe they'd see that too.

The wooden door burst open. Karl heard it swing. There was a light below. But they couldn't see the narrow slot behind the ledge, they couldn't even see the ledge, Karl knew that. So unless they climbed with the ladder he'd be safe; and if they came up the ladder he might have time. Time to squeeze high up that narrow shaft with the chiseled steps. And if he didn't make it . . . Well, he wouldn't think about that now. He couldn't shoot. It would be trouble enough for Oma and Opa without that.

First there was silence and the light flashing around below. Then the noise of empty barrels kicked over. And finally, "No one here!"

Karl waited for a moment, and when he was certain they'd left the storeroom below, he inched up the granite shaft, wedging his bag against the stone wall and moving it up a step at a time until he reached the top, high over the villa.

He'd left a note, telling his old grandparents he'd return someday. It was the only thing to do. They hadn't seen the SS uniform, and he didn't want to change in a station bathroom. That was too risky. So the SS would find the note, unless Opa had destroyed it. But there wasn't time for that.

All the better, he thought, they'd think he was gone long before they came.

When he crawled out through the brush and paused at the iron rail overlooking the villa, he heard voices from the yard one hundred feet below. "The storage room lock?" Well, who knows how long it had been broken. Opa didn't know. It could've been anyone. Food was short and maybe they were after the apples. No one was hidden there. That wouldn't make sense. Why would Opa break the lock and leave it on the ground?

"Leave the old fart alone and get on to the next house! There's no one here." Then the storm troopers were running again.

Karl worked his way along the high cliffs and found the old path which led through the woods behind the park. On the other side of the woods he stepped into the narrow road leading down to Weinstrasse, where he caught the morning work bus which followed the old Pass Road to Perchtoldsdorf. From there he went by street car to Vienna and the Franz Josefs train station.

"The Salzburg train is running about an hour late," the German sergeant in the movement control office at the station said. "I'd suggest you have a nice breakfast at the Wehrmacht canteen. I'll issue a voucher." With these words he took Karl's paybook, glanced at the last page which contained the entry made in Berne for his leave to Vienna, and looked briefly at his identification photograph. "Sergeant!" He looked up sharply. "What are you doing in an SS uniform?"

Karl froze. My God! He'd handed over the wrong paybook! He'd mixed them up in the dark and packed his Waffen SS papers back in the bag!

Karl stepped back, swaying there in utter disbelief. The Sergeant reached for a telephone. Karl turned and ran, slamming the door open as he went; and he ran wildly down the long platform, pushing and shoving people. Behind him he heard a shrill whistle. Ahead, German MPs were checking all passengers on their way to the trains. He ducked into a large waiting room, ran through the crowd of workers, and women and children and piles of baggage and out the opposite door. "Out of the way, SS!" he shouted to the German sergeant checking passes there. The MP fell back, the commotion was on the other side of the building, and he glanced that way and then at Karl, and then he let him pass. Karl was no longer running, but moving fast now, along the line of cars. A German officer ran onto the other end of the platform and bellowed: "You there! Halt!"

Spinning and grabbing a door, Karl jerked it open and jumped into the coach next to him. He ran the length of the car and jumped down on the other side. Then across tracks and up onto another platform. Down the other side of that and across more tracks. Running harder now, he grabbed a rail and swung up onto the steps of a moving coach as it left the station.

The train was crowded with civilians, old men and women with young children who stared at him blankly from wood benches along the sides.

They had no idea what was going on, whether he was the pursued or the pursurer, in his SS uniform.

The train was slowing again for the Heiligenstadt station. Karl stepped to the other side of the car, and when the coach slowed to a crawl, he stepped off. If they were waiting for him inside the station, he would disappoint them. He strode quickly across the yards, caught the first street car heading west along the Danube; left it at Nussdorf. There, in the security of the station toilet, he took his Waffen SS papers from his bag.

The ticket-taker looked at his pass and motioned over a German MP. The MP corporal glanced at his papers. "Have a good trip, sir."

Karl boarded the crowded train, on his way to Salzburg, where he would change trains for Munich. He smiled to himself. Who'd suspect Sergeant Mueller had the audacity to take another train? Hadn't the Englishman, Harvey, told him the most obvious was the least likely to be suspected?

He found a seat in a crowded officer's compartment, stowed his luggage on the overhead rack, and sat down next to a Wehrmacht captain. Several miles later, the compartment door opened. "Security patrol, gentlemen," the SS corporal said. "I need to see your paybooks and movement orders." He started with the young lieutenant across from Karl and worked his way around the compartment. He opened Karl's paybook, looked up for a moment, then took a notebook from his pocket, scribbled an entry, and closed the paybook. "Thank you, sir." Karl nodded. No one else had received the special treatment, and his hands were sweating now. The train was moving fast. If he overpowered the man, there would be no place to go. The corporal took a long look at Karl, and left the compartment.

A few minutes later the corporal was back. "Would you please come with me sir?"

"What's the problem, Corporal?"

"The major would like to talk to you, sir. He's in the last coach."

They were starting the climb to Linz and the train was slowing. As Karl followed the young corporal to the last car, he paused and stepped across to the door. This was his last chance, there was nothing left to do, maybe he'd get lucky and something would break his fall; and just as he put his hand on the door handle there was a roar like thunder as an express passed close on its way to Vienna. The corporal looked back, a questioning look on his face. "Are you coming, sir?"

Karl stepped around the soldier and into the coach. A quick "Hail Mary" ran through his mind. The scene swam before his eyes. A major was standing there in the all black uniform of the elite SS security units, hand outstretched, and saying, "Thank you for coming, Lieutenant." The blood slamming through Karl's head slowed. "I thought you could give us a hand here," the major continued. "We'll never make it through the train before we reach Salzburg. And you being SS, well I thought you might be used to this sort of thing." The SS major asked Karl if he'd lend a hand checking the officer compartments. "This is all you need," and he gave Karl a large security forces badge on a braided rope to hang around his neck.

Wesermuende

Spring, 1944

While the Americans pounded the German industrial cities by day in precision bombing attacks at high altitude, and the British pulverized the civilian population at night in low-level attacks, Karl sat at the communications center in the Intercept Unit overlooking the Weser River and sent coded messages to Dover. It was simple now, since he was commander of the unit.

In the last eleven months, he had counted a total of sixty-three new submarines coming down the shallow river from the A. G. Weser factory at Bremen. Eighteen additional U-Boats had been built at Wesermuende and launched at the Third-Harbor Basin. These, Karl added to his list and sent to the British.

Now he felt safe. The foolish incident at Vienna was forgotten. No one had recognized his photograph in the false Hans Mueller paybook. The edges had already yellowed when he handed it over to the control sergeant at the station. The chemicals were working. By now the picture was no more than a black blob. Temporary meant just that, Dulles had told him. After ten days the pass would no longer be usable.

But what Karl didn't know was that the Gestapo had seen those OSS forgeries before. The first thing they did was to bathe them in a chemical solution.

So Karl went about his OSS mission—collecting information. He was ultimately accepted by the foreman at the Lloyd shipyards, eager to impress an SS officer he'd seen there for almost a year now.

Karl watched the submarines take shape. On May 30, 1944, he learned from the foreman that a new type was ready to slide down the ways. Karl raised Dover and passed on the information. It was the U.3001, an advanced snorkel design, fitted with automatic depth-keeping gear and a 5000 horsepower diesel/electric engine, giving it a range of 12,000 miles. This U-Boat was a great advance over the previous snorkel subs, which were simply older models modified to take the underwater breathing apparatus. The new U-Boat, the foreman had said, was capable of very high speeds above and below the water. It was a test boat. And assuming sea trials went as expected, full production would start immediately at Bremen, Kiel, and Luebeck, in addition to the yards at Wesermuende.

All of this, Karl had transmitted to Dover, along with a complete description of a new Z-Class destroyer, which had come down the river from Bremen on the high tide.

Karl sat, waiting for his acknowledgement, and thinking of the amusing story the foreman had told him. The *Graf Zeppelin*, the only aircraft carrier of the German Navy, had been started when the foreman was at the Bremen yards; and it was absolute confusion from the start in 1940. "The Luftwaffe refused to cooperate with the Navy," he had said with a grin; and then, with what was popularly known as, "The German Look," where the speaker would straighten and look about him to see who might be listening, the foreman told Karl the carrier's anti-aircraft guns were placed before and behind the superstructure, where they could only engage enemy targets to port by firing across the flight deck at low-levels, during which times no planes could be on deck. "Then, after many foul-ups, production was halted with the ship eighty-percent complete. It was resumed again in 1942, with a modified design. Eight, six-inch guns were carried on the lower deck. But they were totally useless fore and aft, and gave no protection to the flight deck. When the AA guns, which had been purloined for shore use, could not be recovered, and armaments refused to supply replacements, production was halted again in 1943." Then he told Karl a new worker had been transferred from the Bremen yard; and the new worker said the ship was under construction again, and that any day they might see Germany's one and only aircraft carrier coming down the river.

It was while waiting for the Dover acknowledgement, and formulating this message, that Karl heard the door slam sharply behind him.

"Another Dover transmission, Lieutenant?"

Karl swiveled in his chair and faced a Luger in the hand of an SS Colonel. "Alex!"

"Yes, Karl. Alex. Now unbuckle your service revolver and drop it on the floor."

Karl, facing the gun, couldn't think. He didn't breathe, and his stomach was cold fear. I should rush him. Draw my gun. I might have a chance. But he sat doggedly in his seat, unable to move.

"Drop the gun, Karl. Now!"

So this was what it was really like facing a loaded gun three feet away. Not like in the cowboy stories, where the hero sprang into action, facing death without fear. With trembling hands, he unbuckled his service revolver and let it slide to the floor. Alex stepped forward and scooped up the gun, stopping for a moment with the cold barrel of his forty-five resting against Karl's head.

Alex stepped back and lowered his gun. "Don't make a noise." Alex was glaring at him now. "When the radioman returns, act natural," he said. "Turn the set over to him. Then walk out slowly. Go to your office. I'll be right behind you—with this." He waved the Luger in Karl's face. "There's no reason to cause a lot of excitement."

In Karl's office, Alex reached behind and locked the door, and taking Karl's seat behind the desk, laid his pistol on the blotter and leaned back in his chair. His face was colorless, with the skin stretched tight over the bones, and he had a frozen, somber smile. His face twitched. "Well, Karl, you've been busy, haven't you?" He spoke the words in a dry montone and his voice was hollow.

"Busy, sir?"

"Don't be so formal, Karl," he said sarcastically. "Alex will do," and pulling an envelope from his breast pocket, said, "Yes, Karl, very busy." Alex took papers from the envelope and unfolded them on the desk. "Peter to Dover." He paused and looked at Karl. "You are Peter, aren't you, Karl?"

Karl said nothing, and watched his cousin calmly read off the dates and contents of fourteen additional transmissions. Well, Karl thought, if he knows I'm Peter, there's no reason for him to ask. If he doesn't know, it certainly won't help if I tell him.

"Oh, yes, Karl. We know you're Peter. You needn't answer."

"Then why are you here, Alex?"

"You're a bungler, Karl. But strangely enough—you're valuable. You can be of use."

"To whom?"

"To Germany, Karl. To Germany. Now, who told you to contact the British? Why are you spotting ships for them?"

"Me?"

"Come now, Karl." Alex lifted the revolver from the desk and pointed it at Karl. "If you're not Peter," he said squinting an eye down the barrel at Karl, "you're no use to us."

"If you know so much why don't you just shoot me, Alex?" But Karl wasn't being brave. Alex wasn't the Gestapo. And if he hadn't turned Karl in, with what he knew or had guessed, Alex could be in serious trouble. How would he ever explain simply walking into the Intercept Unit and shooting the commander, even if Karl was his cousin. This type of dirty work wasn't done by Berlin SS.

"Because we need your contacts," Alex said. "We have a man working with the British. Some of your messages were turned over to the English, the less harmful ones. But most were sent back to Germany by courier. To the Abwehr, Karl. Admiral Canaris. So we know you can get through."

"Now wait a minute, Alex," Karl said, leaning over the desk, "You tell me what you're doing here, then maybe I'll tell you what I know."

"You forget," Alex said, quickly pulling the gun to his chest, leaning back in his chair, and pointing it at Karl, "that I have the gun. Not you."

"But I don't think your little trip here is authorized. You're bluffing, Alex. Now put that damned thing down!" Karl was more angry at himself than Alex for having been such a coward in the radio room. Alex laid the gun on the desk. "Now give me my revolver," Karl said.

Alex shoved Karl's Luger across the desk. "You always were an asshole, Karl. Now where did you get the idea we should transmit military information to the British?"

"It was my idea."

"And the frequencies? The codes?"

"I intercepted them," Karl lied. "And then I took the name Peter when nothing further was heard from that agent. I assume he was captured, or killed. That's all there is to it."

"You're stupid, Karl. We want to bring Hitler down, but not at the expense of the country. Who'd listen to a defeated Germany?"

"Germany? I thought we were Austrians, Alex."

"Austria can't stand alone, We're economically dependant on Germany. Germany's fate is ours." Alex tossed a paybook on the desk. "And thanks to our organization, Sergeant Hans Mueller, this never got to the Gestapo. Now let's not argue. The important thing is to dispose of Hitler. And then we need to make contact with the British and Americans. And for that we need someone—you."

"What is it you propose to ask them, Alex, to forgive the sins of the nation?"

"Karl, you weren't here. You were sitting comfortably in America. Thousands have opposed Hitler, since before the war. And hundreds have died. But we can't make the Allies understand. We have a shadow government waiting to take over. But without support from the Allies it's hopeless."

"What's the Schildwache role in this?"

"Our role, Karl? To save Germany."

"How strong are they? Do they have control of the shadow government?"

"Actually, Karl we're a minority—"

"How are you different from the Nazis, Alex?"

"You were supposed to cover this in your indoctrination, Karl. Rule would be by consent, based on the lines of ancient Sparta—"

"How did you get my British messages from the Abwehr?"

"They're with us. The Nazis installed Admiral Canaris as head of

Intelligence because he was known to be a die-hard conservative and anti-Communist. They assumed he'd be an ardent Nazi supporter. But they were wrong. Although he was cautious, and stayed in the background, he gave his assistant, General Oster, a free hand, knowing of his anti-Nazi activities. And wherever possible, covered for him. Oster contacted General Beck. Then Beck contacted the Chief of the Berlin Police and the head of the Central Criminal Office, both Nazi-party members."

Alex then explained that this small nucleus led to an organization, which now numbered several thousand. "The less you know, Karl the better." He opened Karl's fake paybook. "And in case you get any ideas, I've got this, Sergeant Mueller."

"But I thought—"

"Yes, Karl. You thought the picture would self-destruct. How stupid do you think we are?" Alex folded the pass and put it in his breast pocket.

"So what now, Alex?"

"The time has come. We're moving on Hitler. We can't just arrest him. There's too much support in the army and with the workers. And this time we won't miss."

Alex explained that the first attempt was made in March, 1943. "Two bombs, wrapped together and disguised as brandy bottles, were given to one of Hitler's military aides as a present to another general at Hitler's headquarters in East Prussia. The plane left the Center Army base in Russia. Fighter escorts covered the skies. The bomb was set to go off in half an hour. The signal went out. The shadow government was alerted. Everyone stood by, ready to march on Berlin. The anguished cry from the fighter escorts, advising that Hitler's plane had blown up, was to be the signal to arrest the Nazis. The signal never came."

"What happened?"

"It was incredible. The major who planted the bomb followed in another plane. He explained to the aide that he'd made a mistake and substituted two, real bottles of brandy. Then he took a train to Berlin, and dismantled the bomb in his compartment. The time fuse had worked. The hammer had tripped. But the percussion cap failed." Alex paused and shook his head. "One wonders whose side God is on."

Karl poured coffee into two porcelain mugs. "What do I have to do get back Hans Mueller, there." He pointed to Alex's breast pocket.

"Things are becoming desperate now—cracks in the organization—and we're losing our cover." Alex took the coffee. "Thanks. Some damned fool, I think his name is Schmidthuberr, decided to use the Abwehr for his own purposes. He was arrested for smuggling. And he tried to buy himself out—and he knew a lot, but not all. Some were arrested and executed. General Oster was sent to prison."

Alex then told Karl that the Nazis infiltrated the Free German Group in Berlin. "Abwehr agents, working under cover in Instanbul, were members of the Berlin group," Alex said. "When they heard of the arrests, and received an order to return to Berlin at the same time, they defected to the British."

Alex held out his cup. "Do you have any whiskey?"

Karl took a bottle from the filing cabinet. First he waves that damned gun around and now he wants to drink my whiskey. And he's got my fake pass in his pocket. Well, I'll give him all he wants. I'd drown the bastard in it if I could.

Karl filled his cup with a generous amount of whiskey. Alex rose from the desk, and continued his story, pacing up and down the room.

"Admiral Canaris was removed immediately. And now the SS man, Kaltenbrunner, has taken over all intelligence from the Abwehr. Its the end for Canaris. He's been reassigned to a non-security position, no longer effective for us. They suspect him, Karl. And Kaltenbrunner, 'the calculator' will get him yet—and the rest of us too."

Alex stopped at the window, and peered out over the river. Then he looked down to the dyke. "Nice view," he said to Karl, "I understand how your identifications are so accurate. With binoculars, you only need look down to read the captain's orders as he passes through." Alex smiled coldly, and looked at Karl. He patted the fake paybook in his pocket. "But you must not send any further messages, understand?"

"Yes, Alex. I understand," Karl said. He knew it would be foolish to attempt messages the British weren't receiving in any case.

"It's for your own good, Karl. Streicher, your old commander, is Kaltenbruner's aide. And he seems to have a personal dislike for you."

"I see," Karl answered, rubbing his chin. "Now what?"

"We're looking to von Stauffenberg." Alex paused and pointed to Karl's hand. "He was badly wounded in Tunis, same as you."

"Tunis? I wasn't wounded in Tunis."

"But... you told Hesse in Munich—"

"He was one of yours?"

"He's Gestapo, Karl. But in Berlin . . . well, I work very closely with him . . . Just where were you wounded?"

"I wasn't. It was an accident. A long time ago, a boating accident."

"Well Karl, old Hesse was impressed with you. He knew the name Meister. I told him we were cousins. I suspect, Karl, that he rather liked you. But then, he didn't know you, did he?"

Karl looked over his coffee mug at Alex, and then went to the chair near the window, where he sat and tilted back against the wall. "You were talking about von Stauffenberg."

"Yes. Lost an eye, his right arm, and two fingers of his left hand. A gutsy bastard, though. Returned to duty as soon as he could. But General Olbrecht thought he was essential to our cause and took him out of combat. He's now Chief of Staff of the Home Army, under Olbrecht. From there, Karl, he has access to all of the commands. He's a great coordinator, and as a staff officer, he even has access to Hitler."

"I see," said Karl.

"The operation is code-named Valkyrie," Alex said. "The plan was developed by von Stauffenberg. There are so many foreigners in Germany, workers as well as prisoners, and we had no army at home. So von Stauffenberg persuaded Hitler to develop a contingency plan called 'Valkyrie.' If an emergency breaks out, Valkyrie is put into operation, all government offices are sealed off for their protection; the tanks move on Berlin, the Berlin Luftwaffe seals off the city from the air; the police and the Berlin commandos take control of the city." The skin grew tighter on Alex's face. "It's fantastic, Karl, every unit in Valkyrie is part of the revolt. And Hitler signed his own death sentence, von Stauffenberg's plan, creating Valkyrie!"

"And when do they try again?"

"Now, that's why I'm here, Karl."

"What do you want?"

"We have an agent in Switzerland. He passes on to the Americans all the communications which come across his desk. His contact in Berne is Allen Dulles. We'll arrange for you to meet Dulles. When you do, Karl, you must convince the Americans. Without some hope of support, some indication they'll deal with us, we may not be able to carry it off, even if we eliminate Hitler. But if the Allies mean to destroy Germany, if they will not negotiate a just peace, then we'll lose it all. Because then we must fight on. We must have a Germany. We must have hope, Karl."

"How do you propose that I meet with this man, Dulles?"

"First, Karl, I'll arrange for your transfer to Vienna. The Waffen SS commander there will arrange for your trip as a special courier. And I know Dulles will be waiting to meet you—you've already been to Berne." He looked Karl square in the eye. "Now I know Dulles has been through this before. But make him understand. He doesn't need Roosevelt's approval. He has influence with Eisenhower. The invasion is coming. We'll open the Western Front. And then we'll turn all our forces on the Russians. It'll be over before Washington knows what's happening. And then the Schildwache will negotiate a political solution. But we haven't much time. Tell Dulles that."

Alex returned to the desk, where he sat heavily into the chair. "You must succeed. Do you understand?"

Karl nodded. Now he knew it was time to get out. "Yes, Alex. I understand."

"Good. Then let's drink a toast."

Karl poured the remainder of the whiskey into their empty mugs. Alex rose slowly from his chair, and standing there stiffly raised his mug. "To the new Germany."

"Prosit," Karl said. "To the new Germany."

As Alex turned to leave, Karl said to him, "I heard from Oma that you married Hannelore. How is she?"

"She's fine, Karl. Fine. We live in Berlin-Zehlendorf, very comfortably, with a two-story house and gardens. And we have two fine boys." Then a cloud passed over Alex's face. "Fourteen and sixteen, both members of the Hitler Youth. And you know, Karl, either one would report me, if he knew what I were doing." Saying that, Alex shook Karl's hand and left.

***

Karl waited until the end of June. The Allies had landed at Normandy. But still no orders for Vienna came from Berlin. At last, he called Berlin and asked for Alex. The SS operator told him there was no Colonel Meister listed for Berlin; and then Karl asked for Elska, and when he inquired about Alex, she said in a strained voice, "Karl, he's not in Berlin. He's on the Russian front."

Twelve

Wesermuende

July, 1944

Karl Meister sat in shirt sleeves looking out the open window to the river, where the sun burned off the morning fog. The heavy humidity rolled into the room, where everything smelled damp and close. Tapping his pencil on the desk, he watched now for the *Graf Zeppelin* which was to have left Bremen on the morning tide.

The Allies had broken out of Normandy and were rolling across the French plains—the ground war was coming home to Germany. Well, there was still a chance for victory, the German high command was saying, if the carrier gets out, gets across to Norway, where it can be defended by the AA guns high in the cliffs around the narrow North Sea inlets by day, slipping from fjord to fjord at night, launching stinging raids from its decks against the English each dawn, and providing a safe nest for the returning aircraft. The Germans would cover it's dash north along the Danish peninsula with heavy shore guns, and it's short run across the open water to Norway by every available aircraft and by dozens of U-Boats below.

The weakness in this plan was in the shallow waters off Wesermuende. That's where the British would strike. They would hit fast and hard before the aircraft carrier reached the umbrella of those big guns along the Danish coast. All the English needed to know was when the giant ship cleared port, and that Karl would tell them.

He glanced at his calendar, where he had marked the afternoon off for his weekly reconnaissance flight with Baumwolle. The captain had been promoted, and in addition to his regular duties, now flew missions along the Friesen coast, dipping low over the uninhabited, marshy islands, where the Germans expected landings by Allied ship spotters and saboteurs. On Wednesdays, Karl flew with him in the old Henschel 127.

They never saw any English or Americans on those barren islands. But there were times when they'd spot B-17s high above them; and then they would go even lower, running along the brown-green coast, so that the camouflaged Henschel blended in with the landscape, and being then invisible to the aircraft overhead, they would break radio silence, and warn of the bombers winging into Germany.

But mostly, they saw nothing on those missions. On the way back, Baumwolle would give Karl the controls, letting him learn the feel of the slow plane which practically flew itself.

Intercept operations had come to a stand-still. Dover radar no longer reported fighter scrambles because the German bombers were gone from the English skies. The German radio operators monitored what they could, while Berlin struggled to break the new code and give them some meaningful call signs. The Abwehr agent on the ground was no longer a help, and they learned he actually never was. They had been duped. The Allies wanted their code broken, and then they'd set up a command structure for an entire army which never existed, the one the German's waited for at Calais, while the real invasion force went the long route south to the Normandy beaches.

Before she slipped off to hide in Norway, Elska Banghardt warned Karl the Wesermuende unit would be mobilized for the Russian front once the Red Army reached the Baltic states. They were not far from there now. So it was time to get out. As soon as the *Graf Zeppelin* made its run for the sea, Karl was free to go. That was what his last message from Dover said.

Seeing now that it was past ten o'clock, and that the German aircraft carrier had missed the tide, he decided to leave early and drive to Bremen. He could make a quick check on the ship and be back in time to send a message to Dover and still meet Baumwolle at the weather station for their short drive to the Fliegerhorst and their afternoon flight.

From the bridge over the Weser at Bremen, he could see the carrier sitting in ways under camouflage netting. Twice the British had tried to bomb it in low level attacks. But it was well concealed. The planes had trouble getting bearings; and then they had to make the run up the river against a solid wall of flak. None got through.

Workmen scrambled over the flat-top. Karl could see sparks from welders on the lower deck. High tide had pushed through Bremen at nine that morning. He knew the carrier had missed its opportunity to sail. She can't leave now, he thought, until around five this afternoon. Otherwise, she'll run aground on the sandbar where the Geeste flows into the Weser. And if she leaves on the afternoon tide, I'll have a beautiful view of her from the air.

***

Leaving his uniform jacket in the hot car, Karl walked up the stone steps to the weather service building and pushed open the heavy door. The crippled old Sergeant who had replaced him there, rose slowly from the long table and saluted with a weak Heil Hitler. "Major Baumwolle's gone sir."

"Gone?"

"Yes, sir. He left very suddenly."

"And Fraulein Baumwolle?"

"Operations, sir," the old man said, pointing to the closed door at the end of the hall.

There was a rustling noise inside when Karl rapped on the door. After a few minutes he heard Ingrid say, "Come in."

She stood next to the open window. Her face was drawn and white.

"Your father's left already, Ingrid. He must've forgotten it's Wednesday.... You look tired. Are you all right?"

"Yes, Karl. I'm fine," she said, looking at him anxiously. Her voice was low and quiet.

"It's the strain, Ingrid, the war . . . and you've been working too hard." Karl reached out and took her in his arms. But she seemed distant, and her eyes were red.

"You've been crying, Ingrid. What is it?"

"Nothing, Karl. Really."

He'd seen smoke from the chimney as he drove up. The weather was too warm for a fire. He put a hand on the stove in the corner. The brown enamel was warm. Karl opened the door and saw there the glowing ashes of what looked like sheets of burned paper.

Turning suddenly to her, he said, "Just where is your father, Ingrid?" When she didn't answer, he said again, firmly, "Ingrid, where's he gone. I need to know."

"Berlin."

"When?"

"Last night."

"What were his orders?" When there was no reply, he moved closer to her and said tensely, "Ingrid, what were his orders?"

She looked at him for a moment. "Go away, Karl. Leave us alone."

"You're burning documents, Ingrid . . . Why?"

"Leave us alone, Karl. Don't ask. Just go away."

"I need to know what's happening, Ingrid."

She glared at him. "You wouldn't understand?"

"It's Valkyrie, isn't it?"

She looked up, a startled look on her face. "How did you know?"

"Ingrid, it makes no difference now. Tell me, what were your father's orders?"

"He had no orders."

"No orders. My God, Ingrid. And he went to Berlin. Was the code word sent out?

"The first alert. There's been nothing since."

"And that's why you started burning the papers?"

"Yes. At least there won't be anything here. And when Vati gets back—"

"How did he go? It's not safe to drive. And the trains barely run." Not waiting for an answer, he said to her with a quick smile, "Ingrid, there's hope. He's probably not there yet!"

"Karl, he flew."

"He went by plane?"

"Yes. He commandeered the Henschel, and flew it to Berlin."

"In the dark?"

"Yes Karl." She nodded slowly, an anquished look on her face. "He said it'd be no problem. He'd contact his old friend, Hans. And Hans would clear the way into Berlin. There was a good moon and enough light. He'd land the plane in the street."

"Ingrid, he's a good pilot. He'll make it. But if the coup fails, he's taken a plane, without orders, and flown to Berlin . . . without orders . . ."

"Yes." She sank into a chair next to the desk; and holding her head in her hands, said to Karl, "What can I do?"

"Give the sergeant the afternoon off, Ingrid."

"I don't have that authority. I'm not military."

"But I am."

Karl opened the door. "Sarge, it's terribly hot. Take the afternoon off. Fraulein Baumwolle says there's nothing for you to do. Go see your family?"

"Yes, sir," the Sergeant said with a broad grin. "But I need orders, sir."

Ingrid typed leave papers for the old man. Karl signed them with a flourish and handed it to the excited Sergeant. "Thank you, sir. Heil Hitler, sir," the old man said, backing to the door.

Following him down the hall, Karl watched him hurry down the steps and then pedal rapidly through the iron gate toward the city.

"Now let's get busy," Karl said, turning to Ingrid behind him. "Burn every scrap of evidence."

They went through the files. Karl found notes everywhere. Many were scribbled in pencil, with the black square in the corner. Others were messages to and from Black Square members; and then he saw the word "Viereck."

"Of course," he said to Ingrid, "Viereck, and the Black Square." Now remembering the indoctrination Elska gave him in New York, he said, "It's the monarchist group, isn't it?"

"Yes," she said to him, looking up from a file cabinet in the corner. "Now you know everything . . ." He knew about Valkyrie. He knew about the Black Square, and George Viereck. And he was helping destroy the evidence. But who was he? Was he really with the Schildwache? He said he loved her. It had gone too far, all the pretending. She wasn't sure about her feelings anymore. Could she still do it when the time came? Could she still kill this man she'd come to know so well? And if she couldn't, could she trust him? She looked at the dark eyes in the lean face. Passion had pushed things too far, and she'd lost control that night, and after that there wasn't any going back. But she had to know. "Karl, you have to tell me how you know about Valkyrie."

He spoke the words she feared most. He'd been recruited to work for the Schildwache; and he told her they had infiltrated the SS; and when he mentioned the plan and von Stauffenberg, she stopped him saying, "Yes, but Valkyrie isn't a Schildwache group."

"I know. And it's not your monarchists, either. It seems to be a widespread group, mostly Army officers. You know they plan to kill Hitler?"

She nodded.

"Then they'll try for a separate peace with the English and Americans. But the Allies won't deal with them, Ingrid. That's already been announced."

She drew a deep breath. Her resolve was returning. Karl Meister was a Schildwache, a member of that deranged group who planned to take over the revolt once Hitler was dead. Well, maybe she could go on with the pretending, if it was pretending anymore. If the Schildwache succeeded, Karl might be able to protect her father. And if he turned against them, well, she'd have to deal with that when the time came. "We must keep our strength. Without strength, they have nothing to negotiate. That's the plan, Karl. And if it doesn't work, they'll throw everything against the Russians and let the Allies in. It's the only hope."

"Well," Karl said with a strange smile, "it'll end this damned war. One way or another."

When they had finally found and burned all papers with any mention of the Black Square, they sat in darkness in the operations room, listening to the radio and waiting for news of Valkyrie. What did Karl mean, she wondered—the war would end one way or another?

Suddenly Karl jumped to his feet. "Ingrid, your apartment! There must be dozens of documents there!"

"No, no, Karl. Nothing. Father left everything here. Thank God he had that much sense."

Then with a start, she said, "Mutti! She's expecting us." Ingrid went to the phone and told her mother that her father would be working very late, perhaps all night again, and her mother shouldn't wait up for them.

"Mother's a dear," Ingrid said returning. "If only things were as simple as she sees them. She told me to make sure Vati took his walk after supper." Ingrid ran a hand through her blonde hair and smiled wanly at Karl. "And she told me the same thing last night. 'It's good for the digestion, a thousand steps after the evening meal,' she told me. And she's always made us take a little walk after supper . . . It's a family tradition . . ." Her voice choked.

Karl reached and took Ingrid's slim hand as she sank quietly into the leather chair next to him. "Sometimes that's all we have left, old customs," she said. "It's that thin thread of reality with which we stitch one day onto another."

"Yes," Karl replied quietly. "While the world crumbles under our feet."

They sat quietly, holding hands, and listening to the Berlin Philharmonic on the radio. The music stopped. They stared at the glowing dial, listening to crackling static.

Karl glanced at his watch; and rising slowly from his chair and walking to the radio, he said, "It's nine o'clock. Either they've taken a direct hit or stopped broadcasting to save electricity." As he reached for the knob, a woman's voice, soft and calm, came from the speaker. "This is Radio Berlin," the woman said, "please stand by. Our Fuehrer has a special message."

Again static crackled in the speaker while Karl and Ingrid, now also on her feet, waited near the radio. Soon the woman's voice came again. "We are having technical problems," the pleasant voice said. "So while we wait for link-up with the Fuehrer, we ask for your patience. Meanwhile, we will feature music by Richard Wagner."

At nine-thirty the music stopped a second time. After a short pause, a man's voice came over the air. This voice was tense and hurried, and the man announced cryptically, "Our technical problems persist. Please stand by." Without further announcement, the station played music until after midnight while Karl and Ingrid waited in the hot room.

"Well," Karl said thoughtfully, "something's happening in Berlin. If the woman comes back, the coup is a failure. That man wasn't an experienced announcer—he's probably part of the coup. And if they hold the station and there's no broadcast from Hitler, we've succeeded."

"But, Karl, It's been over three hours. The coup must have succeed. Unless . . ." She paused, trembling in the soft breeze from the window. "Unless there's street fighting," she said.

Karl took her by the shoulders, and looking into her eyes, said, "Hitler isn't in Berlin. He's in East Prussia. So there could be technical difficulties. And yes, there could be fighting in Berlin, too. It won't be simple, this revolt."

"My God, Karl. It's been too long. Too long." Collapsing into the leather chair with a heavy sign, her face drawn and worried, she said, "It's over. They're all arrested, or shot. It's over for Vati now, Karl."

"Maybe so, Ingrid. But I think time is on our side."

"Stand by for a message from the Fuehrer," the woman's pleasant voice returned to the radio. Then in a higher, but still controlled and calm voice, she said, "Sieg Heil!"

"This is the Fuehrer speaking," Karl heard the familiar, gutteral voice of Adolph Hitler over the radio, screaming with voice breaking at a high pitch. "Today will stand as a day of infamy for a very small clique of ambitious officers, devoid of conscience and crimminally stupid!" the Nazi leader shouted. "All were members of the despicable aristocracy. This small band of gangsters planted a bomb at my headquarters. It exploded at noon, killing General Berger and the official stenographer. The building was destroyed. The roof fell in! But I survived! Germany survived! The Third Reich survived! And the spineless assassins have been given the death penalty. Each and everyone of the cowardly swine are being shot, even now as I talk to you, and all who are associated with them will meet the same fate!"

The special broadcast ended with a brief, official report of the incident, giving few details not already disclosed by Hitler. The airways returned to military music followed by the crescendos of Richard Wagner.

All this time Ingrid sat silently in her father's leather chair staring straight ahead, as if seeing the bloody execution scenes on the blank wall.

Karl said nothing. It had come to this. The years of careful planning. The thousands of good men recruited to a lost cause. Now he knew the Gestapo were moving through the moonlit streets.

Unable to speak, he walked slowly to where Ingrid sat in the chair by the window, and putting a hand on her shoulder, looked out. Overhead was a brilliant display of Northern Lights. Peculiar streams of colored light of great beauty rose from the horizon as far around as Karl could see. The light paths arched high to the middle of the black night, where they met a fiery circle there. The rays were transient and constantly in motion, varying in color from a greenish hue to a deep, blood red. Ingrid rose and stood silently beside Karl. Behind him, the radio played Wagner's *Gotterdammerung*. "Yes," Ingrid whispered, "the twilight of the gods."

***

Karl awoke to the shrill cry of sea gulls following a fishing trawler down the wide river. It was six o'clock in the morning. Ingrid, looking very fragile curled in the leather chair under the window, slept at last.

What now? Karl wondered, walking to the typing room where he heated yesterday's coffee. He knew there would be mass arrests—Gestapo tactics would soon produce a list of thousands to be rounded up and shot, or shipped to the Nazi concentration camps. The Allies were still far away in France. It would be months before the Western Armies fought their way into the German heartland. He sipped the stale coffee. "Well," he said to himself, rubbing his face awake, "now it is time to get out."

"Yahoo! Heinz!" he heard from the open window overlooking the courtyard. He pushed aside the heavy blackout curtain and saw Ingrid's mother stop her bicycle at the entrance steps where she chained it to the iron rail.

"Heinz," she called again, "fresh rolls! Ingrid! Hot soup." She took a metal pot and a small basket from the wicker carrier which hung from the handlebars, and holding them in front of her as she walked up the steps, called out, "Liverwurst, Heinz! Are you there, Ingrid?"

Karl met her at the door.

"You!" she said. "What are you doing here?"

Ingrid closed the door behind her mother. "It's all right Mutti."

Her mother stood there, looking nervously at Karl out of the corner of her eye. "Where's Vati?"

"He's in Berlin, Mutti." Ingrid took the basket from her mother.

"Berlin! What's he doing in Berlin!"

"Come, Mutti," Ingrid said, leading her mother to the operations room where she sat her in the brown leather chair by the window. Ingrid told her about the revolt, that her father was part of it and that he had flown to Berlin. Her mother stared into the room, saying nothing. Then Ingrid explained that the revolt had failed, Hitler had broadcast his survival of the bomb attempt, and that Karl, too, was a member of the anti-Hitler movement. And still her mother said nothing.

"Mrs. Baumwolle," Karl said to her, "we must escape. I think I can get a fishing boat for a crossing to England. Will you come with us?"

"No," was her soft reply. "I'll wait here. I will wait for my husband. I won't leave Heinz now."

Ingrid poured steaming broth into cups, cut the hard rolls, and spread them with liverwurst. "Mutti," she said, stopping and turning to her mother, "Vati isn't coming back. There have been arrests. There'll be more. Karl is right. We must go now."

"Thank you, Ingrid," her mother said, refusing the soup and roll, "I'm not hungry. But I will wait. I'll wait here. You go, Ingrid. They won't arrest this old woman." She sighed heavily, and still looking up at Ingrid, continued, "We've been married a long time, Ingrid. I've always waited for Vati. It's like the first war. They said his plane was shot down. That he crashed in flames behind the French lines. But I waited, Ingrid. After the war—he came home."

Karl jumped to his feet. "I hear a plane." Running to the window at the far end of the room, he saw a brown and green single-engine plane coming down the river, flying very slow and low over the water.

The plane swept past, almost as low as the window. Karl recognized the figure hunched over the controls. "My God!" he cried out. "It's your father, Ingrid. He's followed the river home."

Karl and Ingrid ran to the courtyard with Mrs. Baumwolle close behind. There, they saw the plane climb over the dyke, turning to the north. Then it circled back toward the weather station. It came over very low, and flew south, where the high-winged plane circled to the left, and coming toward them again, settled upon the road.

Running across the courtyard to the iron gate, they saw the plane bumping along the uneven cobblestones. It reached the iron gate—it stopped—the engine roared. Its tail lifted and bounced around in a circle until the plane faced down the road upon which it had landed. Then they heard the engine throttle back.

Ingrid rushed past Karl. "Vati," she screamed. Karl ran after her; and when they reached the plane, her father leaned down and threw an arm around Ingrid. It was then, that Karl saw the line of bullet holes which marched from just behind the engine, low across the cabin door, and down the fuselage to the tail.

"Karl," Major Baumwolle said, opening the door, "help me down."

Ingrid stepped back, her face in her hands. "Oh, Vati," she said. "Vati, you've been hit."

Supporting him at each side, Karl and Ingrid walked the major to the weather building, his left leg dragging along the courtyard. Ingrid's mother ran along in front of them, crying and asking, "Heinz, Heinz, what happened?"

When they reached the steps, the major sagged and Karl picked him up and carried him through the door, down the hall and laid him on a low couch in the operations room.

He was bleeding heavily from his chest and left thigh. Karl removed the major's belt, and strapped it around Baumwolle's leg, pulling it tight, until the bleeding stopped. Ingrid unbottoned her father's jacket. His shirt was crimson. "Oh my God, my God," she cried.

Her mother pushed forward and tore the major's shirt down to his waist. "We need a compress," she said. "Quick, Ingrid, get a towel."

"Well, Hanna" Major Baumwolle said, smiling wanly as she pressed the towel firmly against his chest, "I didn't expect you here."

"Lie still, Heinz. We must get you to a hospital. Ingrid, call an ambulance."

"No!" The major rose on an elbow. "Not yet. Karl . . . you . . . and Ingrid. You must get out. It's over for me. But you two . . . you must get out."

"Major," Karl said, "we'll take a boat. I'll bring it alongside the dyke. Can you make it to England?"

The major sank back on the couch. "The harbor's sealed. Patrol boats everywhere...."

"The Mercedes," Karl said. "We'll take the car."

"No, Karl. All roads are blocked . . . Nothing can get through . . . the plane . . . it's the only way out now."

"But, major, it's a two-seater."

"Karl . . . I'm not going anywhere."

"But, sir, I can't fly."

"Listen carefully, Karl . . . you know it flies itself . . . I left the engine running." The major was talking very slowly, his voice little more than a whisper, and his breathing was labored. "Stand on the brakes, the floor pedals . . . seconds—then release the brakes. But be careful, let them both go at the same time. Otherwise it'll swerve. Now, Karl . . . listen to me, go straight down the road—those pedals also turn the rudder, you remember—if it drifts, touch the opposite pedal. Just like when we were in the air. Just tap it lightly, that'll bring it back. If not, touch the pedal again, lightly."

Karl leaned forward, straining to hear the major's weak voice. "Keep the stick between your knees, with very light pressure—you'll feel it—remember—just rest your palm on the stick. It'll take off by itself. Go to a thousand meters. Push the throttle in very slowly—keep the speed at one-hundred-ten." Karl nodded. Yes. Yes. One-hundred-ten kilometers—sixty miles an hour.

"At that speed it's very stable . . . and you'll have enough fuel . . . for England . . . radio ahead . . . land at a bomber field. Those fields are long. Line it up . . . ease the throttle in . . . when the wheels touch . . . cut the power and take your hands off everything . . . it'll come to a stop by itself . . ." Major Baumwolle closed his eyes for a moment. "And, Karl," his voice was very faint now, "once you're in the air, to turn, just bank—that turns the plane, remember. You don't use the pedals. Keep a light pressure backwards—use the throttle to maintain altitude—to turn right, move the stick right . . . just a little. You'll be banked—so it'll lose altitude—just pull back on the stick, or give it more power. Do you understand, Karl?"

"Yes." Karl stared at the white-faced man who now felt for Mrs. Baumwolle's hand. "I understand, sir."

"Good . . . good. Now go. There isn't much time . . . goodbye Ingrid. Good luck Karl."

"Aufwiedersehen," Karl said, "we'll meet again."

Ingrid kissed her father, and then Karl pulled her into the hall, where he whispered, "He's lost a lot of blood, but if we can get him to the car, I think my SS badge and uniform will get us through. We'll head for the American lines. I can't leave him or your mother."

Before Ingrid could answer, her mother was beside them in the hall. "He's gone," she said. "Vati's gone, Ingrid. Now go, like he told you." Mrs. Baumwolle turned to Karl. "Take Ingrid and go."

"But Mutti," tears streamed down Ingrid's face, "I can't leave. What will happen to you?"

"Go Ingrid. There's nothing they can do with this old woman. We've had a good life, Vati and I. I won't leave him now," and taking Karl's arm, Ingrid's mother said, "Quick. Take her. For God's sake! Go!"

They ran to the plane. Karl helped Ingrid into the rear seat, and strapped her belt tight; and swinging up into the cockpit, he waved to her mother who stood on the steps holding a white handkerchief high in the air, swinging it slowly back and forth in farewell.

Karl adjusted his feet on the pedals and held the control stick between his knees. Pushing hard on the brakes, he pulled the throttle wide open. The engine roared. He reached out and pulled up the hinged window, locking it in place by a tab at the top. He felt the seat rising under him, and the tail was coming up. With the plane vibrating level now, he waited while the engine's roar filled the cockpit. He released the brakes. The plane lurched forward. Faster and faster it rolled down the road; and when the right wheel strayed off the cobblestones, he gave the left pedal a short punch. "Too hard," he muttered, as the plane veered sharply left; and he pushed on the right pedal. The plane drifted back to the center of the road.

Then he realized he was pressing on both pedals, slowing the plane. He released the pressure. It surged forward again. He watched the speedometer needle climb slowly. "Forty!" he shouted to Ingrid. "Sixty!" The rumble of wheels against cobblestone stopped, and they were in the air.

The plane rose slowly. The airspeed needle climbed toward the one-hundred-ten mark. Below the plane, the sheds, warehouses, and old boats of the fish harbor, where nets dried on huge racks, grew smaller and smaller. Good God, Karl thought to himself, Baumwolle was right, it practically flies itself.

Tightening his hand on the control lever, he inched the stick back. They were past the fish harbor now and over the Geestemuende section of town with the plane climbing more steeply. The pastel-colored buildings, with their red and black tile roofs, looked like child's toys.

A few moments later, when the altimeter read 1,000 meters, Karl eased in the throttle. The air speed, which had climbed to 150 kilometers, dropped until it reached 110. Karl pulled the throttle out a little. There it is, he thought to himself, 1,000 meters, air speed about sixty miles an hour. And all I have to do now is turn this damned thing.

He dropped the right wing a little. Slowly, the compass swung from south to past west and then to northwest and he leveled the plane. The turn had taken almost ten minutes. Looking back over his right shoulder, he saw the Weser River, stretching toward Bremen, the bridge over the river there, and below the plane, the *Graf Zeppelin*, which now steamed slowly down river toward Wesermuende and the North Sea. He switched on the radio and raised British air control. In a clear voice, he told them the carrier had sailed. When the transmission was acknowledged, he pointed over his shoulder and said to Ingrid, "Well, the German Navy finally has its carrier."

She nodded, grimly.

Leave her alone, Karl thought. She needs time now.

Five minutes later, the North Sea Coast crawled slowly past below the plane.

"Helgoland!" Ingrid shouted, tapping Karl's shoulder, and pointing ahead to the right.

His eyes followed her finger to where he saw the high cliffs of the small German island in the North Sea.

Thirteen

Southport

November 11, 1965

The Lake Michigan wind blew cold down the Black River and snapped the flags flying over the assembled throng. "That's your float, there, Mr. Meister," a young man said to Karl, pointing to a flat, four-wheeled trailer, wrapped in red-white-and-blue crepe, and pulled by a new Dodge convertible with a huge banner stretched along its side which read: "1965 TWENTY-FIFTH ANNIVERSARY OF THE BIG STORM." Four folding chairs stood in a half-circle at the rear of the trailer facing a cardboard model of a Coast Guard lifeboat.

"Your wife goes too, Mr. Meister," the young man said with a laugh. "We need some beauty on the float."

"Where are the twins?" Karl asked his wife, as they took their seats on the folding chairs.

"Oh, this is too dull for the girls," Ingrid said to him. "They've gone to a rock concert in Kalamazoo."

"Ingrid—there he is—it's Billy." Karl pointed to a blue Cadillac with California plates from which a heavy-set man with curly gray hair and wearing a tan suit emerged and walked around to the passenger door. "And that's Muriel," said Karl, as Billy opened the car door.

Karl and Ingrid rose as Billy, walking with a cane, Muriel on his arm, came slowly across the grass and up the steps of the trailer. Billy grinned his big bear-like smile, and took Karl's hand, then Ingrid's. "So this is your German bride, Karl." The two brothers who had not seen each other for twenty-five years slapped each other on the shoulders. The women hugged.

"Football," Billy said, rubbing his knees, as he took the chair next to Ingrid, "the doctor says I have to learn to live with it." And looking past Ingrid to Karl, Billy said, "I saw the boat. You're fishing again, then?"

"I don't know anything else," Karl answered, pushing his gray hair back from his forehead. "And you?"

"Oh, we manage some apartments," Billy said, "in West Covena."

"Don't be so modest," Muriel said with a grin, "We own them, Karl. And you must come out for a visit. Bring the girls, we've lots of room. They'll go crazy over California."

"Smile!" a photographer said in front of them.

Then a thin reporter in shorts next to the photographer stepped forward. "Okay," he said, laughing. "Who's Karl and who's Billy."

The reporter knelt on the green carpet before them and made notes on a small pad while the photographer moved in and out, clicking a 35mm camera. "Let's see," the reporter said to Karl, you rescued the seamen with your fish tug, right?"

"Yes," Karl said, "But Billy, here, is the real hero of that storm."

"I know. I know," the reporter said, sliding closer to where Billy sat. "Get that profile," the reporter said to the photographer. Then turning back to Billy, he said, "Now tell me about the storm."

Billy told him of the huge waves, and how they lost a man over the side, and pulled him into the boat by his lifeline, and finally arrived in Chicago.

The reporter turned to Karl. "I understand two other men were with you."

"Yes. Corky Reiley and Joe Bear. Injun Joe, we called him."

"Where are they now?" the reporter asked.

"Joe was killed at Iwo Jima," Karl said quietly. "With the marines."

"And Reiley. What happened to him."

"He was killed in Ireland during the war."

"Ireland?"

"North Ireland. He landed supplies for the IRA from a German sub. The British were in the hills over the beach. A firefight broke out. The munitions exploded."

"I see," the reporter said, chewing on his pencil. "I'll bet there's a good story in that." And motioning to the photographer he said, "Get this man's profile too, from down low, so that his beard stands out against the blue sky." The photographer crouched low and clicked his camera.

"And what did you do in the war?" the reporter asked Karl.

"Oh, not much. I was in the Army. Communications."

"Did you see any action?"

"No. Not really."

"And you, sir?" the reporter asked, turning to Billy

"I was in the Coast Guard. Submarine patrol on the east coast."

"And did you spot any subs?" the reporter asked, making notes in his small pad.

"Well, there was this time off the North Carolina coast. I was commanding this forty-foot Chris Craft, requisitioned from a New York yachtsman, it was. And along comes this periscope. What a shock—and we had no guns—nothing. I got on the radio—and then one of the men cries out it's just a floating log. So—"

"Give me your telephone number," the reporter said, interrupting Billy. "I'll call you on that."

And shaking first Billy's hand and then Karl's, he said, "But right now the parade's starting, and I've got to cover those fellows in the VFW." Waving goodbye, he hurried down the steps, followed by the photographer, who turned on the bottom step and took one last picture of the two waving men and their wives.

Then the reporter pointed to the three VFW men with flags flying at the front of the parade, the photographer snapped two quick pictures, and the newsmen climbed into an old Pontiac, drove quickly over the Dunckley Street Bridge, and disappeared up the hill.

George Viereck, the anti-Nazi founder of the Black Square, was arrested in 1943 and tried for treason against the United States. The FBI found a letter to him from the Nazi Propaganda Ministry. In it, Goebbels thanked Viereck for his efforts on behalf of the Reich. Viereck claimed it was false, a plant by the Nazis—an attempt to quash the monarchist organization—I've been framed, he said. Viereck was acquitted on technical grounds.

The People's Court, which had sentenced the White Rose students to death at Munich, was hastily convened in Berlin. While news cameras rolled, Germans suspected of taking part in the revolt of July 20, 1944 were dragged before Judge Freisler to confess their crimes.

The court reporters protested—they couldn't take down the Judge's frenzied screaming—and there must be a record.

One by one they stood there. None were given more than a few minutes—there wasn't time—and Judge Freisler's high-pitched acquisitions went unanswered. But when Freisler coughed and gasped for breath, General von Schwanenfeld seized the opportunity. Standing calmly before the outraged judge who'd momentarily lost his voice, the General adjusted his scholarly glasses and spoke of Nazi murders in Poland. He was quickly drowned out by cries of "M U R D E R E R" from the bench.

Generals on the Russian front committed suicide, rather than face the inevitable in Berlin. On the Western Front, General Rommel was driven into the countryside. He had a choice. Suicide or be shot. He was too popular to chance a public trial. I'll do it myself, he told them.

On August 8, 1944 the executions started. "I want them to be hung up!" Hitler screamed. "Like carcasses!"

So they were stripped to the waste as the cameras ground on in the Berlin prison, then slowly strangled with piano wire and hung like slabs of meat on the hooks Hitler had ordered up.

The death toll passed five thousand. The film-makers, working in that stench of vomit, blood and excrement, sickened and couldn't go on. They were replaced by others who went into convulsions, and soon the cameras stopped. Hitler was furious—he'd reviewed each session at night for his evening pleasure.

Then Goebbels ordered the films shown to the troops—and they refused to watch.

Judge Freisler worked at a maddening pace, feeding the meathooks. When the air-raid warnings sounded, he refused to adjourn court. He had a schedule to keep.

A bomb from an American plane scored a direct hit on the courtroom.

Judge Freisler was blown to pieces; and a few remaining members of the underground escaped in the confusion.